The Conversos

V.E.H. Masters

Books by VEH Masters

The Seton Chronicles:

The Castilians
The Conversos
The Apostates

First Published in Scotland in 2021 by Nydie Books

A CIP catalogue record for this book is available from the
British Library

Paperback ISBN: 978-1-8382515-3-6

Also available as an ebook

Cover Design: Mike Masters

Map of Antwerp by Hieronymous Cock (1557) printed by
Symon Novelanus, Zuid-Nederlands (1542–1600).

www.vehmasters.com

For Mike, of course

And in memory of my in laws,
Len and Paula Masters

ANTVERPIA

Die Schelde Flus

Part One

Bethia

August 1547 to March 1548

Chapter One

The Ship

Bethia watches her town grow smaller and smaller. The cathedral towers are narrow pinpricks now, but, close by, St Rules is visible still, an oblong of grey against the bank of clouds fluffing high as a mountain of combed flax behind it. She understands why pilgrims even from as far away as Russia come to worship and do penance in St Andrews, for, seen from the sea, it is a most wondrous sight.

The ship alters course and they head south-east. She'll feel safer the further they stand out from the coast, for they'll soon be in English waters, and England is Scotland's greatest enemy.

She glances up at Mainard, her husband of a few hours, and then at his hand lying next to hers on the rail: brown against white. The ship lurches in an increasingly choppy sea and he steadies her, leaving his arm around her waist. His touch is strange but will soon grow familiar.

Bethia nudges his shoulder with her head, and he pulls her closer. 'You must teach me some Dutch before we reach Antwerp.' A shiver runs down her spine. She knows nothing about where she's going nor what she's going to.

He looks down and smiles. 'Yes, you are an Antwerpse now.'

She tries to catch the hair whipping around her face

with one hand, while gripping the rail with the other. 'I'm what?'

He bends down and shouts in her ear. 'An Antwerpse. The Dutch for a girl who belongs to Antwerp, although amongst us merchants it's mostly French spoken, not Dutch.'

'That's good. I will be able to speak with your family in French then,' she shouts.

He frowns and shakes his head. 'My mother has only Spanish.'

'What?'

The ship slides down the back of a wave and crashes into the next one, dousing them in spray. Bethia wipes her eyes with her sleeve. Wet strands of hair cling to her face, and her cloak billows out behind like a small sail. He lets go of her to grab his bonnet before it takes to the air, his hair and beard glistening, although the spray slides off the tight black curls.

She can no longer see the town, and only the occasional glimpse of rocky coastline. All around, foaming grey sea is rushing past, and the rising wind snaps the sails. The captain shouts and points, and she gazes wide-eyed as sailors scramble up the rigging, bare feet on swinging ropes. She remembers how painful the climb was on her own, shod feet, up the long rope ladder to St Andrews Castle. It's over a year since she crept in to persuade her brother Will to leave the renegade group holding it against the government troops, and return home, both for his own safety and to protect their family from retribution. Indeed, were it not for Will's refusal, she wouldn't now be fleeing her homeland.

The ship rises and her belly rises with it, then down it thumps, her belly dropping like a stone. Mainard points towards a doorway beneath the quarterdeck, and she nods understanding and lets go of the rail. The ship rolls and she staggers, thumping her back and head hard against the mast behind. Then she's thrust forward and

4

grabs the railing again. Mainard too is struggling to regain his balance. Above them the sail cracks and flails while the sailors fight to restrain it.

She's feeling most strange, made worse by the way the ship leaps up and crashes down at the mercy of the waves. This is not fear – she knows what fear is after being trapped inside the ruined castle, hiding in the rubble, while soldiers searched for her. She remembers Father telling that a sea voyage is better than any purge to cleanse him. She feels no urge to vomit, yet has never experienced such a distortion of the senses.

Mainard is at her side once more, tugging on her arm and urging her to let go of the rail. She doesn't want to move, needs to stay here, with the spray fresh upon her face and her eyes fixed upon the horizon. He unwraps her hands and they move at a run, impelled by the tilting deck, then she stumbles through the swinging door, down a few steps, and into quiet.

'The captain has given up his cabin for our use,' Mainard says, looking down at his feet.

The small cabin is made even smaller, for Grissel is crouched in the corner.

'We must find somewhere else for her to sleep,' Mainard mumbles.

Grissel's face is white and sweating, as though she'd covered it with a layer of goose fat. Bethia swallows; goose fat is not a good thought at the moment. Grissel moans, rocking back and forward on her haunches. She opens her mouth and a gush of watery flux sprays out, splashing Mainard's legs and filling the airless cabin with the sour smell of vomit.

Bethia groans and clambers onto the narrow bunk. Perhaps she'll feel less dizzy if she lies down. She groans again, rolls over and presses her forehead to the side of the cabin. A whiff of stale sweat rises from the covers to mingle with the stench of vomit. The cabin door opens and slams shut behind Mainard. She hopes he's gone for

5

assistance. The ship rolls and Bethia rolls with it but is contained within the sides of the narrow bunk. She should get up and help Grissel but she's afraid to move. The dizzy sinking sensation is marginally less if she can but stay still; if only the ship would stay still too.

She hears Mainard speaking but keeps her face to the wall. 'This is the servant to my wife.'

She wants to correct him. Grissel is much more to her than a servant, but the sense of whirling is worsening – how is it possible – and she dare not move, nor speak.

'We must find a bunk for her.'

'There is no other,' a gruff voice responds.

The door opens and bangs shut many times; there's the clang of a bucket, and more retching from Grissel. Mainard comes to persuade Bethia to sit up and drink some brandy, but she shakes her head and then wishes she had not as waves of dizziness cascade over her. He goes, returning some time later to bathe her brow with a cold cloth.

'Thank you,' she whispers.

The sea thumps and batters the ship, like a bad husband beating his wife, and the ship creaks and groans in response. She's sure the vessel cannot resist much longer, that they will all be drowned.

By day three she doesn't care if they do all drown. Indeed, if she had the strength to climb out of the bunk, she'd go out on deck and fling herself overboard. She swears by the Virgin Birth she will not step foot on a ship once she is released from this one, even if it means she'll never see Scotland, and her family, again. She drifts in the half-awake, half-asleep otherworld that's now her reality, broken only by regular visits from Mainard. He bathes her forehead, forces brandy down her throat and even removes her clothes, leaving her wearing only a shift. She's blind to modesty, only wants to be left lying still.

When next she surfaces she can feel the change. The ship is rising and falling smoothly, gently creaking as it thrums through the water. She sits up slowly and feels a steadiness deep inside which she'd always taken for granted before. The pallet with its strew of blankets lies empty on the floor and she hopes Grissel is feeling better too. She swings her legs around ready to try standing, when the motion of the ship suddenly changes. There are shouts from above and the sound of distant thunder. She goes still; the thunder is drawing closer. She leaps off the bunk and huddles in a corner. The ship shudders and she covers her ears at the explosion of splintering wood above.

Chapter Two

Attacked

Bethia hears the sound of running feet and men shouting. She stays crouched, arms protecting her head. She knows it won't save her from injury if the cabin is hit, but she doesn't know what else to do. She can hear her breath loud in her ears and wishes Mainard would come. And Grissel, where is she?

The smooth passage of the ship becomes restless. It slows, waves slapping loud against the sides, the uneven motion setting her belly to rocking once more. She pushes herself up and, holding onto the side of the bunk, looks around for her clothes.

The cabin door bursts open and Mainard rushes in, bringing a gust of sea air. He kicks Grissel's pallet to one side and kneels down to untie the rope which is securing the kist tucked underneath the bunk. 'I must have my sword,' he says, fumbling with the knots.

She kneels beside him, pushing his hand out of the way, and frees the kist.

He flings the lid wide and grabs the sword from where it lies on top.

'But what is happening?'

'Stay here.' The cabin door crashes behind him.

She sits back on her heels and then topples over as the ship wallows. It seems as though they have come to a halt.

Her bundle of clothes is in the kist and she pulls out her skirt and slides it over her head, rising onto her knees to tie it at her waist. Leaning against the bunk she raises her hands to smooth her hair, the smell of sweat pungent. She must wash…later.

There's a thump of something heavy knocking against the side of the boat. It thumps again and she hears voices close enough to touch the speaker, were it not for the ship between them. She flings her shawl over her shoulders and draws it across her chest to cover the shift, tying it around the back of her waist. Then she opens the cabin door, stumbles up the steps and onto the deck. Blinking in the light she sees Mainard close by, his back to her and sword drawn. The sailors are crowded together by the mainmast, heads hanging, while men clamber over the ship's side.

'Get below, Bethia,' hisses Mainard, glancing over his shoulder. 'Quickly. And hide.'

There are two men striding towards him, pistols pointing. She squints, eyes still adjusting to sun sparkling on the water. One of them is long of body, short of leg and very familiar. 'Geordie?' she says.

Mainard looks over his shoulder frowning.

She pushes past him and stands in front of Geordie, eyes wide. 'What are you doing here?'

Geordie's companion reaches out to grab her, the last two fingers of his hand only stumps.

Geordie knocks the mutilated hand away. 'Dinna do that, Androu, she's one of us, ye gowk. Leave her alone, else her father will hae your head upon a platter.'

Bethia, arms akimbo, places her feet wide to keep her balance. 'Geordie, in the name of the Blessed Virgin, what is going on?'

The sailors watch from their penned-in space and the captain descends from the quarterdeck, the sword by his side clattering against the railing. He issues an instruction and a sailor slides past Androu, who shoves him back so that his head hits a stanchion. He bounces forward, red-faced and fists clenched. Androu raises his pistol and fires. The shot skims past its target and lodges in the railing. A second sailor lifts a hand, blood dripping where flying splinters have pierced the skin.

'Stop!' shouts Bethia.

Again all eyes are upon her. She grabs Geordie by the arm. 'Is my father involved in this piracy?' she hisses in his ear.

He won't meet her eyes. She remembers a conversation with Father about the Hollanders great fishery every year, starting in June off Shetland and then moving down the coast of Scotland until they reached the Forth Estuary, for the Lammas Drave in August – and now is Lammas.

'They've these great herring busses with three masts,' Father said. 'Oh, they're braw big boats, which drag the nets ahint. And what nets... why, they can cover over forty foot.'

'But surely the fish are rotten before they can get them back to Holland?' Bethia wondered, and she remembers how her question pleased him.

'Nay a bit of it, for they Dutchie folk are canny. They bring ither boats alongside which run back and forward to their country with the gutted herring salted and packed in barrels. They have a wee bittie of a problem with privateers attacking and robbing them, so they have to be well armed. Still, 'tis a grand trade, if Scotland would only learn from it, for there's good livings to be made in the export of herring and salmon to the Baltic.'

And Scotland seems to have learnt from it, she thinks – learned that it's easier to rob the ships than do the work. Although she can't entirely blame Father after the losses he took when his ship was impounded at Veere in Holland, and all his cargo confiscated near two years ago. She, helping him with his accounts, had wondered at how quick their fortunes seemed to revive. The privateering explains all. But this ship is not a herring bus, it has only two masts and a foresail – why have they been attacked? She suspects it may be nothing more than a chance sighting.

Geordie shakes his head at Androu and confirms her suspicions. 'I telt ye this ship was no worth bothering with.'

Mainard spreads his hands wide. 'We have almost no cargo, only a few hides. With all the troubles in St Andrews there was little to trade, and the trip was all about fetching my bride.' In spite of their peril, Bethia cannot help the glimmer of a smile at the note of pride in his voice.

Androu spits. 'There's aye something for the taking, and her father will never ken if we…'

He doesn't get a chance to finish, for Mainard takes the flat of his sword, and using it like a staff, he sweeps the feet out from under Androu, who thumps down onto the decking. Placing the tip of the sword on Androu's breastbone, Mainard pins him down.

Geordie raises his hands, palms outward, short legs spread wide to keep his balance. 'Aye, aye. Calm down, nae need for that. We're leaving.'

Mainard presses the tip of the sword into the soft skin under Androu's chin, forcing him to tilt his head back. A trickle of blood runs down his neck. Mainard presses harder and Androu eyes widen. Mainard lifts the sword and taps Androu's ear lobe, one side then the other. Bethia holds her breath, as convinced as the quaking Androu clearly is that Mainard is going to slice his ears off. But Mainard raises his sword and takes a step back.

Suddenly Bethia is knocked from behind and falls against Mainard.

Grissel shoves past. 'Uncle Geordie, Uncle Geordie!' She drops to her knees before him.

Geordie stares down at her; indeed, everyone is staring at her.

11

'Dinna be sae daft. Stand up, lassie.'

Grissel gets slowly to her feet and Androu too rises. Bethia sees the glint of a dagger in his hand. She shrieks a warning and hauls on Mainard's arm. The knife misses Mainard by a hairbreadth. Off balance, Androu staggers into Grissel and seizes her. He holds the blade across her neck, hauling her with him until his back is against the railing.

He shouts over Grissel's shoulder to his crew. 'See what you can find. This laddie will hae some fine clothes and Seton no doubt gie'd him a chest full of gold for his daughter's dowry.'

Bethia clenches her fists. Father, tears glinting in his eyes, pressed a fat purse into her hands when they said their farewells only a few days ago. She was surprised that he gave the purse to her and not, as would be expected, to her new husband. She doesn't know what happened to it, was too ill to care. She hopes Mainard has hid it well; it's all she has in the world.

Geordie, face flushed with anger, advances on Androu. 'Let the lass go, you bluidy fool.'

Androu presses the knife into Grissel's flesh. 'Stay there, or I'll gie her a nice wee necklace to remember me by.'

'You'll be sorry if you do.'

'Hah!' says Androu smirking at Geordie.

The men reappear with arms full of clothing, bottles of wine, and a cask of ale.

Androu sniffs and spits. 'Poor pickings for a rich merchant's daughter.'

Grissel, with Androu's attention elsewhere, seizes her moment. She's a tall lass, the same height as Androu, and strong with it. She thumps him full in the face with the back of her head. He goes still, as though he can't quite believe what's happened, and she does it again. He drops the knife and howls in pain, blood dripping from a nose that is most likely broke. Freed, Grissel escapes behind her uncle.

'Harpy,' hisses Androu, and Bethia sees one of his few remaining teeth is broken, blood running from his mouth as well as nose. He wipes his nose with back of his sleeve, spits out a mouthful of blood and dives for Grissel.

But Geordie is ready, grabbing Androu's arm and twisting it up his back. 'We're leaving. Drop what you hae – t'will bring us naething but ill luck to take it, and is not worth the risk of Master Seton finding out. He is no a man to cross.'

Bethia is surprised to hear Father spoken of thus; it's not a side she's seen of him.

The privateers' ship is brought in close and they clamber back, a glowering Androu among them, the skin around his eyes already purpling and nose swollen.

Geordie is about to follow when Grissel clutches his arm. 'Take me with you, dinna leave me here. I need to go hame. I've been so sick.'

Geordie glares at her. 'You will do yer duty, as we all must, and stay wi' the young mistress.'

'Please, Uncle Geordie, please,' Grissel pleads, sticking tight as a burr. Geordie, trying to disengage himself, looks to Bethia.

Bethia sniffs. 'You'll be as sick on that ship as on this. But if you want to leave me, then go. I do not want you here.' She turns, lifting bare feet sticky from the tarry deck caulking, and retreats to her cabin.

Chapter Three

Antwerp

The river is broad and busy. Their ship tacks from one side to the other, the wind blustery, so that one moment they are barely moving and the next thrust forward at a great pace, endangering smaller craft which are expected to get out of the way. It's a narrow miss for some, and, even though there are no collisions, the boats are at grave risk of being overturned by the ship's bow wave. A caravel is making its way up the river in front of them, and Bethia can see several following behind, but the heart-stopping moment is when a galleon suddenly appears around the wide bend ahead. She cannot look as it looms larger and larger, pressing her face into Mainard's arm.

Mainard pats her shoulder. 'They know what they're about, my love.'

She squeezes his arm in response. There are shouted instructions but both captains do indeed know what they are about and turn their ships away from one another. The other ship, though, ploughs into a small fishing ketch and does not stop. There are tiny figures bobbing in the water and other small boats converge on them.

She gazes at the land, which she is most happy to see close by. There are many woods with tall slender spires of a tree the like of which she has never seen before. Through the occasional breaks in the trees she spies villages and farms. She can see people working in the fields, and this too contributes to her rising sense of well-being.

'How much longer before we arrive?' she asks Mainard.

He shouts a question to the helmsman, who shouts back. She must begin to learn Dutch, as well as Spanish, and quickly, if she is to be an asset and not a burden in this life together. She wonders again why Mainard's mama speaks Spanish. When she asked, he said it was because his family came from Spain, but she thought that was a long time ago – and anyway she's sure he once told her they came from Portugal.

She still has little idea of what their life will be like. There was no time for discussion when she agreed to be his wife and fled Scotland. She doesn't even know where they are going to live, feels a tightness in her belly that is different from the malaise de mer, but almost as unwelcome. She detaches herself from him and goes to her cabin to prepare for arrival – and to find a place of calm.

The cabin stinks of vomit and stale bodies. Even without the inconvenience of Grissel sleeping here, it's no wonder Mainard did not join her in the narrow bunk. Grissel is huddled in her corner, dirty yellow hair falling over her big, usually sonsy, face. She's barely moved since her uncle refused to take her back to Scotland.

Bethia stares at her, but Grissel doesn't look up. 'We will soon arrive; you must prepare yourself.'

Grissel hunches down further, peering up at Bethia through the tangle of hair.

'Fetch us some water so we can freshen ourselves; we must smell as bad as this cabin.'

Grissel shakes her head. 'I'm no moving – I'll stay here till I'm took home.'

'This ship isn't going back to Scotland. It's for the West Indies, for sugar.' Bethia has no idea if this is so, but

Grissel is her responsibility. She cannot leave her unprotected, wherever the ship is going.

She goes to fetch the basin of water herself. If she stays in the cabin she'll likely shake Grissel. 'It's not as if I forced her to come,' she mutters to herself, remembering Grissel's eagerness to escape from under her mother's control, and even more so from Bethia's own mother's constant disparagement.

She returns with the water, hauls Grissel to her feet, washes her face and brushes her hair. Just as though I am the servant and she the mistress, she thinks. She clenches her teeth, feeling a wave of longing for home. A tear rolls down her cheek and she brushes it away. This will not do, as Father himself would say, as she's made her bed, so she must lie. And Father would say this most especially if he could see her now, for he told her to marry a soldier and local man, Gilbert Logie – not Mainard.

She sends Grissel to tip the dirty water out and fetch a fresh basin, and this time Grissel obeys. While Bethia waits, she tugs the kist from underneath the bunk, which is in a sad jumble after the privateers' rummaging. She wonders where Mainard hid the purse of money. It is her tocher, she supposes, although truly she should have a greater dowry than one purse of gold coin. She hopes Mainard will not entirely claim it as his property. No, he's a better man than that, else she would not be here. And where is Grissel with her water? She goes out on deck to find a much-recovered servant, laughing with the group of sailors surrounding her as Mainard stands by, clearly amused too.

They have reached a stretch where the river seems to flow due north, as though they are returning from whence they came. Then they are rounding a great bend, and she knows she will remember this moment all her days. The river, already wide, opens into a vast basin, and along one bank is sited the great city of Antwerp. Guarding the entrance to the city is a fortress, built on a scale far greater than St Andrews Castle – which Bethia had, up till now, always considered to be mighty. Its turrets rise high, overseeing all that passes beneath, the stonework a mellow grey rather than the yellow sandstone she is used to. All the colours here seem different, from the grey of the buildings to the deep green of the tall trees to the brightly dressed dots of people visible on the quayside.

'That is the King's Stone Castle,' says Mainard coming to lean next to her. 'It is called the Het Steen, and our Emperor Charles is never done remodelling it, and indeed that's very necessary to protect our city.'

Bethia nods but doesn't respond, for now they are passing the fortress and the city is revealed in all its glory. It crowds the bank and stretches away as far as she can see. The roof line of its houses reach ever higher in a series of jagged points, as though to pierce the sky, poking at God himself for attention. Tallest among them are the spires of what she assumes must be the cathedral, which again is grander than that of St Andrews, but then this is the richest city in the world.

They draw closer to the quays and she sees the many boats moored at the long wharves, prows facing in like a line of obedient suppliants, while others await their turn to dock, rocking at anchor mid-river.

Grissel joins them and Bethia wrinkles her nose; Grissel does smell bad after days of vomiting. 'Oh, it's a braw place, bonniest I've ever seen,' says Grissel in her loud voice.

Bethia snorts. 'You haven't seen any others, apart from St Andrews.'

'Aye, well it's still the bonniest. But what are they long pole things that rise so high?'

'Cranes,' says Mainard. 'We have many new cranes to make the unloading of even large cargos quick. There's even a crane-operators guild now.'

'Is that another river joining there?' Bethia asks.

'That's a canal. They were dug to ease the transport of

goods around the city and beyond.'

She feels a thrill of excitement. There's so much for her to learn, and she hopes the skills she has, so helpful to Father in his business, will be of value in Antwerp.

Bethia assumes a space will be found for them at the quayside, but Mainard says if they wait for one they could be stuck on the ship for up to two weeks. She submits to being lowered over the side in a bosun's chair, the ropes twisting the chair as she descends. She looks down between her feet and sees water below. The chair swings wide as the river grows closer, and then she is hooked over the rowboat and Mainard helps her out. She sits down in the stern, gazing around her. She's entirely happy in a small boat, after the times Geordie rowed her from the harbour to the castle during the siege. She thinks of her brother Will and hopes the punishment for his participation is not too long, nor too severe. He will no doubt be a prisoner in France by now.

Grissel is less sanguine, and shrieks as she is lowered, clinging onto the sides of the chair so tightly that Bethia has to un-grip her fingers. Grissel clambers out, and the small boat is set rocking while she shrieks even more. Eventually all is settled and they are soon standing on the quay.

Grissel grabs Bethia's arm. 'Still it moves. 'Tis makin' me dizzy.'

'You'll soon adjust to being ashore,' says Mainard, offering his arm to Bethia. She is glad of it, feels the ground unsteady beneath her own feet. She hands her satchel to Grissel and they set off, with Grissel's head swivelling as she trails behind.

There are so many people and she hears many languages: Dutch and Flemish she now recognises from listening to the sailors on board; French she understands; the guttural sound of German; and here the familiarity of English; now the exotic sounds of Africa and the Orient. She can feel the wealth and commerce pulsing through the city.

They pass under a gateway and are now enclosed within the high city walls. Mainard finds a carriage, which she is glad of. The sun is bright above and it's hot work to move through this crowded place. The cab looks most strange with large rear wheels and only a single horse to pull it, but the seat is cushioned and comfortable. Mainard sits with his back to the driver, 'so that you two ladies may see all, and I may watch your enjoyment.'

Grissel giggles to be so described, and shrieks as the cab takes off with a jerk and picks up speed. Then she's nudging Bethia as the horse lifts its tail, and the driver stretches a leather bucket on a long pole to catch the droppings. Mainard looks over his shoulder and grins at the reason for the girls' laughter. They are turning away from the river, clopping down long streets lined by so many tall buildings it's as if she is in a city of giants, and the crow-stepped gables of these lofty houses the giants' stairway to heaven. But soon her eyes are drawn back to ground level, for the streets are bustling with people. She turns her head this way and that: so much to see, and each sight more astonishing than the last.

The cab rounds a corner at a fast clip and they enter a square, drawing up outside one of its many houses. The home of Mainard's parents, she supposes, for he mentioned this was where they would live – for a short while. Mainard jumps down and holds his hand out. Bethia descends and Grissel clambers down after her. The young women stand on the pavement and gaze up at the tall house before them. Mainard takes off his cap and smooths his hair, an almost impossible task because it's so very curly. He hesitates, his forehead wrinkling, and she feels a knot in her belly. They walk slowly towards the front door and she grips his hand tight. He squeezes back. The door opens before they reach it. She leaves the sunlit square and enters into darkness.

Chapter Four

The Family

Bethia stands before her new parents, with her new husband by her side. The family are sat at the board, the many dishes piled with food steaming in front of them. Mainard's father gazes on her with a puzzled frown. Then he inclines his head, rises and bows, but the look of puzzlement doesn't leave his face.

Mainard turns to Bethia. 'My father you have met, of course, but may I introduce my mother.' He gestures towards an older woman with a gentle face who's gazing at him in confusion. 'And' – he waves towards the girl sitting on the settle staring at Bethia with bright curiosity – 'Katheline, my sister.'

Bethia curtsies and the women rise and curtsey back.

The mother looks to her husband and he shrugs.

Mainard gestures to the settle and Bethia slides in next to Katheline, with Mainard next to her. A bell is rung and a servant instructed in Dutch. Bethia looks around at the green-painted walls hung with engravings, the paintings each draped with its own curtain, the large cupboard where rich-painted china is displayed, and the marble fireplace – the first she's ever seen. She looks to her new parents. Mainard's father has raised his eyebrows and is staring at Mainard.

Then suddenly both parents are speaking in quick

bursts, firing questions in what she assumes is Spanish. She touches Mainard's sleeve and looks up at him questioningly. He takes her hand, under cover of the board. She's not reassured.

She watches, eyes moving from one speaker to the next. She looks to Mainard, who shifts on his seat as though he's on hot coals. Then Mainard speaks and Master de Lange's head jerks back. The mother gasps and replies, her soft voice growing shrill. The sister turns and stares at Bethia.

A sense of doom is descending upon Bethia, like a thick haar on the sea coast of her home. It is clear that Mainard's parents were not expecting him to return with a bride, and they are not greeting the news of his nuptials joyfully. She thinks how easily their marriage could be annulled, given it is yet to be consummated. She would be sent back to Scotland divorced and unmarriageable. And it's not safe for her there.

Master de Lange shakes his head, speaking slowly in his deep voice. He sounds sad. The mother, brow furrowed and darting gaze, looks fearful. The servant returns with a plate and a glass of wine. The cut glass is finely engraved, the rich ruby-red of the wine showing to perfection through it. Katheline passes a platter of spinach mixed with collops of mutton to Bethia. Mainard stabs the haunch of beef with his knife, hacks at it and tosses the piece onto her platter. She picks at the food and chews on a lump of meat. It's well spiced, yet somehow delicately flavoured, but she's finding it difficult to swallow.

There's a lull in the conversation, as though no one knows what to say.

Mainard's mother speaks.

'Bethia,' says Mainard in response.

Bethia looks at him curiously.

'Mama asked your name.'

Bethia thinks what it must be like to be presented with a new daughter whose name you don't know.

Mistress de Lange stands up and smiles at Bethia, a smile of such sweetness that Bethia cannot help but smile back even through her worry.

'Venga,' she says, curling her fingers in beckoning.

Bethia lets go of Mainard's hand and rises with alacrity. Her skirt catches on the corner of the board as she slides out, hauling her back. She flicks it free but doesn't stop to look it over, hurrying to catch up with Mama as she glides from the room. She wonders if she should refer to Mistress de Lange as her mama. She has not been so invited, and how are they to communicate without any shared language? She clenches and unclenches her fingers, but then Mainard's sister comes from behind and takes her arm.

She smiles at the girl, who's a slender version of her mother, much like Mainard is a taller, and darker, version of his handsome father.

Katheline has bright brown eyes, which gaze curiously on Bethia. 'Mainard told me of you.'

'Clearly he's not mentioned me to your mama,' says Bethia, relief that this girl speaks French well enough for them to converse, making her response sharper than she meant.

'Do not fear, Mama is truly kind. It was a big surprise.'

'You didn't know where Mainard had gone?'

'No, but that's not unusual. Mainard is a very private man who follows his own path.'

Bethia bites her lip. She hears her own mother's voice in her head – you must make the best of it, as girls the world over have to. But that was when Mother was ordering her to marry Fat Norman. She chose Mainard, but it's becoming more and more evident that she barely knows him.

They climb the broad staircase, the wooden panelling which lines it heavy with paintings. The spindles of the staircase, too, are thick posts of polished oak, the banister broad and carved, smooth to the touch. This house exudes wealth, much as the city does. Mama and Katheline lead the way to a chamber stabbed with sunlight from the tall leaded windows which line one wall. There is a large bed with a red cover, and its canopy and curtains are of pale yellow silk. A tapestry of unicorns and roses hangs on the door-side wall; she's only seen one on such a scale before in St Andrews Castle.

Near the ample fireplace there's a low door set in the wooden panelling which lines this wall. She's guided through it and finds a tub in the centre of this garde-robe and the same plump servant who served them at dinner, tidy in her white kerchief and apron, filling it with buckets of water. The steam rises and Bethia wipes her forehead with the back of her hand, made uncomfortable by the clammy heat in this small chamber.

Katheline and her mother stand back and the servant comes towards Bethia, reaching out to unfasten her clothes.

Bethia backs away. 'I will have my own servant,' she says to Katheline.

Grissel was led away when they entered the house and she hasn't given her a thought since, but, knowing Grissel, she'll no doubt be managing despite the language barrier.

Mama raises her eyebrows when Katheline translates. Sirvienta, Bethia hears repeated. She rolls the word around her tongue.

'Your sirvienta is in the kitchens. Mama says she may come above stairs once she's clean. Marisse will help you for now.'

Marisse's fat fingers fumble to undo her lacing while Katheline and Mama stand and watch. Once the lacing is undone, Bethia stops the servant. She cannot take all her clothes off under these watchful eyes.

She looks to Katheline. 'Please, I must bathe alone.'

There's another exchange and the mama nods slowly.

'We will leave you,' says Katheline, moving towards

23

the door. They glide out, closing it behind them, and Bethia is left with the servant. She wants to tell her to go too. What was her name, Mar… something? Bethia waves the girl towards the door but her face wrinkles in seeming confusion; Bethia wonders if it's feigned.

Bethia stands for a moment considering if she's making too much fuffle about this bathing. But no, she must begin as she means to go on, and if she wants the servant to leave her, then the servant must go. She opens the door and ushers the girl out.

She gazes at the tub, has never submerged her whole body in this fashion before, except when she fell into the sea trying to escape from the castle – and was near drowned. She swirls the water with her fingers. It feels pleasantly warm. She removes her bodice, folds and lays it on a stool. She unties her skirt and stands in her shift. She's reluctant to remove it, will keep it on in the tub, but then she has no other to wear, doesn't know where the kist containing her clothes is. Reluctantly she lifts it over her head, dropping it on the floor.

Then she's staring at the red stain on the white linen. Blushing, she tugs the shift and her skirt back on again. She kneels by the tub and washes herself as best she can, making use of the soft linen squares left neatly folded with which to dry herself, embarrassed that she is making bloody rags of such fine cloth, but she has no other.

She finishes dressing and retreats back into the chamber. Her kist has been brought and placed on the floor at the end of the bed, but, when she hurriedly packed it, she did not remember to include a supply of rags. She doesn't know what to do but sit and wait on the big chair by the ower-grand fireplace – for a bed-chamber – which is now filling with shadows while the sun sets.

There's a tap on the door, and after a moment Mainard's face appears around it, eyebrows raised. Bethia feels a softening within her core at the sight of him.

'I can come in?'

She nods.

'All is well with you?' he asks, head inclined.

She flushes, red as beetroot water. 'Not so well.'

He hurries towards her. 'You are sick?'

She shakes her head, holding her hand out to ward him off.

'Tell me.'

She fidgets on her seat. 'It's not something I've ever had to explain to a man before.'

He folds his arms. 'Out with it. I'm strong enough.'

A ghost of a smile crosses her face. 'You know about women's bodies…'

He grins at her. 'Not so much, but I'm hoping to learn.'

She glances down, cannot meet his eyes as she speaks. 'It is the time for me, the thing that happens for us every month when we have our courses.' She can feel the flush spreading across her whole body now.

'Ah.' He nods thoughtfully. 'Of course, I know. And Plato speaks of this. It is when women bleed to cool their natures.'

She looks up, grateful that she need explain no further. 'But it means…' She gazes towards the bed.

He blinks. 'Yes, naturally.'

Bethia blushes and blushes until it feels as though her whole body is on fire. 'I am sorry.'

He reaches down and takes her hand. 'We will have time very soon. But for now I will leave you to rest.' He squeezes her hand and goes.

Suddenly Bethia is so tired she doesn't care what happens, so long as she can sleep. She unties her skirt, removes her bodice, and crawls into bed.

Chapter Five

Shopping

It is evident that Mainard has said something, for the yellow-haired servant awakens Bethia the next morning with a supply of rags.

Bethia asks 'Mainard?' several times in what she hopes is a questioning tone.

The servant's blue eyes grow larger. 'Uitgaan,' she eventually responds.

Bethia thinks the words sounds like a reversed Scots gone oot, which she assumes is what Mainard indeed has done. She presses her thumb into the palm of the opposite hand, rubbing it up and down, wondering what she is to do with herself, left alone in this house without him. The servant watches her. Then she produces a comb from her apron pocket and indicates that Bethia should sit down.

Bethia sits very still as the servant combs and plaits her hair. What is her name – something unfamiliar, and Dutch. She's plumply curvaceous and would be pretty if she didn't have a gap where one of her front teeth is missing; she is young to have lost it already.

Bethia pats her hair. It feels most elaborate, and over-tightly knotted, but she smiles her thanks and nods that the girl may go, for she wants to dress alone, without strange hands upon her. The servant passes her a pouch gesturing that Bethia should tie it around her waist, on top of her shift. Bethia opens it expecting lavender or some such herb but finds only ashes. She shrugs, but nevertheless affixes it.

She's crossing the square hallway, bigger than any room in her old home, in search of Grissel, when Katheline appears.

'You will come out with me.'

Relieved to be given some direction, Bethia nods. 'Yes, let me get my shawl.'

'Marisse can fetch it, but I do not think you will need a shawl. The day is warm.'

'Is Marisse the servant who's been helping me?'

'Yes, she's good with hair, is she not?' says Katheline inspecting Bethia's coiffeur. 'But she's not as pretty as your servant – now she is made clean.'

'Have you ever been on a sea voyage?'

Katheline shakes her head. 'I've been on the river but never all the way to the coast.'

'Avoid it if you can. I would happily have flung myself into the German Ocean if I'd had the strength, and Grissel vomited until it seemed her insides would come outside.'

Katheline laughs, and after a moment Bethia allows herself to smile. Mainard's sister has a laugh like the tinkling of small bells, and the sound gives Bethia a sense of well-being deep inside. Katheline's rather solemn face, set in its halo of soft curls, comes alive, and her smile lights up the dim hallway. She is not pretty so much as unusual in an exotic way, especially her eyes.

'I must see Grissel, then we can go,' says Bethia, and her new sister inclines her head and leads the way to the servant's quarters.

Grissel is found outside, in what seems a very small yard. Her hair is bundled in a knot on top of her head and she sits on a stool plucking a dead rooster.

She looks up, wrinkling her nose. 'They chop the heads off instead of ringing their necks. It's daft, for now I've got blood on my skirt. Although,' she says, smirking, 'it's gey funny to watch the rooster run around with no head and the blood spurting.'

'I see you are fully recovered.'

'Aye, although I canna understand a word they say. Lucky there's a laddie here has got some Scots, for he fought next to our mercenaries in one of those wars they're aye having.' She wipes the sweat off her brow with the back of her hand, leaving a smear of blood. 'Och, but it's ower warm in this place.'

They leave Grissel to her labours. Bethia is relieved to see her settling in, although, truth be told, she's still a little hurt by Grissel's willingness, indeed desperation, to return to Scotland with her uncle. It did not show the loyalty to be expected, and desired, from a servant – especially one who has been with the Seton family since birth.

Katheline passes Bethia a bonnet of a most unusual style as they prepare to leave the house.

'It's like a cone of sugar, except wider in the base,' Bethia says, twisting it around and around in her hands. 'I would prefer to wear my own cap.' She hands it back but Katheline shakes her head.

'That small cap is not seemly. Your head must be fully covered, so you will place this on top of your cap. It will give you protection from the sun… and rain.'

'And obscure my vision,' says Bethia placing it on her head reluctantly. 'I can see very little around me and it weighs heavy upon my neck.'

'Come, Coort,' Katheline calls, and a young man with a long staff appears. He opens the door wide and out they go into the heat of the day.

'How come you don't have to wear a cone upon your head?'

'I'm not a married woman.'

Bethia looks over her shoulder. 'Why is your man following us? Is it dangerous to walk the streets of Antwerp?'

'Sometimes, but in any case we shouldn't be

unattended, and Coort will take good care of us.'

There is a warmth in Katheline's voice when she speaks of Coort and his protection, and she notices out of the corner of her eye that he's nodding at Katheline's words.

'Mama has said I am to take you to choose fabric for new clothes.'

'I have no coin with me.' She wonders where Mainard has hid the purse from Father.

'That's not necessary. We'll buy on account and all will be settled later.'

'I'd prefer to purchase my own clothes.'

'As you wish.'

There is a silkiness about Katheline which is hard to pin down. Bethia suspects she wins an argument by refusing to engage in it. She smiles, remembering how easily she could arouse her brother Will to fury by becoming unnaturally calm the angrier he became. It seems she is not the only lass to employ such a tactic. Poor Will; she hopes Father has done something to enable his release – although it's perhaps early days; he has not long been imprisoned.

The streets are as busy as yesterday, but Katheline moves with confidence: swerving around gossiping groups; dodging the reaching hands of beggars, one of whom has no legs and rides upon a low board with wheels, another with the mark of a leper upon him; ducking down dark alleyways which are pleasantly cool, although putrid smelling; always shadowed by the faithful Coort. Everywhere they go the cathedral dominates, rising above like a great watcher whose eye is inescapable.

They pass down a street that is longer and broader than any in St Andrews.

'It's called the Meir,' says Katheline in answer to Bethia's inquiry.

Bethia is slowing to look around, does not want to be

rushed; it's all so new and strange.

'What is this?' She points into a large gilded entranceway, through which she sees a huge courtyard enclosed within a covered arcade supported by fluted arches and elaborately carved and decorated in the Frankish style. There are groups of men gathered within, bright in their coloured hose, dress swords hanging by their sides. They wear hats of such height she is surprised they don't fall off their heads given the energy with which the men are gesticulating.

'That is the Bourse, where the exchange happens.'

Bethia bends to see further through the twin doorways. 'The exchange of what?'

'Everything that men will buy and sell is brought from all over the world to Antwerp. Here they make their agreements and borrow what money they may need.'

Curious, Bethia goes to walk beneath the archway.

'No, no.' Katheline grabs her arm. 'You cannot go in unattended… and we shouldn't loiter.'

'But we are attended?'

'You must have Mainard with you.'

'That would be agreeable.'

Katheline glances at her as they walk on. Bethia is aware of an edge to her voice. She wants to ask where Mainard is but doesn't want his sister to know that he has not confided his movements to his own wife.

They stop before a house which Katheline enters without knocking. Stepping over the doorstep, Bethia realises they're in a shop. This is not like the Mercatgait shops of home where booths extend from the front of houses and purchases are made at the broad windowsill. And the fleshers market must be elsewhere, for there are no cattle, pigs, goats, nor sheep penned mid-street, the blood from the slaughtered running in the gutters.

The cloth displayed in this shop is the most varied she's ever seen. She rubs a length of woollen weave between her fingers; it's soft and the dye pure, all of unsurpassed quality. She becomes aware of whispering and looks up to catch a group of women in the corner staring. She smiles but they sniff and look away. She turns her back on them but can still feel their hostility.

Katheline comes to stand next to her. It's comforting to feel her close.

'Why are they staring at me?' Bethia whispers.

Katheline, face wiped of expression, reaches to stroke the cloth spread before Bethia. 'Have you made your choice? Mama said enough for three gowns and then there is the cotton for new shifts. We have plenty of lace at home, for Marisse is skilled at fine work.'

They make their purchases and Coort carries the packages. Bethia thinks that bringing a man-servant out with you has it uses. It's hotter in the street now. The sweat trickles down her face from under the cone, which may protect her from burning by the sun but does not give any coolness from its heat. She's glad when they reach home but disappointed that Mainard has not returned. She wonders at it – there's nothing to prevent them conversing, even if they must wait some days before intimacy.

'Katheline?' she calls to the young woman's disappearing back.

Katheline stops climbing the stairs and swivels to look down upon Bethia.

'Marisse,' – she stumbles over the unfamiliar name, – 'gave me a pouch to wear, you know.' She gestures at her waist. 'What is in it? I was expecting lavender.'

'Did she not give you herbs?'

Bethia shakes her head.

Katheline purses her lips. 'That was remiss of her. I shall speak to Mama.'

'No, no, I didn't mean to complain. I'm curious what it contains.'

The frown disappears from Katheline's face and she comes back down the stairs and draws close to Bethia. 'It will help ease the cramps...' – she waves her hand – '...down there.'

'But what is in the pouch?'

'Ah.' Katheline nods. 'Ashes of burnt toad.'

'You burn a toad?'

'Well, not me. But yes, we find it most efficacious. If you come to the kitchens, we'll tell Marisse to place some herbs in a pouch to wear around your neck. I like to use rose petals. It will disguise...' – she leans in close and whispers – '...the blood smell.'

Bethia nods. 'I am fond of rose petals myself.'

Katheline takes her arm and they head for the kitchens together.

Chapter Six

Waiting

It's the anniversary of her birth eighteen years ago but Bethia doesn't mention it.

When Katheline brings her a book, she thinks that, somehow, it's been discovered, but no. 'Mainard thought you might like this,' Katheline says. 'He said to tell you that he peeked into your chamber' – and peers over her knuckles like a wee mouse – 'but you were so deep asleep he didn't want to awaken you from your slumbers.'

Bethia turns the book over in her hands. She's heard of Thomas More's Utopia and is curious how he will describe his fancy. 'Have you read it?'

Katheline shakes her head. 'It's in Latin.'

'So's the Bible.'

'I don't have to read the Bible, the priest does that.'

Bethia thinks of George Wishart burned at the stake, in part for insisting that all should read the holy book for themselves and stand before the Lord on their own cognisance. It was Wishart's death which precipitated the chain of events that led to her coming to Antwerp, and her brother a prisoner of the French. She feels a rising curiosity to read More's words, remembering that he too died for his faith, and refusal to accept that his master, the king of England, could supplant the Pope as head of the Church. She unclasps the book, spreads it across her knees and bends over it. Soon she's absorbed, and only raises her head when the light fades and she must find a candle to continue.

The next day she stays tucked away in her chamber, reading. Although Katheline treats her kindly, Mainard's family don't seem to know what to do with her. But then she doesn't know what to do with herself, adrift in this strange time of waiting. Mainard's out, working with his father, she assumes. And when he came to visit with her, in the privacy of what will soon, she hopes, be their chamber, Mama appeared and chased him away. Then she took Bethia's face between her hands and spoke most earnestly before slipping out the door.

She soon returned accompanied by Katheline. 'Mama says she knows you are eager to be together, but you must not invite Mainard into your chamber at this time.' Katheline, listening to what her mother had to say next, put her hand over her mouth and giggled. Mama nudged her. 'Mama says she can remember what it's like in the beginning, when you are overflowing with love… and things may occur without you meaning it. She says I too must understand, for any child born as a result of congress at this time is likely to be sickly and malformed.' Katheline paused, blushing, but her mother gesticulated. 'It is also dangerous' – she inclined her head downwards – 'to the member.'

Bethia bit her lip. 'We most certainly do not want that.'

Katheline translated and Mama stared at Bethia, then she too giggled.

That had been a good moment, Bethia reflects, but still, it does not get away from this feeling of being stuck in transition – almost like she's in a kind of purgatory. Every so often she rises to ease her stiff back. She wanders around the room and comes to stand by the leaded glass windows, rubbing her neck as she watches the activity in the street below. The milk cart clops by and she sees Marisse, trailed by Grissel, come out to speak to the milk boy. The lad nudges Marisse and grins at Grissel, reaching out to take her hand and bow over it, and Grissel gives a mock curtsey.

When Bethia's called for the meal, Mainard is already seated at the board. He looks up at her and smiles.

'Perhaps we may take a walk,' she whispers as she slides in beside him.

He mouths, 'Soon.'

The food tastes strange to her palate.

'Pepper,' says Mainard in response to her inquiry about what is so liberally sprinkled upon it.

'You use much more than we do in Scotland,' she mumbles, realising as she speaks that they are wealthy and can afford to be generous with their spices.

Then Mainard's father speaks directly to her, asking after her family and even apologising for not inquiring about them sooner for, 'your arrival surprised us.'

She wants to tell him that she was as much surprised as he, that Mainard didn't forewarn her, but it would be disloyal. Instead, there is discussion about how Bethia will learn Spanish. She wants to say that surely it would be useful for their mama to learn French, but holds her tongue.

Master de Lange, who is talking now of a school that Bethia might attend where they teach French, Spanish, and Latin all together to their students.

'But Bethia has good French and her knowledge of Latin is greater than mine,' says Mainard smiling at her. 'When I was at the university we were taught Dutch by reading stories, verhaal Brabantic, every day, after meals – perhaps we might do that.'

'When I think on it, school is best avoided for now.' Papa looks to Mainard. 'You know they executed that teacher.'

Mainard sits up. 'I thought he was protected.'

'The aldermen bowed to pressure and revoked his rights as a citizen of Antwerp. The man was a fool to stage that play – a clear case of heresy, and of corrupting young minds.'

'How was he killed?'

Papa looks to Katheline and Bethia, both leaning forward to listen, and shrugs. 'The sword, but I think he endured much before that merciful end. I fear he lacked friends in high places... always very necessary to us all.'

Bethia wonders why the de Langes might need friends in high places. They are wealthy and must already be well connected; surely they would be the high-placed friends. It niggles at her, like a small stone caught in her shoe. After the meal she tries to detain Mainard but is called away, for the dressmaker has come. She's glad to be distracted from thoughts of the teacher's execution and passively submits to: being measured and turned; her back straightened; pins and tucks; the Spanish farthingale so much wider than she is used to; and the dressmaker, Mama, and Katheline discussing her as though she's not there. Mama takes Bethia's chin in her hand and strokes her face. She speaks, smiling gently, then shakes her head. As the door closes behind her and the dressmaker, Bethia looks inquiringly at Katheline.

'She says your eyes are blue as the sea, your skin is smooth as a baby's, and your figure is as light as thistledown.'

Bethia looks up hopefully. 'Did she truly say that?'

Katheline grins and tugs on Bethia's hair. Then gives it a further tug. 'And that your hair is thick and strong as a rope.'

'But what did she say,' pleads Bethia.

'She said she can feel you have a good heart... I told you, Mama is a kind one. But she also says you must stop chewing on your skin.' Katheline picks up Bethia's hand and touches the raw skin with her fingertip. 'And, from my own experience, I would advise that you do so.' Katheline shudders. 'Mama has a most noxious substance she will paint upon your fingers to discourage any further

36

gnawing.' She wanders over to the door as she speaks.

'Please don't go,' says Bethia. 'I don't understand…'

Katheline, hand on the latch, waits.

'I don't understand where Mainard goes.'

'I think you must speak with him,' says Katheline, and she whisks out the chamber before Bethia can ask anything further.

Bethia takes up her station at the window once more, rubbing her cramping belly. The light wanes; it seems to get dark so much earlier here than in Scotland. She's turning from the window to curl up on the bed when she sees Mainard striding along the cobbles, the feather in his cap fluttering in the wind. Her heart flutters watching him.

A woman emerges from the front door of their house. Bethia can see the top of her cone hat, but little else. The woman is too large to be either Mama or Katheline, and too well dressed for a servant. She sees Mainard and makes for him, blocking his way. He stumbles, managing a quick sidestep to avoid falling over her. She's surprisingly nimble for a large woman and steps in front of him once more, clutching his sleeve.

Bethia bites at the skin around her thumb while she studies the woman's profile – she's a tall woman with a fat belly. Bethia leans against the wall for support – not a fat belly, a pregnant one. The woman is shouting after Mainard, who waves her away with his hand as he makes for the door. She goes to follow him, then thinks better of it and walks slowly down the street.

Bethia feels an utter weariness sweep over her. She doesn't understand this place, and who is this woman to Mainard?

Chapter Seven

Confrontation

Six days have passed since Bethia arrived in Antwerp, and her menses are now over. She has her new clothes, which she would normally much enjoy, especially the gown of rich vermilion, although the low square neckline and tight corset feel strange to her. And the wide sleeves are pretty but most impractical, forever sliding over her hands when she tries to do anything. Mama has said, through Katheline, that of course Bethia must call her Mama, and her husband Papa. She finds it easy to say Mama but so far has been too diffident before the imposing master of the house to even speak to him uninvited, never mind call him Papa. As for Mainard, she has seen him only once in the past few days, and that again in the presence of his family. Today an armoire is slid into her chamber, with much heaving and pushing from Coort, Marisse and a giggling Grissel, and Mainard's clothes placed within.

Then she goes out into the corridor in time to see the back of Mama whisking though a door. There is the soft click of a key turning. She wonders what's behind the door, another bed-chamber she supposes, although not Mama's, which is on the floor above. She sighs. This begins to feels like a house of secrets.

Mainard is there at the meal that evening, smiling and

trying to take her hand. She tugs it out of his grip. It will take more than a smile and squeeze of the hand for her to tumble at his feet once more. And he will not be climbing into her bed… until they have spoken.

Their repast is over and Mama leads Bethia by the hand to Bethia's chamber. The steaming tub again awaits. She undresses, keeping her shift on, climbs in and leans back, enjoying the gentle touch of warm water on her skin. Marisse picks up the soap and washes her hair. Bethia wants to point out that it will take hours to dry and be impossible to smooth for days, but instead submits. She would prefer to have Grissel wait upon her but the family seem determined to keep Grissel within the confines of the kitchens. Marisse massages her shoulders and Bethia closes her eyes and drifts away.

'No te duermas,' calls Mama softly, tapping Bethia on the shoulder.

Bethia jumps.

She steps out and is dried, her dripping hair rubbed and rubbed. She's led to the fireplace, where a fire has been kindled despite the warm September night. Marisse brushes and spreads the hair wide, and, although still damp underneath, it is judged dry enough for the nightdress to be slid over Bethia's head, and for her to slip between the sheets. Mama kisses her on the forehead, and Bethia catches Mama's hand and kisses the back of it. She eases herself up so she's sitting as upright as she can with the bolster behind her, folds her hands on top of the pristine sheet with its edging of lace, and waits.

The door opens slowly and Mainard enters as though pushed from behind. He stands in his nightshirt with his long brown legs and long bony feet and grins at her.

When he doesn't move, she beckons. 'Venga,' she says, to show she has learnt something in the past week. He moves towards her, a smile creeping over his face, but she points to the kist which sits at the end of the bed. 'We must talk.'

He keeps moving towards her. 'Bethia,' he says,

holding his hands out, 'I know this first time in a strange place is not so easy but soon it will be better.' He reaches the bed and goes to lift the bedclothes to climb in.

He's so handsome, with that earnest look and the appeal in his voice, she almost allows it, but instead she holds tight the covers. 'No, you cannot join me until we have spoken.'

He tweaks the covers from under her hand. 'I can explain as well in the bed as out of it.'

She scrambles out the other side and stands with the bed between them. 'Sit!' She points to the kist and goes to sit on the carved chair with its tapestry-upholstered seat, finer than anything in her old home – and this in a bed-chamber.

He sits, tugging his nightshirt down over his knees, then folds his arms.

She swallows and keeps her eyes on his face. 'Why did you not tell me that your parents were unaware of our marriage?'

'How could I? I didn't know that you would agree to marry me when I arrived in Scotland. Indeed, I told you that I came there because I suspected my father had been destroying your letters, so why would I tell him I was going to seek you out?'

'But it was my father who was destroying your letters.'

'Yes, and we did not know this until you forced an admission from him.'

'But why did you wait so long to come?'

'I was not certain of you. Perhaps you didn't want me after all. And then there were rumours the French were sending a fleet to attack the castle and break the siege. I was afraid for you and needed to know you were safe.'

She stands up, ready to come to him, to hold him, to thank him.

Smiling, he opens his arms to her.

She drops back into the chair and flaps her hands at

him, as though she's shooing a rooster away. 'Mainard, this does not answer why you led me to assume that your parents would approve our marriage.'

He leans forward, a hand on each knee. 'My love, I never led you to assume any such thing.'

She flings herself back in the chair. 'You never told me otherwise.'

Now it's his turn to sigh. 'I expected us to have time on the voyage to prepare for our arrival, to plan our life together. But then…'

'I couldn't help being ill.' She shudders at the memory.

He stands up and comes closer, reaching out to stroke her hair, but she raises her arm to stop him.

'No, you will not distract me. I will not be left in confusion – I must know all.'

'There is no confusion. My parents were surprised, nothing more.'

'It was more than surprise.' Bethia thinks back. 'Your papa was most upset and your mama seemed… almost fearful.'

'No, you misunderstood.'

'You are certain it was only surprise? They didn't have other plans for you?'

'Parents always have plans for their children – look at your father. And those plans change with circumstances.'

She nods. 'That is very true.'

He pauses. 'Although, to be fair, my parents were concerned that you came from Scotland when relations between the Holy Roman Empire and your country are not so good. Not helped, as we discovered on our voyage, by Scots privateers. But to you, my sweet wife, they have can have no objection.'

He reaches out offering his hand and she reaches to take it, then as suddenly withdraws her hand. 'I am not finished. Who was that woman I saw you speaking to?'

'What woman?'

'I saw you, from this very window.' She points at the

41

window, bathed in golden light from the last rays of the setting sun. 'The woman was leaving this house, and she was heavy with child.'

He stands up. 'Oh her. That's Geertruyt.'

'And who is Geertruyt?'

He leans down and takes her hand. 'A woman big with child.' He grins at her.

'And why was a pregnant woman confronting you? She appeared most agitated.'

He tugs her to her feet and she allows it, but when he pulls her towards the bed she will go no further.

'I am waiting.'

'Geertruyt is often angry. I pity her husband.'

He places his arm around Bethia's shoulder and leans in to kiss her. She places her hand in front of her lips, so he kisses the back of her hand instead.

'Why was she here?'

He drops his arm and steps back. 'She's my sister.'

'Your sister! Why has no one told me of her, and why have I not met her? She was here and no one thought to introduce us…'

'Come, Bethia. You make too much of this. You'll meet her soon enough, God help you, for she is a difficult woman.' He reaches out and strokes her arm, then tugs her towards him. Encircling her with his arms, he looks down into her face.

'What is that Scottish word for beautiful?'

'Bonny,' she whispers.

'You are my Bethia, and the bonniest thing to ever come out of Scotland.' He bends to kiss her, and this time she slides her arms up around his neck and kisses him back.

Chapter Eight

Rapprochement

Bethia shuffles across the bed, carefully pushes herself up, and drops her feet to the floor. There's a rug beneath them; she still cannot get over its softness. She moves slowly, quietly, stiffly across the room. The light is bright around the shutters and she wonders what time of day it might be. She opens the door to the garde-robe and goes to relieve herself.

It is a relief now too, of a different kind, to bathe. She washes her body gently, carefully, tenderly. She dries herself with the soft linen squares folded neatly on the stand, beside the jug of water, and turns towards the door. She opens it slowly and peers around it, body half-hidden. Picking up a square of muslin, she tries to cover herself, but it's too flimsy to be of much use and she drops it, ready to run for the bed. She didn't feel so exposed walking naked across the room with her back to the bed, but to return with all of her on view seems most immodest.

She peeps around the door again. Mainard is sprawled on his front, hasn't moved, must still be asleep. She creeps around the room searching for her nightdress, which she had not expected would be removed; had imagined a more secret fumbling than the tender exploration and shared curiosity which has filled their night. There's a crumpled bundle of white in the corner. She shakes it out with her back to the bed and slips it on. It falls in large folds to the floor. A shaft of sunlight pierces the gap in the shutters and dazzles her and she blinks.

'I like you better without any covering.'

She turns to find Mainard has rolled over and is propped up on the bolster, arms behind his head, watching her. Dust motes dance along the beam of light reaching towards him.

She smiles shyly.

He stretches languidly then holds out his arms, beckoning her. 'We'll have it off soon enough.'

They have fallen asleep again when there's banging on the door. Bethia realises she's been hearing a gentle knocking for a while, through her swirling dreams. She sits up, searching again for her nightgown.

'Who is it?' Mainard calls, while Bethia scurries around the room. He swings his legs out of the bed and, sighing, stands up. Bethia finally spies her gown and goes to pull it on but Mainard grabs her round the waist. She squeals as they topple back onto the bed.

'Shush,' he whispers, and she giggles as his breath tickles her ear.

They sense someone waiting outside the door, then hear the sound of retreating footsteps loud on the tiled floor. She squirms away from him and scrambles off the bed to peer through the shutters. The sun is high now, the street busy, and she glimpses goods being unloaded onto a handcart from a schuyt on the canal at the end of the alley opposite. She rolls the word around in her mouth: schuyt – a barge – another Dutch word she has learned.

Mainard slips his arms around her, and she leans back against him then quickly straightens up. The male body is... strange.

'Your city is surprisingly clean, especially given its size.'

'Yes it is,' he says, kissing her shoulder.

'Using the barges to transport goods must help. There are few horses coming into the streets.' She points to where a small boy is shovelling dung off the brick pathway and into a bucket. 'And any muck they leave is quickly removed.'

'Mmm,' he says, nibbling her ear.

'You must have found St Andrews to be very dirty by comparison.'

He lifts his head. 'Do we really want to discuss the cleanliness, or otherwise, of our respective cities when there are so many more interesting ways we could pass our time?'

'What would you suggest?' she says, eyebrows raised.

'Enough talk' – he bends to kiss her – 'much better to show you.'

There's a banging on the door. 'Mistress, the mama wants to speak with you.'

Bethia jumps. 'Your mother is asking for me,' she whispers to Mainard. 'I had better quickly dress.'

Mainard keeps a hold of her. 'Grissel,' he calls, 'be a good girl and fetch us a tray of food.'

There's a snort of laughter from the other side of the door. Grissel's soon back and kicking on the lower panel for the door to be unlocked.

Mainard pulls on a robe and opens the door, shutting it behind Grissel, but not before Bethia glimpses the curious faces of Marisse and Coort peeping in from the hallway. She raises her hand to smooth her hair, discovering it in a huge tangle at the back of her head.

Mainard points to the kist at the bottom of the bed. 'Leave it there, Grissel.'

'Shall I serve you?'

Mainard shakes his head. 'Bethia and I will serve each other.'

Grissel bursts out laughing. Mainard opens the door again. Marisse and Coort, caught with their ears to it, stumble into the room.

'Out. All of you!' shouts Mainard, although Bethia can see he wants to laugh.

'I am glad to see you happy, mistress,' hisses Grissel as she leaves.

'What is all this mistressing Grissel is suddenly doing?' asks Mainard as he stabs a hunk of venison with a knife.

'I don't know. She never called me mistress in her life before, but I'm glad to see she's settling. I thought I'd have to send her back to Scotland.' She looks up smiling. 'Perhaps Coort has something to do with her contentment.'

'If he does then she'll have to fight Marisse for him.'

'Not to mention your sister.'

'What? I hope you're not serious.'

'No, no. I'm only jesting,' she says, swallowing.

'Nevertheless, I will mention it to Papa.'

She jumps off the bed and grabs his sleeve. 'No, Mainard, please. T'would be most unfair to Katheline to have her father mistrust her because of something foolish I've said.'

'You promise me there's nothing to it?'

She looks him straight in the eye. 'I promise.'

She thinks of how Mainard may marry where he chooses yet Katheline cannot. And she remembers her friend Elspeth who ran off with the painter Antonio, only to end up in a nunnery when it was discovered he already had a wife. She picks up a leg of duck, sits down in the wooden chair and gnaws on it. The food here always tastes strange, but she is growing used to it.

'Do you think your parents are reconciled to our marriage now?'

He leans back in his chair. 'Too late if they are not.'

She tosses the half-chewed bone on the wooden platter and rises to fetch her comb. 'But why was their astonishment so very great, and especially your mama seemed most upset.'

46

He rubs his forehead. 'Mama has supported us.'

She sits down and tries to untangle her hair. 'And your papa has not?'

'Bethia, must we go over this again?' He leans forward, resting his elbows on his knees. 'We are man and wife now, and no one can come between us.'

She smiles at him, although she is aware he is evading her. Patience, Bethia, she thinks.

'Time discovers truth.'

'What!'

She puts her hand over her mouth; did not mean to say the words aloud. 'It is a saying from Seneca,' she mutters.

'You're thinking about Greek philosophers. I see I shall have to assert myself.' He rises and, taking the comb from her hand, picks up a lock of hair and gently draws the comb through it.

'Roman.'

'What?'

Seneca was a Roman philosopher. '

He narrows his eyes. 'I must take care with such a clever wife.'

She sighs loudly. Her cleverness was frequently remarked on within her own family, and Mother especially, who could barely read, did not consider it a useful attribute in a woman. Then she straightens up; Father, in the end, found her ability with figures most useful in his business.

'Yes,' she says. 'You most certainly must take care.'

Mainard, tugging hard on a knot of hair, drops the comb and roars with laughter.

Chapter Nine

Joy

It's autumn now and the poplar trees turn gold, whispering in the wind as their leaves flutter to the ground and spread, like red-brown cloaks, across the pathways and the surface of the canals. There's much whispering in the house too and sideways glances at Bethia. She supposes they're still entertained by how long she and Mainard remained closeted in their chamber – but that was more than a month ago. Now they are almost an old married couple. She smiles; the first month of marriage is said to be the sweetest – she prays that they can keep that sweetness with them for as long as they both live, even into old age, if God so grants them one together.

Marisse brings her a letter. Bethia opens and devours it before the servant has closed the door behind her. There's much news of Father's latest trading deals, mention of Scots losses at the most recent battle against the English invaders, and, as she skims it, nothing about Will – which she is most desperate to know. Then, in his cramped writing, up the side she spies a few lines saying that he has, so far, been unable to discover where that wretch of a brother is being held. She sighs, wishing Mainard was here to comfort her, but he is out, as ever. He's told her he is working with Papa, working so that he may one day branch out on his own, and she can become his helpmeet just as she once assisted her father, and then they will buy their own home. He becomes vague when she asks about Papa's business, which is disappointing, and she doesn't understand why she's being held at arm's length. Actually, to be as close as arm's length would be good, to at least see the offices and warehouse a cause for celebration, but Mainard says there are clerks to do the work she once did, and they are busy – she would only be a distraction. He kisses her when he says this, saying no man is to be distracted by his wife but him.

'So you will keep me locked up in my chamber, like a jealous husband.'

'Yes,' he says, drawing her towards the bed. 'I want you only for myself.'

'And what about what I want?' she asks, placing her palm against his chest and pushing him away.

He bows. 'Your wish will forever be my command.'

'Except when I want to go to the offices of the de Langes.'

'Patience, my love. Patience.'

The curious glances grow more rather than less, as the days pass and the air outside grows chill. Bethia thinks she's rarely seen anything as beautiful as the sparkling ice-encrusted grasses and leaves on a frosty morning. She is kneeling on the window seat watching the passers-by one day when Mainard comes to find her.

'No book to read, today?'

'I'm finding it unusually difficult to concentrate. My head feels light as thistledown floating on the breeze, yet I should be improving my Dutch by reading.' She waves her hand at two copies of More's Utopia which lie neglected on the kist.

'Why two copies?'

'It's not so easy to find books in Dutch, and More's Utopia is here with the Latin and Dutch for comparison – and what better book for me to read. I can learn of his great conception, and in a new language.'

His brown eyes gaze upon her with approval. 'The more we can all fit in the better.'

She wonders what he means but is distracted, noticing his hands are behind his back. She tugs on his arm to find out what he's hiding. He twists away and she tussles with him, eventually capturing a square box. Sitting down again she opens the parcel, smooths the polished leather and sighs with delight. The dressing case holds a silver-backed mirror and ivory comb. She looks up at him. 'It is the most beautiful gift I have ever received.'

He takes the comb from her, picks up a strand of hair and runs the teeth through it. 'Bethia, do you have aught to tell me?'

'Should I have something to tell you?' She searches her mind; she's mostly kept to her room apart from a few outings with Katheline, and they were harmless enough.

He lets her hair fall and kneels before her. 'Mama thought perhaps there was some news.'

She has an inkling now of what he's hinting but chooses not to understand. 'I showed you the last letter from Father. He's promised to locate Will, if he can.'

Mainard shakes his head and stands up. 'I must away then.' He walks slowly towards the door and she does not stop him. She feels a strange reluctance to speak the words she knows he wants to hear… is weary of the watchers in the house. Of course, Marisse, or even Grissel, will have reported that her courses have not come. Her breasts ache and she feels a heaviness, which she guesses must mean she is with child. A part of her is delighted to prove her worth as a wife so soon, but she also resents this constant sense of being like an insect caught in fine Venetian glass. The freedom that she expected from being a wife has not been realised. Indeed, she has less liberty in Antwerp than when she was a maid in Scotland.

Mainard is closing the door and still she does not call out to him. She picks up the dressing case, heavy in her lap, and holds it close to her chest. It is a generous gift. She goes to him, whispering her secret that is no secret. The smile is wide enough to split his face and he hugs her tight, then quickly slackens his grip and holds gently.

'I am no fragile flower, you know.'

He touches her belly. 'You carry our child, and I will take very good care of you both.'

She strokes the side of his face. 'I thank you, but Mainard, please do not suffocate me. Sometimes I feel as though I can barely breathe in this house.'

He frowns. 'What do you mean? Is anyone unkind to you? You must tell me, I will not have it.'

Her hand falls and she gazes out the window. 'Everyone is very attentive… but sometimes I'm lonely.'

He places his hand under her chin and turns her face to look up at him.

'It will get easier… for us all.'

The rejoicing throughout the house is great. Master de Lange smiles upon her, the worried frown leaves Mistress de Lange's face, albeit briefly, and Katheline hugs her close. But even more than before, Bethia cannot easily leave home. They are too busy around her when she tries to go, and always she is offered Marisse or Katheline to attend her, with Coort trailing behind. It is not safe, she will become lost, she cannot speak the language well enough, it will look as though the de Langes are not caring for her. But she senses that more is behind it than her well-being.

And she does not believe Mainard is always with Papa. Why would his fingers, and sometimes sleeves, be paint-stained if he was merely clerking for his father? Perhaps Papa likes the ledger entries colourful. She stands in the hallway and gazes up at the large painting on the wall above her head. It shows Antwerp from the other side of the river and is, yet again, a confirmation of the size and grandeur of this city. Bethia is drawn, however, to the depiction of the fields, trees, and farmhouse in the foreground. She feels a longing for such space, which is almost unbearable. She moves closer to the painting and reaches to touch it with her fingertip, then she cradles her belly. Better days are coming. Once she has her child, surely she will have more liberty.

And then one day she can bear it no longer. She creeps down the stairs, grabs her cloak and hat from the peg, slides the front door open and escapes. She hurries down the street and round the corner, expecting any moment to be stopped. If she can only get amongst the crowds of people that are invariably to be found even on a day when the breath fogs in the air. But the streets are empty, even the canals are deserted, no children shrieking as they slide up and down cursed by the skaters. She creeps along staying close to the walls of the houses until she spies small groups of people up ahead, moving purposively. She hesitates, then follows them. They join others until she is part of a stream of folk who are heading towards the marketplace. There's little chatter among them but a sense of suppressed excitement. She can smell smoke… a fire in the market. She clutches her cloak around her with a rising feeling of dread as she's carried forward by the crowd. Then, over their heads she can see a man being raised, bound to a stake. She turns, blindly pushing against those who have come up behind her, who brush past her as though she wasn't there, all eyes on the spectacle that is unfolding. Once before she has seen a burning, in St Andrews. She will not stay for another.

Mainard is waiting for her when she returns. 'Not a good day on which to make your escape,' he says, arms folded.

She sits down, covers her face with her hands and shakes her head.

He drops down beside her, placing his arm around her, drawing her close.

'I thought there was some safety for the people of Antwerp from this, that they were protected by a charter,' she says.

'Not for Anabaptists.'

'Why not?'

'The Anabaptists are mostly poor people – the man being burned was only a baker – so have little protection, especially when Mary of Hungary has taken agin them.' Mainard sniffs. 'Papa says she's a hypocrite,' he pauses, face flushing, 'although you must never repeat that.'

'I will not, I promise. But why is she… that thing?'

'She was much taken with the works of Erasmus for a time and even had him at her court. Her own chaplain came under suspicion of heresy. But our governor, whatever reforming leanings she may have, hates the Anabaptists.'

Bethia wonders why it should matter so whether you are baptised as an infant or request it as an adult. But clearly it does. 'I think I will stay safe at home in future.'

He holds her close. 'Do not be afraid. It is usually safe enough for us, but better you're escorted.'

She shakes her head; all desire to roam has left her. She will rest in her gilded cage.

Chapter Ten

Geertruyt

There is a family in the servants' quarters. They jump when Bethia enters the kitchen and the mother draws a small child to her, while the older one hangs onto her skirts. Bethia cannot think why they should look at her so warily, even fearfully. Perhaps they are some relations of Marisse's or Coort's that shouldn't be here. She gazes over the woman's head, looking for Grissel, frowning when she cannot be found. Retreating, she finds Mama hurrying into the hallway, and Katheline chasing behind. An urgent message has come from Geertruyt's husband.

Bethia helps Mama on with her cloak, and out Mama and Katheline go in a great rush of excitement. She closes the door on the chill air; the mist rising above the canals is as cold as any wind blowing off the sea in her old home. She wonders how long they will be, and shivers part in fear and part in anticipation, for Geertruyt's labour has begun and Mama and Katheline's attendance, and support, are wanted.

Bethia has yet to meet Geertruyt, who's been confined to her home since the day Bethia witnessed her altercation with Mainard. Geertruyt is, it seems, exhausted and cannot bear the strain of a visit from anyone, not even her new sister. Bethia is, however, introduced to Geertruyt's husband – a much older man who looks to be ages with

Master de Lange. He seems kindly enough, bowing over her hand and welcoming her to the family. Bethia is reminded of Norman Wardlaw, the man she was once, most unwillingly, promised to. He was also older, and so fat he wheezed as he walked, but kindly too. Peter Schyuder, unlike Fat Norman, is whip thin, his shoulders bowed as though he is carrying a great burden on his back.

He is a printer – a trade Bethia knows little of, for Scotland has few printers, and none in her home town. Peter Schyuder is but one among many in this city. It seems that Antwerp is at the forefront of every new innovation: art, writing, building, transport, finance, as well as ways of thinking. Indeed, Mainard tells her that where Antwerp leads, the world follows. But then being the wealthiest city in the world also brings its challenges. She thinks of Mainard's tale of Antwerp under siege only four years ago and the motto of the duke who attacked the city: 'Burning and torching is the jewel of war'. For some men the fight is all, and she's glad her husband is of finer stock, even if she doesn't know where he is and what he's doing much of the time.

Mama is away all day and the following night. Bethia doesn't want to think of Geertruyt's suffering. After two days, Katheline comes running with the news that Geertruyt is safely delivered of a son. She's well but very tired. Nevertheless, Bethia is permitted entry to the house and nursery, although not Geertruyt's chamber.

Bethia bends over the crib but can only see the slight hump of a small body under its hood. Mama sits in the chair, rocking the cradle with her foot whenever there's a snuffling from within, her eyes drooping.

'If you would care to lie down, Mama,' she says, stumbling over the word, still not entirely confident in their relationship, 'then I can tend the baby.'

Mama blinks and Bethia repeats, this time with gestures, for her Spanish is halting – although Mainard has told her several times how good it has become already and how proud he is of both her diligence and quick learning.

Mama nods and leans forward to push herself up from the low chair. Bethia hurries to help and Mama leans on her for support.

'Eres es una buena chica,' Mama says, patting Bethia's face.

Bethia thinks that Mama, like Peter Schyuder, looks as though she's carrying the weight of the world on her shoulders. Bethia wonders at this, for, although there is danger everywhere, at least they do not have England constantly on their doorstep – Father's most recent letter has told how Protector Somerset is harrying all up and down the east coast of Scotland.

She kneels down by the side of the cradle and peeps under the hood. She can see the tiny face now and feels a tug of longing for the moment when she will hold her own child. The nurse bustles in and Bethia rises. The woman smiles at her and bends to pick up the baby, offering him to Bethia. Bethia is afraid. She's not held a baby since her brother John was born, and that's now ten years ago, but the nurse is insistent. She takes the small bundle and looks into his sleeping face, bending to kiss his forehead. There's a call from the neighbouring chamber and the nurse reclaims the baby. Bethia, drifting from the chamber, can still feel him warm in her arms.

She returns the next day and the next. Sometimes with Mama and Katheline, sometimes alone with Marisse, and once with only Grissel for company – which felt a great achievement. Geertruyt's lying-in goes well and Bethia is invited into the chamber. Geertruyt greets her, eyes flicking up and down, then begins a conversation with Mama in such rapid Spanish that Bethia gives up any attempt to follow. She shuffles from one foot to the other and eventually perches on the window seat. The nurse brings the baby and goes to give him to Bethia but is redirected to Mama. Geertruyt talks and talks, words coming in angry bursts, eyes bulging as her voice rises, and the baby joins in with a shrill cry of his own, while Mama responds low and quiet, to soothe both daughter and grandson.

Bethia picks out a few of Mama's words, chiefly the repetition of 'do not fear'. Mama leans forward and, catching Geertruyt's face between her hands, kisses her forehead. Geertruyt closes her eyes and allows it. Bethia realises that Geertruyt is an attractive woman when her face isn't scrunched with vexation. She's not beautiful in the way of Katheline and Mama, with their almond eyes, full lips, and straight noses; Mama especially has a serenity – when she's not worrying about her family – that Bethia would wish to emulate. She watches Mama stroke Geertruyt's large face with her long, be-ringed fingers and misses the tenderness of a mother. Then she cannot help but smile; her own mother isn't a tender woman but much more of the ilk of Geertruyt: fretful and complaining. Unfortunately, Geertruyt opens her eyes in time to catch Bethia's smile. She flushes with anger and, pushing Mama's hands away, points at Bethia.

'Fuera de acqui,' she shrieks over and over, waving her arms as though chasing away a wild beast.

Bethia's eyes grow wide. She understands enough Spanish to know she's being ordered from the room. She's suddenly exhausted with the strangeness of this new country – her new country – and stands her ground.

'Why do you not like me?' she asks, in halting Spanish.

Geertruyt's face contorts and she shouts a jumble of words which Bethia cannot untangle. Her husband comes running and she cries to him. He takes Bethia's arm.

'Come,' he says quietly. 'I am sorry but you must leave. Come back when she's calmer.'

'But what have I done?' she asks, as he leads her away.

'It is nothing. Geertruyt needs to rest.' But she notices his eyes flick away as he speaks.

Later Mama tells her not to worry, that Geertruyt is emotional, as women often are after the birth of a child. Mainard too says there's no reason for Geertruyt to shout, and anyway she's exaggerating. Of course Geertruyt doesn't hate her. Bethia wants to stamp her foot in frustration. She determines to pin Katheline down. Katheline is younger than her. She will not allow Katheline to slide away, as is Katheline's wont.

There's a reliquary procession the next day and Bethia joins Katheline to watch it pass from the safety of their doorstep. 'We have such processions often to celebrate holy days in St Andrews,' says Bethia, when Katheline begins to explain the feast. She stands tall. 'For our cathedral holds the bones of Saint Andrew.'

'Ah,' says Katheline grinning, 'but do you hold a part of Christ Jesus himself, for this is the Feast of the Holy Prepuce.'

Bethia doesn't know what the Holy Prepuce is. Presumably some part of Christ's body, but she's not going to show her ignorance by asking. The one thing she felt sure of, in this secular city of trade and finance, was that her town, although poor by comparison, was the more holy. She stares at the reliquary, a golden casket with a carving of the Virgin cradling the baby Jesus in its centre flanked by the apostles, as it is carried past, but is none the wiser.

The streets empty behind the procession and Bethia takes Katheline's arm as they walk to church for Mass. Bethia feels a rising determination to get some answers to her many questions. Katheline tries to release her arm but Bethia grips all the tighter.

'Ouch! That hurts.'

'Not as much as it hurts me to be in this constant haar of confusion. No one will give me a straight answer. Please Katheline, if we are to be true sisters to one another, tell me why Geertruyt doesn't like me.'

Katheline frowns, shaking her head, and Bethia stops

so suddenly Coort barrels into them.

'Do not say it,' says Bethia.

'Say what?'

'That of course Geertruyt does not hate me. She does, she could not have made it plainer. Please speak the truth.'

Katheline stares at the ground, then looks Bethia straight in the face. 'It is a long and complicated tale and I do not precisely know why Geertruyt is so upset. She had hoped that Mainard would marry Peter Schyuder's sister, I think. Come, let us walk, we're blocking the path,' she says, as a matron huffs and puffs her way past glaring as she goes.

'So,' says Bethia slowly, 'was Mainard promised to this woman?'

'It was discussed. I don't know how far the negotiations had got.'

'Is this why your parents were upset when they met me?'

'Ask Mainard.'

And although Bethia presses hard, her new sister will say no more.

Chapter Eleven

Sadness

Bethia is awake, sitting up in bed when Mainard returns. The candle has burnt low, but there's little smoke. These beeswax candles are untold luxury, unlike the ones in her old home which reeked of animal fat and made the eyes water excessively.

Mainard jumps when he opens the door and finds her, arms folded, waiting. 'I'm sorry, my love. Would you prefer if I slept elsewhere so I do not disturb you when I'm so late? Especially now you need your rest.' He smiles and comes to take her hand.

She does not return the gentle pressure, and leaves her hand lying limply in his. He sighs and, releasing it, moves away to undress, dropping his clothes on the kist. She feels herself weakening as she watches him – the lean body, golden skin, and long fingers. She shuffles back against the bolster so she's sitting completely upright, and when Mainard lifts the covers to join her in the bed, she holds them down.

He sighs again. 'Please, Bethia, I'm very tired.'

She shakes her head. 'Not as tired as I am of all this subterfuge. I am your wife, Mainard. I left my home and family to be with you. I trusted you. Can you not share with me in return?'

He stands by the bed holding the edge of the covers.

'And can you not trust me enough to believe that everything I do is for us, for our future and the future of our unborn child?'

'Very well, I'll not ask you where you have been all day and all evening. Tell me about Beverielle Schyuder.'

'Can we talk about this tomorrow, Bethia, please.'

He flicks the covers out of her hands and climbs into bed. Kissing the top of her head, he lies down with his back to her.

'That is a promise, Mainard?'

He grunts.

She feels him slide from the bed as the early morning light pierces the shutters, and she pushes herself up, following him into the garde-robe.

He turns as she opens the door. 'God's wounds, woman. Can a man not relieve himself in peace?'

She retreats. Picking up her shawl and wrapping it around her shoulders, she sits in the big chair, hands crossed over her belly. It feels rounder than before. She strokes it; there truly is a baby in there, and it's growing.

Mainard emerges, still naked, and strides across the chamber.

'Stop trying to distract me,' she says.

He grins at her as he pulls his shirt over his head. 'I wish it were so easily done.' He opens the shutters and sits down on the kist. The light streaming in is dazzling and she squints and twists in her seat.

'What is it that my lady wishes to know?'

But she is not to be charmed. 'Beverielle Schyuder…'

'Is the sister of Peter Schyuder.'

She glares at him. 'If this is going to take all day then so be it. But if you want to be released any time soon then I would suggest you are more forthcoming.'

'There's nothing to say. My parents thought she and I might be a match and Geertruyt promoted it. Nothing more.'

'Why all the secrecy? If that is all why not explain it to

61

me before? It's not as though I didn't have other suitors before we were wed.'

'It was of no significance. I did not intend to become the husband of Beverielle Schyuder however much our families may have desired the match.'

She nods – she of all people can understand how it is to be pressed into an alliance that is repugnant. 'But why not tell me from the start instead of leaving me befuddled by Mama's fearful face, Papa's horrified face, and Geertruyt's angry one?'

'I know. I should've done better by you.'

She stands up and walks towards him. He looks up, but she doesn't put her arms around him as she suspects he's hoping and instead grabs his beard, pulling his face towards hers. 'Our alliance will be stronger if we work together – and to do so successfully there must be no secrets.'

He grabs her around the waist and tugs her onto his lap. 'I married a wise-woman,' he whispers, kissing her neck.

'And don't you forget it,' she says, leaning into him. 'Mainard…'

'Mmm?'

'What's a Holy Prepuce?'

He sits up and stares at her.

'You don't know?'

'I know it's a relict of Jesus Christ. I don't know which part.'

He gives a great bellow of laughter. 'It is a most tender part.'

'What?'

He whispers in her ear.

'Nooo! Truly?'

He nods. 'Truly.'

'That is… unusual.' She grows solemn-faced. 'But really we should not smile, for it is still a holy relict to be venerated.'

They look to one another, then they are both laughing.

62

She stops suddenly. 'It is what's done to Jews but…' her voice tails away.

He pushes her gently off his lap and stands up. 'I was baptised as an infant. I am a Christian whatever my antecedents, and whatever whisperings there may be around us. We are doing our best to belong, and no such thing was done to me.'

She opens her mouth to ask a question and Mainard puts his hand up. 'Please, Bethia, let it go.'

And she does.

Later, Mama, Katheline, and she walk out, with Coort following. Their breath clouds in the chill air and crystals of ice hang from the frost-encrusted trees and eaves of the tall houses. The mist rising above the canals, like a field of ghosts, freezes the very marrow: blood and bones. They pass a group of men playing the roaring game. Katheline starts an explanation and Bethia murmurs that the men of Scotland are curlers too. She feels Coort behind draw close: always listening, always watching. 'Is Antwerp really so unsafe that we must have an attendant?' she says loudly, knowing she sounds peevish.

She's aware that Mama and Katheline are gazing at one another over the top of her head. They are no taller than she, yet there is something about the way they carry themselves that makes her feel small.

'Sometimes there are Spanish soldiers and others who will attack for no reason, but especially women who are unprotected.' Mama speaks in a low tone and Bethia has to twist her head to hear.

'Are they in the city now?'

'Perhaps.' Mama walks faster and Bethia has to skip to keep up.

'They do not like us,' Mama mutters.

Bethia wonders if she's heard correctly.

'The Spanish soldiers do not like anyone,' says Katheline. 'And they especially do not like those from Portugal who have escaped to Antwerp.'

Bethia stares at her. 'You escaped?'

'Hush,' says Mama. 'Enough of this talk. It does not help.'

It doesn't help what, wonders Bethia as they divest themselves of their thick cloaks and gloves in Geertruyt's entrance hall. And why then does Mama speak Spanish and not Portuguese?

Geertruyt, who is out of bed for the first time when they arrive, doesn't have the same elegance as her mother and sister – although perhaps it's not fair to compare given that she has recently given birth. She greets Bethia with a nod, has told her mother that Bethia may visit, but there has been no explanation, or apology, for the vehemence of her attack. Bethia determines that if she gets the chance to be alone with Geertruyt, she will have it out. She senses that Geertruyt likely will overpower her, if she allows it, and she did not escape the jurisdiction of her mother to fall under Geertruyt's withering scorn.

Mama, Katheline and Geertruyt blether, and Bethia, although understanding some of what they have to say, lets her mind drift. Sometimes she needs a rest; it requires much concentration to listen to a language when she must stumble around inside her head to find the meaning. She studies Geertruyt's chamber. It's not as fine as her own, is smaller and lacking the Persian rug upon the floor, which Bethia so loves to run her toes through, but is still much better appointed than the bed-chamber she once shared with Mother. Printers must also be rich men, she concludes. She wonders if she and Mainard might set up a printshop; she would like to have a business in which they could work together. But Mainard seems to think her only task is to grow babies. She smiles and places her hand on her belly. It is enough – for the moment.

She becomes aware the tone of the conversation has changed. Geertruyt is spitting words out at Katheline at great pace and Mama is making soothing noises, telling Geertruyt she must be calm. 'Estar tranquila,' she repeats, hands extended wide apart, palms downwards. 'Tranquila, tranquila.'

Geertruyt takes a deep breath and shifts in her seat. Katheline speaks slowly and, after a moment, Geertruyt nods. Bethia looks from one to the other to the other but no one will meet her eyes.

Mama rises. 'Ven a ver a la bebe,' she says, nodding at Bethia.

Bethia follows her. The nurse is sitting on a low stool, feeding the baby, who's making small, snuffly grunts as he suckles. Mama sits down on the other stool, smiling and nodding. Bethia sees Katheline whisk past the door, which has been left ajar, and then hears the noise of the street door slamming. She excuses herself.

Geertruyt is hunched over, folded arms pressing into her breasts. She looks up grimacing, as Bethia comes in. Bethia turns to close the door behind her, giving Geertruyt time to compose herself. Geertruyt straightens up, tugging her shawl across her chest, but not before Bethia sees the damp circles on her nightdress.

'How are you feeling?' she asks. She's fairly certain Geertruyt can speak at least some English; after all, both Katheline and Mainard can.

Geertruyt grunts. 'Childbirth is difficult, as I understand you will soon discover.'

Bethia assumes this is the nearest to felicitations that she will receive from Geertruyt. Nevertheless, she smiles and nods. 'Geertruyt,' she says, edging closer, 'I'm sorry you're upset that Mainard didn't marry Master Schyuder's sister.'

Geertruyt glares. 'You think this is about Beverielle. It is about protecting our family.' Her face grows more and more flushed. 'Mainard's a fool who will get us all thrown out of this country, our wealth taken from us, or worse.' She stabs her finger at Bethia, as a torrent of words burst forth. Bethia leans back, eyes wide and heart thumping. 'You may be a Christian, as Mainard keeps pointing out, but you come from a country we are at war with. How can that help our family?'

'B-b-but we are all Christians.'

'Stupid girl. We are Nuevos Cristianos, Conversos. Do you even understand what that means? Ask Mainard to tell you what happened to Gracia Mendes – and she richer by far than we. You prance around here with your simpering ways and false modesty.' Geertruyt is shouting now. 'What kind of girl just turns up without any agreement between families? I'm sure you're not even properly wed.'

Bethia turns and runs blindly down the stairs and into the street, leaving the front door wide behind her. She lifts her skirts and flees, not caring that people are staring at her. She left the cone hat behind and can actually see where she's going – except she doesn't know where to go. The cathedral looms up on her right and she heads there, turning aside before she reaches it. She's too agitated to sit, and the Lord feels very far away at the moment; even the Virgin has deserted her. She shivers, wrapping her arms around herself, wishing she had grabbed her cloak.

The city walls rise at the end of the street. Again, she lifts her skirts, hurrying towards the gate… and escape. She pauses on the small humped bridge over a canal and presses her side, feeling a sharp pain. She walks slowly through the gate, weaving her way among the people entering the city. It's the first time she's been to the quayside since the day she arrived.

Even though it's winter, the harbour is still surprisingly busy. She walks slowly, holding her shawl tight around her and shaking with cold.

'Dinna be so daft,' says a man to his companion as they stride towards her. Impulsively, she moves in front of them and the man bumps into her. 'Sorry lass,' he says, steadying her.

'You're from Scotland?'

'Aye, as are you too, I am suspecting.'

'Och, it is good to hear your voice.' Her eyes fill with tears.

'There, there, lass,' he says, patting her shoulder clumsily. 'What are you doing here and so far from home? Are ye lost?'

She wipes her eyes with the back of her hands. 'No, I'm fine. Thank you for your concern.' Her voice shakes and she takes a deep breath to get control of herself.

The men bow and move on, looking back as they stride away.

She's trailing home – for where else can she go – when she feels the first twinge: a tugging deep in her groin. Mama comes running when she sees Bethia's face and helps her upstairs to her chamber.

'Decansas,' Mama whispers.

Bethia rolls onto her side and falls into a place that is not sleep, and yet she's not awake. There's a buzzing in her ears as though wasps are busy around her head, and pinpricks of light explode beneath her eyelids. She draws her knees tight to her chest, protecting the baby in her belly.

Later, she doesn't know how much later, she hears Mainard's voice and then there's whispering. He strokes her back and a groan escapes her. She bites down on her lip. She's not in pain, just has a fever; it must be something she ate. 'I am well,' she whispers. But the whisper is followed by a cramping, and she curls in on herself again.

Mama is there, leaning over. She hears her send Mainard from the room and then the covers are lifted, and there's a gasp. She does not want to look, does not want to move. There is more whispering. She's told to lift her hips and something soft and thick is pushed beneath them. Mainard returns and is ordered to leave – this is women's work and he can do nothing. Nevertheless, he sits on the bed, then lies down curving along her back, disregarding Mama when she remonstrates.

She falls asleep. Then it's morning, the light seeping

through the shutters. Mainard is gone and Grissel is asleep on a pallet nearby. She has had no more cramping; perhaps all will be well.

She slides down from the bed. Grissel is awake immediately, taking her arm and supporting her while she uses the pot. As she straightens up, she hears Grissel sigh. Looking down she sees her waters are bloody, and as she crawls back into bed a groan of pain escapes her. She curls tightly, holding... holding... holding...

But it doesn't stop the cramps. By evening her baby is gone.

Chapter Twelve

Despair

Bethia lies in her bed, face to the window, back to the door. She hears the bells ringing out the hours throughout the day, the streets grow loud and quiet, a final burst of noise when the taverns close and curfew falls, and then there is silence. She watches the light brighten and fade through the gap in the shutters. It will be cold outside, she supposes. She draws her knees into her chest, holds tight and rocks.

People come and go: Mama, Katheline, Grissel, Mainard. They sit on her bed; they stroke her back; they tell her she will have other babies; they open the shutters and try to persuade her to get up, wash, eat the food they have brought, join the family. She curls up tighter as they speak, eyes squeezed shut, turns away, pulling the covers over her head to block out the light.

On the seventh day she awakes from her uneasy slumber to find Mama and Katheline standing over her. Mama speaks, Katheline translates, and both are emphatic. 'Mama says it smells bad in here. She says that this happens to many women; it is the lot of women to bear children and have them die, and often to lose them before they have even left the womb. She says it is much worse to see them grow and hold them in your arms and watch the life fade from them. She says that Mainard is sad and worried; that you must be his helpmeet and not a burden to him.'

Bethia wants to shout, how can I be Mainard's helpmeet if he will not share anything with me – but she lies still as though she's asleep, still as though she's a corpse. She hears them leave, the door clicking behind them.

Another day comes and goes. She is brought no food but doesn't care; she wasn't eating anyway. The fire burns low and the embers fade; she tucks her face under the blankets, warm and fusty. She goes to use the pot, and it hasn't been emptied since the previous day. This she does mind. She opens the shutters enough to allow a small amount of light in and, turning, catches a glimpse of herself in the Venetian mirror hanging on the opposite wall: her thick hair, of which she is normally so proud, is limp around her wan face. Everything about her drags downwards, as though the Devil has a grip around her ankles, tugging her to him. She is unresistant.

She crawls back into bed. It's enough to allow some light into the room. She awakes to candlelight and the weight of someone sitting heavily down upon the bed.

'Bethia!' Mainard shakes her shoulder. 'Come, let me help you sit.' He tugs her arm and then leans over, half lifting her against the bolster. She doesn't resist, but doesn't help either. He takes her face between his hands. 'Look at me.'

She lifts her eyes slowly to gaze into his brown eyes, fringed with the curly lashes. She's sure his beard has grown longer, wants to touch it, but somehow her arm will not move. She drops her gaze and he drops his hands from her face.

'Wherever you have gone, Bethia, please come back,' he whispers.

She falls back against the bolster and closes her eyes.

She hears a sigh, then feels his weight lift off the bed, senses he's standing, gazing down at her. When she opens her eyes he's gone. She's drifting back to her disquieting dreamworld when the door is flung wide, banging off the wooden panelling. She jerks awake and pushes herself up.

Mainard sits down on the bed again. 'What has happened to you?' he says in a low voice as he grips her shoulders. 'Where is the girl who found her way up a long rope ladder and into the siege castle full of angry men? Is this the girl who hid from the soldiers for a day and most of a night when the castle was overrun and escaped down a cliff-face – all by herself? What's happened to the spirited woman who told her father she would make her own choice of husband?'

He lifts the covers, swings her legs to the floor and kneels at her feet. 'Come back to me, my Bethia, please come back.'

A tear runs down her cheek and she brushes it away.

Mainard put his arms around her waist and rests his head in her lap. She strokes his soft curly hair.

He looks up. 'I see a glimmer you may be with me again.'

'I promise I will try… but it's hard, Mainard. The baby lost… and I miss home so much.'

'Do you want to go back?'

'Will you come?'

'What would I do there?'

'Perhaps my father…' She stops herself, knows it wouldn't work. She gazes into his face. 'I will stay with you.'

He stands up and lifts her to her feet. 'Thank the Blessed Virgin,' he whispers in her ear. Then he stands back and says in his normal voice, 'And for the sake of the Virgin, and your loving husband, please wash.'

The noise comes from deep inside; she doesn't recognise it at first. She's laughing, and then Mainard is laughing with her.

He opens the door. 'Grissel,' he shouts. Grissel

appears immediately; he must've had her waiting in the passageway. 'Bring hot water and cloths – and quickly.'

Grissel curtsies, unprompted, and scurries away. When she returns with the jug and soft linen, Mainard leads Bethia to the garde-robe, but she gently pushes him out. This is an intimacy she does not want.

Washed and refreshed, she sits in the chair and takes the beaker of ale and a plate of bread, cheese, and apples, small and wizened, yet sweet, from the tray that Grissel has brought. No meat, it must be Friday. Grissel strips the bed, turns and fluffs up the wool-stuffed mattress. The smell of lavender, from clean sheets, fills the room. The candle is burning low and Grissel lights another from its flame, pressing it into the holder, gathers the dirty linen into her arms and fumbles for the latch. Mainard rises, opening the door wide and bowing as she passes. Grissel snorts with laughter.

'I see you like my servant.'

He looks startled, then smiles broadly as he comes towards her. 'Grissel is a most diverting wench, and bonny with it.'

He raises his hand to pat Bethia's cheek. She hits it away and he dissolves into laughter. 'It is good to know there's one way I may gain your attention.'

After a moment he sits down on the kist, arms resting on his knees as he leans forward, studying the floorboards.

'You're tired?' She wants to reach out and stroke his bent head again but, instead, she sits watching him.

He nods, not looking at her.

'What were you doing today?'

'The usual.'

'Working with your papa?'

He shifts the weight from one hip to the other.

She presses. 'You were with Papa all day?'

He looks up and tugs on his ear. 'What is this – an Inquisition?'

She stands up quickly, and then has to hold the back of

the chair to stop herself from falling.

He leaps up to catch her, his face full of concern. 'Come, I think you have been up for long enough.' He leads her to the bed.

'You will stay with me?'

He lifts the covers and she slides beneath them, then he strips off his clothes and climbs in after her.

'I will stay and hold you,' he says, curving into her back.

Chapter Thirteen

Discovery

Day after day, the air rises chill and white from the ice on the canals, creeping in through gaps in casements and under doors. Bethia feels she may never be warm again. She stands at the window rubbing the glass with her sleeve to remove the runnel of water inside and leans close to peer out. She's been here near seven months; will she ever grow used to this place?

Nevertheless, she is recovering. She is still sad but no longer despairing. She may have lost what little value she had to Mainard's family when she lost the child, but Mainard has made it clear he's her loving husband despite her failure. One day, she determines, cold or not, she will go out. When first Katheline, and then Mama, insist she should have Marisse and Coort to accompany her, she refuses. 'I will take Grissel. She knows her way around, and between us we have sufficient Dutch to manage.'

'But where do you want to go? There can be no requirement for you to go out. The servants can fetch whatever you need. It's bitter cold, even for March.'

'I'm going out and Grissel will accompany me.' She pats Mama on the arm. 'See, I have my stout boots on.' She pokes a toe out from beneath her skirts. 'And it will do me good to take the air.'

Katheline translates and a smile transforms Mama's face. She wraps a shawl around Bethia's head, over the hat, to add to the one already tied around her shoulders, and strokes her cheek. Bethia pulls on the heavy cloak, woven from the best wool cloth brought from England.

The young women run out into the sparkling sunshine; the white mist of their breath clouding the air around them, yet the cold is invigorating. Bethia stops suddenly and Grissel barrels into her.

'What's wrong?'

'Nothing, it is good to breathe and all so fresh. Even the stench of the privies are dulled in the cold. I almost feel the sea nearby. Almost.'

Grissel shrugs.

'Do you not miss the sea? I didn't realise how much a part of my life it was until I came to live here. There's the river but it's not the same. Not the same at all.'

'I dinna care if I never see the sea again.' Grissel shudders. 'I wasna ever so sick, even when mither fed me red caps as a purge.'

'So you are content to stay in Antwerp for the rest of your days?'

Grissel shrugs and half turns. 'It's no sae bad, and there's some awfy braw things aboot it.'

Glancing behind, Bethia sees that Coort is following them, at a discreet distance.

Despite the cold, the traders have set up their stalls and are touting their wares. They pass the Bourse, busy with merchants standing in groups beneath its arched quadrangle intent on their buying and selling. Money must be made, regardless of the weather, although they're clustered close to the braziers. She picks up an orange and holds it close to her nose, breathing in the sweet aroma. She's never seen oranges and lemons in such profusion before she lived here. She beckons to Grissel, who barters loudly over the price, with Coort standing silently at her shoulder.

Bethia moves to another stall, while surreptitiously

studying Coort, wondering what it is about him that has all the ladies clustering around. He's muscled yet small... but then, in comparison to Mainard and her giant of a brother Will, all men are short. His hair is already receding, his face sullen. She stares at him, puzzling. Grissel makes some aside and he smiles. It is a smile of such warmth, his face lights up like the sun emerging from behind a cloud. It's no wonder the receiver of such a smile melts before it. She resolves to speak to Grissel, otherwise there will likely be fighting among the servants over who is to be the recipient of this man's smiles. Although she's fairly certain, if it comes to blows between Marisse and Grissel, that Grissel will be the victor. And as for Katheline, she must be protected from him.

Turning her back, she picks up a bundle of kale, smoothing the ribbed grey-green leaves through her fingers. This they do have in abundance in Scotland. To her right a trader is selling cat skins. She runs her fingers over them while he waits hopefully. They're well cured and of the softest kitten underbelly. Father exports these, and others, for good-quality hides from Scotland are much in demand in France and the Low Countries. Her mind drifts and she feels a longing for her home that tugs hard in her belly, as though the umbilical cord has not been cut.

Grissel nudges her. 'Whit are you standing there, all glaikit like.'

'Mind your manners,' she says sharply. Grissel is become too familiar again, and it's time Bethia put a stop to it.

Grissel bobs her shawl-wrapped head, but not before Bethia sees the grin. She marches off. It's too much to have her servant goading her – somehow made worse by the knowledge that Grissel no doubt thinks she's doing it for Bethia's own good.

And suddenly there's Mainard, striding towards the Rue d'Esprit: the street of ghosts. She looks to Grissel, but

Grissel's preoccupied between her bartering and Coort's smiles. Bethia ducks her head and hurries after Mainard. He may be going to his own father's warehouses; perhaps she might even discover the reason for his green-stained fingers.

Mainard is moving swiftly and she has to hurry to catch up, although she wouldn't want to dally in this alley of unquiet spirits in any case. He reaches the end and disappears around the corner. She picks up her skirts and runs. It feels good, although she knows Mama wouldn't approve. Bethia slows as she reaches the corner, her breath billowing white clouds in the air.

He's at the door of a house opposite. It swings wide and a young woman stands on the threshold, her long yellow hair falling in waves to her waist as she welcomes Mainard with her smile. She stands aside and he passes into the house, turning his head to speak as he goes. She touches his arm, gazing up into his eyes, and then the door closes.

Bethia drops to her haunches and crouches against the alley wall. She knows men are not as women; she knows they find comfort elsewhere; and Bethia has been not been available to Mainard recently. She searches for a handkerchief. A hand is thrust in front of her holding one.

Grissel takes her arm. 'Come, mistress, 'tis time we tak ye hame.' Bethia allows herself to be led back to the house, with a curious Coort following in their wake.

Mama makes a great to do when she spies them from her casement and runs down to open the door. 'Too soon,' Bethia hears her say over and over. At any other time she would be pleased she was following the Spanish, but all she wants is to escape to her chamber. She pushes her way past Mama and climbs the stairs, flings the door of her chamber wide and slams it shut, making the casement rattle.

She looks at her bed, wants to burrow beneath the blankets and stay there. Instead, she paces up and down the room. The armoire containing Mainard's clothes faces her. She opens the door and tugs the few jerkins and breeches from their hooks, flinging them onto the floor. She kicks them around, but it's not helping. She picks up a doublet slashed with green. He was wearing this when he returned to Scotland for her. Why did he come back, if he already has a pretty woman to part her legs for him? It doesn't make sense. She holds it to her face. It smells of him: strong and male.

Sitting down on the chair, she leans back, holding the jacket to her like a child seeking comfort. Her eyes droop. When she awakens some time later, Mainard is standing before her.

Part Two

Will

April to July 1548

Chapter Fourteen

Forsare

It is a Saturday, but Will is not certain which month – March or maybe April. He knows it's Saturday because that's the day the anthem to the Blessed Virgin is sung on this galley of France.

Salve Regina, Mater misericordiae
Vita, dulcedo, et spes nostra salve.
Ad te clamamus exsules filii Hevae

They are indeed *exsules filii Hevae – poor banished children of Eve.* The words are so apposite Will clenches his fists to stop the howl of pain. And he's not the only one who near forgets himself that first week it is sung. James of Nydie joins in, with a voice of such sweetness that Will, amongst others, is blinking the tears away.

Et Jesum benedictum fructum ventris tui
nobis post hoc exsilium ostende
O clemens, o pia, o dulcis virgo Maria

But if he forgot himself, John Knox certainly did not. There is a sudden roar, most powerfully leonine, and Knox brings them back to themselves.

'We are Reformers and God's cause must triumph,' he bellows. 'The worship of Mary is false doctrine. Close your ears to this sweet song of the Devil lest it corrupt ye.

Our souls will stay pure like Christ Jesus, even when he was in agony upon the Cross.'

Will hangs his head. Truth be told, he is not entirely sure what he's more shamed by – his forgetting for a moment a core tenet of the Protestant faith, or that Knox has destroyed the beauty of the singing with his harsh, uncompromising spirit.

Now, like the other Heretics Écossais, he refuses to sing the anthem and they have taken their rebellion one step further: none of the Scots will remove their cap for the service. Instead, they tug them hard over their ears, holding them tight down. Knox regularly begins a prayer of his own, sometimes the words of Matthew and sometimes as the spirit moves him, loud enough so that the Scots forsares, who are gathered at one end of this ship of more than one hundred galley slaves, can hear.

It's a great comfort to them, although the commander of the galley furrows his pretty Gallic face at their protest yet seems reluctant to order the whip wielded, at least during the service. And, Will thinks, they're afraid of Knox's indomitable spirit. He's heard them muttering that Knox is habité par le diable. Truth to tell, when Knox starts up, he is most fearsome, but that's not because Satan lives within him, but because he is a channel through which the true word of the Lord God Almighty is heard on earth.

Once the service is over they bend to their oars. They have yet to leave the shelter of the river but spend each day upon it practising and learning their craft. 'It is our apprenticeship,' mutters Nydie. Will laughs. He can hear Nydie's words being repeated, passed among them like a balm. It's through such shared moments that they will survive this monstrous injustice.

Will is relieved to see Nydie's thin face light up at the laughter. He worries about his friend, doubts he is strong enough to survive the privations of life as a galley slave. He bends to rub at the shackle around one ankle, the skin raw and tender. The other end is around Nydie's ankle, and neither can move without the other. Not that they're free to move from their station, for a chain runs through the shackles into an iron ring screwed to the deck and binding them to their places on the bench. Indeed, they must sleep, eat, and do the necessary where they are chained.

When they were first brought on board, after the winter spent imprisoned in the castle at Nantes, he feared he would be kept permanently seated. He's a tall man – Will the Giant, his fellows have named him – and there's no space at the oar for him to stretch his long legs out, crammed as they are between the rows in front and behind. Indeed, even the smallest among them struggle. If he can never extend his legs, nor bear weight upon them, he may end up unable to walk. He soon discovers he need have no concerns, about this at least. To wield the long oar, the four men that line each bench must rise, arms extended to push it away, then sit as they pull it back. The strain on his knees, thighs and back is relentless, and now he fears he's going to end up with his legs permanently bent, like a mason crippled after a lifetime shifting stone.

The whisperings among the Scots had been to row ineptly but they soon learn how perilous that is. Rowing out of rhythm, you risk being clouted by the oars of those in front and behind. In any case, the commander is wise to such tricks and makes certain they all pull their weight. In each section of the ship the sous-comites carry whips, and the noise that makes as it cracks over them is one thing, but the burning pain which accompanies a direct hit is much worse, even than the whippings from his father, which Will endured as a lad. It only takes a few flicks of the nerf de bouef, and Will, and his fellows, bend to the task.

He watches as the sous-comites stride up and down lashing out at the galérien, the French convicts, as well as the Scottish contingent. Their handsome boy commander soon orders them to stop. One sous-comite clearly relishes his task for he cracks the whip a few times more before desisting, grinning as he does.

The commander tells his men that the Scottish heretics will suffer so much in the next world they do not need severe punishment in this one. It's of some relief for Will to know that the whip will be used only as necessary, without overmuch cruelty, but he knows there's no kindness here – the galley slaves must be subdued yet still able to work.

They row up the river and out the broad estuary to the sea. The river isn't too bad and soon their strokes are smooth, the rhythm easy, as they keep time with the whistle that a sous-comite blows to set the beat. And there is a certain satisfaction in all pulling together. When they reach the open sea, the work becomes harder as the waves grow higher. He hopes that the wind will favour whatever journey they are to make and push the ship along. But these galleys surely cannot go far into the oceans; the sides are too low. It doesn't need a restless sea, but only a gentle undulation, for the waves to splash over them.

Initially the cold water is refreshing to their over-heated bodies, but Will quickly discovers how the salt dries the skin, stinging cuts and blisters. He gazes down at his hands. He cannot straighten his fingers, the skin so taut they are held clawlike, perpetually. He could force it, but then the skin will tear further. He supposes his hands will eventually toughen like they did when he was forced to help dig the countermine during the siege of St Andrews Castle. He groans. Is this his future – to become an expert forsare… such a romantic-sounding word for a cruel life.

The commander, flicking dust off his sleeves as he watches, seems satisfied, and they go back up the river to Nantes. The first time, Will expected to disembark and be returned to the castle, where they were imprisoned overwinter. He was soon disabused of that notion; it's too much trouble to unshackle them from their station.

Today they are fed a bean stew, and soon the ship is loud with farts, the air around them even more noxious than usual.

"Tis a shame we cannot harness the power of our expulsions to blow us on our journey,' says Nydie.

There are loud guffaws, and again Nydie's words are passed among them, but soon the laughter is changed to groans. It's fortunate that the breeches they are provided with are without the usual division for legs, since, with the impediment of fetters, they must be donned over the head. These women's petticoats, as some have named them, at least make it easy to relieve themselves. The leather bucket does its rounds and is quickly full, the faeces slopping over the top. Will empties and empties and empties over the side, retching at the smell. There's a sudden gust of wind and he's covered by the blowback. He drops onto the bench and wipes the spray off his face with the back of his hand as best he can. After that he directs the bucket to be passed to the other side of the galley: doesn't care if its contents hit the quayside. Let these Frenchies suffer for giving them food which passes straight through.

Chapter Fifteen

Let Her Swim

Will awakens at sunrise, head resting on his knees, and jerks upright. There are guns being fired, and soon it is passed among them that two of the galérien have escaped. Will thinks they won't get far unless they can slip their fetters. And certainly, it's not long before they're recaptured. Peasants with long staves, accompanied by a couple of huge, slavering hounds, arrive with much shouting from the men and barking from the dogs. They drag the captured galérien by the ropes twisted tight around their necks, with more labourers prodding from behind. All seek the reward, which it is whispered among the forsares is as much as five of these men will make in a whole year.

The prisoners are hung upside down from the mast while the sailors take turns to beat the soles of their feet with a bastinado. Will notices that they apply the wooden rod skilfully, only hitting the arches, careful to inflict great pain without permanent damage. When the men are eventually let down, they do indeed manage to hobble back to their seats and are still capable of rowing.

That evening, the sous-comites move among them issuing tunics of coarse brown fibre, much like the sailors wear. It seems to have properties whereby it repels water, up to a point, but is a weighty garment which will no doubt grow even heavier when soaked by high seas. Nevertheless, he's grateful to be afforded some protection from the cold waters in the Bay of Biscay. He's less enthusiastic about the red cap, with which he's also issued. He jams it on his head; it's a good fit and covers his ears nicely, but the flopping tail, which Nydie flicks back and forward skimming his hand over Will's head, has them all laughing. Once they're dressed in their tunics and caps, there's nothing to differentiate them from the common criminals who form the bulk of the galley slaves – nothing, that is, except the branding. All of the French prisoners have the letters GAL seared onto their skin.

Sailors move among them wielding clippers. Will looks at the pile of hair at his feet, the same yellow-red as Father's, but not as bright red as his little brother John's. He brushes his eyes with the back of his hand, wondering if he'll ever see John's freckled face again, wondering if Father will exert himself to pay a ransom and have Will released. But none of the Castilians have gained their freedom, not even the instigators of the siege, the powerful lairds of Fife. He notices they don't have to take up the oars but are presumably still ensconced in reasonable comfort in their respective chateaux prisons. Even that horse-penis Carmichael seems to have evaded the galleys. Will clenches his fists remembering the beating he took from Carmichael, but in the end Will returned as good as he got.

He's not sorry to be freed from his mop of filthy hair, for the lice had become most troublesome, and is grateful for the red cap to protect his head from cold air and hot sun alike. Yet, when the barber comes at Knox with the clippers, Knox hits the barber's hand away, shaking his head of thick hair violently. The sous-comite arrives with his whip, and more sailors come to hold Knox down, but he will not be subdued and continues to buckle and roar. A command is shouted from the foredeck and the sailors let go. Knox is to be left with his long black hair and thick

87

black beard, like the latter-day Jeremiah that he is. The Scots smile to one another. It's a small victory, but significant – and lifts their spirits exponentially.

Will gazes in puzzlement at the piece of cork with the long cord attached, which each galérien is given. A sailor demonstrates. The cord is to go around the neck and the cork in the mouth. Knox mutters about French devilry while the Castilians look to one another in confusion. The sailor mimics rowing.

'I think we are to row with great effort but little noise,' says Nydie. He twists the cork between his fingers. 'This looks to be a plug for our mouths – no doubt for use when we are under attack.' He leans in to whisper in Will's ear. 'But nothing will keep our John quiet.'

Will guffaws. He sees the sous-comite raise his whip, a smile spreading over his face, and the laughter dies as quickly as it came.

A priest comes on board, clean-shaven face wrinkling with distaste. The strong pine scent of the pitch with which the whole ship is smeared combined with the stench arising from the galley slaves, worse than any privy, is indeed eye-watering until you grow used to it. The priest's biretta bobs up and down as he recites the Mass, the words tumbling out of his mouth like a stream rushing downhill. The Scots sit upright, as ever refusing to bow their heads. The French crew seem puzzled by the Scots intransigent behaviour. The Latin babble flows over Will. He remembers last year when the Castilians were excommunicated by the Pope, and how much he was affected. The terror he felt to be excluded, cast out, denied was very great. And when their pardon was received, and rejected, indeed set alight by Knox himself, Will believed he was destined to burn in the firepits of Hell for all eternity. But after a winter in a French prison sharing a cell with the great John Knox, he no longer has any doubts about the rightness of the Reformer's beliefs.

Now a sous-comite is moving among them, eyes cast

down in reverence, holding an image of the Virgin. The painting is exquisite: serene blue eyes in a delicately moulded face, and a halo shining bright above her. The priest intones on and on, while the sailor moves slowly along the rows holding the image before each of the galley slaves so that they may kiss it and invoke the protection of the Blessed Virgin.

It is so very beautiful that Will feels drawn towards it, as though an invisible force is tugging at his core. The sous-comite comes closer, his usual sinister smile replaced by an expression of reverential bliss, and Will finds himself leaning forward thinking what harm can it do; they need whatever blessings they can get for a safe voyage. He doesn't want to drown at sea – having near drowned in the harbour at St Andrews, he remembers the choking terror too well. And fettered as he is, if their ship sinks it means certain death. He feels the stillness of peace in his heart as the Virgin comes to him. He will kiss the image; he does not, in this moment, care what his fellows think.

The reverential sailor and the Virgin reach John Knox first. Knox waves it away.

'Trouble me not. Such an idol is accursed, and I will not touch it.'

Will jerks as though he's awoken from a stupor.

'Thou shalt not make unto thee any graven image. Thou shalt not bow down thyself to them, nor serve them, for the Lord thy God is a jealous God, and will visit the iniquity of the fathers upon the children unto the third and fourth generation.'

Although Knox is shouting the words of the Old Testament out in Scots, it's clear, from his red face and waving arms, that he's not willing to kiss the image. The sailor appears confused rather than determined and looks to an officer who has hurried over to prevent any further resistance.

The officer fires French at Knox, and Will translates the

words in his head. In essence, the officer is saying why would even heretics choose to go to sea without invoking whatever help they can. The sous-comite gestures, punching his fist towards Knox. The image is thrust forward, hitting Knox on the face so that his lips touch it.

The sous-comite calls over his shoulder. 'I'll la embrasse.'

There's laughter among the Frenchmen, convicts, sailors, and officers, for once united in shared pleasure at the obdurate Scot being forced to kiss the image.

Knox jerks the Virgin out of the man's hands and tosses it overboard. 'Let her save herself, for we do not need her,' he shouts. 'She is light enough and can learn to swim.'

There is a shared gasp from both the French sailors and the galérien.Will sees the image sink slowly into the river. The priest is shouting his outrage but the Scots do not care. Will feels sure it's a sign from God that the effigy vanishes with such ease. The Scots nod to one another – no one may quash the indomitable John Knox.

Will expects them all to be punished, but beyond feeding them a diet only of biscuit so hard that it breaks the teeth to bite, alongside the usual water with dead insects floating on the surface, no further punishment is inflicted. And truth to tell, the lack of bean stew is not greatly mourned.

Chapter Sixteen

Scotland

The drowning of the Virgin is the last time they have anything to smile about, and Will's surmise that they cannot go far out to sea in galleys clearly built to guard coastal waters proves erroneous; it's many days since they last saw land. The fetters rattle around his ankles as he shifts on the plank of wood that is his home. He needs to sleep, but there's something under his right arse cheek that, among his innumerable discomforts, is impossible to ignore. He squirms and twists to ease himself, but still it's there, pressing into the last area of tender flesh on his body.

'God's blood, man, keep still and let us get some rest while we can.'

Will turns to gaze at his shackle-twin. Nydie does not look good. He corrects himself; none of his fellows look good. Nydie, with his thin face and pallor apparent beneath the sunburn, looks frailer and sicker than most. Of course, they cannot expect a long and hearty life as forsares, but surely the French won't hold them forever; they aren't criminals but prisoners of war. But then a criminal is given a sentence, which he serves and is surely then released. They were given no sentence and release may only come if the French galleys are attacked and they are freed. And that is dependent on who the attackers are.

If it's the Spanish or Ottomans, then there will be no release, only a change of master. But should they be captured by English ships, then they will certainly be freed. He and his fellow Scots killed Cardinal Beaton and took his castle at St Andrews in part at the behest of King Henry VIII of England. And that now-deceased king did not keep his promise to send a relief force. England owes them some restitution. But the galley, as well as carrying many forsares, also carries troops ready to fight off any attack, be it English, Dutch, Portuguese, Spanish, or Ottoman. Release or escape is most unlikely.

He reflects that the soldiers and sailors do not live in much greater comfort than the galley slaves while they are at sea. Even the officers rest only in chairs set out on the small deck, while the soldiers are confined to a raised enclosure where, tucked in beside the cannon, they sleep with their heads resting on their knapsacks. They at least do not have the indignity of the bucket, but do the necessary in seats that have been made to hang over the sea. Will does not envy the oarsmen who sit nearby.

The wind is rising. He knows this, not only because the galley is rocked, but mostly because the dark waves are splashing over the side and soaking him – for night does not bring a halt in rowing when they are this far out to sea. He has the best and the worst seat of a forsare at the same time. Best because it's the least strenuous position for rowing and he can lean against the ship's side to sleep during the rest periods. Worst because he's soon soaked whenever there's the slightest of waves.

He gazes at his bare feet. They sit, soft and luminous, in the swill of seawater and piss which slops over the board on which they rest and is slow to drain away in these heavier seas. He thinks of Agnes, the family servant back in Scotland, and how she used urine as a bleach to rinse their clothes. His feet are well-cleansed – Agnes would approve.

He falls into a half-doze, awakened only when a

92

particularly large wave dumps water over him. There's activity as the sails are raised, and the rowers on shift can gratefully take a break, although those on the other side of the ship are knee deep in foaming water as the lee side dips into the sea while they race along. He slips back into a dream where his sister Bethia is standing, finger-pointing and berating him, while Grissel behind her is laughing. Then his father is there, with an angry face and bitter words. He comes to once more: that dream was not so far removed from the reality of his former family life.

Nydie is vomiting again. He calls to the sous-comite on duty, this one a more kindly sailor than his sinister-looking colleague. The man makes his way between the lines of forsares, whip hanging over one shoulder.

'My friend is ill,' he says, the French words forming easily. 'Please help him.'

The sailor's face softens at the please.

Nydie retches again and a thin stream of bile trails from his mouth.

'I think the pottage of vegetables was not good for him.'

The man pats James on the shoulder. 'Not the vegetables, only malaise de mer, he will grow accustomed.' He retreats back up the narrow walkway between the rowers and Will does not blame him. The stench of sweat, dirt, and bilge is bad enough, but the smell of fresh vomit overlaying all is gut-wrenching. Will's on the verge of emptying what little is in his own stomach. He chews on a crust of dry bread, which he'd tucked away in his waistband for just such a reason, and it settles him.

He turns his attention to Nydie again. A rat is running around Nydie's feet; surely he must see it with his head hanging so low, but James is beyond caring. Will shifts, kicks out – and finally eases the pressure on his hip. Thanks be to the Lord God Almighty for small mercies.

The sky lightens, glowing red in the east as the sun

begins to lift its face over the horizon. The wind dies and one third of the forsares must take to the oars once more. John Knox, on Nydie's other side, awakens from his doze. He rolls his shoulders and stretches his arms as best as he can when they are each pressing into the person next to them and the rowers behind are close enough that they can feel their breath upon their necks – and smell it too. And the man in front of James, a French convict, has had his back splashed with James's watery flux. It's fortunate it's his shift to row and he can spare no attention for retaliation.

Will looks over the top of James's drooping head at Knox. His hair is luxuriant as a woman's, although all their hair has grown since their heads were shaved at the start of the season. For Will, it's a great relief to have the beard grown back upon his face. He suffers more than most from the burning of the sun. He protects his head with the red cap but his skin goes from white to flaming red, never turning brown as the others do – and is always painful to touch. He hopes he can grow a beard the like of Knox's, which spreads as wide as a blanket over Knox's chest. Will stretches over and picks a flea off it, squashing the beastie between his fingers. Perhaps he should eat it; t'would be the first meat he's tasted in weeks.

There's activity at the mast, and a flag is hoisted. He squints as it unfurls, trying to work out the insignia. Why are they raising the saltire, surely it should be a French flag they fly? Signals are passed between the galleys that form their fleet. He peers out to ascertain whether they're drawing close to land and about to anchor, or about to come under attack. No, there's no activity around the cannons, no sense of that rising fear and frenetic energy that comes when death is threatening. He bends again, peering to his left in an attempt to see through the oar holes on the other side. Hills are visible, some cliffs and a beach. If only his fellows would keep still he could better determine.

Then he hears the French galley slaves chattering

excitedly. 'Ecosse,' they say. His heart lifts; he is home. He tugs at the fetters; perhaps there is someway he can slip these chains and swim. A wave soaks him, a reminder that his swimming is, at best, rudimentary. But there might be a landfall. He gazes again at his pulpy feet, wondering how long they'd last on stony ground. He doesn't care, if If he ever gets on land he'll walk barefoot to reach St Andrews.

He nudges James, then places his arm around him to help him sit up, to see Scotland. Knox begins to pray in sonorous tones. It's a long prayer, said loudly so all the French can hear, even though they won't understand, as though Knox thinks the rightness of his words will be sucked in through their skin, pass through the flesh, and be deposited into their very bones. As though he believes that through loud prayers, viscerally, their captors will know the true path to the Lord.

Nydie groans in Will's arms, his head rolling against Will's shoulder. Knox continues to intone, the words flowing from his mouth like the beat of a drum. Will shakes his head to get rid of a rising irritation as Knox drones on. He becomes aware of a churning deep in his belly and realises it's fear, for if he loses his faith in John Knox's power and rightness of thinking he has nothing to sustain him.

It's their shift now. They take up their oars, and only when they have done at least two dozen strokes and are up to the speed set by the sous-comite are the rowers in front allowed to stop. The men lean on their oar, too exhausted to even lift their heads. But Will doesn't care, for his body is already screaming at the strain. He jerks as his back spasms, but he cannot stop. And he has near four hours of this. Yet he keeps pulling, in rhythm with his fellows, as the sous-comite strides up and down the narrow gangway shouting tirer, tirer, tirer. He falls into a waking nightmare, thinking that he cannot keep going, but somehow he always does.

The bell rings; their shift must surely soon be over. Will glimpses a sandy beach strewn with small stones, trees, and the land rising away from the shore, but cannot pause to look. There are shouted instructions; the rowers are to go slow; then the anchor is dropped. Will stands up, stretching out to ease his back. There's a castle before them but they're moored well out from it, for the tide is also well out. He studies it. Built on a rocky promontory, the stout curtain walls enclose a keep which towers above them. But the walls themselves are of no mean height. He squints, head tilted. The walls come to a sharp point, like the prow of a ship facing out to sea.

'I think this could be Blackness Castle,' he says to James.

Nydie's head comes up. He struggles to rise to his feet, Will supporting him. There's a rustle of excitement among the Scots as others confirm it. Will twists to look over his shoulder. On the other side of the Forth Estuary, in which they are moored, is the kingdom of Fife – and home.

He drops back onto his bench, rubbing his neck. Then picks up the fetters, wrenching on them. They are as firmly fixed as the last time he tried.

'The French must be using the castle as a base,' says Nydie. 'It's their flag that's flying from the keep.'

Once the tide comes in sufficiently, there is much to and froing between the French garrison and galleys. Supplies are offloaded and soldiers too. The word amongst the forsares is that England holds Inchcolm Island, which sits at the mouth of the Firth of Forth. No wonder their ship stayed near to land as they rowed up the estuary. He stands up again, twisting to catch sight of the island, but it's blocked by a spit of land, and even if it were not, they sit low in the water.

His heart thumps in his chest. His home is immediately to the north and the English to the east – the hope of freedom so very close. But it soon dissipates, for they leave early the next morning on a still sea, keeping close to land. Unless the English are ready to attack with ships, there is little chance of rescue. Will swallows hard and rows, for what else can he do.

Chapter Seventeen

Aground

There's a strange sensation beneath his feet. It is not the sound of galley cleaving smoothly through water but a vibration: a shuddering rasping. They look to one another in bafflement. A crash, and the ship comes to a sudden halt and he's flung forward into the row in front. The shackle chain goes tight and Will's tossed back, hitting the face of the man behind with the back of his head.

Will opens his eyes to find Nydie patting his face and calling his name. He has fallen between benches, free leg in the air, and the prisoner behind is complaining loudly about the weight of Will's body across his feet. Will tries to rise. It's not easy, trapped as he is between two rows and his leg fettered to Nydie's. The other prisoner shoves at him, with no attempt to assist. The man is a common criminal, brutal and brutalised, so what does Will expect, but when the fellow kicks him, he lashes back with his fist. Soon there's a flurry of fists, feet and rattling chains, until the sous-comite clambers over waving his whip. The lash catches Will across the cheek, and he is roaring and the French prisoner is roaring, and then Knox is roaring. Knox has the bellowing power of an enraged bull, and drowns them all out.

The ship, which seems held firm by whatever it has hit, lists with a suddenness that sends them sliding towards the downward side, along with the great tangle of manifold ropes which snake everywhere. One of the rowing boats above breaks free from its tethers and swings loose, narrowly missing Will as he and Nydie are brought to an abrupt, and jarring, halt by the pinioned shackles. The sous-comite, with nothing to hold him, keeps tumbling, hitting the men and benches on the sunken side, and the small boat comes crashing after him. It all comes to an abrupt end when both sous-comite and boat hit the lower side. Will winces at the flying splinters of wood and the cries from those who have been hurt.

He lies still for a moment. Then struggles to sit up, looking down at Nydie. 'A sandbank, I swear we've run aground on a sandbank.' He tugs James under the arms, which is not easy with their legs shackled together, back up to the oar hole so he can see out and confirm his suspicions. Then he is sliding back down the sloping deck once more. The shackle still holds around his ankle but the pinion breaks. They are free – although not from each other.

Will looks for Knox; the long hair defines him. But Knox is no longer close by; has somehow reached the far end of the deck. All attention is on the side dipping into the sea, with men shouting and fighting to avoid falling in and others helping those crushed beneath the smashed rowing boat.

Again he grabs Nydie's arm, holding onto a stanchion with his other hand. 'Quick, we must get out.'

They stagger to their feet and Will uses all his strength to haul James to the upside. Even if he wanted to, he cannot escape without his conjoined friend. Galériens shout for help as water creeps along the deck, but sailors clamber over them to get out. Will and Nydie cling to the top-side staring down at the confusion.

'We should help them,' mutters Nydie.

Will knocks his foot against Nydie's. 'What we can do, fettered as we are?'

'How then do you propose to escape?'

Will looks over his shoulder. 'I will swing my free leg over first, then the other, and you must of course' – he rolls his eyes – 'follow.'

James stares at him. 'Go on then.'

Will swings his long leg up and hooks it, with some difficulty, over the top. The ship rolls further onto its side and both men cling to the railing.

'You need to lift your leg up now.'

Nydie, a good head shorter than Will, struggles to lift the shackled leg high enough. Will can do nothing to help without losing his balance.

'It's too high,' Nydie groans.

Will swings his free leg back and drops into the galley once more, and hauls Nydie along to where there's a bench still attached to the deck, which they both step on. Up Will goes again, and Nydie, clenching his jaw, this time manages to heave his leg over, and Will's shackled leg follows. Now both Will's legs are over the side and he's facing into the ship, his chest pressed hard against the top of the rail.

'Get your other leg out,' he gasps.

James swings round to rest his chest on the railing, and both pairs of legs dangle against the outer curve of the ship.

Will takes a last look at the tumult inside. 'When I count to three, we'll let go, together.'

James nods and Will prays that the sea is not deep – nor too shallow. But when they let go, the ship has settled so far on its side they have to push themselves backwards over the curve, and then they are falling.

Will wants to laugh with relief. He's landed on his back in shallow water, the sand soft beneath him. He rolls onto his hands and knees, kicking his foot out to untangle the chain, and pushes himself upright, bringing Nydie with him. The water rises barely to their calves. They are on a long spit of sand, the galley high in front of them, hull

100

exposed. Beyond, more banks of sand poke through the sea like the humps of a lolling sea monster. He glances at James, whose face is as white as the crunched shells lying in swathes on the banks, thinking what to do.

Miles away, he can see land… a long line of soft hills to the foreground, with a backdrop of much higher ones behind. That's where home is; he recognises the peak of East Lomond. Even a good swimmer would most probably drown trying to reach it. He turns, noting and dismissing the small island, no more than a grassy knoll, to his right – nowhere to hide there. Facing him is land they can reach: a long low rocky beach with trees delineating its shoreline. He tries to move but his feet are sucked into the sand, holding him tight to this place. He tugs until one foot breaks free while James stands glaikit.

'Come on, Nydie, we must away.'

Nydie fights his foot free of the suckering sand. Will puts his arm around Nydie's waist.

'Together,' he hisses.

They try to run, and manage a shuffle, emerging from the shadow of the long galley.

Nydie hauls on Will's arm. 'Stop!' he wheezes

They tuck themselves back in and Will peers around the prow. All is confusion as men tumble out of the ship, splashing into the water. The galley lists further, and there are more shouts of alarm from men fearful it will roll, trapping them beneath it.

'We need to go this way,' Nydie points. 'We can work our way in line with the shore but stay hidden by the galley. When we've got far enough along, we should make a run for the trees.'

Will nods and they move, the sound of their splashing feet loud in his ears. He guesses they'll be visible to at least one of the galleys coming towards their stricken ship but hopes, for the moment, all attention will be on rescuing the crew and capturing the rest of the forsares.

They shuffle-run as fast as they can, but Nydie is going

slower and slower and out of rhythm. He stumbles and falls.

'Nydie, we cannot stop.'

'I cannot breathe.'

'We must work together. You count to keep us in sequence.'

James shakes his head

'Please, Nydie, we're so close. I think we've run aground on the sandbanks at Cramond. Could anything be more fortuitous?'

James struggles to his feet. They begin their shuffle-run once more. Will glances out to sea; more galleys are drawing close and some have lowered small boats. They are moving with greater speed than he and Nydie. Christ's blood this is hard.

'Not far now, just keep going,' he encourages.

Their fetters restrict movement enough without the added challenge of sea against his legs and the sand clutching his feet. But they are drawing near the shore and the water barely laps their ankles. Nydie is stumbling, on the verge of falling, leaning more and more of his weight on Will. He's surprisingly heavy given how little they get to eat and, in James's case, that mostly expelled. They reach the shore and Will slithers on wet seaweed, one leg slipping out from under him. Staggering, he holds onto Nydie and manages to regain his balance. Over the rock-strewn shore they go, Will half carrying, half dragging James into the shelter of the trees.

He glances over his shoulder. One of the boats is close but they won't be able to beach it here, not unless they are going to risk dragging it over stones. He and Nydie might actually make it. He looks back before the beach is blocked from view, just in time to see the French sailors clambering out and leaving one among them to stand in the water holding their rowboat. Surely the Lord could've granted them a little more time to make good their escape.

The undergrowth beneath the trees is sparse. He looks

up, wondering if they could hide in a tree, and realises the climb is impossible, shackled as they are. James stumbles and Will drags him forward. If they weren't chained at the ankle he could sling James over his shoulder and carry him.

Then Will can hold him up no longer and Nydie topples to the sandy earth and lies there, insensible. Will stands over him, hands resting on his hips as he catches his breath. He bends to tug on the chain that binds them but it holds fast.

'Yes, break it and go, please,' pleads Nydie.

Will ignores him, gazing around. There's a small glade ahead filled with a dense swathe of gorse, its yellow flowers dazzling in the sunshine. He bends, and taking hold of Nydie by the ankles, he steps backwards, dragging Nydie with him. He doesn't think he can keep this up. He tries rolling Nydie over. Bits of earth, tree bark, dead leaves stick to James's wet clothing. Will feels like a giant ant rolling its prey safely home. He crawls, pushing James over, kicking his chained foot free when it gets caught, not caring that James's face is coated in dirt. Picking up a broken branch of Scots pine he ruffles the ground as best he can to remove the trail they're leaving.

'I can walk. Help me up,' pleads Nydie.

'I only need you to squirm in here with me,' says Will, panting. 'Can you do that?'

Nydie nods.

Will, face skimming the needle-strewn earth, slithers in beneath the gorse with James by his side. The thorns catch, gripping as tight as a drowning man. Tugging his clothes free, feeling his skin prickled by a thousand tiny needles, he keeps moving. The gorse pulls his hair and tears at his forehead. Again he frees himself, blood trickling down his face, and pushes in further. Then he's caught, a branch pinning him to the earth, and he cannot move. He thrashes but the gorse catches his arms, legs, and hair as effectively as any four soldiers holding him down.

103

'Keep still. I'll get you loose.'

How Nydie manages to extricate him, pinned down as he himself is, Will doesn't know. His skin stings and the gorse tears at him while they squirm in further.

'We're in deep enough, do you think?' whispers Nydie

'Well, we're not going back out to check.'

Nydie giggles. It's a curiously high-pitched sound. 'Wheesht.'

They lie still. A breeze rustles the leaves of the nearby trees, bees buzz above their head, large and clumsy. The earth beneath them is dry and warm, the scent of the bright yellow flowers above so strong it catches in his throat. He feels his eyelids drooping and struggles to keep them open. He jerks awake and turns his head, face skimming the ground, to look at Nydie, who's very still.

Nydie's eyes glitter in a shaft of sunlight. He responds to Will's poke with a groan. Will places his finger over James's lips. 'Quiet, as a wee mouse.'

James stifles another groan.

Will wriggles to find a spot where he isn't being pricked by a thousand gorse needles but it's impossible. He makes himself go still. This is a discomfort of a minor sort, he reminds himself, as nothing to the anguish of effort required of him every day at the long oar. And really it's pleasantly warm beneath the bushes, the heat of the sun nicely contained, the pungent scent of the bright yellow flowers enticing. With a long sigh, he lets himself drift.

Chapter Eighteen

Escape

Will awakens with a jolt. Something is sliding across his unshod feet. He lies rigid, then lifts his head to peer down the length of his body in time to see the tail slither away. An adder most likely; lucky he didn't move, for he's heard their bite is painful. He cannot believe he let sleep overcome him at such a perilous moment. It must be well into the long Scottish spring evening for the light is beginning to fail, a grey dusk creeping over the earth. Of course, it's May, so a deep twilight is as dark as it gets, and first light is by four bells. He remembers, almost two years ago, how they took St Andrews Castle by stealth and killed its cardinal on just such a day.

He turns his mind back to their current predicament. The sailors he saw landing on the beach will be fully occupied with containing the slaves they found close to the galley. And then they will look to refloat the ship, which by a strange twist of fate is called The Cardinal. John Knox had been most disconsolate at sailing in a ship so named, but said at least it was a cardinal that could be put to some use. It's strange it ran aground on such a calm day. He must stop his mind from wandering and make a plan. They need to head inland with all possible speed. Then they must find a hammersmith to remove the leg irons, which means finding the nearest habitation. They're roughly midway between Leith and Queensferry, a long hobble in either direction. His heart fails him as he considers the difficulty of movement even for a short distance, but they must just get further from this shore. And if they manage, by the grace of God, to rid themselves of their fetters, what then? A fishing boat is what they need. If they can steal a fishing boat then they can row to St Andrews. It's a long way in a small boat, but they can do it, they've had enough practice. And, although Father may turn him away, Bethia will help them – she may even be married to Gilbert Logie of Clatto. He's fairly certain that Logie had a strong hankering for Bethia, and Father would approve the match since Logie is of good family.

He can feel his muscles unclench now he has a plan. He will not think of all the ways in which it may fail or of the long journey to get to Clatto, which sits above Garrbridge. One step at a time, one very small step at a time. First the fetters. Nydie mutters in his sleep. Will covers Nydie's mouth and shakes him gently. Immediately he realises it was a mistake, for Nydie thrashes around.

'Christ's blood, be quiet man.'

Will feels something tickling his face; it moves across his lips, and now Will is the one thrashing as he knocks the spider away.

Nydie's leg is caught in the thorns. Will has to swivel around, staying low, face skimming the dirt, to release him. The gorse catches onto his hair as soon as he moves, but, after what seems an eternity, he releases Nydie and frees himself, although the bush retains a goodly clump of his hair.

Eventually they're out and on their feet. Will shivers. It's chilly after the smothering heat beneath the whin. He can hear distant calls from the shoreline and see torchlight through the trees. They'll be waiting for high tide, no doubt, to refloat the beached Cardinal. He swallows, his dry mouth feels as though it's coated with a thick layer of dirt.

James stands by his side, panting. Will's empty belly tenses; how they are ever to successfully escape if Nydie is already exhausted? The chains rattle loud in his ears as they begin the shuffle out of the glade.

'Take your stocking off,' Nydie hisses.

'What?'

'We need to wrap it around the chain to deaden the noise, and you'll be quicker.'

They have been provided with footless stockings such as the sailors wear as part of their few items of clothing, and Will, leaning on Nydie's shoulder, balances on one foot, tugs it off and winds it around the chain.

Will can see a fingernail moon hanging high above the trees. He hopes they're going in the right direction as they move away from the sound of voices. But then the voices grow louder, the light closer. He hauls Nydie behind the broad trunk of a nearby tree. They lean against it, Will sweating – and shivering.

He can hear the conversation now. A gruff voice calls, 'Nous vous trouverons.'

He clenches his fists and can feel the tension shoot up his arm, becomes aware his body is as tight as a skin stretched out to dry. The light is moving away. He sags with relief.

'They are looking for us,' Nydie whispers.

'I fear you're right.' Will thinks of the beating they'll get if caught, but giving themselves up now will not save them from it.

The darkness is already waning as they emerge from beneath the trees. He can hear a bell ringing, a nearby monastery calling the monks to early matins. It will have tools for them to break these chains… and food. No, it's the first place they'll search. He hobble-runs past its walls, dragging Nydie with him. Ahead, another clump of trees rise, tall shadows in the dim light. They stop beneath them, bent over, hands resting on their knees. The grass is soft underfoot after the stony track, but the nettles grow high, ready to sting the unwary.

'We must break our fetters,' pants Nydie. They both search the ground around them, kicking the long grass aside.

'Here,' says Will, hefting a large stone in his hands. He bends, unwraps the stocking and hits the chain binding their ankles together. And hits and hits. But it's difficult to get enough momentum and the stone bounces off the links.

He looks up, breathlessly, at the watching Nydie. 'We need a hard surface.'

Nydie points. 'There, a stump.'

The chain is taut... and resistant. The stone leaps out of Will's hand, hitting him in the face. He groans and leans forward, hand to forehead.

He locates the stone and resumes his task. 'It's no good. All that's happening is I'm denting the wood beneath. We need a flat stone.'

He doesn't want to tarry here. It's too close to the beach and the monastery, but they'll move so much faster freed from one another.

'We'll go on, but keep a look-out for something suitable.'

'And, at the same time, a look-out for our pursuers,' mutters James.

Will doesn't know how Nydie, so much frailer than him, keeps going. Will is biting on his lips to stop the groans as his hips and knees stab with every shuffle. It grows lighter, long streaks of golden light like the halo of the Virgin Mary. But he and his fellows have rejected the Virgin – she will not be watching over him. And he knows they must find somewhere to hide now daylight is almost upon them.

'Here,' calls Nydie. 'This might work.' He halts before a smooth stone, half-buried in the earth.

Kneeling, Will studies the chain as best he can in the light, turning it in his hands. He stretches out his leg and waves Nydie away until the chain is taut over the stone. Then he smashes stone on stone, again and again, until suddenly Nydie is staggering as the link gives way. Will leaps to his feet, grabs Nydie's wrist and runs. He's been left with the longer end of chain, which rattles behind him. Quickly he wraps it around his ankle, tying it in place with the useful stocking.

There's a settlement further along the path: a sorry-looking group of cottages, the turf roofs in much need of repair. He knows the further away they can get from the coast the safer they will be – from their French guards at least. But Nydie is running the half stagger of a man who will soon fall face first onto the earth.

One house standing alone looms in the distance, with a nearby shed. He points. 'Just keep going, man, and we will be hid.'

Nydie puts on a spurt of speed and passes Will, running with all the awkwardness of a goose being chased by a fox. As they cross the rough ground in front of the byre, past a mountain of dung, Will feels something sharp pierce his foot, but he doesn't stop. Inside, the cows shift restlessly in their stall and the calves complain loudly in theirs.

'They will soon come to milk,' says Will. 'I think we must go on.'

'Leave me, Seton, I can go no further.' Nydie drops to his hands and knees.

'Then we will bide here.'

Chapter Nineteen

Dung Heap

The centre of the heap has, at least, the benefit of being of long standing and the dung is old and dry. They scoop at it with their hands, then Will attacks it with the stone he's unaccountably kept a hold of. Nydie finds a long sharp sliver of planking broken from the wall of the dilapidated shed and uses it to dig. The freedom of having their chain broken and each being able to move without the other has revived them and they work with fresh purpose. Soon they have shifted enough shite to crawl inside. Will looks down upon Nydie, curled up like a rat in its hole, and covers him, while James creates a breathing passage with his outstretched arm. Will crawls in and covers himself. At least it's warm, and he has been in places that smelt worse: the galley being the most prominent example, but St Andrews Castle, after months of siege, coming a close second.

He wriggles inside his rathole trying to stretch his legs out. His foot throbs; he must've cut it on something sharp, but really it's nothing. His whole body has hurt ever since he took up his new trade as a galley slave. He clenches his fists; they must make good their escape.

Again he falls asleep in this cocooning warmth, coming awake with a start. His heart is thumping, sweat pooling in his oxters and pouring down the side of his body. He can't breathe, is suffocating as he tries to take in great gulps of air, impossible beneath the weight of dung, and has to restrain himself from bursting out. After what feels like a lifetime, his breathing slows and the sense of suffocation recedes. But it quickly rises again, for he can hear voices.

'Fetch me yon bucket, and be quick aboot it, laddie.'

The farmer must have come to do the milking. He lies taut, but the fear is not so great. If they're discovered, then he and Nydie between them will likely overpower him, and the laddie. But for the moment he will stay hid, for their pursuers may not be far. The laddie has returned with the bucket it seems, for the next words Will hears is him being offered a sup of milk by the gruff voice. Oh, it's good to hear Scots spoken, to know he's in his ane country and even to think upon his equally gruff father. He hears the bleat of calves shuffling in their pen and eventually the sound of their release. All goes quiet now, and he guesses the calves are being allowed their share of the milk.

Suddenly the peace of the milking is shattered as the shed door crashes wide. The farmer cries out and men shout. The French soldiers are among them.

There seem to be many of them milling about outside the byre; he can see the flash of blue uniform through his small air hole, hear them shouting at the farmer. Then the laddie is crying and pleading. Why are the French so determined the farmer and his son must know something or even have hidden them? An officer comes, one that can speak some English.

'We know they are here. You must give them up or we'll take the boy – he is strong, will make un bon galérien.'

The farmer is pleading, begging… he has hid no one, is only a poor man with a few cows. There is nowhere to hide in this byre. They can search. Please let his son, his only child, go.

111

'Du sang,' the soldiers are muttering among themselves.

Will searches his mind for the translation. Blood? Is it blood they're chattering about? Then he can feel movement above him. He lies rigid. A sword is stabbed through, so close to his face it strokes the side of his cheek. And Nydie has given himself up, is shouting at them to stop.

'Come out,' a voice commands. It's him they're speaking to. He debates whether it's better to stay hid and risk being stabbed or accept a return to the galleys. It's the Devil's choice, but on balance he decides he wants to survive uninjured. He rises like Lazarus, but it's from the dung heap and not the dead he comes.

Sliding down the heap he sees it. The telltale drops of blood from his cut heel leading to their hiding place. He looks over ruefully at Nydie, who shrugs. And then they're being hustled back towards the ship while the farmer's cries follow them, for the soldiers, smacking their lips at the prospect of some tender veal, have tied a rope around the two young calves' necks and are dragging them along. At least they spared the lad.

They're back on the beach far quicker than it took them to stumble inland. The oars flash in and out of the water. What a joy it would be to have a short oar which did not require all your strength to pull. The warm bodies of the calves slaughtered on the beach, their blood soaking into the sand, lie before him – indeed have been allocated more space than he. Hunched over, his back aching already at the prospect of being fettered to an oar once more, he fears what their punishment will be. They row out past their stricken ship, which lies on its side filling with water as the tide comes in. They're still some distance from the fleet but the stench is already nigh unbearable. He remembers Father telling that he could smell a galley a mile to windward. No wonder the officers douse themselves in scent, but what are the forsares to do when their only means of washing is a soaking from a wave.

Nydie and he are greeted with a great shout of welcome by their compatriots, almost as though they're returning heroes not failed escapees. Will is allocated a new place by the walkway. It has the benefit of being amongst the driest seats, since it's furthest from the ship's side and thus he will not be constantly dowsed in seawater, but the much graver disadvantage of being the position that demands the most of the rower as he must push the oar from his feet to high above his head with each stroke. But he knows he has been fortunate not to suffer worse punishment, and is grateful that Nydie, presumably in recognition of his weakened state, has again been allocated a mid-row seat.

The captain of their former ship stands next to the commander of this ship, his face tripping him, as their old servant Agnes would say. A whisper is passed around the forsares: that The Cardinal ran aground due to handsome boy's incompetence; that the other ships easily avoided the sandbank on such a fine day; that the fairest ship among the French fleet is lost. And then Knox is speaking. Will no longer sits close by, cannot hear the words, but soon they're being passed among them. 'Scotland can bear no Cardinals.' It's repeated over and over and soon the Castilians on the ship are shouting with laughter as the French look on, angrily. They do not understand the joke but know it's at their expense. Will rolls the words around his mouth. Scotland indeed tolerates no cardinals, and surely the grounding of The Cardinal is a sign from God. He feels a small kernel of hope; the Lord looks after his own.

Chapter Twenty

St Andrews

They row hard out of the Forth, staying wide of Inchcolm Island, and head up the Fife coast. Night comes and they anchor off Wemyss, at least that's where Will guesses they are because of the castle dominating the shoreline. The French soldiers take a small boat to the beach, build a fire and spit-roast the calves. The smell of roasting meat drifts out over the water. Will's belly knots; it must be nigh on two years since he last ate a good meal, in the early days of the siege, when Cardinal Beaton's stores were still plentiful. The sun drops low in the late evening sky and the warmth of the day goes with it and they're permitted to stretch a sailcloth above them, which provides shelter from the cool breeze.

Will is apart from the rest of his fellow Castilians now, fettered to a convict. They negotiate who is to sleep on the bench and who along the boards their feet rest upon. Will gets the boards, but truth to tell, he prefers them really, for his long body can stretch out fully, although there's always the risk of being splashed in piss by someone relieving themselves during the night. Remarkably, his spare pair of canvas breeches, spare shirt, and heavy brown sailor's jerkin have been rescued from the beached Cardinal. He covers himself with them as best he can and quickly falls into a deep sleep from which he is only dimly aware of the snoring of his new shackle-mate.

There are fewer Scots onboard, the crew and slaves from the foundered ship having been dispersed among the fleet. Knox and Nydie sit together, for which Will is grateful. Nydie needs to be watched over and Will worries that he cannot long survive such relentless hardship. John Knox too is far from well, suffering from a gripe of the belly. He hunches over, clutching it, and Will can hear his groans from many rows behind.

They row on up the coast the next day and, during his rest period, Will half turns on his bench, watching Knox writhing on his seat as though there's a nest of ants stinging him. Nydie speaks soothing words; he can see him whispering in Knox's ear. As the afternoon wanes, Knox's groans grow louder until they can be heard all over the ship. The sous-comite grow impatient and insist the cork bung is placed in Knox's mouth. Will asks to be moved, saying he is Knox's friend and can help, but moving positions is not easily accomplished when you're shackled to another. The sous-comite preoccupied with keeping the oars moving in rhythm to the steady beat of the drum raises his bullwhip threateningly until Will desists.

All too soon it's his turn to row again and, once rowing, he cannot attend to anything else. But as he grips the huge oar, rises to standing and pushes it to its full extent – away from him and over the backs of the rowers in front – he can see out. Then he's back down on the seat, his knees and thighs screaming from the effort, but his heart lifting. He knows this coastline, can see his home. The spires of the cathedral, the tall towers of St Rules and St Salvators, the dumpy tower of Holy Trinity, where Knox first preached to the town's congregation. He cannot pause or turn to tell Knox and Nydie of his discovery for it will disrupt the rhythm and bring down the wrath of the comite upon him. He tries to twist his head and shout but has no spare breath to do anything but rise, push, pull, sit… rise, push, pull, sit. They are sliding past his town. There is his nemesis the castle, protruding out to sea on its rock. He can see men swarming over it; they must be rebuilding where the cannons of the besiegers tore through the walls. And now the long stretch of golden sands behind which Will played golf when he was a laddie, not so long ago. The broad expanse of the yawning Eden Estuary is visible ahead. He's in despair – Knox and Nydie will not see it.

The sous-comite blows his whistle, giving the signal that the shift change is upon them. Will collapses onto his bench, panting to catch his breath. He turns and gesticulates. Wants to shout but cannot for, again, it will disturb the rhythm – and lead to a whipping. Then, oh thanks be to the Lord for his great gifts and foresight, the comite calls a halt and they all rest, rocking on a gentle sea while there's talk between the commanders. Perhaps they are going to land at St Andrews, but nevertheless he must seize this moment to alert Knox.

'Did you see, did you see?' he turns and shouts. 'Look where we are.'

Nydie helps raise Knox, but he's not strong enough to hold the dead weight up, for Knox seems near to fainting with pain. The French prisoner in front swings around and lends a hand. Between them, and the man behind giving a push, they get Knox to his feet. There is silence as all watch.

'Do ye ken where we are?' calls Will.

A slow smile spreads over Knox's face. 'I ken it very well,' he says. His voice can be heard clearly, for the seagulls who were squabbling in the sky above not a moment ago are floating silent on the wing.

Knox raises his arm and points. 'There is the steeple of that place where God first opened my mouth to proclaim His Glory.' He straightens, as though the power of the Lord has indeed infused his spirit, his voice growing stronger. 'I am persuaded. However weak I may now

116

appear, I shall not depart this life until my tongue again shall glorify His name in that very church.'

There's a cheer from the Castilians and Will himself can feel the power of Knox's words shoot through him, bringing comfort and strength so he's more able to endure the disappointment which follows. The consultation is over, a signal given. They are to commence rowing once more, are not to land at St Andrews. There's to be no respite, and no opportunity, however unlikely achieved, for Will to hear news of, or even see, his family.

They stand out to sea, away from the sandbanks of the Eden Estuary. Now it's evening, yet the sun sits well above the horizon still, shining a light upon their efforts. They make good speed in such an unusually calm sea, but as the moon rises, a white slice in a blue sky, a breeze gets up, rippling the water. Will feels the tears on his cheek as his town shrinks small and disappears. They row past Tentsmuir and abreast of the Tay Estuary, where Broughty Castle stands guard, and then they heave to.

By daylight they see figures busy upon the castle ramparts and cannons being swung in their direction. Do they not see that it is their allies the French? Then it is passed among them that this castle, like Inchcolm Island, is held by England. Will feels his spirits rise once more… until they're being fired upon. If they're sunk then he will go to the bottom of the German Ocean chained to a French convict.

He rows with all his not inconsiderable strength, while those at rest are also ordered to take up their oars and all to place the bung between their teeth. The comite shouts instructions, the drum beats loud, the whistle blows shrilly, and cannon balls land around, soaking them in spray. Will bends to the task Christ Jesus has set him and soon he can think of nothing else.

Part Three

Bethia

March to July 1548

Chapter Twenty-One

A Partnership

Mainard is holding a rolled-up parchment in one hand as Bethia opens her eyes. He smiles down at her, offering it. She returns the smile, forgetting for a moment that she's upset and disillusioned. But the tenderness slides away to be replaced by anger and she jerks upright and grabs it.

'Gently,' he says, placing his hand on her wrist. 'Let me.'

She climbs out of bed, rubbing her eye, while he carefully unrolls the parchment and spreads it on the kist. She comes to stand behind him and sees it's a piece of chorography. Kneeling down, she looks more closely: a mapping of the area around Antwerp's grand cathedral. She's only ever seen such a drawing once before when Richard Lee quickly sketched her explanation of where the siege tunnel had been begun. She remembers nodding at Will over Lee's head. May Mary Mother of Christ watch over her brother, for the last letter she had from Father said that there was little possibility of his release.

Mainard kneels beside her and they study the map together. She reaches out and gently draws her fingertip across the map. 'Blue for the river and civic buildings, sienna for the houses and city walls, white for the streets, green and ochre for the fields,' she recites. 'I had not understood we had so many fields within the city walls.'

'Very necessary for when the city is besieged.'

'I've never seen anything so skilfully drawn and coloured too.' She glances at Mainard, who seems, how does he seem... proud. 'You made this?'

'Alas, I did not draw the map, but I was its colourist.'

'You're learning to be a map-maker? Is there even such a trade?'

'There's a growing demand, and a group who're working to map the world. I want to be among them. But first I must start as a colourist, and this way I may join the Guild of St Luke. My friend Abram Ortel, although he now prefers Abramus Ortelius since he became a guild member, is teaching me.'

'Why the name change?'

'It's a tradition, when you join, to Latinise your name.'

'So what will you become – Mainardus Dui et Alta?'

He laughs. 'Not both long and tall, one or the other, I think.' He grows serious. 'I would very much like to go to the Buckmesse in Frankfurt. It's a very large fair for books and I'd learn a lot.'

She lets go the map and stands up. He rolls it carefully. She thinks he looks hurt that she's not studied it for longer, but she needs answers, cannot allow herself to become distracted, feels annoyed that he's hoping to disappear off to Germany, no doubt leaving her here.

'I saw you today,' she says, staring down at him.

'That's good you were out. Was I far away, why did you not call out to me?'

'Mainard, you've been secretive since I arrived here and I'm tired of it. Why am I only learning now of your ambitions to be a map-maker, and who was the bonny yellow-haired lassie?'

'You were following me?'

'Aye, I was following you.' She folds her arms.

He gets off his knees, sits on the kist, then he reaches down and picks a pair of crumpled breeches off the floor. They dangle from his hand as he looks at them, forehead wrinkling. He gazes around the room. 'Why are my clothes scattered over the floor?'

She bends to pick the doublet up, smoothing it out and returning it to the armoire. Opening the door, the scent of sandalwood assails her, its dense cloying smell making it difficult to breathe comfortably. She looks up, sees he's waiting for an answer, and tosses her head. 'What do you expect when you tell me nothing? You called me back the other day; you wanted the wife who scaled the castle walls, the girl who defied her father to marry you. That comes at a price, Mainard.'

'Everything in this world has consequences.'

'And the unexamined life is not worth living.'

'Oh, we're trading Greek philosophers now.'

She shrugs. 'I always liked trying to read Socrates when Will was learning Greek.'

He leans back, arms folded. 'Know thyself. He that is not contented with what he has, would not be contented with what he would like to have.'

She picks at the skin around her thumbnail, then lifts her head and stares into his eyes. 'And is Socrates describing you? Are you not contented?'

He stands up and paces around the room, tugging ever harder on his ear. 'Papa trades in cloth. Then he had some interest in gunpowder and sulphur – which are in great demand from Russia and England – but it was discovered that England was selling it on to France, to use in the Italian Wars against our emperor, so that trade became restricted. Now building materials are much needed as Antwerp grows and grows, so he moves into that – and also he's trying to get a foothold in silver thread, if only the Italians will allow it. So far, spice has eluded him even though it's where the Portuguese traders have control.' He takes a deep breath. 'Papa is a restless soul. It's difficult for him to settle.'

'I'm certainly made dizzy by that exposition of his interests, but where does the map-colouring fit in?'

123

He sits down on the kist, elbows resting on his knees, leaning towards her. 'The maps hold my attention. Not only the colouring, it is the drawing of them, the science behind and…' His voice drops to a whisper and she has to lean forward to hear him, '…the exploration.'

Bethia stands over him, arms akimbo. 'Are you telling me you have aspirations to be a Vasco de Gama or Christopher Columbus, seeking out new lands?'

'I don't know, Bethia. Perhaps not so far afield' – his face lightens – 'to Italy most certainly. Ortelius and I are most eager to visit there.' He gazes at his hands. 'My life feels like it should have a greater purpose than ledgers.'

She begins to pace. 'I'm listening to Will all over again. He didn't want to work with Father, he wanted a higher purpose – and look at him now. All this searching for the true faith, and he is a prisoner.'

'This has nothing to do with religion. I am of Jewish extraction, baptised in the Holy Church and have no wish for any Holy Father but the Pope.'

'But you have the same restlessness as Will – you want adventure. I see now why my father advised marriage to an older man, for, as well as having built a secure living, they have outgrown this hunger. And, as for women, our adventure, it seems, is to bear children… or at least attempt to.' She drops onto her chair and stares at the floor.

There is silence in the room. The daylight is failing and the room grows dimmer. A log rolls in the grate sending sparks up the chimney. Mainard rises to light a candle and Bethia tends the fire, then closes the shutters to shut out the Devil and his darkness.

'I still don't understand why you did not tell me of your ambitions? Why the secrecy?'

He stares at his feet. 'I was not sure, until now, if I could master the necessary skills to even become a colourist.'

'How much did my father give in my dowry purse?'

He rummages around in the kist, releasing the bag from a secret compartment which she was unaware of. They spread out the contents and stand gazing down on them.

Bethia picks up an engraved silver bracelet. 'This is beautiful, look at the quality of the work. I've never seen it before. I wonder where Father got one so fine.'

She holds it out for Mainard to inspect, and he takes it from her hand and studies it with a quiet smile. 'I sent it to you, Bethia, as a token that I would soon return.'

She bites her lip. 'And Father hid it when he burned your letters.'

'There was a small locket too.' He rifles among the coins. 'Here it is.'

She takes it from his hand. 'It opens,' she says in surprise. 'How cunning is that!' She looks at him. 'A lock of your hair.' She bites her lip, remembering that time of waiting, when the longing for him was a burning ache and she had no word. And not only had he written, but sent tokens of his love. Yet since she has been with him in Antwerp, it's been painful too – the longing for the familiarity of home and her family very great.

'We must find a way to make this work.'

He takes her hand. 'And we will.'

Chapter Twenty-Two

A Way Forward

It's Good Friday and they are in the dimly lit church, all eyes drawn to the candles burning on the Communion table. The priest snuffs each out in turn until there's only a tall central one left; one flame to light the darkness. Bethia, kneeling in the nave along with the rest of the congregation, feels a deep sense of peace. She's always loved this celebration: the remembrance of what Christ Jesus suffered, and how he brought light to the world. Then she walks home with Mainard by her side, his parents and Katheline ahead and the servants behind, feeling a sense of connection created by them all worshipping together.

The family are up before dawn on Sunday and Bethia dresses quickly in her new Easter clothes. The sun rises behind the church while the congregation sing, their voices rising to the blue sky above. Bethia, standing next to Mama, notices she only mouths the words, and wonders at it. Then the doors are flung wide and she forgets as they move, with the throng, inside.

The abstinence of Lent is over and the rich smell of roasting meat pervades the house. There's haunch of spit-roasted beef that the pot-boy has spent many hours turning, but no boiled boar's head – which Bethia hoped for and would have eaten at home on this day, the strips of snout especially delicious. She asks Mama, who wrinkles her nose and directs Bethia to the waterzooi, saying it's a traditional dish of Antwerp. It's Bethia's turn to wrinkle her nose; she doesn't like either the appearance or the smell of this watery stew made with fish and egg, but the pie of small stuffed birds she concedes is most flavourful. They drink wine and toast to a joyous holy day. When she and Mainard finally fall into bed, he reaches for her and she turns to him.

'So our abstinence is over too,' he murmurs.

'I do not think you are suitably holy.'

'You can be holy enough for us both,' he says, pulling her close.

The family make gifts of their old clothes to the poor, Grissel whispering that Marisse has pauchled much of it for her family. The celebrations continue for twelve days and are as rowdy as anything in Scotland. Bethia particularly enjoys watching the juggling and the fire-eating. There are plays too, and songs, but after she sees one about rocking a baby to sleep she turns away. She catches sight of Grissel in the watching crowd, and Coort too. He sees her staring and whips behind a fat man. Grissel looks around, clearly baffled by his sudden disappearance. Bethia resolves to speak to Grissel, for she does not think Coort is a man who can be relied upon and, judging by Marisse's sour face, this romance is creating disharmony.

Mainard takes her hand and tugs her homeward. He is again as eager a lover as he was last year. She's happy they're together once more, happy they spend all day in each other's company during the Easter celebrations, but she cannot give herself as completely as she once did. She's determined too that they will continue their recent conversation, for she suspects that when Easter is over he will again spend little time with her.

Geertruyt and she have not met since the day Bethia lost her child but they cannot avoid one another forever.

Sooner or later she'll want to bring her son to the family home, and Bethia still has no idea why Geertruyt hates her. But of greater urgency is for Bethia to find some purpose, to feel she is useful. She can hear Will's voice in her head as she thinks on this. He was forever harping on about a higher purpose, but his was all in service of God. Bethia is in service of family, for the Lord can well look out for himself.

Early one morning while they both lie half-awake, Bethia rolls on one elbow and looks down upon Mainard's face. She strokes the line of his eyebrow. 'Such a beautiful shape, and without the need for plucking.'

'Hah! I would not subject myself to the pain of tweezers.'

She runs her finger along her own eyebrow line and then touches the edge of her brow, feeling the prickle and thinking it's time Katheline and she did one another's hairline again. Then she hears the soft click of a door being carefully shut in the passageway outside. There's a mystery about that chamber she must uncover, but Mainard tugs gently on her hair and she forgets about any mystery.

'May I come to the map-makers with you?' she asks later.

He closes his eyes. She studies his face. He doesn't look annoyed, only as though he is trying to work something out. 'You may, but I must warn you that Beverielle Schyuder is sometimes there.'

She climbs out of bed and picks up her nightdress.

'Is she a colourist too?'

'No, but she's friends with Elizabeth, who is sister to Ortelius.'

'Elizabeth is the bonny yellow-head.'

He shrugs. 'She has yellow hair, but she's not bonny like you.'

'You are such a beguiler.'

He grins.

'But it would be good to meet other young women. I have only Katheline and she seems often distracted.' She ponders this and realises it's true. Katheline is her friend, but always there's a sense of watchfulness. 'And perhaps I may learn to paint, as Elizabeth does.'

He rises and crosses the room, turning to look at her with his hand on the latch. 'Elizabeth is not married.'

'Some married women work – you said Geertruyt helps her husband in his printing shop.'

He sighs. 'That is true but she must fit the work around caring for her child.'

'Let me come, please, Mainard. I'm lonely in this house.'

'As you wish,' he says, and escapes to the garde-robe.

She rings for Grissel to help her dress in her vermilion gown and fix her hair. Mainard, finished his ablutions, is summoned by Papa. Bethia waits, gazing at the large painting hanging above the stairs, thinking of Mother and her painted ceiling. There was a great fuffle, as Mother would say – Bethia can almost hear Mother's querulous voice – about that painted ceiling, with Father resisting every step of the way.

'Vedute,' says Mainard coming to stand next to her. 'It's what we call this type of painting. And we were careful to ascertain it was not a forgery.'

'What do you mean?'

'The sale of art is a profitable business and inevitably people make copies of what's in greatest demand – and the city fathers deal most severely with anyone caught doing so.'

She turns her attention to the view of the city once more.

'It's painted from the far bank of the Scheldt,' says Mainard, leaning close. 'We must go there and you can study the vedute of Antwerp in all its glory.'

The painting is beautiful but she feels a tightness in her chest, as though an iron band is gripping it, for there's no space in this landscape. 'How many people live in Antwerp?' she asks as she follows Mainard towards the front door.

'Papa says we may have as many as eighty thousand, but that rises and falls with the foreign merchants who come and go. Papa has certainly made money bringing building materials into the city to sell, but demand is recently dropping.' Mainard sighs as he wraps Bethia's cloak around her shoulders.

She picks up the cone hat and twists it in her hands. 'Do I really have to wear this ugly thing.'

'Yes, it's better if you do. We must show that we fit in.'

Seeing his anxious face, she places it on her head without another word, and stepping out into the street, takes his arm. Someone walking behind mutters a word she doesn't understand, then hawks and spits. She goes to turn but Mainard stops her. 'Let's not spoil our day because of a fool.'

She looks up at him but he gazes ahead. After a moment she asks, 'You were saying about Papa?'

'Oh Papa! He's forever following something new, and he wants me there too, but he doesn't want my opinion. He wants to get into diamonds now but needs contacts for that – and it's sewn up tight as a pot-boy's anus.'

'What!'

'Have I offended you? But you are a married woman, I need not be so careful in my words now.'

'Mainard de Lange, what a terrible expression. And as for the poor pot-boy…'

'Yes, they are careful to keep a skewer handy to repel any unwelcome advances.'

She covers her ears with her hands. 'Enough!'

'Come,' he says, drawing her arm through his once more. 'I will take you first to Our Lady's Pand on Cammerstraat, since you enjoy art. There's much there to study and learn from.'

They stroll along the broad street together. It's the first

time she has felt truly content since she arrived in Antwerp.

Chapter Twenty-Three

Theatrum

Bethia is entranced by the many stalls to be found within Our Lady's Pand. She wonders why Katheline has never brought her here, but Katheline seems ill at ease when she's away from home. She forgets about Katheline as she stops before a painting small enough to cradle in her hand. They move on to the next stall, where a joiner is making frames.

'There is everything needed in this one place.'

'This is the oldest permanent art market, but we have other panden now, especially on the upper floor of the Bourse, which took much business from Our Lady when it opened a few years ago. There used to be booksellers here too but they're now gathered around the area where the perkament huis is.'

'I don't know that word.'

'Perkament, it means parchment.' He stops, takes her hand and kisses it. 'You're doing very well, nevertheless, in learning Dutch, and especially Spanish, so quickly. I'm proud of my clever wife.'

She flushes and slides her hand away, conscious that they're being watched by shoppers, but pleased to be so praised, for it has not been easy to learn.

'We will go into De Vette Hinne next, since it's close by.'

She puzzles over the words, keen to show off her

Dutch after his words of praise, but it doesn't make sense and her answer will no doubt make him laugh. 'The Fat Hen?'

He pats her on the back. 'Well done! It's the pand where tapestries are sold.'

'I'm the wrong women to take there then – my mother said it was impossible to teach me fine needlework.' She stops suddenly and grabs his arm.

'That man…' And she's off, running with Mainard following.

The man glances over his shoulder and a look of alarm crosses his face. He dodges between stalls and is gone before Bethia reaches him.

She bends over breathless and then stands up and stares all around, searching for him.

'Bethia, what's going on,' says Mainard, catching up with her.

'That was Antonio, and I vowed if I ever saw him again I would beat him until his pretty face could no longer ruin the life of another girl.'

Mainard stares at her.

She takes his arm. 'I do not mean me. Antonio is the one Elspeth ran off with… to Antwerp. Then she discovered he already had a wife. Remember, your father helped her return to Scotland.'

Mainard's face lightens. 'Ah, of course. But there's no requirement for you to beat him, you have a husband who will do it gladly.'

She squeezes his arm.

'I'll make inquiries and let you know what I discover. But come, there's the weekly auction at the Friday market. Let us go there and watch the oudecleercoopers at work.'

'You are testing me again,' she says, trying to recapture the lightness of mood.

'I am indeed.'

'Old… clothes?'

'Very good. Soon we will speak Dutch together as

easily we do your Scottish-English.'

'Hah! But I thought we were to meet your friend Ortegus and his sister, Elizabeth?'

'Ortelius. His name is Abram Ortelius. We'll go later.'

She wonders if he's trying to distract her but she's curious enough to allow it. The auction includes used clothing, tools, jewels, and even the contents of a house whose owner died in debt. Bethia, watching, and trying to follow as best she can, is aware of Mainard's amusement at her eager face, but she's too absorbed to care. Then books and engravings come up for sale and she feels a jolt run through her body – as though the Virgin is telling her something.

'Do you need a permit to buy and sell?' she asks as the sale finishes and they leave.

'There are restrictions – or else anyone could do it, and it would no longer be such a profitable enterprise.'

She scratches the back of her neck where she's sweating under her hat. 'If I was buying on behalf of my father, who already does some trade here, would that be permitted?'

'You are married to a sinjoor – this man of Antwerp' – he thumps his chest – 'and I think that will be of more import to the guilds than who your father is.'

Glancing up at him she catches sight of Mama and Katheline, emerging from a house up a side alley, and points to them.

Mainard frowns. 'I thought they'd stopped going there.'

'Where do they go?'

Mama and Katheline walk away, heads down. There's a quiet absorption about them which she is reluctant to disturb by calling out.

'Does this have something to do with the secret room?'

'I don't know what you're talking about.' He sets off in the opposite direction, taking big strides so she has to run to keep up with him.

'Slow down, Mainard,' she says breathlessly as he thrusts his way through the crowded street. She grabs his arm. 'What is a Marrano?'

He stops, staring down at her. 'Where did you hear that word?'

'Once when I was out with Katheline, and when we left the house today I'm sure that man hissed it. You must've heard him, he was calling us Marranos, wasn't he?'

'I heard nothing.' He's walking quickly again and she has to do a little run to keep up with him, twisting to look up into his face. He stares straight ahead, striding even faster until she's too breathless to speak.

'Here we are at the Ortelius's,' he says, stopping in front of a carved oak door. The wood is panelled, the panels curved not straight. But she doesn't get a chance to study it, for the door is quickly opened in response to Mainard's knock.

'Ah, my friend, you have come to work, even during Easter.' The man smiling on the doorstep is already beginning to lose his hair, although he has a rich beard growth which may compensate for the balding dome of his forehead.

He turns his grey eyes on Bethia and she takes a step back. He has an intensity about his gaze that's surprising in one so young. He's friendly enough when Mainard introduces her, but not much interested beyond a quick bow and a few words of welcome. He takes Mainard by the arm, talking all the way, while Bethia follows behind. They go through a central courtyard pretty with small trees in bud, early flowers pushing through, and even a cage of songbirds. The men don't stop and, after a moment, she hurries after them into a gallery where several easels are positioned in the light, holding work in various stages of progress.

'There's a problem with the drawing here,' says Ortelius stabbing his finger at the work. 'The dimensions are wrong; see, the church is too large and the surrounding houses too small. It is incorrect.'

Bethia wanders along the gallery looking at what's spread across the boards. Then she sits down to examine the work more closely and is soon absorbed in the cosmography. It's a mapping of the world, she's never seen such a thing before, and so vast it's beyond comprehension. She thinks of the quays of Antwerp and the great mix – colour, hair, eye shape, size – and feels overwhelmed by all the different peoples in the world.

'Antwerp is here,' says Ortelius, pointing to an area near the top of the map. She jumps, unaware he had come up behind her. He leans over and lightly touches the map. 'Here is Italy, where your husband and I would very much like to go. And this is your country, I think.'

She touches it with her fingertip.

'But it's now thirty years since Waldseemuller's cartography and already we know more, especially of the Americas.' He glances over at Mainard who's still engrossed in the engraving propped on the easel. 'It is our ambition to produce a book which will show the world in all its component parts: a Theatrum.'

A young woman glides along the gallery. 'Mainard, you have surprised us. We did not expect you today.' Bethia watches as Elizabeth touches his sleeve and looks up into his face, smiling. 'Come, see how my colouring is progressing.' She leads him over to another easel and sits down on the stool before it.

Mainard stands behind Elizabeth and studies her work. He does not invite Bethia to join them, nor introduce her. 'You have missed a corner,' he says, pointing.

Bethia can see he's teasing Elizabeth. The girl gazes up at him, tip of pink tongue touching her upper lip. Bethia sucks in a breath of air.

She stands up and walks over to the pair, aware that Ortelius is watching her with his large grey eyes. He calls out, 'Elizabeth, this is de Lange's wife.'

Elizabeth turns, the luscious lips pouting now. She dips a curtsy. Bethia inclines her head, thinking it unlikely that Elizabeth will become the friend she had hoped for.

They leave soon after, and Bethia, her uneasiness renewed, resolves to again pin down this husband at her side, who is slippery as an eel. But when they reach home, all is in uproar: Peter Schyuder has been arrested.

Chapter Twenty-Four

Peter Schyuder

Geertruyt paces up and down, the tears dripping from her face and rolling down her neck unchecked. 'What are we to do, oh what are we to do?'

Katheline tries to catch her, to get her to sit down, but Geertruyt knocks her hand away. Papa is not at home so Mainard takes command. They fire Spanish at one another in great bursts and Bethia struggles to follow. Mama wrings her hands, Geertruyt wails, and the baby screams.

Bethia lifts him onto her shoulder, whispering in his ear. She remembers this used to calm her brother John. 'Good little Pauwels Schyuder, be calm, be calm. All will be well,' she says over and over. He snuffles, the soft milky breath warm in her ear. She can feel him grow heavy as he drops off to sleep.

Geertruyt shouts at Mainard and the baby jerks awake and howls. Bethia slides towards the door, expecting any moment to be prevented from removing Pauwels, but Geertruyt is too intent on waving her arms and crying to notice. The baby, damp in Bethia's arms, needs to be freshened anywise. She'll find Grissel and together they will attend to perfect Pauwels.

Laid gently upon a blanket, the bairn kicks his legs in the air and waves his hands in fascination before his face as Bethia and Grissel sing.

Wha wadna be in love
Wi' bonnie Maggie Lauder?
A piper met her guan to Fife,
And spier'd what was't they ca'd her;
Right scornfully she answer'd him,
Begon you hall shaker,
Jog on your gate,
ye bladderscate,
My name is Maggie Lauder.

Maggie, quo he, and by my bags
I'm fidgin' fain to see ye;
Sit down by me, my bonnie bird,
In troth I winna steer thee:
My name is Rob the Ranter;
The lasses loup as they were daft,
When I blaw up my chanter.

Katheline's head appears round the door and smiles to see them. 'I find you worshipping at the feet of Master Pauwels, and well deserving he is of it too,' she says, coming to stand before him.

Bethia scrambles to her feet. 'Please tell me what's going on?'

'You may leave us,' Katheline says to Grissel, who's quivering with curiosity, although she climbs to her feet and goes without evincing any reluctance. Bethia knows she'll listen at the door.

'Peter Schyuder has been arrested,' says Katheline.

'Yes, I understood that much, but not why.'

'He's charged with disobeying an edict.' Katheline sighs and says softly, almost to herself, 'He was not the safe choice of husband after all, for now we are caught up in this new religion as we try to distance ourselves from our old one.'

139

Bethia's head feels overfull and she fears she will never understand what's going on in this family. 'No wonder Geertruyt is in despair,' is all she says. 'But what is this edict that you speak of?'

'Our emperor – you know of him?'

Bethia tries not to roll her eyes. 'Yes, your emperor is Charles.'

'And he's yours also. 'Tis better you do not forget, for although all may seem easy in an Antwerp led by city fathers, it's still Charles who rules over us through the governorship of his sister, Mary of Hungary.'

Bethia stiffens, annoyed to be lectured by the younger girl. 'Tell me of the edict and how it has caused Schyuder to be arrested.'

Katheline opens her mouth to speak but Pauwels yelps and they both turn to where he lies. Bethia picks him up and places him in the cradle that was once Mainard's and which she had hoped, and now prays, to one day use for their children. When he's settled she waits, hands in her lap, as she sits on Papa's large chair.

Katheline sits down upon Mama's smaller chair and rests her hands in her lap too. Bethia stares at her. She doesn't know if the mimicry is unconscious on Katheline's part. It's hard to tell anything from Katheline's face sometimes, hidden beneath her mask of impassivity – which Bethia no longer confuses with serenity.

'It is about books.'

'Isn't it always about books!'

Katheline blinks, but continues. 'The edict states that any works relating to the Bible cannot be translated from the Latin into any language without permission from the aldermen. To do so is considered heresy which is punishable by death.'

Bethia listens as Katheline speaks in a strangely formal way, which somehow makes the words she says more terrible.

'Should the perpetrator repent then, if they are a man

they will be decapitated, a woman they will be drowned, and, for the impenitent, it is death by fire. Peter Schyuder is suspected of printing books which have not been approved, and is now in prison as a consequence.' Katheline pauses then, as though she has run out of breath.

Bethia can feel her own heart racing; she understands now why Geertruyt is in despair. 'What will happen next?'

Katheline shrugs. 'I do not know.'

Bethia bends to lift the baby from his cradle. He's not crying but she needs the comfort of holding him. She walks up and down stroking his cheek with her finger. There's a rumble of noise from the hallway and Geertruyt clatters into the salon, followed by her mother and brother. Her face softens when she sees her son, and, although she does not thank Bethia, she takes him gently.

Bethia pats her on the arm. 'I will do whatever I can to help you,' she says.

'I must find out more,' Geertruyt blurts out.

'I've already sent a message to Papa. Let him speak to the aldermen and learn what we must do to secure Peter's release,' says Mama, hands fluttering.

Geertruyt drops into a chair and sits, tapping her foot. She stands up again and Pauwels grizzles. Bethia opens her arms and Geertruyt places him back there. 'I cannot stay here waiting. I must do something. Perhaps I might go and meet Papa.'

'No,' says Mama, placing her hand on Geertruyt's arm. 'Leave Papa to speak; he knows many people.'

The door opens and Geertruyt looks up hopefully, but it's only Grissel bringing refreshments. She twists her hair with her fingers, round and around. Bethia tucks Pauwels back in the cradle once more as Geertruyt waves the proffered drink away, knocking Grissel's hand in the process so most of it spills on the rug. Mainard mutters he will go and find Papa while Geertruyt twists her hair

141

further as the door slams behind him.

'Come,' says Bethia, taking Geertruyt by the arm. She's surprised when Geertruyt does indeed come, and without any resistance. She leads her in silence to her chamber.

Geertruyt looks around curiously. 'Katheline and I once shared this room, did you know?'

Bethia shakes her head and gestures for Geertruyt to sit.

'It's not much different, although the armoire is new and the smell is more... masculine.'

Bethia flushes and picks up the comb.

'That's beautiful.' Geertruyt waves at it.

'It was a gift from Mainard.'

'I hope you know what a fortunate woman you are to have such a husband.' Her lips pucker and eyes flare into her more usual expression of angry discontent. 'He was a prize for any woman, our Mainard – young, good-looking and of wealthy family.'

Bethia wants to retort, as was I. Instead, she picks up a strand of Geertruyt's hair and begins to comb. Geertruyt goes rigid but doesn't stop her. Soon Geertruyt's shoulders relax and she holds her head still. Bethia combs and detangles in silence.

'Your hair is such a rich black,' says Bethia, after some time has passed. 'And very strong too.'

Geertruyt's head droops and she doesn't reply.

There is the sound of voices loud in the hallway below and Geertruyt's starts. They run down the stairs to find Papa has returned, but without much news.

'He is being held at the castle.'

Geertruyt cries out and Papa pats her awkwardly on the shoulder, continuing in his deep voice. 'Do not fear, my dear. It is a comfortable enough prison – provided you are kept on the upper floor, which, of course, Schyuder will be.'

'Can I see him?'

'You may, and take him food and what comforts you can.' He pauses. 'And Bethia should be the one to accompany you.'

Bethia looks up.

'I will accompany my sister,' says Mainard.

Papa shakes his head. 'Much better to have Bethia. She's of good Catholic stock, even if it is from Scotland, and her father is not unknown amongst the merchants.'

Bethia stands up straighter to be so described.

'I would not place your wife at risk, my son, and it will help your sister to have her support.' He pauses, and then looks Bethia in the eye. She is startled to have his gaze so direct upon her. 'We will need to raise considerable funds to secure Schyuder's release. Do you think your father might be prevailed upon to help, since we are all family together?'

Bethia resists chewing on her finger. 'I will write to him,' she promises.

Chapter Twenty-Five

Imprisoned

'Is Geertruyt a Protestant sympathiser?' Bethia asks Mainard as she dresses slowly, while he lies in bed watching. Today is Beltane, and she remembers, as she slips on the farthingale, how she would once go with all the other young girls of St Andrews to wash her face in the early morning dew. Katheline told her that here too in Antwerp 'tis a ritual to bring health and beauty to girls. But Bethia is no longer a maid and it does not apply.

Mainard looks puzzled. 'Why would you think that? She's my sister and has already converted from one religion.'

'It hasn't stopped my brother – belief knows no boundaries.'

'I can assure you that Geertruyt has no Protestant leanings; she's more a follower of pragma.'

She bends over to kiss him, then hauls him upright. He comes unresistant.

'What does that mean?'

'Ah,' he says, climbing out of bed. 'This is a rare occasion, to find something my clever wife does not know.'

She reaches up and gives a sharp tug on his beard.

'Ouch! Take care, it took long enough to grow and I would not want to lose any. Geertruyt believes in the power of family; that's her faith and religion all tied up in one.'

'I can understand that,' she says slowly, wondering why she and Geertruyt do not have a better relationship since their thinking is aligned, on this at least. 'But why did she marry Peter Schyuder, who, it seems, has leanings towards the teachings of Luther.'

Mainard snorts. 'I doubt that. The Schyuders are a long-established and well-respected German family.'

'And Germany is the home of Luther.'

'My love, I can be fairly certain that Schyuder is not a Protestant.' He pauses. 'There was an issue about five years ago, before he was married to Geertruyt and when Antwerp was besieged by that bloodthirsty monster Van Rossum.'

Bethia stands head to one side, happy that Mainard is sharing his thoughts with her.

'A stream of pamphlets came out asking which Maarten was the more evil… Maarten Van Rossum or Martin Luther. Our lovely poetess, Anna Bijns, coined a phrase which went something like' – he taps his brow – 'Van Rossum torments bodies but Luther's crime is far greater, for he destroys souls. I believe Schyuder was involved in printing them.'

'So why is he in prison?'

'We do not yet know precisely what his crime is.'

'But what else could it be than support of the Protestant cause – or is he an Anabaptist?'

'God's blood, I hope not. The aldermen will not turn a blind eye to that, as you know. But, knowing Schyuder, it's unlikely he's aligned to any cause. There's much money to be made from printing forbidden books, and pamphlets.'

'But to risk torture and decapitation – surely it is a matter of faith.'

Mainard slams his hand against the shutter and it bangs off the window. 'What I do not understand is why

145

he would place his wife and child in such a perilous position.'

Bethia thinks of her brother Will. The need of men to show that they can endure pain as Christ Jesus did will forever baffle her. She puzzles over whether Will would have made the same choices if he had a wife and child.

'Where are you off to today?'

Mainard, rifling in the armoire, keeps his back to her. 'The Ortelius's. I will take my chance while Papa is distracted.'

'Where does he think you are?'

He shrugs. 'Papa has agreed that I may go, as long as my work for him doesn't suffer.'

'And has he left work for you?'

'Yes, I will do it later.'

'I wish I could help.'

'There's no need. And soon you will no doubt be kept fully occupied in other ways. I take it you have no news for me on this?'

She shakes her head, staring at the ground.

He wraps his arms around her. 'I'm sorry. That was not kind of me.'

She pulls away, then, after a moment, leans into him closing her eyes. He holds her tight as the grey light of a dull day seeps in through the casement.

When he's gone, Bethia prepares to go out herself. She hurries; she must not keep Geertruyt waiting. But she also needs to speak with Grissel, and without the watchful eyes of others upon them. Once out in the street, she walks slowly, allowing Grissel to come abreast. 'Grissel, is there something improper occurring between you and Coort?'

Grissel tosses her head. 'There's naething going on.'

'Mistress.'

'Aye, right. There's naething going on, mistress.'

'Do you think I was born yesterday? I can see the looks and nudges, hear the giggles, and most of all watch

Marisse's face grow more anguished with each day that passes.'

Grissel raises her eyebrows so high they disappear under the kerchief wrapped tightly around her head. 'What care I for Marisse. She's nothing but a sour-faced besom.'

'Grissel, that is not kind. I won't have you speak of her in such fashion.' She catches Grissel's arm and gives it a shake. 'You will behave yourself. Promise me, Grissel.'

'I will try… mistress,' says Grissel.

Her tone is meek, but Bethia is by no means convinced.

'But I canna help it if Coort prefers me.'

'Grissel!'

'Aye, aye, mistress. I'll no gie him ony encouragement.'

Bethia is about to tell Grissel that she is to do more than that, but suddenly there's a woman with a young girl, clinging to her side, blocking the way. Bethia goes to swerve around them but the woman grasps Bethia's arm.

'Please, mistress, my husband said you would help us.'

Bethia goes to walk on, then pauses. 'Who is your husband?'

'Antonio, the painter.'

'Then I'm sorry for you to have such a husband.'

The woman holds her hands out, pleading. 'They have imprisoned him and claim he's guilty of forgery.'

Somehow Bethia's not surprised to learn of the painter's crime. She fumbles in her pocket and passes the woman a few coins.

Antonio's wife dips a curtsey as her hand closes over them.

'How did you know who I was?'

The wife tosses her head. 'Your husband's family are known.'

The rain, which has been threatening, begins to fall.

Bethia and Grissel pick up their skirts and hurry to the Schyuder house. Bethia has come each day to accompany Geertruyt to the prison, happy to know that she's a useful family member, while anxiously awaiting a response from Father to her request for funds.

When they emerge, the rain has gone and the sun is shining in a cloudless blue sky. 'Oh, 'tis hot,' Bethia says.

Geertruyt, face more pinched than usual, ignores her comment. 'You may send your girl home.'

Bethia is by no means certain she wants Grissel out of her sight, but decides it's better, on balance, to placate Geertruyt. Grissel leaves, with a smile on her face. The streets get busier as they walk towards the river. People emerge from their homes shielding their eyes until they adjust to the dazzling light, and the stallholders in the Groetmart wipe the sweat from their faces.

Elrick, one of the workers from Schyuder's printing business, follows behind, carrying the food that Geertruyt has had prepared for her husband. While the investigation into Schyuder's activities continues, their print shop is closed, and Bethia is impressed that Geertruyt has kept the men on.

'How else are they to feed their families,' Geertruyt said sharply, when her father asked the question.

He took a step back, but replied mildly enough. 'They are skilled men and will find employment with other printers.' He paused. 'I suppose that may not be so easy while it's surmised they may have assisted in the production of heretical books. You may keep them on, but only for the time being. We will discuss it again if your husband is not soon released.'

Geertruyt tossed her head and Bethia wanted to laugh. It reminded her of arguing with her own father... yet Geertruyt is a married woman and her obedience is to her husband, not her father. 'Peter says he will be released, that it's all a mistake which will soon be rectified.'

Bethia thinks on all of this as she speeds towards the

prison in Geertruyt's wake. Schyuder has been held for a month and the authorities seem in no hurry to either investigate or sanction his release. They draw nearer the river, where the castle rises, huge and solid above the flimsy wooden houses.

Geertruyt always insists on coming early in the day. She tells Bethia that it's not a good place to be after dark, and not only because of the thieves and pickpockets who are watching for the distracted and unwary, but also because the area is haunted by a giant. She nods to Elrick, who has kept close behind them. 'Ask Elrick, he will tell you, for his father has seen the Druon Antigoon.'

Elrick shifts his hand along the staff he carries, gripping it more tightly. 'Yes, indeed, meuvrou. My father was attacked, he fell to the ground, and the giant rose over him and blew the foul breath upon him. My father was never the same again.' Elrick taps the side of his head. 'In here he was all wrong.'

Bethia is listening intently. She finds Elrick's Dutch dense and hard to follow, made worse by the words whistling through the gaps between his few teeth.

'Come,' says Geertruyt, waving her own hand impatiently, 'we mustn't dally.'

They cross the causeway which spans the river lapping at the castle's foundations. A dead bird, wings outspread, floats past, and children are foraging amongst the rubbish trapped in an eddy against the castle, wading into the filthy water to grab what they can.

In they go under the archway to the wide courtyard. The prison is housed in the turreted building to their left; to their right is the home of the marquise who controls it, and before them fishwives ply their trade, gutting fish as they shout out today's catch and prices. Behind are stairs and archways leading to further courtyards, and a church, its coloured glass winking pink and blue in the sunlight. Bethia reminds herself to find out about the saint, Walpurgis, after whom the church is named.

149

'You may as well return home, Bethia, if you're going to wander in a trance,' snaps Geertruyt.

Bethia dips her head in apology.

After the guards have thoroughly investigated their bundles and Geertruyt has paid the bribe to make certain the food they bring is not confiscated, they're led to the gaol where Peter is being held. The chamber itself is up two flights of stairs and, Bethia suspects, is of a comfort that the wretches held in the foetid cellars beneath could only dream of.

They're not permitted much time with Schyuder. The skin of his face is tight, cheekbones and jawline sharply protruding and his eyes sunken, but nevertheless he smiles and nods and urges his wife to be of good cheer as though there's nothing to worry about. She clings to his arm, anxious face upturned, and, when the guard comes to say they must leave, he gently prises her fingers loose, kissing her on the forehead.

A fishwife strolls in front of them as they leave the castle, carrying a bucket full of guts which she upends onto the causeway below. The weans are soon slithering amongst it and kicking the fish heads at one another. Bethia tucks her arm into Geertruyt's and Geertruyt does not resist. They walk back to her home in silence and part on the doorstep.

'Elrick will see you home.'

Bethia nods absent-mindedly.

Chapter Twenty-Six

The Print Shop

When the door closes on Geertruyt, Bethia turns to Elrick, who is waiting, arms hanging limply. 'Will you take me to the print shop?'

A smile spreads, lighting up his dour face. 'It would be my pleasure, my lady, but I do not hold the key.'

'Where is it kept?'

'Usually I have it, for I open up every day for Master Schyuder,' says Elrick, the whistle through the gap in his teeth even more pronounced on the 'sch'. 'But Master de Lange took possession when my master went to prison.'

She's leaning forward, eyes fixed on him, intent on following his words. 'So you say Master de Lange holds it?'

He nods, and she's pleased that she understood, but less pleased with the answer she's been given.

'Come. I will collect it from home,' she says with a confidence that she hopes is not misplaced.

She finds the key with ease, inside the kist that sits in the entrance hall, next to the row of hooks from which cloaks, capes, and bonnets are hung. If it's noticed the key is gone, she will say Elrick needed it. In her haste, and curiosity, she doesn't consider, until later, the vulnerable position she may be placing Elrick in with her subterfuge. All she can think on is that now she will finally get to see inside a business in Antwerp.

Elrick leads Bethia through a series of interlinking alleys, which grow narrower until they are walking single file. Bethia wonders if she's being unwise following this man, of whom she knows little, into such deep corners of Antwerp. It certainly heightens the sense of doing what she should not be doing. Nevertheless, she keeps going. They squeeze out the end of a narrow close and into a square, which Bethia cannot remember having visited before, where there are several shops next to one another, all selling books.

Elrick stops in front of one that's shuttered. 'The printing press, of course, is elsewhere. Here at Steenhouwerstraat is where we sell what we print.'

He takes the heavy key from her outstretched hand and unlocks the door. She follows him into the gloom with rising excitement. He opens the shutters and the light illuminates the solid wooden counter which bisects the small space. Behind it are rows of shelves with books stacked on them. Bethia goes around the counter to look and finds a stool lying on the floor. She picks it up, glancing at Elrick.

'I don't know why it's knocked over, for Master Schyuder was arrested at his home. The authorities have not been here... yet.'

Bethia stares at him. 'Do you work here or at the printing press?'

'I help the master wherever he may need me.'

'No doubt Master de Lange has visited the shop to make certain everything is in order.' She doesn't speak aloud what they are no doubt both thinking, which is that he will also have removed anything incriminating.

She picks a book off the shelf, curious to see what's in demand by the good people of Antwerp. It's a book of songs. She's never seen such a thing before and turns the pages over in wonder.

'We hope to print music as well,' says Elrick, 'but it

requires the making of a special typeset of punches and matrices that will be costly.'

She sets the book carefully back on the shelf and picks up another larger tome, opening it on the polished wooden counter; the engravings are executed most delicately.

'Engraving with copperplate permits more detail than using woodcuts,' says Elrick looking over her shoulder. He points. 'See how fine the lines are, but it does require to be pressed hard, and the greater pressure leaves its mark too.' His finger traces the indentation around the border.

She can feel the warmth of his breath on her ear and tugs her shawl close.

Turning, she thrusts the book at him. 'Put it back. We will go now.'

He steps back. 'Yes, mistress.'

She can detect no lasciviousness in his expression, perhaps she has misunderstood – and she does want to learn more about this business, for the kernel of an idea is growing. 'Tell me about the printing process.'

'It has many costs involved… but once the press and all the equipment has been purchased, then those are eventually written off.'

She looks at him with new respect. He's clearly a man who understands accounting.

'Paper is our greatest expense and must be paid for before we can start production. Fortunately, it's readily available; the best vellum comes from Lyon. Nevertheless, it's a heavy burden, and so we always look to print those books which we know will sell well.'

'And they are?'

He looks down, scuffing at something on the floor with his heel. The light is growing dim as the sun sinks behind the tall houses on the other side of the square. 'Devotional works are in great demand.'

'Bibles? Printed in Dutch?'

'Bibles printed in Dutch, and other languages… and in the Lutheran spirit.'

She thinks she understands but repeats it back to check. 'And Lutheran works are prohibited by order of the Crown.'

'So they are the most profitable, because they're not so easy to acquire.' Elrick rubs his brow. 'But we, of course, do not print them. We only do what's permitted. Truly, mistress, I do not understand why the master has been arrested. I think it must be someone who wants to take his business.'

She nods, although she's not sure she believes him. 'Is the day book here, or any of the ledgers? I would very much like to see them.'

He opens a drawer which contains ink and quills, slides it out and kneels down, feeling in behind. She picks up the ink horn and twists it absently in her hand. The quality of the ink is so much better than what she used in Scotland, but then it comes from some strange beast of the sea, whose name she has forgot, and not from chimney soot.

A shadow blocks the light from the window. She looks over, to see faces staring in, and feels a shiver of cold, as though someone has walked over her future grave.

Elrick is pulling out large ledgers, laying them on the counter. Hid among them, she spies a smaller book. She stares again at the window; the faces have gone. Quickly she slips the book out, as he tugs to extricate another ledger. Unclasping it, she looks inside. It contains a script the like of which she has never seen before: square and strong, yet with a great elegance of line.

'What is this?'

Elrick pushes himself to his feet and snatches it from her. 'P-p-please do not mention you saw this. The master would be most upset.' He looks at her, appealing… almost tearfully, she thinks.

'Put it back, quick.' She gathers up the ledgers. 'Can

we make a parcel of these to carry? I'll take them home.'

He looks dubious.

'I will tell no one of the book you inadvertently showed me.' She feels a little guilty about employing such tactics, but she wants time to study the ledgers. 'Don't worry, Elrick, I'll not keep them for long.'

'You must return them tomorrow,' he mumbles.

'Till tomorrow then.' She smiles at him, and the frown fades from his face. Now all she wants to do is reach home and shut herself up in her chamber. She looks around as Elrick locks up the shop, relieved to find no watching faces. He walks behind her carrying the package, but she waits for him to draw level.

'What is that book you hid?'

He hangs his head and slows, tries to drop behind her again, but she slows her pace too.

'Tell me.' She knows she shouldn't probe a servant of the Schyuders in this way. It's like she's been infested with some tapeworm feeding off her curiosity and cannot rest until it's satisfied.

'A holy book,' Elrick mumbles, 'of the Jews.'

'Why would your master have such a book?'

'The master is a man of business. Many of the Conversos from Portugal will pay richly for a copy of their holy texts.'

'Even though it's perilous?'

'The greater the peril, the greater the revenue.'

'Is this why he's imprisoned?'

'I do not think so, for the copy is still hid. It may be for some Bibles in Dutch.'

She ponders Elrick's words and what they mean as she smuggles the ledgers into the house and replaces the key in the kist. She's called to the board immediately, Mama fussing about how long Bethia's been out. Katheline glances at Bethia as she sits down, but says nothing.

'How is Geertruyt?' Mama asks.

Bethia gives an account of her visit to the prison, all the time wondering at Katheline, and where it is that Katheline so often goes that Bethia is never invited to accompany her. But then Bethia thinks of the ledgers and forgets Katheline's secrets, hugging herself with pleasure at the trove awaiting her inspection as soon as she may escape the meal.

Chapter Twenty-Seven

Discovery

Bethia readies herself to go to church. Mainard will accompany her, but the rest of the family are going to worship in the house of an acquaintance, which has a chapel. Bethia doesn't understand why she and Mainard are not invited to join them. She's never worshipped in a private chapel and would infinitely prefer to sit in comfort in a small quiet space, no doubt well appointed, and enjoy the connection of an intimate service. When she said as much to Mainard he tugged on his ear, as is often his way when he doesn't know how to respond.

She stands at the window looking down on the tops of their heads as they depart. There was much washing before they left. Grissel and Marisse were running up and downstairs with buckets, both filling and emptying. She's noticed this is often the case on Fridays, has never been among people who wash so often, is sure it cannot be good for the skin.

Katheline glances up, as though she feels Bethia's gaze, and Bethia waves. They're barely gone when Marisse and Coort emerge followed by the pot-boy, whose name Bethia has yet to discover. When once she asked, he flushed, hung his head and shuffled his feet, and she gave up in the face of his embarrassment. They walk away in the opposite direction to the de Langes and are halfway along the street when the front door bangs again and Grissel comes running, calling for them to wait. Marisse walks faster, but Coort and the pot-boy turn, smiling.

Apart from Mainard, who is still in the garde-robe, Bethia realises that she is, for the first time, alone in the house. She shivers, wonders if she dare do what's she's thinking...

It seems she will, for she's already at the door of her chamber and creeping along the passageway. Her breath seems loud in her ears as she lifts the latch. She expected the door would be locked, indeed has caught Mama locking it on more than one occasion. The latch clicks, the sound loud in the empty hallway. Shoulders bunched at her ears, she waits, but Mainard doesn't come.

She opens the door slowly, not sure what she'll find. There is a bed, a kist, and an armoire in the dim light from the window, where the shutters hang ajar. She can see nothing to explain why Katheline, in particular, spends so much time in here. She walks around, hand trailing along the bed, and lifts the lid of the kist. There are blankets neatly folded. She slides her hand under them, feeling to the bottom. Only blankets here. She continues around the bed and stands in the corner, staring across the chamber, sure she's missing something. If this is all it contains, she cannot understand why it's usually kept locked.

She gets down on her knees and peers under the bed... nothing there. Straightening up, she smooths her skirts out. They are of finest sarcenet, purchased for her by Mainard's family. She casts her eyes at the ground as though Mama is before her, finger-pointing accusingly, and knows she should be ashamed of herself to be prying when Mainard's parents have treated her so generously.

She goes to leave and, on impulse, tugs the door of the armoire wide as she passes. It's empty. She closes it slowly and stands in front of it, forehead wrinkling. Then she opens it wide once more. Lifting her skirt, she fumbles at her waist and, releasing the farthingale, gathers her long skirt high and climbs inside. The door creaks shut. She's in darkness. The space is too small, she cannot turn around, cannot breathe. She's trapped. She kicks her heels and bangs her elbows against the door.

It opens suddenly and she falls back. Caught by strong arms, she looks up into Mainard's face.

'What are you doing, Bethia?' he asks, pushing her upright and releasing her.

'Nothing,' she mumbles. She can think of no reason why she should be found inside an empty armoire. Yet, as Mainard slams the door shut, there is a rattle from within. 'What's that noise?'

She goes to open the armoire once more, but he takes her firmly by the elbow, picks up the farthingale with the other hand, and guides her from the room. 'We'll be late for the service.'

She pulls on the farthingale and looks up into his face. He stares ahead, leads the way downstairs and places her cloak over her shoulders. Out on the streets she's too hot in the cloak. Mainard stalks at her side still staring ahead and she soon falls behind, as is proper for a good wife.

They both take confession. She thinks on it as they sit quietly through Mass. Many times she's been to church with Katheline but she cannot ever remember her entering the confessional. And yet Katheline is a most quietly obedient young woman.

She kneels to pray, covering her face with her hands. Ever since she arrived in this country she's always been one step behind, never fully understanding what's going on. Of course, it's much easier now that she and Geertruyt are, at least superficially, friends. They even have a plan to reopen Schyuder's shop.

'I cannot sit by while others take the trade that Peter has built with such effort,' Geertruyt said. 'I am his wife and do not need permission or approval from my father to reopen. Will you help me, Bethia?'

Bethia resisted the urge to jump up and hug Geertruyt.

The two of them sat together and studied the day book.

'I do not understand this, do you?'

'Yes,' said Bethia, not admitting to having pored over it a few days earlier. 'Look, you can see who bought each book and how much they paid for it.' She ran her finger along the line of cramped writing.

'Yes, I understand that part. What I do not understand is the tally and how it is arrived at.' Geertruyt pointed to the figure at the bottom of the left-hand column.

'Give me a piece of parchment, some ink and a quill, and I will show you.'

Bethia smiles as she sits in the pew remembering, for however much she explained the system of calculating, Geertruyt could not understand.

'This is almost as bad as being back at school with a master who thought if he flicked my fingers enough with the ruler, that it enabled learning. Perhaps Elrick might be of assistance.'

But they soon discovered that Elrick's skill is in sizing the materials and attending to the printing so that the books they produce are of the highest quality, and he has no understanding of written calculations, although he clearly carries much information in his head.

'You will do it,' Geertruyt declared, and Bethia did not demur, for she very much wanted the task. 'But you must seek Mainard's permission first.'

Bethia agreed, certain he would give it, but, now, as she looks sideways at his stern face, she's less certain. She determines to speak to him as they rise up and follow the congregation out into the sunshine. She flicks her cloak over her shoulder. It's as warm here in May as the hottest of summer's days in Scotland.

There are street musicians at play, performing to the crowds who are readying themselves to watch a procession. Mainard tosses them some coins, which proves a mistake, for they gather around to serenade further. He grabs Bethia by the hand and they push their way through, much to the disapproval of a watching burgher and his wife.

'Marranos,' she hears. There it is again.

Chapter Twenty-Eight

The Book

Bethia and Geertruyt are bent over the big accounting book while Bethia tallies the figures for what has been a good day's sales.

Geertruyt is watching her intently, as though the skills Bethia has may be transferred through staring at her. 'It is fortunate that you are family and I trust you.'

Bethia loses count. The words *you are family* run around and around inside her head. She saviours them, doesn't think she's ever tasted anything sweeter – and from Geertruyt!

Geertruyt rises from her tall stool at the counter and walks around the shop. 'We must have more Spanish and French grammar. It was a good suggestion of yours that we add them to our stock.'

Bethia grunts. 'I needed the Spanish grammar myself – how else can I learn to speak easily with your Mama. Although she does not follow the rules, I have discovered.'

Geertruyt stares at her but says nothing. Bethia starts counting the figures again but Geertruyt's restlessness is making it hard for her to concentrate. 'Why don't you go home, and I will close up and follow you.'

Geertruyt snorts. 'And leave a pretty girl like you alone? The only reason Mainard permits you to assist is a promise that you will be protected. If he was to discover that Elrick is not always with us, he'd be furious.'

'Well, please sit down, or at least stay still. I cannot think with all this movement around me.'

'I will count the stock.'

'And that will require movement.' Bethia lays her quill down. 'Perhaps I will take it home and do the calculations in the quiet of my chamber.'

Geertruyt looks doubtful. 'I don't want to carry the accounts through the streets, better to keep them here.'

'In their secret place.'

'Yes, they contain much information that would be useful to a competitor. Wait for me outside while I hide them.'

Bethia places her hat on her head and stands outside. A funeral procession makes its way down the street, the coffin on a cart, the mourners following in their tall hats and long back cloaks. Street urchins have tucked in behind hoping for alms to be scattered, an act of virtue which may help assure the deceased a place in heaven.

She shifts from one foot to the other. It's too hot to stand here without any shade; she can't think what Geertruyt's doing that's taking so long. Then she shivers as though something is creeping down her spine. She stares around her but all eyes are on the procession… yet still she has the sensation of being watched. She retreats inside the shop, which is empty. Panicking, she rushes over to the counter. There's a book lying on it and she picks it up as she leans over.

Geertruyt's face bobs up from behind the counter. Bethia jumps and drops the book. It falls on the floor, the pages fluttering open. She bends to pick it up.

'Give me that,' demands Geertruyt, thrusting out her hand.

Bethia passes the book back and Geertruyt snatches it, ducking behind the counter. Bethia leans over and stares down at her.

'I don't recognise the script – what language is that?'

Geertruyt stands up and fits the drawer in place. 'Haven't you ever seen Hebrew before?'

'I don't think so.'

'I am sure they must teach it in your university at St Andrews. They do here.'

Geertruyt comes around the counter. Suddenly there are two men between them and the door. They've had customers today, but none that exuded such an air of menace. Bethia feels Geertruyt stiffen next to her.

'We are closed,' says Geertruyt, the quiver in her voice palpable. 'Come back tomorrow.'

The men ignore her, strolling behind the counter to the shelves. Bethia and Geertruyt draw closer, turning as one to watch the intruders. The taller one picks up a book, flicks through it and tosses it face down on the floor. He picks up another, tugging at the binding so the spine splits. 'Oops,' he says as he throws it on the floor.

The other stands behind the counter, legs spread wide and hands flat upon it. 'Now, my girlies, just give us the takings and we'll be on our way.'

Strangely, Bethia feels almost relief at these words; they are thieves not inquisitors. And cocky thieves at that, for they have left the way to the door unguarded. Hidden by the counter, she grabs Geertruyt's hand, twitching it backwards and hoping Geertruyt understands.

The man lifts one hand off the counter and runs a finger down the side of Bethia's face. 'Pretty,' he says.

She hits his hand away.

'And even better – a spirited one.'

Geertruyt runs for the door with a suddenness that leaves Bethia trailing behind. And Bethia's wrong, for outside there is a third thief standing guard. He grabs at Geertruyt, but Geertruyt's a big woman and he's only a lad, skinny and underfed; she barrels into him, sending him flying. Now both women are in the street running and shouting for help. People turn to stare and some men working on a nearby building slide down the scaffolding and surround them. Bethia turns, red-faced and breathless, to find their pursuers have vanished into the crowd.

'Thank you, thank you,' says Geertruyt, fumbling in her pocket and distributing largesse like a queen. The men bow and tug their forelock, looking anxiously towards the building where their foreman is calling them back to work.

Bethia walks towards the site, calling up in a voice still shaking with fear. 'We are much obliged, sir. Could one man please attend us while we lock up our shop?'

He waves his agreement, shouting down to the burly fellow still by their side, 'I'm watching. You'll return promptly else there will be no job to return to.'

Their rescuer stays only long enough for Geertruyt to lock up and leaves them. The women walk quickly towards home, arm in arm, but are soon forced to slow down to navigate around a pedlar playing the pipes with a monkey hunched quivering on his shoulder.

Bethia is shaking still and can feel Geertruyt's plump arm is taut.

'I think we will arrange for Elrick always to be with us in future,' says Geertruyt, as the pedlar, glaring at the tumbler and his assistant, plays louder. 'And for a man to guard the shop.'

'That would be wise,' says Bethia, who has no intention of returning to the shop without protection; indeed, at this moment she is by no means certain she will ever return.

'You will be fine to go home from here,' says Geertruyt at the corner of the street which leads to the de Lange house. She pauses, looking fiercely at Bethia. 'Do not tell anyone what happened, especially Mainard, or we'll be made to close the shop.'

Bethia hesitates, then nods her agreement. She hurries down the wide and busy street towards home.

A woman with a young girl stuck to her side blocks Bethia's path, and she, moving swiftly, tries to swerve around them. The woman grasps Bethia's arm and she realises it's Antonio's wife.

'You must help us. They will not release Antonio without a ransom paid.'

Bethia, feeling her heart thumping in her chest for the second time today, shakes her arm free. 'There is nothing I can do,' she says, and hurries on.

The woman and her child, both with cheeks more sunken than the last time, chase after her, persistent as flies. Bethia touches the purse tucked deep in her pocket and the wife's eyes follow.

'I can give you a few coins, that is all. And I do it only for your sake – he deserves whatever punishment is meted out to him after what he did to my friend.'

The woman is still watching Bethia's hand. Bethia extracts some coins.

The wife snatches them, saying, 'I need much more than this to pay for his release. You must help – Antonio knows about your husband's family, things you would not want revealed.'

'If you come near me again I'll report you for begging without a licence.' Bethia doesn't know if such a thing is required in Antwerp, but in any case, the woman's already gone, as fast as she can.

Still shaking when she reaches the sanctuary of home, Bethia finds Grissel in the hallway. Marisse is lurking in the background, ever watchful, ever suspicious. Coort appears, leather apron on. Bethia is sure she sees him pinch Grissel as he passes, although her eyes are still adjusting to the dim light after the brightness outside. She takes off her hat, giving it to Grissel, who steps forward with a smirk on her face as Coort disappears upstairs. Marisse stands her ground, feet wide apart, hands on her hips glaring at them.

'Marisse!' says Bethia, who is in no humour for badly

behaved servants. Marisse flounces through the kitchen door.

'Come,' Bethia orders Grissel, and leads the way upstairs, where she finds the bed still unmade and the room uncleaned. She folds back the half-open shutters and flings wide the casement. Truly she's had enough today without this. She turns and glares at Grissel. 'I'm not going to say anything about the condition of my chamber, nor about Coort and his unsuitable behaviour – although you deserve a whipping on both counts. What I am going to say is this. If you do not mend your ways, from this very moment, then I will send you back to your mother.'

Grissel drops to her knees, pressing her palms together as though in prayer. 'Mistress dinna dae that. I will be a good girl, I promise.'

'Stand up at once,' says Bethia, swallowing a smile.

Grissel clambers to her feet, tripping on the edge of her skirt and grabbing Bethia's arm to keep her balance.

'Go and fetch water and cloths and clean this chamber thoroughly. I shall look under the bed, mind.'

Grissel lets go Bethia's arm and stands uncertainly.

'What are you waiting for?'

'I haven't telt awbody, mistress, but your courses – they didna come.'

'Then make sure you keep it that way. I want complete silence on this, Grissel, or I truly will send you home. Now get about your work.'

Chapter Twenty-Nine

Judaisers

It is their quiet time of the evening together and Mainard sprawls in the chair by the fireplace, while Bethia perches on the kist. The heat from the candles is making the room over-warm and she rises to pull the shutters ajar. It's after curfew but she can hear singing in the distance. The street smells rise up, more pungent now the weather is hot, but nothing like St Andrews. She's still amazed by the cleverness of the Antwerpen to have made pipes to carry waste from the top floors of their houses to the street level; no emptying buckets out of windows for them. It does mean that the canals which encircle the city are noxious, but all waste flows into the rivers, eventually.

The moon is rising above the serried rooftops of the houses opposite. It looks small, not like the same moon as the one she'd watch rising over the glistening sea of home. She suddenly remembers it's bad for a woman with child to look upon the moon and quickly drops back down onto the kist.

She looks to Mainard, who's lazily watching her. She should tell him she may be with child but knows if she does that it will most probably be the end of her work with Geertruyt, and despite the terror of the day, she wants the work, badly. She stills her face and lifts her feet, showing off her new shoes come today from the cordiner.

'Very pretty,' says Mainard, 'but of greater interest is the dainty feet inside.' He reaches to grab a foot but she evades him with a giggle. She wants to avoid intimacy until she can be sure that the baby which she's likely carrying is established, but Mainard is a vigorous man.

'Geertruyt says that they teach Hebrew at the university.' She contains a shudder, pushing away the memory of what happened immediately after that conversation.

'Oh, ho, we're being very serious now.' He reaches out a long leg and taps her foot.

'Did you learn Hebrew?'

'Of course we did. It's one of the sacred languages, along with Latin and Greek, as you should know since it's the language of the Old Testament.'

'Did you understand it before university?'

'Bethia, you know my family were once of the Jewish faith. I've never made any secret of this, almost from our first meeting I told you.'

She leans forward. 'But if you've been a Christian since birth, why would you learn Hebrew as a child? Are your family Judaisers?' She covers her mouth with her hand, didn't mean to be so blunt.

He flings himself back in his chair so hard it nearly oversets. 'We have converted, and that does not make us any less faithful followers of Christ than any other child of the Holy Father, although we are constantly beset with suspicion. Where did you even hear that expression?'

'I don't remember, on the streets I think,' she says, gazing at her feet.

She looks up to find him staring at her. 'My life is here, Bethia, with Ortelius and his cosmography and cartography. I am as much a Christian as the next man, and as you know I take confession, I attend Mass. I am no relapser.'

She goes to stand beside him and stroke his head, but he twists away from her. Standing up, he undresses,

169

dropping his clothes on the floor, and climbs into bed. Eyes cast down to avoid the moon, she closes the shutters, shutting out the noxious night air, and follows him. He rolls away from her when she touches his back with her fingertips. She sighs. It is as well he's not attending to her, but this is a most unhappy means of keeping him away.

Mainard is all affection by the next morning as he turns over to hold her close. It's as though their discord never happened, but still the words worry away at her. What does it mean to be a converso, and what does a Judaiser do? It does not sound good, whatever it may be.

'I forgot,' she says. 'Antonio's wife stopped me in the street. You know, the painter. She says he is in prison for forgery.'

Mainard shrugs. 'It is no concern of ours.'

'And so I told her. I did give her a few coins,' she says. Somehow to tell him this tale assuages her guilt at not disclosing the much bigger story of yesterday.

Later, at dinner, there's word that Peter Schyuder's case may soon be heard, but in the meantime another Brabant printer has also been taken prisoner, this time outwith Antwerp.

'Much better that Schyuder was arrested and imprisoned within the city,' says Papa. 'The city fathers have special arrangements with the governor and the king, for it would not do for their source of ready borrowing to disappear if all the foreign merchants left.'

Geertruyt sits at the board with them, Pauwels bouncing on her knees. Bethia's never seen Geertruyt looking so well before.''Tis said my husband may be released very soon,' she says, and the baby crows and waves his fists, happy in his mother's relaxed arms.

'We do not know how soon,' says Papa. 'I must caution patience.'

'But you are working hard for his release.'

'Certainly, my daughter.'

170

When they climb the stairs to their chamber, Mainard slings his arm over Bethia's shoulders.

'Do you have something to tell me, my love.'

She starts guiltily, but his tone is warm so it cannot have anything to do with the print shop.

He drops his arm, opens the door and looks down into her eyes. 'I can count, almost as well as you. I would say it is some time since your last…' – he casts his eyes at her belly – 'you know.'

'Oh,' she says. 'Yes, I think you may be right.'

'I thought women kept a note of these times, especially when there was hope of a child.'

She flushes.

He frowns. 'Why the secretiveness when you know I can only receive such news with joy?'

'After the last time…'

'Ah, forgive me. I did not think.' He shuts the door and puts his arms around her, gently.

She looks down. It's not with modesty but shame that she should so deceive him.

By the next week she does not care either way for the result is the same. A day of spasms and bleeding, and whatever was growing inside has left her. This time Mama insists that the foremost physician of Antwerp must attend.

The physician, a man high of forehead and long of jaw, studies her and sighs. The midwife who assists him sighs too. 'The fullness of blood opens the veins and strangles the infant while he is in the womb,' he begins.

'Strangles him in the womb,' says the midwife, gazing reverentially at the physician.

'It is a case of the bad humours.'

The midwife nods sagely, while Mama wrings her hands.

Bethia flinches. Any previous attempts to rebalance her humours have involved the ingestion of red caps, followed by days of vomiting.

'Women in general tend towards a cold and moist temperament.'

'Cold and moist,' repeats the midwife.

Bethia, propped up against her bolster, stares at the physician. Spittle gathers at the corners of his mouth and glistens on his lips… it appears he is overly moist.

'Cold drinks or cold food tend to constipation. Excess of heat produces coagulation and prevents food absorption.'

Bethia looks to the midwife, who is hesitating. 'Constipation and coagulation,' she mumbles.

Mama is evidently growing weary of this performance and bursts forth, 'So what would you recommend?'

'This we must consider,' he says, stroking his long chin.

'Consider,' echoes the midwife, patting her bosom.

They turn to one another.

'A bleeding,' says the midwife.

'And all meats too hot or too cold are to be avoided,' says the physician.

'Her meats should be pigeon, turtles, larks, veal, and mutton only, and she must not take any meat that provokes urine. For herbs she may use endive and borage and abstain from raw salads. She is permitted to eat pears, cherries, and damsons,' lists the midwife.

They turn to one another, nod, apply leaches, take much blood, present Mama with their bill, and leave. Then Mama insists Bethia wear an amulet around each wrist. 'Los de abasho,' she mutters, tying them on.

'Huh!' says Mainard when he hears of the physician's diagnosis. 'I could do as well myself, with the help of Galen and Hippocrates.'

'What is los de abasho?' Bethia inquires.

Mainard touches the amulet. 'I see Mama has made her own assessment and is appeasing the spirits.'

Bethia shifts in bed wondering if that's akin to witchcraft, but she'll follow all and any directions given.

She begins to doubt she'll ever hold her own bairn in her arms and her body feels heavy with sadness

Mainard strokes her hair and she glances up at him – can see that he's as sad as she.

Chapter Thirty

Grissel and Marisse

Mainard, after his assessment of the physician's diagnosis, again vanishes. Bethia wonders if this is her husband's way of dealing with sadness, to disappear – and when she could most do with his support. Mama comes to sit by Bethia's bedside. She holds Bethia's hand and pats it, then touches Bethia's hot face. 'You have a fever.'

'No, it is just so very hot.'

'It is warm but not excessively so for July. Your servant may sit and fan you.'

Bethia sees Grissel's face over Mama's shoulder. Her smile is so wide, when Bethia translates, it looks as though her cheeks might split. The bowl of cool water she brings is refreshing, and Mama insists Bethia remove her nightdress and sponges her arms and across her chest, talking all the while – more than she has ever heard Mama speak before. Bethia squeezes her eyes shut with embarrassment as the cloth is run over the mound of each breast. Her own mother would never have touched her so intimately.

'Peter Schyuder has been released.'

Bethia tries to sit up. 'That is good news. I'm happy for Geertruyt.'

'And I thank you, my daughter, for the assistance your

father generously gave.'

Bethia thinks of the funds that Father sent at her request. She didn't tell him why they were needed, saying only that she and Mainard wished to start a small trading business. He had replied that she should consider this her dowry, and wished them well.

Mama places a hand on each shoulder and presses Bethia down, staring into her eyes. Bethia shifts under the pressure, doesn't like being pinned down. 'Geertruyt is no longer in need of your help. You must stay quietly at home. There are bad humours which stir inside you and are injurious to any baby you carry.'

Bethia stares at her. Mama, normally so gentle, looks fierce. Then her face softens and she brushes the hair away from Bethia's face. 'All will be well if you follow my instructions. Your first duty as a wife is to bear children, sons where possible. You must devote all your energies to achieving this purpose.' She gives the cloth to Grissel. 'I must away to Geertruyt, for I promised to come this past hour.'

'And that's you telt,' mutters Grissel, as the door closes behind Mama.

Bethia looks at her in surprise. 'You understood what she said?'

Grissel shakes her head. 'No, but it isna difficult tae guess. You're tae bear many sons.'

She drops onto the stool Mama vacated and dips the cloth in the bowl. 'Ach, this water is ower warm. I'll fetch a fresh bowl.' She stands up, grinning down at Bethia. 'And I'll also be telling Marisse I've got new duties.'

Bethia lies, head turned, gazing at the window and thinking on what Mama said. She did not tell Bethia anything she didn't already know. Of course, as a woman, her first duty, unless she devotes her life to the Lord – as her friend Elspeth was forced to – is to give her husband sons, and in this she has so far failed.

Grissel, smile now as wide as the River Scheldt,

returns, slopping water and splashing the woven rug come from Persia.

'Watch out, you'll damage it.'

'Och it's only a wee bittie water.' Grissel plonks the bowl on the floor as Bethia collapses back on the bed. 'Marisse wisnae ower happy when I telt her I wis to bide with you. The pot-boy has disappeared and she's having to turn the spit-roast, for Coort's too grand to lend a hand. Her face is as red as if she's being roasted in Hell.' Grissel wipes the drops of sweat off her own forehead. 'This country is far ower hot, and no breeze from the sea to cool you neither.'

'Would you like to go home?'

Grissel ponders this as she wipes the sweat off her face with the cloth meant for Bethia. Then she shakes her head. 'Nay point in thinking aboot it. We are here and we maun make the best o' it.'

Bethia lies quiet for a moment and then leans on one elbow. 'Grissel, sometimes you can be very wise.'

Grissel looks startled, then sits tall at the unaccustomed words of praise.

'I think I'll sleep now.'

Grissel rises, picks up the bowl and tosses the damp cloth in it as Bethia closes her eyes. She moves around the room as stealthily as Grissel can move. There's a thud followed by a grunt of pain.

Bethia sits up. 'God's blood, it's like having a herd of goats in the chamber. What are ye about?'

Grissel is hopping on one leg, rubbing her ankle.

'Go away, now.'

'If I sit doon quietly, can I stay?'

'No, you're too restless. Go away.'

Grissel sighs heavily and leaves.

Bethia's mouth is dry; she should've asked Grissel to fetch her a drink. She lies still, but it's no good. She must get up whatever the physician and Mama have said. It's better if she does; she won't allow herself to fall into despair like the last time.

She throws the cover off and walks slowly up and down. She feels stronger the longer she is up and moving about, the weight of sadness less heavy upon her. She combs her hair, tying it back in a ribbon. Slipping on her shift, she ferrets around in her kist, pulling out an old skirt and bodice, tucked away at the bottom, that she brought from Scotland. They're not like the long gowns, with the huge sleeves and wide farthingales, that she's worn since she arrived here, but they feel safely familiar.

She opens the door of her chamber. The house feels empty, although no doubt there's work going on below in the kitchen; she wonders who's turning the spit-roast now. She's at the top of the stairs when she hears shouting. Holding tight to the banister, she descends.

Throwing wide the kitchen door she finds Grissel and Marisse each hauling on the other's hair, while they scream in one another's faces. Before Bethia can react, Marisse draws her nails down Grissel's face, gouging a raw red line.

'You wicked besom,' shrieks Grissel, and she swings for Marisse, slapping her hard across the face.

Marisse lets go of Grissel's hair and howls, hand against red cheek.

Bethia, frozen in the doorway, comes to life as Grissel releases Marisse and goes to punch her.

'Stop! Stop it at once.'

Marisse picks up a pot and is advancing on Grissel. Bethia grabs the broom and thrusts it between them. Coort appears at the back door, takes stock and grabs Marisse around the waist. Marisse throws the pot at Grissel as Coort hauls her backwards.

'Come with me,' orders Bethia, dragging Grissel by the arm. In the hallway she turns on her. 'What were you thinking?'

'It was her what attacked me,' says Grissel staring at the floor, blood trickling down her cheek.

Bethia points up the stairs to the attics. 'Go and tidy yourself.'

She returns to the kitchens to find a dishevelled Marisse standing glowering, while Coort berates her.

There's a knocking on the front door.

'Get that, Coort,' she orders

Bethia retreats quickly back up the stairs; feeling dizzy, she drops down onto a step. The knocking comes again, louder, and Marisse, not Coort, emerges slowly from the kitchen, red-faced and muttering.

Then Marisse is speaking to someone on the doorstep. Bethia can't see who it is, nor hear properly what they're saying, for Marisse's broad back blocks her view. Bethia remembers meeting Marisse when she first arrived ten months ago. She thought Marisse bonny enough then, but not so much now with the pinched lips and the way she's taken to glaring at Bethia from under lowered brows. She must sort this, cannot allow the rivalry between Marisse and Grissel to continue. It's poisoning the house.

The rumble of voices goes on as she muses. A deep male voice is sounding insistent; perhaps Marisse needs help. Bethia stands up and creeps down a few steps. Over the top of Marisse's head, framed in the sunlight, she can see… red hair. It is red hair. She runs down the last few steps and pushes Marisse aside.

'Gilbert!' she shrieks, and flings herself into his arms

Chapter Thirty-One

A Visitor

Bethia sits on a heavy chair in the salon. Despite also being invited to sit, Logie stands gazing at the gilt leather panels adorning one wall. She suspects it's to allow her to compose herself and is grateful for his thoughtfulness. She can't think what led her to behave in such an unrestrained fashion, especially now she's a married woman. She gazes at the floor and blushes and blushes, while Gilbert leans in close to study the artwork.

'This is very fine craftsmanship.'

She looks up, had forgotten how very red his hair is. 'They come from Spain.'

'Ah, of course, the Spanish are most skilled at this work.'

Marisse bangs through the door with a tray, carrying glasses and a decanter. The tray wobbles and the glasses slide. Before Bethia can stand up, Gilbert strides forward, takes the tray from Marisse's hands and lays it on the small table. A glimmer of a smile appears on Marisse's face at this rare offer of help from those she serves. She stands, rough hands dangling, her hair still a-tangle from the fight.

'That will be all, Marisse. You may go.'

Marisse shuffles from the room, taking a last look at Gilbert as she closes the door slowly behind her. Bethia pours the claret into the glasses, enjoying its rich ruby-red and knowing that Gilbert is unlikely to have tasted better.

He takes the proffered glass, sits down and looks at her. 'You can speak Dutch well.'

'Do you know Dutch?'

He shrugs. 'A little. French is mostly all I need to get by in Antwerp.'

'Then how do you know I speak it well?'

He leans his head back and laughs. 'Still the same Bethia Seton.'

'How I wish that were so.'

'You're not happy here?'

They're straying into difficult terrain. She shifts in her seat and, ever the gentleman, he begins to speak as though he had not asked the question. But it lies there, between them.

'Your family is well. I visit them whenever I'm in St Andrews, which is not often' – he smiles ruefully – 'now the siege is finally over. Your father does not say it, but 'tis clear that he misses you greatly.'

Tears fill her eyes.

Gilbert continues, as she dabs her eyes with her handkerchief. 'I'm travelling with a deputation at the behest of Regent Arran to make peace with Charles V. The difficulties between the Holy Roman Empire and Scotland, encouraged by Henry of England, have continued after his death.'

She leans forward. 'It's strange that Charles is allied with England when he is at this moment initiating an Inquisition in the Low Lands to stop the spread of Protestantism.'

'Perhaps, but we in Scotland have our great alliance with France, and the Holy Roman Empire does not love France. We need at least to be tolerated by Charles, and especially his sister. It's greatly affecting the merchants that we cannot trade freely.'

She thinks of their ship being attacked by Scottish

privateers. 'We Scots could endear ourselves more to foreign merchants trading across the German Sea.'

'Ah, your father told me your ship was attacked. The easy pickings are all too tempting.'

She stiffens, feeling a flash of annoyance at the inference of easy pickings. 'We resisted as best we could, but our attackers had cannon.'

He waves his hand gently in a gesture meant to sooth her obvious agitation.

She's charmed, had forgot what a skilled courtier Gilbert is. 'And what of Scotland?'

He looks weary. 'The attacks from England continue. Your father may have mentioned in his letters that it has been much worse since you left. King Edward's uncle, now regent, is most determined that our queen will marry his nephew.'

'I think Father does not like to worry me overmuch.'

Gilbert smiles, but it doesn't reach his eyes. 'Your father is a good man,' he says, his voice dropping so low she has to lean forward to hear him.

'I hoped he might have come to Antwerp… you know, for trade,' she says.

'I'm certain he will come, but not in these treacherous times.'

She nods, accepting Father has good reason not to travel, and hopes the application made to him for funds has not influenced his decision. 'And is there any news of Will?'

'I'm not aware of any, but it's many weeks since I last saw your father.' He touches the scar puckering his face with his fingertips.

'What is it?'

'We think that some of the Scots prisoners may be used as forsares.'

She bites her lip. 'I had suspected as much but pray that it is not so.'

'If I hear anything of him I will be sure to let you know,

now that I have a place of residence to address any communication.'

She looks at him but says nothing. They both know it's not seemly for him to write to her, but she won't reject the offer.

'Your brother John' – his smile does light up his face now – 'is as wild a young devil as ever.'

'Oh John!' She smiles, prepared to be entertained by tales of his latest mischief.

The door opens and they both turn to see Mainard, face impassive, enter.

Gilbert rises, and after a moment Bethia follows. She stands, hands clasped tightly, as the men make their bows to one another. She looks to Gilbert and then back to Mainard. Gilbert is stocky and strong, with the long scar puckering his face. The red beard is sparse on that cheek, but what there is, is carefully brushed over the scar. Mainard is tall and dark, with the curly beard which he has such difficulty getting to stay on point, however neatly trimmed, and the easy manner. He is the younger, and truth be told, much the handsomer. Her face softens.

Mainard turns to sit down, and glances at Bethia. She wonders at his arrival. He never normally comes home at this time, indeed is often out until just before curfew. And he does not appear to be surprised to find Gilbert Logie here. Marisse, the meddling besom, no doubt sent a message to him.

Mainard is all interest in Logie's trip, and Gilbert answers well but tells little; a courtier adept at prevarication. It's no doubt the reason he's a trusted member of Regent Arran's troupe. She wants to know more about the attacks on Scotland by England and surely this is safe ground, for it can hardly be a secret.

'How does the English protector hope to succeed in these constant attacks? Is he trying to capture Queen Mary? Poor child, she must be very young still.'

'She's not five years old.' He straightens out his knee,

rubbing it.

'I see your leg pains you,' says Mainard in his deep voice.

Bethia feels a rush of tenderness at its timbre.

'Ach, just an old war wound.' Gilbert snorts. 'Truth to tell it was incurred when I tumbled down some stairs chasing my older brother.'

Mainard smiles. 'I too am scarred from childhood, after falling out of a tree.' He pats his head.

Gilbert grins. 'I'm ashamed to say that I wasn't a child when I fell.'

They both laugh, and Bethia sees that these two men could be friends.

'But this does not answer your question, Mistress Bethia.' He stands up and walks around, and their gaze follows him. 'The wee queen is moved constantly so that the protector's spies do not find it easy to keep abreast of her latest place of hiding. But we are in the summer now, and the protector harries us constantly. Aside from the English garrison on Inchcolm, they also hold Broughty Castle as well as Haddington, so England holds sway along the east coast from Berwick to Dundee.'

She leans forward. 'What of St Andrews? It must be vulnerable, jutting out into the German Ocean as it does.'

'So far, St Andrews is untouched but there was a very recent attack by sea, at St Monans.'

'No!' Bethia says. She looks at Mainard. 'St Monans is within easy march of St Andrews.'

Gilbert grins. 'Fear not. The good people of the village, womenfolk too, rose up to fight the English invader with pitchforks and whatever other weapons they could contrive, and then Sir James Wemyss came over the hill and routed the English troops.' The smile fades. 'It was some small consolation for our defeat at Pinkie last year.'

'Has not France come to Scotland's aid?' She chews on the skin around her thumb, then remembers she's supposed to have given up such childish habits and tucks the bitten thumb into her palm, wrapping her fingers around it.

Gilbert looks towards the window, she suspects to give himself time to consider his response. 'We aye hope for this, but France has her own concerns. And mounting any campaign is a most costly exercise. Indeed, we're surprised the English protector can find the funds for so many mercenaries, cannon, armaments, and ships, not to mention ensuring all his garrisons in Scotland are kept supplied. It's our hope that his government will grow concerned as the coffers empty, and more and more funds are borrowed from the Jews, and call a halt to his profligacy.'

She bites her lip but Mainard sits expressionless.

Gilbert rises to leave soon after and Bethia holds tight to the arms of her chair to restrain herself from jumping up and pleading with him to stay longer.

'You would be most welcome to join us at the board this evening,' says Mainard.

Bethia looks gratefully at him.

'I thank you and will endeavour to do so but, as I'm sure you will understand, my time is not my own.'

'We will hope to see you,' says Mainard as he ushers Gilbert out.

Bethia sits twisting her handkerchief. It doesn't feel nearly so satisfying as chewing on her skin. Mainard returns and stands before her holding out his hands. She places hers in his and he tugs her up to standing, wrapping his arms around her.

'I know it's hard my love, to be so far from your family.'

She leans into him, grateful for the comfort of his long body.

'You do not regret your choice?' he whispers in her ear.

She shakes her head, although truth be told, in this moment, she doesn't know the answer.

He smiles down at her. 'I must return to Ortelius soon,

184

but we have enough time before I leave.'

She casts her eyes down but after a moment nods, which he takes to be a similar eagerness to his own by the way he hurries her from the room. But really she is thinking it's barely any time since she miscarried, and perhaps if she had obeyed her father and gone with the older and more reliable suitor, she would not now be punished by losing her babies.

Chapter Thirty-Two

Conversos

Bethia comes face to face with Gilbert a week later, as she's leaving the house, trailed by Coort.

'I have just returned from Brussels,' Logie says without any preamble. 'I had hoped to meet your family but am called away again urgently.'

'So soon, I too hoped we would have more time to speak.' She can feel her voice wobbling and bites the inside of her cheek.

'But I do need to impart some information to you before I leave.' He holds out his arm. 'Perhaps we may walk together.'

'You may go,' she says to Coort, who suddenly seems as reluctant to return to the house as he had been, only a few moments ago, to leave it.

'This sounds very serious,' she says, taking Gilbert's proffered arm. 'You look most stern.'

He doesn't respond to the levity of her tone but continues in a sombre mood. 'I hope you will not consider it an impertinence to ask, but how much did your father know of your husband and his family before you were wed?'

'Do you mean the reason why Master de Lange was in St Andrews?' she asks, oddly relieved that she can answer the question. 'He was attacked and, in defending himself, his attacker was killed. Papa' – she pauses, glancing at him, aware that his eyes flickered at the Papa – 'was required to pay the man's family a large amount in recompense and to undertake a pilgrimage. Papa's penance was then complete.'

'Ah.' He scratches his head. 'The pilgrimage now makes sense. What I have to impart to you is of a most sensitive nature, and yet it also concerns me how widely known it would seem to be.'

She lets go of his arm and stands, hands outstretched. 'God's death, Gilbert, tell it to me without any more preliminaries.'

He takes her arm once more. 'Let us keep walking. I don't want some sharp-eared sinjoren overhearing what I have to say.'

He leads her towards the city wall and they pass through one of its gates, cross over the canal which encircles the city, and stroll along a road where ripening crops of barley and wheat are brushed by the breeze. It's the first time she's been outside Antwerp since she arrived last year. She feels the sun hot on her head, through her wretched cone hat, but she doesn't care. The tightness in her chest, now such a constant that she barely notices, suddenly releases. She thinks Gilbert must sense her relief for he does not immediately begin his tale, and he too takes deep breaths of the sweet air. 'Do you know the reason there are fields so close to the city walls?'

She shakes her head.

'Antwerp has been held under siege many times, most recently only four years ago.'

'I knew about that, but they did not get inside.'

He nods. 'They did not. But that's why the area outside the walls is fields. Between the destruction wrought by the besiegers and the city's need to have an open space to watch and fire upon, the countryside is close.'

She wrinkles her nose, pointing to a steaming midden.

187

'Perhaps too close.'

They hurry past, flies following them, until they are abreast of rows of cabbages, which have their own pungent aroma under the heat of the sun.

'It's so very flat here,' says Gilbert as they stand aside to make way for a cart of crated chickens, squashed together.

She crouches down, exclaiming with delight. 'Strawberries. Oh the Blessed Virgin.' Popping one in her mouth, she closes her eyes at the burst of sweetness. She picks as many as she can carry, sliding them into her pocket and passing a handful to Gilbert.

An angry woman is before them, the cluster of bairns at her feet wearing little beyond layers of dirt. Bethia can follow some of what she says, but even Gilbert with his limited understanding of Dutch gets the gist. He offers her payment for the stolen strawberries and the woman's face transforms as she looks at the coins he places in her hand. She closes her fingers tight around them and takes to her heels before Gilbert changes his mind, the weans running behind.

'You just made one woman very happy. Growing wild along the roadside – I don't even think they were hers to claim.'

He shrugs. 'Small coin to me, but a big difference to her.' He takes her arm once more and tucks it into his.

She allows it, yet knowing that if Papa were to see her now, far from being granted the small freedoms she's finally achieving, she'd end up confined to her chamber.

'Are you aware that your husband's family are Conversos: New Christians.'

'I know they came from Spain, through Portugal. And yes, that they once were of the Jewish faith but converted to Christianity a long time ago.'

'Your husband told you it was a long time ago?'

She wonders why he keeps saying your husband. Surely he can call Mainard by his name. She squirms, knowing she's not behaving right by either man, but it's such a joy to see Gilbert and hear a good Scots voice. She's as bad as her former suitor Fat Norman when presented with a plate of marchpane to gorge upon, eating until it was all gone, despite knowing he would suffer for it later.

'De Lange is not even their true name – did ye ken that? They took it when they arrived here.' He glances at her but Bethia says nothing. 'As I understand, they're part of a large group who first fled from Spain to Portugal when increasingly there was an Inquisition of any who were not true Christians. Portugal allowed them entry, at a price of course, for kings are always in need of funds. Those who were poor were also taken in, for kings are always in need of slaves, and especially galley slaves.'

They have stopped walking and are standing facing one another, but more carts are coming. They move onto a path snaking through a cluster of spindly trees and Gilbert dusts a fallen log inviting her to sit down.

'All was well, to begin with, and the king of Portugal now had some very wealthy Jews from whom to borrow. But when he married the king of Spain's daughter, he agreed, as part of the marriage settlement, to an Inquisition of Jews in Portugal, and especially Nuevo Cristianos.'

She shifts on the log to find a more comfortable spot. 'But Mainard's family converted willingly and are true Christians. He was baptised as an infant, he told me.'

Gilbert takes off his bonnet and fans his face. 'Mayhap, but King Manuel forcibly converted many Jews – or at least their children. His debts were great and he didn't want to expel such a ready source of income. Most of the spice trade, and the ships to enable it, is controlled by Conversos and Jews.'

'But they did convert, so what is the difficulty now?' She stands up and slides her hand in her pocket. It comes out red and sticky. She had forgot about the strawberries. She licks her fingers, eyeing Gilbert.

189

'They are under constant suspicion. There's a general belief that their conversion is merely expedient and they are secret Judaisers.'

She kicks the ground with the toe of her slipper.

'What's more, it's increasingly evident that Portugal is no longer a place where Conversos are welcome. The very rich merchants, like the famous Mendes family, are already gone – not only from Portugal but also now from Antwerp.'

'Was there a Gracia Mendes?'

'I do not know… perhaps.' He looks at the sun as they hear the bells striking the hour from the nearby city. 'I must get back.'

The road is rutted and baked hard after days of hot sun and no rain, and again she takes his arm to steady herself, realising her strength has not yet fully returned.

'My concern for you is this…'

She knows she should correct him. He need have no concern; she has a husband, and it is he who should have concern for her.

'…the wealthy Conversos are aiding the poor ones to flee Portugal. It is said there's a route set up whereby shiploads arrive in Antwerp and are then passed along the line to Ferrara and Venice.'

Bethia's heart skips a beat as she thinks of the families she has found being fed in the de Lange kitchen. She bites down on her lip, is certainly not going to mention this to Gilbert.

'It is said they even travel to Salonika, for it seems the Turkish infidels are not as troubled by those of another faith as we Christians. Inevitably, the Hapsburgs are concerned that Antwerp is being used as a route by which Conversos, and more importantly their wealth, may escape, and all to the benefit of Suleiman and the Ottoman Empire.'

'This has nothing to do with the de Langes,' she says, realising her voice is shrill.

'On the contrary, it is suspected that Master de Lange is heavily implicated in the escape network.'

Bethia feels as though all the bones in her body have gone soft. She staggers and Gilbert catches her, slipping his arm around her back to support her. But she quickly regains her balance, detaching herself from him. She walks towards the city gates, eager to get home and be rid of Gilbert, never thought she would wish such a thing.

He strides at her side but she looks straight ahead.

'It is not safe for you here, Bethia. Best you come home to Scotland with me.'

'What!' She stops and glares at him.

'I mean,' Gilbert stutters, '…I am not suggesting…'

She walks on and he hurries to catch up with her. 'I mean only that you should travel under my protection and I will return you to your father's house.'

His face is very red. In the midst of her anger Bethia rather enjoys seeing the mask of a polished courtier slip to be replaced by that of a deeply embarrassed lad.

They pass through the gate, Bethia walking in front, as fast as she can, although truly she feels quite unwell and would welcome a chance to sit down.

'Bethia, wait. Let me finish before we reach the de Langes.'

She slows and turns.

'Please do not misunderstand me.' He looks down at his feet, then lifts his head, staring into her eyes. 'This has nothing… no, let me be honest… this has little to do with the hopes I once had. It is about your safety. I don't think you realise the danger you are in. Remember Wishart – you saw his burning – the inquisitors do much, much worse to anyone they take. And the Inquisition is coming. Even Antwerp cannot evade it.'

She walks on, head down, thinking. Gilbert walks silently by her side. In this way they arrive at her door.

'Gilbert, I thank you most truly for your concern, and your friendship, but I will not leave.'

She holds out her hand.

'I hope, and pray, you will never have cause to regret your decision,' he says as he bends to kiss it. He starts to walk away then stops. 'I am here for one more night. If you should reconsider, I can be found at the large inn close by the docks. Your husband will know – and Bethia, I think you should talk to him. I have a sense that he too would agree it's best you should leave, at least for the time being.'

He bows again and walks away, while Bethia watches from the doorstep.

Chapter Thirty-Three

Don Juan

Bethia doesn't know what to do with herself as she wanders around the house, thinking on Gilbert's words. Mainard is out, as are Mama and Katheline. She would very much like to speak with her husband, although she has not decided if she will relay all of what Gilbert had to say. Indeed, perhaps she had better not mention she saw Gilbert again. No, that's wrong, there was nothing clandestine about it, and in any case, Coort will no doubt make certain that Mainard knows she went for a walk with Gilbert unattended.

She's dithering in the hallway, wondering whether to enter the salon, where she can see Papa pacing, or retreat to her chamber, when there's a knock on the door. Wondering if Gilbert has returned, she opens it wide, without considering that she should leave it for a servant to answer.

There's a man on the doorstep ready to enter, who steps back when he sees her. He takes off his bonnet, revealing long, shining black hair, and bows low saying, 'I am Don Juan Micas and you must be the beautiful Bethia, of whom I have heard.'

She stares at him, doesn't like to say, but of you I have heard not a word. He's a small man, finely boned with large almond eyes, like Mama's, and skin as rich brown as

Mainard's. She realises he's waiting for her to stand aside and bid him enter.

A voice comes booming over her shoulder. 'Joao, you are come. I did not expect to see you here again.'

Bethia stands aside, and Papa, smiling broadly, places his arm around Don Juan's shoulders and walks him into the salon, bending his head to speak. 'I take it you have returned to retrieve what you can?'

'The negotiations go on, and I would hope that I may extract some of what we are owed, but I am here principally to sell the house and land.'

Both men turn, to see that Bethia has followed them. She does not quite know why she has, only that she is in need of distraction, tired of subterfuge, and will no longer be held on the periphery of life with the de Langes. If their sufferings are to become her own, then she must know all.

'Bethia, tell Marisse to bring us refreshments. And to prepare a chamber.' He looks to Don Juan. 'You will stay with us.'

Don Juan tosses the short cape back from one shoulder in a swirl of yellow, revealing a long sheathed sword. Bethia sees a huge emerald inset in its centre which matches his green velvet knee-breeches and large codpiece, while skimming his chin is the highest neck ruff imaginable.

'I thank you for your kind offer but I'm already comfortably set up.' He frowns, and the deep crease between his eyebrows, surprising in one who cannot be much older than Mainard, grows even deeper. 'I would have your advice, my friend. 'Tis is a lonely road I travel, and helpful to speak with someone upon the same perilous journey.' He pauses and they both again look to Bethia, who has halted by the door.

'Some wine, Bethia,' Papa says gruffly.

She goes, closing the door behind her, and stands in the hallway. She's annoyed to have been dismissed, and somehow that makes what she does next seems justified.

194

She walks towards the kitchen door, making her footsteps loud, and calls out as though speaking to someone. Then she turns, creeping back to press her ear against the door.

'I have met with Charles,' she hears Don Juan say. She hadn't noticed before, so taken was she by the manner of his dress and fine face, but his voice is surprisingly high, almost girlish, for a man.

'And what was his response? Is our emperor willing to return all that he has confiscated?' says Papa in his deep voice.

There's the sound of footsteps as one of them moves across the floorboards, and she leaps away from the door, ready to run to the kitchen. But it doesn't open and, after a moment, shaking at her own temerity, she's drawn back to listen.

Papa is speaking again and she's missed whatever Don Juan's response to his question was.

'…Mary of Hungary is an obdurate woman.'

'I did feel that Charles wished to do right by us. He is an honourable man… for a king. The king of France, however, is a different matter. He claims his debt is cancelled, saying he borrowed from Christians and, since it is determined that we are Judaisers, then he need make no repayment.'

There's a thump as though the board is banged.

'Our troubles are never-ending. Only today an alderman warned me that some painter has claimed I commissioned him to copy Bosch's work. A forgery, I ask you! As if I would ever bother when I can afford the original.'

Bethia, clutching at her dress, hears the creak of a floorboard and runs down the passageway. Hardly knowing what she's saying, she orders Grissel to take the tray in and follows behind. The men fall silent as the claret is poured and some sweet cake offered. Bethia takes the glass that she included for herself and sits down. Papa stares at her again and, when she does not rise, says that he and his friend have private business to discuss. She dare not risk lingering by the door a second time, and it's as well she does not, for it is opened as she walks across the entrance hall.

When Mainard returns she hurries down the stairs, saying, 'Don Juan is here.'

'I must join them,' he says, picking up the hand that was detaining him and kissing it. 'It's good to have Joao among us again.'

'Wait, Mainard, I need to tell you something. That… that… horse-penis Antonio…'

'Bethia, where did you ever learn such words?'

'It doesn't matter, from Will most probably, and he is a horse-penis… Antonio, I mean, not Will. He's claiming Papa paid him to forge a painting.'

Mainard frowns. 'I doubt anyone will believe him.'

'I'm so sorry. It's my fault for ever helping his wife.'

'You are my kind wife,' says Mainard, pats her on the head in a most annoying way and goes into the salon.

She's chewed her skin raw before he emerges and suggests they go out to take the air. 'What of Antonio?' she asks as soon as they're outside on the street, which is quiet now the markets are over for the day.

'It's nothing, forget him. We'll go towards the Carmelite nunnery. There was much upset a few years ago when Jews were accused of burying their dead nearby, on unconsecrated ground.' He sighs. 'But then where are they meant to bury the dead, since they cannot do it on consecrated ground?'

She takes his arm and squeezes it. 'So you're distracting me by telling a grim tale.'

He continues as though she hadn't spoken. 'Do you know Erasmus said that if we are mannered in our dealings with each other then it is a civilising agent which leads to compassionate treatment of all one's fellow human beings? I cannot believe that Jesus Christ, were he alive today, would condone the treatment meted out to

Jews. He was, after all, one himself.'

Bethia gives a sharp intake of breath to hear Christ so described. In a way it is true, but it was the Jews who gave Christ up when they might have saved him. Then again, it was the Romans who crucified him, not the Jews. She shakes her head, doesn't know what to think – decides it's better not to think, easier to go to church and follow the words of the priest.

Instead she says, 'I didn't know you were so well versed in the thoughts of Erasmus. You do like to live dangerously, Mainard.' She blocks from her mind the many other ways in which the family live dangerously. She has not yet decided whether or how to broach Gilbert's words – is enjoying this peaceful interlude together.

They stroll on in silence. The air is thick, holding onto the heat of the day, but less clammy than earlier.

'Here, this is what I wanted to show you.'

They stand before closed gates. A high wall encircles an area of woodland, although they're within the city boundaries. Through the trees she glimpses a large house. 'Is that a fountain?'

'It is, a most beautiful one made of marble brought from Italy.'

The place has an air of abandonment. She presses her face against the bars and can see no sign of life. She's aware of Mainard watching her. 'This is the home of someone of great wealth,' she says.

'They used to have the most wonderful parties here. I came as a child – it was the most exciting place ever. You think we have paintings; it's as nothing to the artwork Diogo had. I wonder what happened to it all… most probably Mary of Hungary has much of it adorning her residencies.'

'Who's Diogo?'

'A crafty but astute, daring but untrustworthy, eloquent and energetic man. At least that's how I once

197

heard him described, but he's dead now. He died… must be near on six years ago. He bought the property when he came to live here and control the Antwerp side of the Mendes trading empire. Then, as life became increasingly perilous in Lisbon, his brother's widow Gracia followed.'

Gracia Mendes, Bethia thinks. So this is where she lived.

'Things grow ever more difficult here, as we know. And the Mendes were the richest Conversos of all. The kings of Portugal, England, France, and our Emperor Charles himself, all borrowed heavily from them. Gracia fled to Venice the year after Diogo died, taking as much of her wealth as she was able to.'

'Why is the house not sold?'

'Ah, that's an interesting tale. Come, it's probably not wise to linger here.'

Arm in arm, they stroll towards home. It's cooler now, a breeze coming off the river. He doesn't speak until finally she nudges him.

'The property, and more, was impounded by the emperor, or at least his sister, on his behalf.'

'Is that why Don Juan has come?'

'Yes. He's a relation of Gracia's – her nephew.'

Finally, things begin to make sense, thinks Bethia.

Chapter Thirty-Four

Secrets and Lies

What a day it's been, Bethia reflects, as she readies for bed. Mainard too seems exhausted, for he is, unusually, already asleep. She has been on the verge of speaking to him, telling him of Gilbert's words several times. Tomorrow will do; there is no hurry, for she has no intention of leaving with Gilbert even if Mainard considers it wise.

She removes the pins and, freed from its coils around her ears, her hair flows thick across her shoulders, falling to her waist. It's too hot to leave it loose; already the drops of sweat gather at the back of her neck and she plaits it as best she can reach. She pauses mid-braid, puzzling over whether the de Langes are Judaisers or true Christians and thinking of the story Don Juan told at the board as they broke fast together.

'Gracia has written to the Pope,' he said in his high fluting voice, 'asking that she may remove her husband's bones from the Lisbon graveyard where they lie. His Holiness has agreed… for a large sum of course.'

There was a ripple of laughter.

'Where will she inter him?' asked Mama.

'Ah that is an interesting question. She has of course told the Pope that she wishes Francisco to lie in her private chapel in Venice.' He steepled his fingers. 'But it is my opinion she will follow her sacred duty and bury him on the Mount of Olives so he may be among the first to rise with the coming of the Messiah.'

'She is a good woman,' Mama had replied.

Bethia jumps; there is a soft tap on the door. Opening it, she finds Marisse standing there.

'Shush,' she says, putting a finger to her lips, and she steps into the hallway, closing the door gently behind her. 'What do you want, Marisse? It's very late.'

'This came for you, mistress,' says Marisse, dipping a curtsy. She holds out a note.

Bethia looks at the well-folded paper held between Marisse's chubby fingers and feels a strange reluctance to take it.

'Who brought it?' In all the time that she has lived here the only written communications she's ever received have been letters from Father and a few scribbled sentences from her wee brother John.

Marisse shrugs. 'A messenger came.'

'What messenger?'

'I do not know,' says Marisse, her voice shrill.

'Be quiet,' says Bethia, snatching the note from Marisse's hand.

Marisse's lips curl; it is a sly smile – verging on contemptuous.

'Get to your bed.'

Marisse pads away and Bethia retreats to her chamber.

She unfolds the paper. The note is brief, to the point, and in French. Reading it, she goes as still as a mouse being tracked by a cat.

> You live amongst Crypto-Jews and are damned to burn in the firepits of Hell for all eternity. Do what you know in your heart is right by the Lord and for the sake of your eternal soul. Give the foul usurers up – or the Inquisition will take you too.

It is as vile a piece of writing as she has ever

encountered. With shaking hands, she rips it into small pieces and burns them in the fireplace. She sits by the ashes for a long time.

Eventually she rises and reaches for the candlestick. Holding it aloft, she slips from the room. It's hot and airless in the passageway, the shadows dancing along the walls and lighting up the contorted figures in the painting which hangs here. Most of the pictures in the de Lange home are the large landscapes of the Low Countries, but this one tucked away, high up in the passageway to the bed-chambers, is very different. Mostly she avoids looking at it, puzzled by why the family would want a painting of Hell, showing women savaged by dogs and men raped by demons, close by where they sleep. She hunches her shoulders as she creeps by, but it still feels as though the creatures from the fevered mind of this man Bosch are about to leap down and seize her – as the writer of the note threatened.

She's before the door now, her hand reaching out to lift the latch. It isn't locked and swings open. She hesitates and then enters, closing the door firmly behind her to shut the demons out.

The armoire creaks as it swings wide. She catches its door and goes still to listen. The house is silent, everyone surely asleep, apart from her. Extending the candle inside she's careful to hold it away from contact with the wood. Making certain the door is wide and will not swing shut, she steps within and feels around the back, pushing with the palm of her hand. Bending down, she finds a narrow gap. Aye, it goes to the base. There's a smell of burning, and she leaps back out, sets down the candle, and hits at her hair, eyes watering at the stench. The smell slowly dissipates, but she keeps patting her head, tugging on her plait and sniffing.

This is foolish. She will return to her chamber and crawl in next to her sleeping husband. But instead, leaving the candlestick on the floor, she steps inside the deep armoire once more and pushes. There's no movement, but she hears a rattle. She steps out again and sits on the kist. Dare she open this Pandora's box...? The flame is guttering, the candle won't last much longer, and she must decide before she's plunged into darkness.

She crawls inside, the wood hard beneath her knees, and feels along the base once more. There it is. She releases the catch and the back of the armoire swings open. She stretches her arm out... into blackness. She leans forward, waving her arms wide trying to work out the dimensions, and then she's falling. She cries out as she tumbles, thumping face first onto the ground. Mary, Mother of Jesus, it hurts. She sits up rubbing her nose and forehead. The candle flickers in the room behind and she crawls back to collect it.

Placing each foot with care, she steps back into the hidden space, holding the candle high. It's a small chamber, not much bigger than a garde-robe. There's nothing in it, apart from three stools. She cannnot see any reason why it is kept hid from her, and others. She picks up a cloth covering one stool. It unravels to the floor, is only a long, fringed shawl. She holds it in one hand, candle in the other, baffled. Resting the candle on the floor, she folds the material and places it back on the stool. She moves around the edges of the chamber; there's nothing here. But tucked behind the third stool she finds a small kist. She draws the candle closer, and opens it. Inside is a finely made eight-branched candlestick. She lifts it out, admiring the delicate workmanship. The burnished gold shines in the light as she twists and turns it in her hand. Laying it gently down, she delves into the kist once more. There's a book inside. She holds it to the light, angling it so as to read the inscription on its cover. It's in the same writing as the book hidden in Peter Schyuder's secret drawer – the sacred language of Hebrew.

'Put the Tefillot down,' says a voice from the darkness.

Bethia shrieks and drops the book, which knocks over the candlestick. It hits the stool and sets alight the trailing fringe of the shawl, the flame bright in the darkness. She bangs on it with her hands. The figure rushes through the armoire, ghostly white in her nightdress, and beats at the flames too, then whips the shawl off her shoulders and smothers the fire. They kneel next to one another, breathing heavily.

'What are you doing in here?' says Katheline. The tone of her voice makes Bethia shiver, in spite of the sweat trickling down the side of her face.

'I-I-I'm sorry,' Bethia mumbles. 'I needed to know.'

'Bethia, you interfere too much and it causes the family trouble.'

'This secret place of worship is most dangerous, and it has nothing to do with me.'

'But you bring us peril nevertheless. I know of your brother and his espousal of the Protestant cause.' She turns and stares at Bethia. 'I like you, you know that, but you were not a wise choice for my brother.'

'I cannot see that Beverielle Schyuder would've been any wiser, given her brother's arrest.'

'The Schyuder's have powerful connections and you have none… here.'

Bethia rises awkwardly to her feet, the reek of smoke much worse now she's standing, and looks down on the top of Katheline's dark head, which is illuminated by the light that Katheline set down in the chamber outside this hidden space. 'Whatever you may wish, I am a member of this family. I will stand or fall as the rest of you do.'

She doesn't wait for a response but clambers back through the armoire and out into the chamber. She expects to find the whole family standing there with arms folded, but it's empty.

She picks up the oil lamp that Katheline was using, not caring that she'll leave Katheline in the dark. The light is much steadier than from a candle. She remembers how impressed she was when first she arrived and saw these lamps fuelled by a plant extract. There's nothing like it in Scotland, but then the Scottish weather is most probably not conducive to growing colza... or whatever the plant is called. She knows she's thinking about this plant because it's too much for her, in this moment, to consider the secrets she's uncovered. When she escaped from Scotland, she believed she was journeying from danger into safety. Now she finally understands that the peril here is greater.

She opens the door to her chamber and slips inside. Mainard's long body is stretched out diagonally across the bed. He groans, turning away from the light, and resumes the soft snoring which punctuates his sleep. She lays the lamp on the kist and goes to sit on the chair. She will not sleep, will wait here for Mainard to awake.

When she next opens her eyes Mainard is standing in front of her, arms folded. 'God's bones, woman, what are you about now,' he says and sighs. 'And why am I smelling smoke?'

She rubs her eyes, which feel dry and gritty.

'What have you been up to?' He reaches down to take her hand and pull her out of the chair.

She knocks it away. 'Sit down,' she says, and points to the kist.

He lifts his eyes heavenwards, but sits down. She looks at his long legs emerging from the nightshirt, with the dark hair curling on them, and wants to reach out and touch them. But she must not. The words tumble out in great disorder. 'Your sister wishes me gone. She found me in the secret place. What is the Tefillot? What is going on in this house?'

He stands up and goes to the shutters. The morning light reaching over the crow-stepped gables of the houses opposite pierces Bethia's eye.

Mainard gazes out, back to her, his long feet firmly

planted. 'What were you doing while I slept?' he asks wearily.

'Do not turn this on me. You feed me small pieces of information like a trail of crumbs to trap a wren. Every time I think I've finally understood, something new comes to light.' She leans back in the chair, feeling its solid wood at her back. 'Why is there a secret place hidden behind an armoire in this house?'

He turns on her, flushed and angry. 'And why are you creeping around at night, and by the smell arising from you, trying to set fire to us all? You have no right to be poking and prying into what does not concern you.'

'No right!' She leaps to her feet. 'No right! Your family are secret Judaisers, or so it would seem from what I saw last night. You think that will not affect me, as your wife. What of the children we may have? Where will it place them? Do you not see that I must know?'

She falls back into the chair exhausted both from the events of the night and the constant challenge of trying to understand. She realises she has never, through all the trials of this first year of their marriage, shouted at him before – and knows there are not many husbands who would tolerate such behaviour from a wife.

'I am only trying to protect you.'

She strokes the side of her forehead, up and down, up and down. 'Is this why Peter Schyuder was arrested? Is he a Crypto-Jew too?'

'No he is not, far from it. And, in any case, it's better you do not know, as I said.'

'This is not protecting me, Mainard. You brought me here falsely. I thought I would be safe, and my father most certainly did. I saw Gilbert yesterday and he says I should return to my father's house with him.'

'Hah! I am sure he would like that.' He stands up and walks around. 'Perhaps it would be best.'

'Is that what you want?'

'It seems to be what you want. And' – he tugs on his

ear – 'it may be wise. When does he leave?'

'Today.'

'I will get a message to him.'

'Very well, if that is what you wish.'

Nothing more is said as they make ready for the day, politely side-stepping one another. She opens the kist and kneels before it, sorting through her clothes. She's aware of Mainard hesitating behind but does not turn to look at him. There's a knock on the door and he answers it. Bethia glances over. Mama stands there, her face white and hands extended, palms upwards. Mainard puts his arm around Mama and leads her away, closing the door behind him.

Part Four

Will

July 1548 to August 1549

Chapter Thirty-Five

La Reale

They are back in France by early July, and Nydie and Knox are taken off the galley and returned to the castle. Will considers that neither could have held up for much longer. Knox had rallied as they rowed up and down the east coast of Scotland, harrying the English garrisons at Broughty, Inchcolm and Eyemouth, and disembarking troops to relieve Haddington. But Nydie had grown as frail as an old man and Will greatly feared for his friend; much more of this life as a forsare and James would soon be entering the next one. He is relieved for them both, but finds his own imprisonment well nigh unendurable without James's companionship and Knox's strength of purpose.

When he, along with a number of others, is taken off the galley, his hopes rise. They are quickly dashed – he should have known when his fetters were not removed that he was simply being moved to another vessel. It's a much larger ship with more rowers. The sails are large too, and the accommodation rich, with cabins on the upper deck and greater storage in the hold. Indeed, it seems like the galleasses of Venice he has heard tell of, combining the best of sail power with slave power to give great manoeuvrability and speed. He groans at the thought of what may be required of him. Then there is a

209

whispering among the galérien that this is the royal galley often used by King Henri himself. Will hopes that the king might want his slaves better tended to, or at least cleaned up, but it would seem not and he is as dirty as ever.

Moored mid-river, they are given a sail to mend, no doubt to keep them occupied as they swing at anchor. Soon he has new callouses on his hands from forcing the needle through the tough sailcloth, to add to the callouses he has built up from wielding the oar. Early next morning he's woken from a deep sleep to row the ship into the quayside. He watches as supplies are loaded, and picks the stripes of blistered skin off his face, trying not to dwell on the torment of being at sea again.

There are soldiers being marched onto the quayside now. They board his ship and the one drawn up behind them. Then they're floated off and two more galleys are brought in and uploaded with supplies. All is bustle as they ready for departure. He wonders where they're bound; it no doubt depends on where France considers their greatest enemies to be. Perhaps they are for the Mediterranean, to fight the Ottoman Empire – or to ally with it against Charles in the constant tug of war over the Italian states. He looks to the Turkish slaves among them and wonders if they'll feel the same desperation to escape that he did when near to Scotland.

A boat is coming towards them, laden down with richly dressed men, the plumes of their bonnets blowing in the wind. He sees a flash of yellow-red hair and beard, and thinks one among them, at least, is likely a Scotsman. Then the sous-comite is shouting and he must attend to his oar.

It is his rest period and, as ever, he leans his elbows on his knees, head hanging. His new shackle-mate is Spanish, probably captured in one of the many skirmishes in the long power struggle between France and the Holy Roman Empire. They have no shared language but Will is determinedly learning some Spanish; it makes for a small distraction. His head droops further and he sleeps. But he's not given long to doze – already it's his turn again. He had hoped for a less strenuous position on the bench when he moved galleys, but is again positioned at the outside of the row, because of his height and strength. He sighs, being a giant among slaves is not a blessing.

They have moored at the mouth of the river overnight. Tomorrow will be the open sea. It's as he's chewing on ship's biscuit – how can it be so hard already when they are only a day out – trying to soften it with spit and sips of water and studying the sores around his ankles, that he becomes aware of someone standing on the high walkway above him.

'Will Seton, as I live and breathe!' a voice calls. 'I would say well met, but that would be an inaccuracy of gross proportion.'

Will looks up and gasps, the biscuit catching in his throat. He coughs, spluttering and spraying crumbs. When he can breathe again he is doubly humiliated. It's bad enough to be fettered, vermin-ridden, and stinking, without also being red-faced and choking.

'Why are you here?' he asks.

Gilbert Logie takes a step back, the smile fading from his face. The commander calls to him. Will can feel Logie hesitating above, but keeps his eyes resolutely on the oar at his feet, which he's about to take up again in any case. Eventually, out of the corner of his eye, he sees Logie moving away.

By the end of his stint, when he has time to think again, he's sorry he didn't speak to Logie, wishes him back so he could at least get news of his own family. Logie will know what happened to Bethia, may even be her husband. Now he's desperate to speak, but reluctant to draw attention to himself by calling out and would probably incur a whipping if he did. He thinks it likely they're going to Scotland, since Logie is on board. He wonders why this ship, which looks to be among the pride of the French galleys, is being used for a coastal blockade and harrying the English emplacements.

Several days pass and Will notices he's receiving better treatment from the sous-comites. He's moved from the walkway side to the ship's side of the bench. Immediately he's aware of how much less strenuous the rowing is, and the constant pain in his back recedes. His shackle-twin is delighted, nudging Will and making what he assumes are ribald comments. Then some meat is included with Will's daily rations, slipped to him surreptitiously. Will doesn't know when he has tasted anything better, nor the skin of wine to follow. He shares the latter with his companions along the bench, and from being derided as a dour Scotsman, he suddenly becomes a popular fellow.

It's an easy journey, the wind favourable and not much work demanded of the rowers. He sees the Bass Rock, with its crown of circling gannets, towering in the Firth of Forth, and knows he's once again near home. It seems they are to make landfall at Leith, and no doubt Logie will disembark. Will can feel his heart, indeed his whole body, straining with longing to once again step foot on his ane country.

They are here for little more than a day. Will had hoped for a longer respite. Logie returns. They quickly cast off and are joined by more ships of the French and Scottish fleet. Perhaps they're going to attack one of the English-held strongholds, possibly Broughty. The English didn't even have to fight to take that castle; it was handed to them by Lord Gray. He remembers Patrick Gray swearing allegiance to the English Crown when he visited St Andrews Castle during a period of truce. It's a thing of wonder, and bafflement, to him that they were ever permitted free movement during the siege, and for as long as five months. He watched that swearing of allegiance, along with the lairds, and felt a strong distaste at the time. He knows he should support

England's ambitions for England has embraced the Protestant cause, but it can never sit comfortably with him to have his country controlled by others – be they English or French.

By the next day they're passing his home. Will turns his head away, cannot bring himself to look on the distinctive spires and towers. He feels tears in his eyes and makes no attempt to brush them away. When he next turns his head he finds Logie standing nearby on the walkway.

'Your family are well.'

Will breathes out, a long exhalation of relief. Had not admitted to himself the anxiety he was carrying that they might have suffered on his behalf.

He nods to Logie. 'Thank you for telling me.'

'They were not punished for your transgressions.'

Will stiffens. He did not transgress. He followed his faith and his conscience; how is that a transgression? He turns his head away, but Logie's next words soon have him turning back.

'I saw your sister when I was recently in Antwerp.'

'Antwerp! Bethia is in Antwerp?'

'Yes, she married her pilgrim.'

Will shakes his head to clear it of the fog which seems to have descended.

'She did not tell you of Mainard de Lange?'

'No.'

The ship slides down a steep wave and Logie staggers, but quickly regains his balance. 'He's a man of Antwerp who came with his father on a pilgrimage to St Andrews. I understand the father had killed someone and was required to atone.'

Will snorts. 'Aye, and a pretty penny the priests will have taken in indulgences from him.'

Logie yawns and Will feels a fool. But he couldn't let that pass, had to remind Logie again that he, Will, is here because of his faith.

213

'Bethia is well, although still adjusting to life in Antwerp.'

Will feels suitably chided that he had not asked after her health. 'What is her husband like?'

'He's a merchant, or more correctly, the son of a merchant from Portugal.'

'Is he young?' Will can hear his voice rising and shakes his head to calm himself.

'He is young… and handsome,' says Logie, voice as dry as hard biscuit.

Will cannot help but smile; trust Bethia to land on her feet. He feels a strange sense suffusing his body. It's so unfamiliar he cannot put a name to it for a moment. He feels… happiness, tinged with relief, and positively beams at Logie. But Logie does not return his smile.

Over the next few days, as they sometimes sail and sometimes row up the sea that bounds the east coast of Scotland, Logie comes frequently when Will is at rest. Will learns of his father and younger brother John, but it's always to Bethia he returns. And the relief he feels is very great. He did not realise how concerned he was about this sister who he left alone and in peril, hid among the rubble of St Andrews Castle. Yet he has a sense Logie is not telling him everything – but then they can be overheard by those around, some of whom may understand English.

There are cliffs now, high cliffs, to their left. He wonders if they're making for the faraway islands at the top of Scotland. Surely that cannot be, for they belong to Denmark. And then one day Logie tells him, in answer to Will's inquiries, that they are to row down the west coast of Scotland, but he will not say where they are going, nor why.

Chapter Thirty-Six

West Coast

It is full summer and the sun rises early and sets late…
and the hours of rowing are long. They are far to the north
now and here the winds come, perhaps unsurprisingly,
from the northlands of ice and snow. There is no shelter to
be had from a coast lined with steep cliffs, green with
grass which takes a hold where a man cannot, before
dropping to narrow rocky shorelines. And the galleys are
ever in danger of being blown onto these unfriendly
shores or the lonely pillars of rock which stand like
sentinels dotted along the coastline, and all this means
endless work for the forsares to keep the ship clear and
safe.

One day Will overhears a comite laughing with his
comrade. 'It does not matter from which direction the
wind blows, the galley is carried by the wind in the
sinews of our slaves.' He would admire the clever turn of
phrase were it not for the sentiment. He sends a prayer to
the Lord that the comite might be captured and have his
sinews so abused.

Eventually they turn a corner and are heading south,
sheltered from the Atlantic swell by strings of islands. The
sea is the richest of turquoise, like to the ring Father gave
Mother when John was born. They stay well out from
coast but he can see the white sand of small beaches and

215

the hummocky boulder-strewn hills which rise immediately behind them. This coast is so very different to the broad sands and rounded hills of the east. It's almost as though they have gone to another country and not the other side of his country. Will smiles to himself. It is the Highlands, after all, which is a wild country of fierce and feuding clans.

There are many islands: long narrow fingers of land; short dumpy circles; islands that are simply a huge lump of rock dropped into the sea; one that is so flat they are upon it before Will realises it's there; and large islands of many hills which take all day to pass. But the sea between the islands has its own perils. Bloodcurdling tales are passed among the forsares of tidal races and turbulence below, masked by treacherously smooth water, where sea monsters and ghosts of the dead entice unwary mariners to the deep. One night, when all are at rest and it's quiet on the ship, Will sees these ghosts draw close, smothering the rows in front of him. There are cries of fear until the sous-comites come with lights and the captain orders them all to take up their oars and get the ship away from this accursed place.

The next day it is as though the unquiet spirits never came calling, and the sea is as still as if the angels rest upon it. Black flies cluster above their heads landing on eyes and lips, and they row faster to escape them. In the early evening they enter a long channel, the land drawing close on either side. The deeper into the estuary they journey the more settlements there are: farms, turf houses huddled together, the occasional tower house, and then they come to a castle fortified by high walls and perched upon a great lump of rock with the broad estuary before it and the mouth of a tributary river to one side. It looks impregnable. Will cannot see how it is entered, except by scaling the rocks – at great risk of tumbling into the sea, as well as being easily picked off by archers from above.

Soon it is passed among them that this is Dumbarton

Castle. Will remembers that one of the reasons the Castilians were able to hold St Andrews Castle under siege unchallenged for the first few months was because the Scottish troops were fully occupied in trying to wrest Dumbarton Castle from the pro-English group holding it. Head tilted back, Will gazes up and considers it a wonder they were ever successful.

They anchor below the castle, sitting well out from the rock-strewn shore. A boat is lowered and Logie is among those who are rowed to the small pier. The sound of the waves gently lapping against the ship's side soon has Will's head nodding but clouds of midges descend in the stillness of the evening to torture them. It is a short lived relief when the wind begins to rise and they are gone. He looks up to find the sky above is dense with cloud. It grows dark and rain falls with an intensity that quickly has them soaked and shivering as they struggle to haul the tarpaulin over and tether it down. Will huddles low and even the heavy coat cannot keep him warm. The French galley slaves mutter and growl about the weather in Scotland, and why so cold when it is midsummer.

They are rocking at anchor in an angry sea the next morning when a large ship comes in and drops anchor. He watches as passengers disembark and the sailors try to keep the rowboats steady. Men clamber down a rope ladder, carefully judging the moment to let go and drop into the rowboat. There is much activity, and Will can sense that the commander of this ship is anxious as he struts up and down shouting orders, his voice floating on the wind. A fine lady with huge skirts comes on deck, with a coterie of women rushing behind her.

Then she is lowered slowly on the bosun's chair. From the anxious faces watching as the chair bumps against the side, it's clearly a woman of great importance. Her skirts catch in the wind, her stocking-clad legs most improperly revealed. She might have been better to do as Bethia once did climbing into St Andrews Castle, and don breeches for this descent… although his sister is the only woman he has ever seen so attired. The shame of it makes him blush still.

There is a muttering amongst the forsares. What are they talking about? Guise and the Duke of Lorraine. A jolt runs though him. No, it cannot be. He leans forward peering through the slot where the oar goes, while the sea, growing stormier by the second, soaks his face. This woman holds herself straight and proud as she descends, no squeals of fear as the chair swings in the wind. She is certainly regal enough to be Marie of Guise, mother to the wee queen. He wonders why she is come here, to this castle.

The wind grows stronger, blowing in from the west in a rising gale. Will refuses his enhanced rations, for any food in his belly seems to be slopping around like the mixture of seawater and piss which is slopping over the boards at his feet.

By the next day the wind has dropped, although the galley is rising and falling on the waves which break against the shore with great spumes of spray. Provisions are brought and loaded onto their ship, many provisions. Four other galleys appear in the bay to add to their fleet. The east coast, where England prowls, must be much depleted of ships.

Great kists are being brought down to the pier and loaded onto the small boats. It requires strength and balance to manoeuvre them so all aren't upended into the sea. They are tied down, rowed out, and distributed among the waiting galleys. Even greater effort is required to haul them on board ship, and Will and his shackle-mate are, unusually, released from their bench to lend a hand. The rope burns his hand as he hangs on with all his might. There's a real danger the load will fall into the sea – and take them with it. The sous-comite roars and wields his whip, extra assistance is called, and eventually they get it onto the deck. More follow and, despite the callouses on his hands from the oars, the rope finds new and tender places and soon his fingers and palms are torn and bleeding. He spits on them, tucking them in his oxters as he's led back to his place.

There's a lull. The baggage loading, which has gone on sporadically over two days, seems over. Will awaits, with greater curiosity than he has felt for a long time, to see who is to join them. A great crowd emerges onto the small pier. They mill around, chattering excitedly. Will can hear the high shrill voices of the ladies and the deeper growl of the men. He sees Logie's red head among them. He is moving people towards the boats lined up waiting to take them to their ship, calm in the centre of confusion.

The galley, although substantial, is blown round and he's facing out to sea. Will bends over trying to peer through the oarlock at the far side of the ship, but all he can see is a line of heads equally bent, twisting and turning to catch a glimpse.

By the time the ship has swung around again, Gilbert Logie has managed to load two boats, which head for the other ships moored in the bay. There's another flurry of activity on the pier and five small girls, each holding the hand of a lady, arrive. The foremost child is a redhead, like Logie, but Will is too far away to make out her features. She is, however, being treated with great deference, everyone standing back to allow her precedence. Will's heart pounds. He guesses who this is… and he does not think his guess is wrong.

Chapter Thirty-Seven

Mary

The child hangs back, tugging on the hand which is pulling her forward. The wind blows her cloak and veil in a great swirl around her small body. What are they thinking of, to bring such a precious cargo out in a rowboat on a day like this, and when there are few places more secure than this castle perched above vertical cliffs. His shackle companion nudges Will, inquiring, in Spanish, if this is indeed the wee queen. Will thinks before responding, then shrugs. It doesn't matter if the man knows.

Eventually courtiers, ladies-in-waiting, soldiers, and small children are all loaded. It's early evening, and although it won't be dark for several hours, a decision has clearly been made to set sail in the morning. Will has nodded off when he becomes aware the bosun's chair is being prepared again, and up comes the Dowager Queen Marie. She is a tall sturdy woman with a firm line to her mouth, indicating great determination, but the worry lines across her high plucked forehead give a sense of the cost of such determination.

A small child bursts from a forward cabin, chased by her ladies.

'Maman, maman,' she calls. 'Venez-vous avec moi?'

The last is said with such hopefulness that Will feels a

lump in his throat and wonders what is wrong with him to be so sentimental about a Catholic monarch, albeit a small child.

The queen mother shakes her head but gathers the child to her and disappears into the cabin.

The two ladies-in-waiting stay out on deck, and Will, whose position is nearby, catches snippets of their conversation. 'This is not wise.… the queen was settling… now we must deal with her distress once more.'

One of the ladies, a dainty, dark-haired, darting creature, is remarkably pretty. His fellow slaves seem to agree. 'La Belle Écossaise,' he hears muttered among them. The sea is calmer, with waves kissing the ship's side rather than slapping it, thanks be to the Lord for the prospect of a rough passage with children and fine ladies on board is not pleasant. He looks up, not a cloud in the blue sky overhead, although long white streaks spear it as the sun drops low.

The queen mother emerges, face impassive. 'She's asleep now, you may go to her.' She waves to the attendants and they scurry through the cabin door.

Logie comes, bows low over her hand and escorts her to the ship's side.

'I will take very good care of our queen,' he promises.

She doesn't speak but taps his arm in acknowledgement. She's swung out, and after a few moments he sees her rowed over to the ship on which she arrived.

Logie comes to lean on the railing nearby. 'It is very sad,' he says. 'Who knows when, or if, our dowager queen will see her only, and much loved, child again.'

He is called away before Will can reply. Will sits unmoving as the dusk falls, feeling weary with sadness. Who knows when any of us may see our loved ones again, he thinks. But still his heart is wrung with pity for the wee motherless queen hounded from one side of her country to the other because of her marriageability. King Edward's

Uncle Seymour is most determined, and he once heard tell that, before his recent death, King Francis of France was trying to broker a marriage contract for Mary with the king of Denmark's son. He wonders if that's where they're taking her now, back along the north of Scotland and across the German Ocean to Denmark.

At first light they weigh anchor and Will bends his back to the oar. The wind is unpredictable, constantly shifting direction. First they are rowing into it, then it's skimming in from the side, and for one brief moment it comes from behind and there are even, blessed relief, preparations to raise the sails. But then it turns once more. The strength increases and it gusts as though the Devil himself is plying the bellows.

The wee lassies emerge on deck, chattering and encircling the taller lass, their queen. She's the most animated of all, shrieking at a toy monkey which Gilbert Logie, who has joined them, produces with suddenness from behind his back and pretends is leaping upon the girls. One child grabs it from Logie and throws it in the air. Blown by the wind it lands close to the board on which Will's feet rest. The wee queen darts along the walkway before anyone can stop her. Will bends to pick up the toy, tossing it at her feet.

She stares down at him; her eyes are soft brown and her red-gold hair, escaping its snood, curls around her face. She reaches for the toy and Will notices how delicate and white her hands are, with remarkably long fingers for a child.

'Are you a bad man?'

'I try to be a good one,' says Will, smiling, but she's picked up by Logie, who carries her to where her ladies are clustered together, holding onto skirts and capes. The wind and rising sea is quickly too much for them, and especially for one of the wee lassies, who empties the contents of her belly onto the deck in a great spume.

Will is surprised the waves are as high, for they are

still in the channel with land on both sides. Soon the galleys are forced to seek shelter, and before nightfall they have anchored in a small bay dominated by a tower house. It's too perilous to lower the boats and get the children to shore so they swing at anchor, still buffeted by the rising wind while all the royal party suffer sickness from the sea except the wee queen, who, it is told around the ship, remains in good spirits. She's occasionally seen sheltering by the cabin door while Gilbert grips her tightly, and her guards balance nearby. Once Will hears her singing, her voice of great sweetness.

After three days of storm, La Belle Écossaise is seen arguing with the captain. 'It is too much, this swinging aimlessly in the sea. Take us ashore.'

The captain shrugs. Will doubts if he even understands what she says since she speaks in Scots. A gust of rain sends her scurrying undercover. She's back the next day demanding, 'Let me off this boat immediately. I must repose myself, and the children too.'

The captain evidently does understand Scots for he bows low saying, 'I give you the choice, my lady. You can either stay on board, or leave and drown.'

She stands for a moment clearly not believing what she's heard, then the ship lurches, rocked by a large wave. She staggers and is only saved from falling overboard by Logie, who has appeared in time to catch her. He escorts her below, and Will can see she has much to say.

The storm blows itself out and they can proceed down the channel and out through the Firth of Clyde. The wind may have died to an eerie stillness but the sea is choppy, causing the motion of the ship to be most unpredictable, constantly lifting and dropping with a jarring crash. They row out between the islands of Bute and Cumbrae, and Will hopes they will now journey in a direction where the wind can aid, rather than impede. But the seas grow rougher and, when he raises his head, he notices huge banks of cloud massing on the horizon – indeed the clouds are so dreary grey they are at one with the sea, and he must squint to make out where the sea ends and the sky begins.

There is an anxious consultation taking place on the foredeck and Logie is shaking his head. They are no longer sailing in a southerly direction but aiming to the southwest towards a large island. All rowers are pressed into service and soon they are again anchored off a settlement. It's passed around among them that they are by Lamlash on the Isle of Arran. Will searches his mind to think what he knows of Arran but, beyond its earl, can remember nothing. They tug the tarpaulin over them as protection from the driving rain, fighting to hold it down as it flaps wildly, and Will is lashed across the face by a flailing rope. God's blood, it stings, making his eyes water, the salt tears mingling with salt water from the sea, which he is soaked in.

Their convoy joins five other ships taking refuge in the curve of the bay, which is further sheltered by the small island which sits across its entranceway. Signal flags are raised and lowered and soon it's passed around that all five ships are part of a Scottish merchant fleet. The next day a boat is lowered from one into a lumpen sea. It carries some provisions as well as passengers, and all arrive on deck unharmed.

Will watches as there is much bowing between the merchant men, Logie, and the queen's Scots guard. The wee queen emerges as the wind calms, and the merchant men bow so low their heads near hit the deck. She stands before them with a calm assurance that belies her years. Will wonders again where they are bound. Clearly not to Denmark, else they would have turned north and safely away from England. They must be for France, and likely for a long time, he thinks, with the queen mother so sad at their parting.

The merchant men do not tarry but take the letters Logie passes, no doubt to inform the dowager queen of her daughter's well-being and the slow progress made. The wind has dropped sufficiently that it's determined they will leave. Up comes the anchor and they head out of the sheltering arms of the bay and south once more. But they have been deceived. The wind veers around, hitting them with such strength they can make no headway, indeed are being pushed backwards, the waves running under them to splash mast-height on the rock-strewn shore. Scotland, it seems, is most reluctant to release her queen.

The captain is compelled to turn the ship around and, barely two hours after their departure, the luckless maid is back again, moored in the same spot in Lamlash Bay. Their fleet is alone this time, for the merchant ships have gone north. Will thinks that the dowager queen will receive her letters with all possible speed, the merchant ships flying before the wind.

The next day all is calm and they head out to sea once more, although with great wariness, any moment expecting the power of the Lord to drive the wee queen back. But it seems they are at last let go, and soon Arran is a speck far behind them. Evening draws in and the setting sun is dazzling red in Will's eyes so that he has to squint to see. He's confused; surely they should be heading south, not west. The next morning the sun rises, a golden orb in the blue sky, behind. He can see land to the left and then finally they turn south, standing well out to sea with the hazy coastline visible in the far distance.

Logie is out on deck, then strolling across the walkway.

'Ireland?' Will hisses.

Logie nods. 'Always best, wherever possible, to keep another country between us and England.'

Will can't help but smile; has to remind himself that Logie is his enemy.

The weather holds and they make good progress over the next few days. Ireland is behind them and they are off the Cape of Cornwall when the sea makes a final attempt to hold them. And here they cannot seek shelter in any nearby bay. Worse, they see ships appear – and soon it is shouted that English ships are giving chase. Will rows, looking out for them each time he's in a standing position when the ship crests a wave. He feels a knot tight in his chest, knows he doesn't want that bonnie wee lassie caught by English corsairs – even if it means he's freed. Bung between his teeth, he pulls as hard as he can, and there's no need for the sous-comite to ply his whip.

Another shout goes up after what feels like hours, but it is no more than one bell. The English are turning back. Will's heart lifts, but only until he realises why… the wind is howling across the bare masts. Soon he is so lashed by the waves it's as though he stands beneath a waterfall. Night falls and the seas rise higher and higher. All around him men cry and shiver with fear as white spumes rush towards them out of the darkness.

The man at the wheel is roped on, so difficult is it to stay in place. Then there's a thump and the ship shudders from stem to stern. They cease to make any headway and lie wallowing. The lamps from the escorting galleys disappear into the darkness and the stars are blacked out by the clouds.

A drag anchor is flung out to keep them pointing into wind, while the rumours run up and down the ship: they have hit a whale; they have holed on a reef; the ship is sinking. But then it transpires the rudder is broken and they cannot steer. The wind dies suddenly; they must be in the eye of the storm. It is eerily still, as the unquiet ghosts, who Will is sure still follow them, dance around in the darkness.

Men are hung over the lee side – Will cannot imagine anything more terrifying – and remarkably are able to replace the rudder.

This is the last attempt by God, or Satan, to prevent Mary reaching France. A few days later, after some easy sailing, they are moored off a town with a tall cathedral, a bishop's palace, and a sandy beach. It looks like St Andrews and Will clenches his fists, thinking of his ane town.

All is peaceful now, the sun sparkling on a blue sea. Already it's hard to believe what they endured, and that a voyage which would normally take five days has taken eighteen, with weather in August worthy of the worst storms of January.

The wee queen disembarks with her coterie of small maids and ladies-in-waiting around her. She is a remarkable child, Will thinks. Not only pretty with her smooth skin and dainty manners but also a child of great courage and steadfastness. He fears she will need it in this precarious life and prays she will be safe and happy in France. He knows John Knox would not approve of Will's sentiments but this is his queen and he owes her his allegiance, whatever her religion.

Chapter Thirty-Eight

John Knox

It is winter again, the second one of Will's imprisonment. Again, he, along with other Castilian forsares, are held in the huge fortress chateau of Nantes, a life of luxurious indulgence in comparison to being a galley slave. There are some terrifying cells of course, such as the quaintly named petite chambre – of such small dimensions that it's impossible for an inmate to stand up once confined within, and barely wide enough for them to lie down. Fortunately, Will has never provoked the guards sufficiently to be constricted therein.

John Knox is much preoccupied with the treatise which Henry Balnaves has written concerning justification by faith alone. Balnaves is held in lordly comfort, a prisoner with much freedom, in the castle at Rouen. William Kirkcaldy of Grange and his father and sons are also held in Normandy, and who knows where the Masters of Rothes, Norman Leslie is. Will snorts. He's probably escaped or even been released. It would be the greatest irony if he were, for he was the instigator of both the siege and the killing of Cardinal Beaton. Yet he is as slippery as wet seaweed on rocks, and nothing seems to stick to him.

Knox considers Balnaves most fortunate that he has been able to argue, debate, and discuss the Protestant cause with learned men brought to him in prison, as his French captors attempt to return him to the papal fold. How Knox would have enjoyed, indeed relished, such an opportunity.

'The French think that we can be turned from right-thinking,' he says, banging his hand down on the board with which he has been provided, along with paper, quills, and ink. 'But how can they even consider that anyone who reads Balnaves' careful doctrine would want to return to a place where they commune with our Lord through an intermediary?'

He picks up the pen, gripping it tightly between his fingers, bends his head, chewing on his lips, and writes rapidly. Will, watching from a stool in the corner, his knees near to skimming his face so long are his legs, nods off to the scratching of the quill. He's startled awake moments later, when Knox leaps to his feet and begins pacing and talking loudly.

'It is only through our faith that God gifts us the holiness of his son. This is the great truth which Martin Luther has uncovered and the foundation on which sound doctrine must be built.' He nods as though agreeing with himself, his black beard waggling.

Thumping down on his seat once more, Knox seizes his quill. Will slides onto the rough stone floor so he can stretch his cramped legs. He looks up to find Knox standing over him. Knox is of small stature, but from Will's position sprawled against the wall, he seems a mighty man – a latter-day prophet who speaks the will of God. Or, more correctly, that is the mantle he takes on. This thought is confirmed when Knox turns to greet an entrant to their chamber come seeking guidance.

Will listens as Knox proclaims. It seems it is now difficult for him to converse in normal tones and all words are spoken at great volume, for John Knox loves to preach. Will shakes his head. What is he doing watching Knox in this way – as though he has any right to sit in judgement on him? After some time the man is released, a relieved smile upon his face, for Knox has given words of comfort as well as guidance. Will scrambles to his feet and offers to scribe so that Knox may let his thoughts flow uninterrupted. Perhaps this way he may imbibe some of Knox's certainty.

They work together well in this fashion for some weeks and Will feels his faith reviving. He spent too long away from Knox and sound doctrine. The journey with the wee queen, watching the parting from her mother, speaking to Logie, all had weakened his resolve. He is ashamed that he could be so easily led from the fold. No, that is not correct; he was not led so much as he developed an understanding he did not have before... certainly of the vulnerability of the infant queen. It still does not sit right that she should be chased from her homeland by English bullies. He bites down on his lips and shakes his head to clear it of any such thoughts. His only consideration should be sound doctrine, and his own justification by the faith.

He studies hard, and prays hard, over the winter months as Knox works on a summary of Balnaves' treatise. Will does not fully understand why a summary of the work is necessary but he shuts down that thought before it's fully formed. Knox speaks the true word and it is neither right nor correct thinking for Will to question it. Debate and discourse are their meat and drink, but the basic tenets of Protestantism are inviolable. Knox links their sufferings to those of the great saints, saying often that they are all bound in chains as St Paul once was. And like St Paul, their sufferings will make them stronger in service of the Lord.

There is much discussion about where the summary might be sent, and Knox determines that it should go to the congregation of Holy Trinity in St Andrews where Knox first found his calling as a preacher. It's also the church of Will and his family. Will doubts that his father will be ower pleased to see Knox's letter nevertheless he forms the words carefully.

'I exhort that ye read diligently this treatise, not only with earnest prayer that ye may understand it...' Knox pauses, fluffing out his beard, which has become as dense as a sheep's pelt, 'but also with humble and due thanksgiving unto our most merciful Father, who of His infinite power hath so strengthened the hearts of His prisoners, that in spite of Satan, and in the most vehemency of tribulation, we work ceaselessly to seek the salvation of others.'

Knox comes to read over Will's shoulder. 'That will do very well,' he says. 'But what think you?'

Will is so startled to be asked that his hand jerks and a blot of ink drops, marring the words he has carefully scripted. Knox tuts and Will's opinion is forgotten.

Over the winter Will's body slowly recovers. He can stretch his fingers out from their previous clawlike state without the skin tearing. He can stretch his long legs out without encountering the bench in front, or indeed kicking the legs of the man in front, which was the subject of much animosity. He almost feels his youthful age once more. The anniversary of his birth comes and goes. He's now eighteen years old, and after what he's suffered can surely be considered a man. Of course, all is not perfect; his back does seize up, with fierce spasms, if he moves heedlessly, and Knox too still suffers from the belly thraw, which had him so ill they feared he might die last summer. But all in all Will's life is tolerable, if only the shadow of the spring sailing did not hang over him as the winter progresses. There is no end to this cruelty either: he may be destined to live and die shackled to the oars.

On a mellow late winter's day, when Will can sense spring around the corner, there is suddenly much unusual activity. Knox is told to gather his papers and what clothes he has, for he is leaving. He goes to sit quietly in his corner. Will knows he is at prayer and must not be disturbed – but it is a strange communion with the Lord, for Knox glances frequently towards Will as his lips move.

Eventually he rises and demands to meet with the governor. He soon returns, saying to Will. 'Collect what things you have.'

Will stands, arms dangling and head to one side. He would be fearful if it were not that Knox is smiling, indeed whistling in a most unmusical fashion.

'I've told them you are my assistant and must come with me.'

Will stands tall to be so described. 'But where…?'

'I will explain all later. Let us just away, while we may.'

There is a ship waiting. They board it as free men. They are not shackled, they are not sat on a bench before the oars, indeed there are no forsares, for this ship is powered by wind alone. They are shown to a small cabin. Will cannot believe the untold luxury of having a space, out of the wind and waves, in which to sleep. He turns to Knox, so close that their faces are almost touching.

'Where are we going?'

'To England,' says Knox, and Will hears the note of triumph in his voice.

Chapter Thirty-Nine

London

They do not quite understand how it has come about that they are free and, even when they arrive in London, are still in a fog of bafflement. Knox and he travel by cart through streets with houses so crowded together Will feels he cannot get any air. And the numbers of people moving and struggling, pushing and fighting, punches thrown between arguing street sellers, children begging and thieving, women openly plying their dissolute trade, is beyond belief.

St Andrews is better laid out than this city, he thinks: no alleyways where you must squeeze between houses to get through, and all streets broad enough for the many processions and holy days. At first the smell is very terrible, the River Thames, which they sailed up, like a great sewer. He saw a dead body floating down it along with several dead dogs, all caught in swirling eddies of excrement. The river is a thick grey flow and yet people are washing in it. But soon he grows accustomed to the pervasive smell of rot, barely noticing it.

At no time are they left to make their own way: arrangements have even been made for their accommodation. It's basic to be sure, but after the privations they have endured, all seems sumptuous. Will finds himself adrift, too used to being a prisoner to know what to do with his freedom. He would explore the streets, but it's not easy to wander where everything is crowded – and perilous. Eventually, one day, while Knox is engaged with new friends who seem much taken by him, Will determines to go out alone. He finds his way to the Palace of Westminster, spread in a great jumble of buildings over Thorney Island, like a huge greedy spider at the centre of its web. The guards are staring as he peers in through a gate. One takes a step forward and Will retreats. He has no desire to be incarcerated in an English prison having just escaped from a French one.

He heads back to the river, and finding himself at the extensive docks, he weaves his way along the quayside. He sees coal being unloaded, the carriers coated in soot. Barrels are rolled off the next ship, the men moving at great speed, and behind them heaps of skins are carried on the bowed shoulders of men. He pauses before the next ship, watching as a large armoire, visible through its wooden packing case, is swung onto the dock. He thinks the sailors are speaking Dutch; perhaps this ship has come from Antwerp where his sister is. He could ask, and if they are returning he might go with them for a short visit, for he is a free man. He says it aloud, 'I am a free man,' and does not think he has ever heard sweeter words.

He keeps walking, even though he knows he should return and find out what news Knox may have. But who knows where they may next be bound, and he should see this great city while he can. He comes up against a crowd ahead.

'What is everyone staring at?' he asks a respectable-looking man, who, Will hopes, is unlikely to seek payment in return for an answer. In any case, Will has none to give, which at least has the benefit of meaning he's not worthy of robbing.

The man looks surprised to be accosted, then grins. 'Ah, a man, indeed a giant, of Scotland... who must be a friend to England?'

Will stares at his feet and then looks up flushing, doesn't care to be so described, but supposes it must be true. He nods slowly.

The man laughs. "Tis as well you count yourself a friend, for here we see what happens to those who are not.'

Will draws closer. He can easily gaze over the heads of the crowd.

A prisoner in chains is shoved off the back of a cart and reappears, struggling, between two constables, the rope ready knotted around his neck. He sees the post they are dragging him towards – death by slow strangulation – and turns away.

'You're not staying to watch?' asks his new friend.

Will shakes his head. 'I must away, should not have tarried this long.'

'Hah,' the man sniffs. 'How else are we to deter piracy? Anyway, 'tis the best entertainment you'll see for many a day.'

Will thinks he's witnessed enough suffering, including his own, to last a long time. He strides away, dodging the people rushing to the spectacle. Boats are clustering on the river, bumping and manoeuvring to keep their spot. They'll be here for some time too; this is not a quick death.

When he reaches the inn, John Knox has returned and is both elated and agitated. They are to meet with Archbishop Cranmer who, it seems, has important work for Knox. 'A ministry,' he says, rubbing his hands together. 'Seton, you must tidy yourself. Where have you been? You stink as bad as the river.'

Knox takes a comb and tugs it through his beard, while Will shouts for a servant to bring him a jug of water. He dunks his whole head in and shakes it out like a dog. Knox takes off the long black robe, which his new friends have purchased for him, dusts it off and sponges the white marks which dot it. Will borrows a needle and thread from the hosteller's wife and, after all the practice he had repairing galley sails, neatly sews up the split seam across the shoulder of his jerkin. When Knox agrees they are both suitably groomed, they set out.

Archbishop Cranmer has a long white beard of whose luxuriant growth he is clearly proud, as he repeatedly touches it, fluffing it out and then stroking it smooth much as Knox himself does. Will wonders if this is now a clerical requirement. Cranmer's cheeks are rosy-red as an apple, his brown eyes large, and he looks like Will has always imagined God to look: benevolent yet fiery. He puzzles over whether it would be right to commission a painting of the Lord, or if that would be a false image, while Cranmer and Knox debate transubstantiation and justification by the faith. They don't agree on all points but both clearly relish the opportunity for discussion. When they part, Cranmer makes a gift of the Book of Common Prayer, which Knox receives with a bow and a smile.

'Was it Archbishop Cranmer who was instrumental in our release?' Will asks as they are led out through long corridors.

'I understand that representations were made by Protector Somerset to the French government. Whether Cranmer was behind it I cannot say for certain, but I think he sees I may be of use. He tells me, which perhaps you did not hear for you seemed distracted' – he glances at Will from under bushy eyebrows – 'that there is a great need in the far reaches of England for priests of sound thinking to support their flocks to follow the true path and turn from Rome.'

They stop, the way forward impeded by workmen extending a long rope which has been thrown from the church tower above. The rope, as great as the cable of a ship, is stretched taut, held down by a huge anchor.

'The tower is unstable,' says Knox in answer to Will's obvious puzzlement.

'No, my lord,' says a labourer tugging his forelock.

Knox, pleased to be so addressed, tolerates the correction.

'It is for the entertainment of our young king. He's much taken by the funambulist who will come sliding down the rope like the arrow out of a bow, and all done with the head first.'

Knox frowns at the man's enthusiasm and walks on. 'I do not have time for games,' he mutters.

Will, who would've enjoyed watching such a spectacle, follows reluctantly. 'Do you think Cranmer will grant you a licence to preach?' he asks, reverting to their interrupted conversation. He sees a slow smile spread over Knox's face and understands that is Knox's great hope and aspiration.

And indeed by early April the Privy Council give Knox his licence and authorise a payment of £5 per annum, which seems a veritable fortune to Will. They are to go to Berwick-on-Tweed, bringing the Word of God to the lawless people of that crowded town perched on the Scottish border. Will hopes it is a sign from God that his future too is as a preacher.

Chapter Forty

Berwick

Will stands on the newly erected Lord's Mount at Berwick and turns around and around. He's never been anywhere so heavily fortified as this town. The walls are high, the gun emplacements many, and the earthworks which were thrown up so very quickly, and which even the Protector Somerset is said to have seized a shovel to help dig, are vast. The town is bounded by the sea to the east, and the river bending around it affords protection on the south and west sides. It's curious, Will thinks, that the town is, in effect, built on the north side of the river: the Scottish side. Anyone arriving from the south has to cross the broad expanse of smooth flowing water to reach here – that or come by sea, which many do. But then he remembers his school days and the dominie's dirge-like tones as he related the story of Berwick, which was once a Scottish town, seized by Edward I of England, and every man, woman, and child in the town killed for their resistance. And in the three hundred years since, it has regularly changed hands, although for sometime now has been held by England. He gazes out at Scotland. Does he miss it? No he does not, for here the true faith is followed and there's much work for him to do. He turns his back on his home and descends into the crowded streets of this overfull town.

When they met with the roughly dressed commander of the garrison soon after their arrival, he told them that there were near on three thousand five hundred additional souls over and above the usual population of the town. 'These consist,' he says, in a voice so weary Will wonders how this soldier finds the strength to lead his men, 'of English soldiers, mercenaries from many parts, as well as the workers brought in to build the fortifications. And we do have much coming and going as we hold our gains within Scotland; Haddington in particular is of grave concern, for we have to move through hostile territory to keep its garrison supplied.'

Will hears an intake of breath from Knox, sitting at his side, and remembers that Knox is from Haddington and has family there.

The commander does not notice anything amiss and continues his briefing. 'And, of course, all will grow worse now, for with summer near upon us the fighting season begins again.'

Will thinks on this as he descends the long sloping street, counting the many languages he hears spoken: English, of course; Polish; Dutch; is that Swedish; and now Scots. He was surprised to find so many of his compatriots here when he first arrived. Some are come for the same reason as he, fleeing a Catholic Scotland, but many have more prosaic matters on their minds, including providing services to the soldiers and relieving them of their money and whatever belongings they have.

He hurries past the many beggars lying where they can, some too sick to even stretch out their hands and plead. Most are soldiers from Haddington, Eyemouth and Lauder who have been returned here and left, unsupported, when they are ill or injured, and no longer of use. But this garrison does not want them either, and since these men have no funds, they are shut out of houses and die of want in the streets. And he has heard tell that even those soldiers who are receiving funds are so poorly paid they can barely afford food, but that is no wonder with the price of all victuals excessive.

Two soldiers emerge suddenly from an alehouse in front of him. One staggers and knocks into Will.

'Watch out, ye fool,' the soldier mutters, then quickly looks at the ground as Will's great height towers above him.

Will, reflecting that there are some advantages to being tall, continues on his way at a leisurely pace. When he reaches St Mary's, the church which Knox has been assigned for his first ministry, he finds him deep in discussion with John Bede, who has come from the Bishop of Durham.

'No man can have anything unstolen,' says Bede, shaking his head with such vehemence that his cap falls off.

Will picks it up and hands it back, and Bede twists it in his hands as he speaks. 'This whole place is one of social disorder and the worst policing. Between blood feuds, murder, and thievery it will require a stern disciplinarian in the pulpit, as well as a strong preacher, to lead both moral and social reform.'

Knox purses his lips and nods, while Will thinks it is good to know how sorely they are needed in this garrisoned town.

Bede reaches out and pats Knox on the arm. 'If anyone can introduce a strong sense of discipline then you are he. Your time in the galley will command respect amongst the soldiers especially, for you will have a deeper understanding of their life than any normal priest. Their commander is too weighed down with the challenges of keeping Haddington fed and fighting off the warring Scots to deal with all the issues arising here in Berwick.'

Knox stares at Bede. 'How ready are the people for church reform?'

Bede turns and looks to the long coloured glass window depicting the Virgin holding the baby Jesus.

'King Edward may be young but he's strong in his Protestant beliefs, and the government equally so. But outside London the following is weaker, with many still practising the old faith – including, I fear, some clergy.'

Knox tuts loudly, the sound bouncing off the stone pillars of the church.

Bede waves his hands, as though to calm Knox. 'I know, I know… but we must have patience. It's better to draw people to reform steadily than hurry them faster than they are willing to go. We want true conviction, and that may take time.'

Knox paces back and forward in front of the pulpit. 'I understand your concerns, Bede, but we cannot wait. If we do not move with an urgency then there is great danger that people will slip back into the old ways – or never leave them at all. And there should be no place in the church for an unreformed clergy. This we must relentlessly root out.'

Bede opens his mouth to speak but Knox talks louder. 'My duty in life is to blow my master's trumpet,' says Knox. 'And I will proclaim the gospel of God's grace in Jesus Christ to all who will listen.'

And true to his word this is what he does. Will feels a new force flow through him, for Knox preaches with such fervour that soon not only locals attend his church, but Scots are crossing the border illegally to hear him speak. And the soldiers like him because he has no airs and graces but speaks to the common man as though the saving of his soul is as important as that of a man of substance.

Inevitably he is controversial, always taking the congregation one step further than any other preacher, causing them to gasp and look to one another, fuelling debate and discourse as they emerge from the church. But such is his strength of purpose and belief he carries all before him. At Whitsun, when they have been in Berwick only a month Knox departs from the newly adopted Book of Common Prayer, which the congregation have barely come to terms with, and issues a command, which Will, holding the cup of wine for Communion at Knox's side, nearly drops when he hears.

'No, no, we do not kneel. To sit is all that is needful… and right.' Knox waves his arms encouraging them to follow his command.

There is great rustling from his listeners. Some are already upon their knees, others in the process of descending. They look to one another, eyes flicking around to ascertain what their neighbours are doing.

'Sit,' commands Knox, in his powerful voice.

As one the congregation rises and sits upon whatever seat or stool they have brought. No one gainsays him, at least within the church, and soon no one thinks much of it – it has become the way of doing things in St Mary's. Indeed, it's a considerable relief for the knees, as well as saving wear and tear on clothing.

There is, of course, much blethering about this and other acts of Knox, outwith St Mary's itself. Will himself is not entirely convinced about sitting. He does not fully understand why they should not kneel before the Lord. There was something about the ritual that felt right – although he supposes Knox's assertion that Jesus and his disciples sat around the board for the Last Supper is correct. Yet they have not been here long; are still establishing Knox's ministry. Surely Knox might have waited before he risked antagonising the senior clergy, and especially the Bishop of Durham, to whom they are accountable. Will shivers at the prospect of being flung out.

The garrison at Berwick grows smaller in number as they move towards summer. There are revolts further south, requiring military intervention, and many of the troops are sent off to subdue the rebels – it seems that not all communities can be led to the true word as quickly and easily as the people of Berwick. But then not all communities are fortunate to have a preacher with fire in their belly the like of John Knox. Will learns that the rebellion in the south is about the use of the Book of Common Prayer, and especially holding services in English. He wonders how the people of Cornwall would react to being instructed not to kneel but perhaps they wouldn't object – as long as they were instructed in Cornish. Will says as much to Knox, but Knox is not amused.

'Levity is all very well and good at the appropriate time and with the appropriate subject. This is neither the time nor the topic on which to employ it.'

Chastened, Will chews on his lower lip. He feels like a small boy standing before his dominie, even though the top of Knox's head barely reaches Will's chest. But his fears are proved right, for the next day Knox receives a summons to answer to the Bishop of Durham for his deviation from the prescribed text.

Chapter Forty-One

Newcastle

'One of my parishioners will provide me with horses,' Knox tells Will, more than once, when they are discussing the journey to Newcastle, where they are to meet with the bishop.

Will wants to say, you've already told me, but he doesn't want to spoil Knox's evident pleasure in rolling the word parishioner around his tongue.

'You are my assistant, of course you must come,' Knox says when Will questions whether Bishop Tunstall will care to see him. He realises that having an assistant, although nowhere near as vital as having parishioners, also brings Knox satisfaction.

He finds it strange to be on horseback again and enjoys the journey greatly, at least for the first day.

'It would have been quicker to travel by sea,' Knox mutters to Will as they climb the stairs of the inn that night, 'but Johnson was most eager to have my company, and discourse, upon the journey. And he has business to attend to so will leave us before Newcastle.'

Will nods; indeed, Knox is sounding quite hoarse from incessant talking.

'I must rest my voice tomorrow, so I have plenty of wind to speak with our bishop.'

Will snorts with laughter. This is one of the many

reasons he so admires the man. Just at the point at which he thinks Knox is getting overfull of himself, Knox comes up with a quip which shows he is a man of true humility – and really how can he help occasionally sounding boastful, when the Lord speaks through him.

The next day they press on hard, for Knox does not want to linger – however much Johnson would like to draw out their conversation. It's as well it's May and late before it grows dark, for they ride all day, stopping briefly only to sup. When the long gloaming finally fades, they are still outwith the city walls and fortunate to find an inn able to accommodate them. Will groans as he climbs down from his horse. He aches all over. Then he smiles to himself; he's growing soft already. A sore arse and bruised thighs from riding are as nothing to a day at the oars.

The next morning they finally enter Newcastle, and Knox is as glad as Will to see the back of the loquacious Johnson, who suddenly found reason to accompany them all the way, and who is blown up with pride at having spent a few days in the company of the famous John Knox. Will thinks it's curious to watch how greatness is more and more being conferred upon Knox by the faithful.

He doesn't expect to meet with Bishop Tunstall but Knox insists he come, saying, 'If you are one day to find your calling, then you need to understand how to deal with senior clerics, and especially those who may question your doctrine.'

'So you expect the bishop to disagree with what you are preaching.'

'I think it very likely.'

'And will he raise remaining seated during the act of Communion?'

'Yes, that in particular. Although since John Hooper, a most faithful and learned exponent of Calvin, has recently been appointed chaplain to the king's uncle, I would expect a change in government views on this subject. But then Tunstall, I fear, has never truly embraced Protestantism and may even be a secret Catholic still, deep in his heart. Yet he is an astute man, having survived King Henry's machinations with the church when disposing of wives, so we must not discount him.'

Will shifts made uncomfortable by these words, and hopes what Knox is saying is not treasonable. He has no desire to be returned to France, or worse. For the first time, in England, he has felt safe to follow right-thinking. He wishes Knox did not feel the need to push quite so hard. Yet the Lord must truly be watching over Knox that he has thus far evaded the burning pyre.

The bishop keeps them waiting for some time. The noon bell rings and still they're standing in the courtyard of his Newcastle residence, the guards impassive in their heavy helmets, gripping tight their pikes. The sun is warm overhead and the courtyard sheltered from the breeze. Will's face grows hot and sticky. Knox is calm beside him, although he too must be sweating beneath his heavy black robes. Eventually they are led into the bishop's presence.

Will is surprised to find Tunstall as clean-shaven as a Catholic priest. He has a deep cleft in his chin and full lips which any woman would be proud of. He bids them welcome and invites Knox to be seated, leaving Will to stand. Will doesn't mind, he can watch better from the side.

'Berwick is a most lawless town, overfull with soldiers and vagrants from Scotland,' says Tunstall.

Knox stiffens at such an opening salvo, shooting straight back, 'And yet, since I have taken up my ministry I have produced a great quietness in the town.'

'So I have heard.'

Will sees a glimmer of pleasure on Knox's face to receive such acknowledgement, however unbending the delivery.

Tunstall's lips grow thin. 'Nevertheless, you go too far,

Master Knox.'

Knox's eyebrows shoot up with such suddenness that Will has to run his hand over his face to conceal a smile.

'I refer to your continued insistence that the bread and wine are not the blood and body of Christ. This denial of transubstantiation is most abhorrent.' He leans forward. 'You have been permitted a certain leeway as a Scot preaching in your own church, especially since I understand many of your congregation are fellow Scots. Nevertheless, I will say it again. You go too far.'

He stands up, as though the strength of his feeling is too great to keep him seated, and stares down upon Knox, who sits unmoving. 'We have you at one end of the country pushing the Protestant cause to its limits, and at the other end we have Devon and Cornwall in uproar about services being held in English.' He raises his eyes to the ceiling as though seeking divine intervention. 'And why, I ask you, should Cornishmen be complaining about services held in English, when before they were held in Latin and they did not understand that either?' Tunstall sits down heavily. 'Though I am not without some sympathy for them.'

Will shifts, made uncomfortable by these sentiments, and Knox's face flushes. Knox opens his mouth to speak, but the bishop waves him silent and continues.

'It is difficult enough for the common man to understand that there is no longer the joy of procession, that they must see all shrines removed, nay even desecrated, but the dissolution of the monastic orders has also meant the end of any formal scholarship in Cornwall.'

As Will listens he begins to be of the opinion that it is Tunstall who goes too far. And Knox is by now very red in the face as he tries to control himself. It's not often these days, Will reflects, that John Knox has to exercise restraint. He is become used to being surrounded by a crowd of unquestioning admirers.

Again Knox opens his mouth to speak but the bishop raises his hand and continues. 'I understand that, as a young man leading your first ministry, you are most eager, and that is to be commended – but you must give way to the greater knowledge and experience of your elders, and betters.'

Will removes all expression from his face. He's most uncomfortable at witnessing Knox's chastisement. If he stays still perhaps he can merge with the stonework and they'll forget he's here, although it seems, from Cuthbert Tunstall's words, he has already forgot.

'I am instructing you that, as of now, you are to follow the liturgical formalities as described within the Book of Common Prayer, and as directed by the king and his government.'

Will risks a glance at Knox and thinks he may well burst. Every part of Knox's body is held tight: fists clenched; lips pursed; eyes bulging; arms folded.

Tunstall waves his hand in dismissal and picks up the papers in front of him. But if the bishop has finished, Knox has yet to begin.

Knox stands up, blowing out the air he was holding in. 'I must have the freedom to speak from the pulpit of God as directed by his Word and Spirit only.'

The final word comes out as a shout. The bishop starts and Will hunches over. 'Any other approach is most wrong, for surely you must agree' – Knox spreads his hands wide, voice softening – 'that the government and the universities should not have any right to direct the clergy.'

Tunstall does not look mollified but nevertheless Knox continues. 'Only on the grounds that I have contradicted Scripture should there be any interference, and then only the church courts should have the right to do so. It is a priest's duty to expound and apply the Word of God as laid down in the Bible, and not as some government, university, or Pope may interpret it.'

Knox stops to draw breath, while Will, fearful that their ministry may be over before it has barely begun, takes a step towards him. Knox flaps his hand at Will, who hesitates, arms dangling as he watches helplessly.

Tunstall, brow deeply furrowed, speaks. 'I am your bishop. I warn you now, do not push this matter further or else you will find yourself in the Tower accused of heresy. I shall write to the archbishop and apprise him of your words. You may leave now.'

Knox gives a slight bow and backs away. Tunstall doesn't acknowledge their departure. Out in the courtyard, Knox swings his arms wide as though warding away evil spirits. 'I hope I may not live to regret my words.'

Will hopes they may both not live to regret them, but still he is proud of Knox. 'They had to be said.'

Knox looks up at Will. 'I thought you did not approve.'

'I didn't fully understand – but you are right-thinking. This is why we suffered nineteen months as forsares, and before that over a year in a stinking castle under siege. To give way now would be a travesty.'

Knox thumps him on the back as they walk out through the gates of the bishop's palace. 'Good lad,' he says.

Chapter Forty-Two

Puffed Up

Will is sent to the docks at Newcastle to arrange their passage back to Berwick. Knox is in a hurry to return, saying it will be far quicker, as well as less painful on the arse, to go by sea.

'We are getting soft already,' he says, grinning. He is in great good humour, feeling that, overall, he bested the bishop during their discussion.

Will wanders along the dockside enjoying the bustle, although the gulls, diving and screeching, squawking and fighting in a great tangle above him, are enough to send anyone scurrying. There are plenty of ships here, loading coal, unloading tiles, carrying great bales of cloth, swinging boxes of shining fish onto the dock. Will swallows; he still struggles at the smell of fish – although there's been times these past two years when he would have been glad to eat it, however repulsive. He swings his arms, as Knox did earlier, enjoying the movement; the joy of being free will never leave him.

Eventually he locates a ship which is doing the short hop to Berwick with supplies for the garrison. He rushes back to collect Knox. Opening the chamber door Will finds him pacing up and down muttering to himself, gesticulating widely and, no doubt, preparing his next sermon. Will stands in the doorway for several minutes before Knox sees him. It looks as though his discourse will be as controversial as ever and create great energy and discussion amongst his flock.

Knox is certainly buoyed up on the return journey, which takes longer than expected. The wind is, unusually, from the north-west, and they must tack far out to sea before making their way into the coast at Berwick. As they draw near, the wind dies and Will worries that he may be asked to take up the oars… or caught by some French galley guarding Scottish waters. In the end a breeze comes up with the turning of the tide, and soon they are safely moored in the Tweed Estuary.

Knox is smiling broadly as they stride up the hill, hailing folk and responding to shouted greetings as though he's lived here all his life.

The next day he's back in harness and again warning from the pulpit of closet Catholics still to be found in high places. 'And what of the royal succession?' he bellows.

Will watches as people shrink, some instinctively covering their ears.

'We all pray for the health and long life of our good young King Edward, a more staunch Protestant it would be hard to find. But his successor is openly a papist, who will not be shifted from her faith, however wrong-thinking, even by all the entreaties of her beloved father. We should not bury our heads from the calamity that would ensue, should she become queen.'

People are shifting where they stand or sit and looking to one another. 'This is treasonous talk,' he hears the man in front mutter to his neighbour as the service ends and everyone leaves the kirk at unusual speed. 'But then Knox knows no better. He's a Scot after all, never had to live through the times of King Henry and all the changes of wives and shifts in the royal succession – not to mention risk having your tongue cut out for breaching the laws forbidding its discussion.'

The man looks behind, espies Will listening, and

pushes through the crowd to escape. Will expects that Knox will be called again to Tunstall to give an account of himself, but all is quiet – on that front at least.

Knox, well satisfied, tells Will he hopes that Protector Somerset will have the good sense to listen to his words, should an account of them reach his ears, and act upon them. 'For, although the young king seems of good health, who knows what may occur. We know this well in Scotland, where our kings, however robust, are frequently struck down in their prime either by illness or the sword. And if the Princess Mary was to take the throne then the life of a Protestant in England will be as nothing.'

Will nods and picks up a quill to transcribe Knox's words. He is grateful to be learning so much. He prays every night that it may lead to a ministry of his own one day, although he knows to hope for it shows an excess of pride unsuitable to the calling. And he wonders if he could he ever be as bold as Knox, who daily risks his life with his words.

He picks up a letter from a parishioner seeking advice and asks Knox how he should respond to it. Knox leans forward and takes it from Will's hand. 'Ah, the young Mistress Marjorie, I will reply to this myself.'

Will shifts in his seat. There is a proprietorial tone to Knox's voice that he has not heard before.

Knox ponders the letter and then sits down to write. Will is slipping from the room when he looks up. 'Stay, Seton, for this is a most thorny issue and perhaps I may better answer by speaking my thoughts aloud first.'

Will takes a seat and prepares to listen and form a viewpoint. It will be useful to have such practice, should he ever have a congregation to lead.

'This earnest young woman is seeking a point of clarification on the Gospel of John and, in particular, how she should behave towards visitors to her home whom she knows to be strong adherents of the Catholic faith.'

Will blinks. The answer seems straightforward,

especially after Knox's uncompromising words to Tunstall. 'She should not allow Catholics entry to her home. Indeed, she should have no friends among them.'

Knox lays down his quill and picks up the letter once more. 'Aye, but it is not so simple as you make out.'

Will shifts on his seat wondering if he'll ever be good enough to become a priest.

Knox moves his papers, quills, and ink around the board, picking them up and laying them down in turn. 'Of course, there will come a time when no Protestant should associate with papist malingerers, but if we cut them entirely from our society then how are we to bring them to the true faith? I think it shows great gentleness of spirit that Marjorie has not cast aside her old friends, be they idolaters or no. Great gentleness.' He nods to himself.

Will wants to counter that it shows great weakness of resolve, but he can see his contribution is neither sought nor desired.

Knox picks up his pen once more and dips it in the ink. 'I will tell her that she is not a partaker in evil deeds, as she fears, by wishing a Catholic visitor Godspeed as they leave her home. Although she must take great care with whom she associates.' He pauses. 'But perhaps it's better that I meet with her to discuss this further.'

'Is this a daughter of Elizabeth Bowes?'

Knox nods absent-mindedly, head still bent over his letter.

Will grins. 'Elizabeth Bowes is a most eager convert to the cause.'

Knox looks up. 'She is a woman most eager to do right by the Lord.'

'Yet she has a fondness for the false ceremony of the Mass.'

Knox stands up so quickly his stool falls to the floor. 'She's taking guidance from me on these matters and is most willing to consider the error of her ways. And do you not have work to do? I still await your commentary on Christ's temptation in the wilderness.'

Will's in no mood to tarry in the wilderness. He grabs his bonnet and heads out the door. If Marjorie Bowes is the daughter he's thinking of, for Elizabeth Bowes has many daughters, she's barely fifteen years old, and very comely. It is not seemly for Knox, a cleric, to spend as much time as he does in the company of women – indeed to seek them out. He decides he'll go to St Mary's and sit quietly in the church. He feels a restlessness deep inside that he cannot account for.

Chapter Forty-Three

Marjorie

Marjorie Bowes is a comely lass. Dainty and fine-boned, she has a sweetness of countenance that is most appealing. She's a good height for Knox, but Will stands very tall next to her, like the tower of St Rules above its small nave. But even if Marjorie did not have to look a long way up to see his face, Knox was always going to be the more appealing prospect, especially as his ministry grows.

There are many women in the congregation now; indeed, Will thinks that women are more drawn to John Knox than their husbands. He attends to their concerns and doctrinal questions with great seriousness, bowing his head to listen as they whisper in his ear. But the one he attends to most is Marjorie's mother, Elizabeth Bowes. Will himself doesn't see what the attraction is. She speaks in a high fluttery voice that is most irritating... and has much to say. Her hands flutter too and her brow furrows as she listens earnestly to Knox's, usually long, responses. If it's after a service and her husband is standing by, a burly man who soon calls, 'Come along Elizabeth,' then she cannot linger. And if she doesn't respond, her husband takes her arm saying, 'We have tarried long enough.' She goes, reluctantly looking back over her shoulder, her unmarried daughters trailing behind.

Knox preens himself, fluffing out like a blackbird seeking a mate, whenever he talks of his ministry. Will doesn't think it shows suitable humility of spirit, but when he listens to Knox speak and watches the response to his words, he doesn't entirely blame him for the sin of pride. And Knox is a good man who struggles with his demons more than most… but the time he spends with the Bowes women Will does not consider easily justified; surely he cannot be contemplating matrimony. He paces up and down his own chamber shaking his head. He knows that George Wishart, amongst others, said a priest should take a wife – indeed it was one, among many, of the reasons he was burned at the stake. And he supposes it is better than taking a concubine as Cardinal David Beaton and most of his ilk did, but still it seems very wrong. Men of God should rise above their carnal needs.

Marjorie Bowes is so very sweet though, as she looks up at Will from under lowered brows. She's delicate in her movements, most obedient to her mother's wishes, and she smells of lavender. Will finds himself watching her often. She is very young, even younger than Bethia was when Father wanted her wed to Fat Norman. And just when he is thinking of his sister, a letter comes. Not from Bethia, of course, for she won't know his whereabouts and he doesn't have the directions to write to her in Antwerp. The letter is from James of Nydie. He's been released from his comfortable castle and risked returning to his home in Scotland. Will suspects that Nydie was probably too junior a player in the great siege for the authorities to take much notice. In any case, the depredations of England into Scotland have grown considerably less recently. With Queen Mary of Scots safely in France – who would know better than Will – the world has changed.

Will is particularly pleased that, along with giving news of himself, Nydie also gives news of Will's family. Although Will has written to Father since he was released, he received no reply. Nydie writes that he visited the

Seton household and was made most welcome by Mistress Mary, Agnes and even John, who Nydie says is growing at a pace where he will soon rival Will himself. Will thinks on it; John was only a wild, freckle-faced boy when he last saw him. He sighs and looks up to see Marjorie watching him, while her mother and John Knox are in deep discussion about Mistress Bowes' pastoral needs.

Marjorie stands up and treads softly across the floor to sit beside Will upon the settle. 'You have received ill news?'

'No, no, on the contrary, my friend writes that all is well with my family in Scotland.'

She looks at him most sympathetically. 'It must be difficult to be so far away.'

'I have my work here… but am happy to receive news of them.' He does not mention that there is no greeting nor message from Father, even though Nydie says he told them he was going to write and asked if they wanted to include a note. Mother can write little more than her name, so he would not expect anything from her – but surely Father might have a care for his elder son and heir. But then he's probably been disinherited and all will go to brother John. He never wanted to be a merchant anyway, still hopes to find his calling as a pastor.

He stands up, needs to move. 'I am going outside for some air. Would you care to join me?' He is holding out his arm for Marjorie to take when Elizabeth Bowes looks over and shakes her head. Marjorie sinks back onto the settle and Will leaves alone.

Elizabeth Bowes seems to be forever at the door seeking guidance, although she always brings Marjorie with her. Will overhears two parishioners wondering if Master Knox has succumbed to the Devil's temptation, in the guise of Elizabeth Bowes, and realises that the frequency of her visits is arousing gossip within Berwick and beyond. He mentions it to Knox, although not in those exact terms.

Knox waves his hands about as though shooing Will away. 'Aye, aye, I ken she's here ower often, but she gets herself in an awfie fash about her former idolatry and other iniquities, and as her spiritual advisor, I canna leave her to be buffeted by Satan.' He pauses and strokes his beard. Will watching, thinks how much comfort Knox derives from his beard, but then it is a powerful symbol of the new order that he, a priest, now wears one. 'And her questions and worries are most helpful to me in my cogitations, and in understanding where the serpent invidiously inserts himself into my own brain. In discussion together we can break down the head of the serpent and guard against it stinging us upon the heel.'

Will thinks that sometimes he does not understand what Knox is talking about. This all sounds like a ruse, although it's only himself that Knox is fooling. Anywise, what does he care, for he can spend time with the fragrant Marjorie. Her long brown tresses, her gentle brown eyes, her sweet earnestness, for she too is beset with fears, are all a balm to Will's soul in a way he's never experienced before. And she looks to him for guidance! He stands taller, moves with confidence, and even Knox referring to him as a clerk, and not his assistant, does not lower his spirits, at least not as much as formerly. And, he does not think he is mistaken, Marjorie likes him in return. He would swear on his Holy Bible, or more correctly, the Book of Common Prayer, to it.

He is, one day, plucking up the courage to reach out and take sweet Marjorie's hand, sitting forward on the edge of the settle to block Elizabeth Bowes, who is whining away in Knox's ear, when he catches what is being said. He goes still, not quite able to believe what he's hearing.

'My husband is most unhappy, but fear not, my good Knox, he will come to see that nothing could be better than an alliance between our families. Greatness is already upon you, and although Bowes considers that you do not have the necessary funds to marry, I am sure that your many supporters will make certain that you want for nothing. So, for myself, I am happy to agree an alliance between you and dearest Marjorie.'

She looks over to where her daughter and Will sit. Will, too, stares at Marjorie. She hangs her head, blushing, but he catches the ghost of a smile on her face. Why did she not tell him, why did she let him think he might have a chance? He stands up and mutters something about a task he must complete and rushes out.

He feels utterly at a loss as he paces the streets, down the hill and back up again, along the walls, to the castle and Lord's Mount. Elizabeth Bowes is treated more as Knox's assistant than he has ever been. It is with her he debates the Bible, it is to her he entrusts his doubts, it is to her he turns for spiritual solace. And now he's to marry her daughter, bonny Marjorie, even though he cannot support her and she is likely to be called a priest's whore by the many who consider any clerical marriage an abomination.

He stays out long enough to make sure Elizabeth Bowes will have exhausted even her long list of questions, and gone. Knox has his head bent over his papers when he returns. Will gazes around the comfortable quarters they have been assigned: the tall casements which look out onto the wide bend of river leading to the sea; the oak furniture, the one tall chair in which Knox always places any visitors, humbly taking the stool on the other side of the board; the kist where Will tucks away his thick pallet and warm blankets each morning; and the door ajar to the chamber with the feather mattress on a high bed in which Knox takes his rest.

There's a tap on the door and their landlady enters carrying a tray containing their evening meal: rabbit pie, collops of bacon, baked eggs, trenchers of ale, and bread so fresh-made that steam is rising from it. Will, for all his agony, feels his mouth grow moist in anticipation.

The landlady rests the tray on the board, sets out the repast, dips a curtsy, and goes. Will lifts his stool over to the board and reaches to break off a hunk of bread. Knox gazes at the meal and groans as he kneads his belly.

'It is still troubling to you?'

'I fear this is a legacy from the galleys that may never leave me. Elizabeth says there is a new physician come to Berwick who is most knowledgeable, and she will arrange for him to visit.'

Will buries his face in a large slice of the rabbit pie.

Knox rises from the board and wanders around the room, clutching his belly. Will glances over but Knox seems deep in thought, rather than in pain. He mops up the juices from the meat with a generous hunk of bread.

Knox smiles and nods to himself. 'It is most satisfying to observe the order that a strong message supported by clear doctrine can bring to a community. The commander was saying to me only yesterday what an improvement he has seen in the streets in the few months since my ministry began.'

Will picks up the last collop of bacon and drops it into his mouth.

'Our next task is to prepare a reasoned case for married clergy.'

Will chokes on the bacon. He coughs and coughs and coughs.

Chapter Forty-Four

Adulterer

Will has avoided any contact with Marjorie since the revelation she is to wed. He therefore considers it most trying, when he is walking back from St Mary's one day, that he encounters Marjorie and her sister Ann in the street. He doffs his bonnet and steps aside to allow the ladies passage, but Marjorie stops in front of him. Sister Ann has been drawn to a small child: bare-footed, dressed in the flimsiest of shifts, dirty and snot-nosed. Avoiding Marjorie's eyes, he watches as Ann crouches before the child, stroking the grubby hand held out to her.

'I hope this day finds you well, Master Seton,' says Marjorie in her soft voice.

'Tolerable,' mumbles Will. Christ's bones she smells good.

'I have not seen you for some time,' she whispers.

Before he can form a reply there's a cry from Ann and the bairn takes to its heels. 'My purse, my purse,' shrieks Ann.

Will takes off after the wean, leaping over a beggar's foot which is suddenly obstructing his passage. Another beggar appears from a nearby close and barges into him but Will easily knocks him aside. He sees the child duck into the space below an outside stairwell and slows down, looking around as though he's lost sight of it, and not wanting to alert anyone else involved in this play to the need for a further distraction. He drifts past the stairs, head turning to search all around, then reaches a long arm in and collars it. The bairn, empty-handed, sets up a great yowling.

Will shakes it. 'Wheesht, or I'll have the soldiers tak ye awa.' The child grows quiet, staring at Will with huge eyes. Will remembers what it is to be hungry, so hungry your belly aches and you can feel all the bones of your body jutting through your thin skin.

'Fetch the purse and I'll gie you these.' Will holds out a handful of coins but the wean shakes its head. He realises the purse is needed else the child will be beaten, and even more than it clearly is judging by the purple bruising showing through the dirt of its skin. Will also realises he needs to move fast, before the other beggars involved arrive. He grips the bairn and shakes it. 'Get me the purse, now, or it's the gallows for you.'

It whimpers, but crawls into the space behind the wooden stairs and fetches the purse. Flinging the purse at Will, the wean tries to take off, but Will's prepared. He grabs the child with one hand and bends to pick up the purse with his other. The bairn wriggles and squeals, and he shakes it like the small rat it is.

The young ladies come hurrying up. 'Thank you so much,' says Ann, 'you were so brave.'

Will looks at the filthy bairn struggling in his grip, who barely reaches above his knee, and wonders if it's sarcasm he's hearing, but both girls are smiling and nodding and gazing wide-eyed upon him.

'What will you do with the child?' asks Marjorie.

'Take it home and feed it well.' Will is surprised to hear those words fall so decisively from his lips, but he knows it's the right action when he hears himself say it.

They gaze upon him with even greater admiration, and Will cannot help sticking his chest out – and feeling some understanding for Knox's similar response when the women of the congregation gaze upon him with adoring eyes.

The girls insist on accompanying Will to his lodgings and the landlady insists the child must be washed before it's allowed food, 'for who knows what beasties it brings.' They are all surprised when she returns with a bonny wee lass, albeit with her hair clipped short. 'I could do nothing else' – the landlady shakes her own head – 'so full o' crawling creatures it was.'

John Knox, to whom the lassie is now being presented, watches as she sits with her arm curved around the bowl of food she's given. She eats slowly, savouring each mouthful. Will sees her slip a hunk of bread into the pocket of the dress the landlady found for her. Perhaps she's keeping it for later, but more likely it will be shared among hungry siblings. And the dress will be taken from her and sold as soon as she returns to whatever hovel she came from. What are they to do with her?

Knox has clearly been pondering the same thing. 'I have spent much time considering how we might help the poor and afflicted of Berwick.' He paces up and down, hands behind his back. 'The destitute soldiers are so many among us, as well as children such as these. Christ Jesus would not have turned his face away as he passed by them, and nor should we.' He pauses. 'The difficulty has been in knowing where to start when there are so many in need. But one child' – he smiles upon the waif – 'we can surely exert ourselves to find a suitable place for.'

It quickly emerges that Knox's suitable place is the Bowes' home. Fortunately, Marjorie is already of the same mind and offers to take the child without much persuasion. Knox smiles, and Will beams, upon her. She is so very modest and truly good… and pretty.

It's agreed that Will is to escort the young ladies home, keeping a tight grip on their charge as he goes. He suspects the child will flee as soon as she gets the opportunity but he's wrong. She stays, seemingly contented, and providing Will with a reason to visit their home, unencumbered by Knox, for it was he, after all, who caught and rescued the bairn. He and Marjorie have much discussion about the best way to guide this lost soul to Christ, and soon he feels a small kernel of hope once more. Her marriage to Knox has not been mentioned recently, and in any case, her father does not sanction it. He pushes away the thought that he has even less to offer than Knox. If he returned to his father's house, then he'd have a good life to give her as the son of a merchant... better than Knox could offer. But even should his father take him back, does he want this fragrant young woman enough to give up his hope of a ministry and return to ledgers and accounting? When they are apart he knows he cannot relinquish his aspirations, but as soon as he's with her, he thinks how very easily he could. And they are again together nearly every day, for Marjorie's mother is going through agonies which demand much guidance and support from her pastor. Knox complains again about the time taken up with her fasherie but he never turns her away, indeed invariably stops what he's doing to attend to her.

One day Will finds Knox alone in St Mary's pacing up and down, shaking his head vehemently. He stands in the doorway of the church until Knox looks up and beckons him in. 'You're aye lurking somewhere,' he mutters.

Will stiffens. He considers that most unfair – he's aye bent on some errand or other for Knox.

'I am most tormented, a most tormented man.'

Will waits. He cannot imagine what's coming next.

'It is Satan who is tempting me, infecting my heart with foul lusts,' he says, spittle spraying from his mouth.

Will nods slowly. 'I was coming to speak with you. There has been more talk about your meetings with Mistress Elizabeth.' It's hard for Will to get those words out as it means he will have less reason to see Marjorie – but surely he can find other ways, especially if Marjorie is willing, which she seems to be. Indeed, he would describe her as eager to be in his company. He smiles to himself and then becomes aware that Knox is glaring at him.

'What is being said?'

'That you are an adulterer.' The words burst from Will's lips. He did not mean to be so brutal, wanted to frame it more tactfully. But it's true, that is what's being said.

Knox tugs on his long nose. 'There is an easy solution,' he mumbles, and pushing past Will he leaves the church.

Will follows slowly homeward. The numbers of destitute soldiers seem greater than ever. He turns to gaze at one man lying against a wall, the stump of his leg covered in filthy bandages and his nose half-eaten away, no doubt by the great pox. Knox has spoken to his parishioners about providing a feeding station for these men but the project has not advanced as it might, so taken up has Knox been by his pastoral care for Elizabeth Bowes. Will resolves to make it a priority to address the soldiers' needs.

But when he arrives at their lodgings all thoughts of anything but his Marjorie are banished. Knox is smiling, Elizabeth Bowes is beaming and Richard Bowes is in the corner looking much put upon. John Knox and Marjorie Bowes are to be wed.

In that moment of telling, and while he tries to compose himself to offer the happy couple his felicitations, Will knows his time with Knox, and hopes of a ministry under his patronage, are at an end. He cannot remain here.

Part Five

Bethia & Will

August to October 1549

Chapter Forty-Five

Preparations

Papa returns home sighing wearily. 'The Florentines and the Genoese are fighting over who gets precedence in the parade,' he says. 'But at least we do not have the Venetians to contend with, for they would demand to be first above all.'

Bethia hurries to the kitchens to fetch him some ale, while Mama leads him to his chair and kneels to remove his boots. He leans back in the seat while Mama, Katheline, and Bethia wait in various stages of impatience for him to recover enough to tell his news. Mainard returns while Papa draws breath, strolling into the room and flinging himself down on the settle next to Bethia, his long legs stretched out in front of him. He reaches to take her hand and squeezes it.

Papa opens his eyes and looks to Mainard. 'Well, my son, how goes it?'

Mainard releases Bethia's hand and stands up. 'We are working as fast as we can, and hope all will be finished on time.'

Bethia winces, pressing her hand against her side. Both men pause and look to her, while Mama half rises and Katheline watches from her seat.

Bethia waves her arm. ''Tis nothing. Only an elbow in my ribs.'

They all relax and Mainard sits down, lightly patting her belly. 'That's my strong boy.'

Mama raises her eyebrows and Papa averts his gaze at such spousal familiarity. Only Katheline smiles.

'Can none of the other merchant groups do anything to resolve the dispute between Florence and Genoa?' inquires Mama.

'We have all had our disagreements. Indeed, we Portuguese merchants needed to be firm with those arrogant Englishmen, who think dominance in the cloth trade means they are superior to all.' A laugh escapes him. 'But, at the end of the day, we, and the Fuggers, prevailed. Trade in cloth is as nothing to having the king in debt to you – and between us and the South Germans, Emperor Charles borrowings have become very great.'

'And how can this dispute be resolved?' asks Bethia.

Papa looks over at her in surprise, and Mainard nudges her foot with his. She ignores him. Soon she will be a mother, and her standing within the house changed from the moment she knew all their secrets and yet, in the end, chose to stay. She waits, refusing to yield to the invisible pressure to lower her eyes.

'Letters are being written,' Papa says slowly, gazing at his son.

Bethia tells herself that she doesn't care if he looks at her or not, at least she's hearing about the state of play between merchants, for she still endeavours, even after two years in Antwerp, to understand the strange workings of this most powerful of cities.

Mainard again squeezes her hand. 'And what do the letters say?'

Papa stands up. 'The Genoese claim that they had precedence in both Granada in 1526 and then at Charles's coronation in Bologna in 1530. The Florentines counterclaim that they were not present at either Granada or Bologna and therefore the Genoese claims are an irrelevance – and refer to events nigh on a quarter of a century ago. The world has changed much since then.'

A ripple of laughter runs through his listeners and Papa's normally solemn face softens into a smile.

'And how is it to be resolved?' asks Bethia.

Mainard shakes his head imperceptibly, but she will not be silenced. Her own father allowed, even encouraged, questions, and she is still his daughter.

Papa shakes his head too, but as he speaks, Bethia understands he's shaking his head about what he has to say, and not at her. 'We have reached an impasse. All that can be done is for the two delegations to lay their case before the emperor and let him decide. My advice to both would be not to do such a thing. It will only incur his displeasure, and this is a time to seek favour.' He stands up. 'Of course, every guild wants to lead the procession, to show that they're the most powerful as well as Charles's most loyal subjects, but sometimes discretion is the wiser course. Of greater concern are the problems with our triumphal arch.' He gestures to Mainard. 'Come, my son, I would appreciate your advice given your growing artistry.'

Colour suffuses Mainard's face to have his father praise him. Bethia feels a lump in her throat as she watches them leave together. She knows how much this moment will mean to Mainard; his future as a maker of maps, and not a trader of goods, finally acknowledged before the family.

She heaves herself off the settle and follows them out.

'Bethia,' Mama calls.

She stops halfway out the door.

'Where are you going?'

'To rest in my chamber.'

'Very good.'

She climbs the stairs wearily. She wants to go out into the streets and watch the triumphal arches grow in size, as each group tries to outdo the next for cleverness of metaphor and intricacy of sculpture. She wants to watch

271

the guilds practise their tableau and the hundreds of carpenters at work. Instead, she bows her head over her sewing knowing that, as her pregnancy advances, she is safer in the cool high-ceilinged rooms of this tall house than out in the crowded, noxious streets where who knows what pestilence may be spreading. And it's not so bad to sew as it would once have been, for she is preparing for the coming of her child, a far more joyous entry than any king and his princely son come to visit.

It is late evening now and she's half dozing in her chair when Mainard peeps his head around the door, placing his finger to his lips when she exclaims at the sight of him. He wraps her shawl around her shoulders and whispers in her ear. 'I know you want to see the preparations, and it cannot hurt to go out into the streets now it's cooler and there are fewer people about.'

She kisses his cheek, pleased by his thoughtfulness and suppressing a twinge of shame that she once, even for a moment, wished she'd chosen Gilbert Logie instead of Mainard as her husband. They creep down the stairs and turn the key slowly in the front door. It clicks loudly in the silent hallway. Bethia covers her mouth with her hand to contain a giggle as Mainard slides the door wide and they make good their escape.

The air in the street is balmy rather than stifling, although the smell rising from the nearby canal, as ever, has her covering her face with the edge of her shawl. It feels as though she's been a prisoner within the house for months, albeit willingly, for she will do anything to be delivered safely of this child. But he is big and active in her womb now; she knows this one is strong.

There are men working even though the sun is long set. The curfew has been relaxed, for the city must work night and day to complete the preparations in time. Many have stripped to the waist, and the torchlight plays across their skin. There's something otherworldly about watching them swarming over the structures like large fiery devils. The designer moves anxiously among them, regularly calling out for them to take care.

'And this is only one of many that van Aelst is overseeing,' Mainard says.

Bethia has glimpsed some of the structures from her window – shifting from one side to the other to see – but nothing has prepared her for the scale of the work.

'Come, I would take you to the gate through which Charles and Philip will enter.'

They pass beneath a triumphal arch and Bethia stands in its centre looking up. 'It's like a temple.'

Mainard nods enthusiastically. 'Good, it is indeed – the design inspired by the Temple of Janus. And see how they have used the colossi to look as though they are supporting the whole structure. It's the story of Antwerp; our wealth and industry is a foundation for the emperor's greatness. But I want to show you the German arch.'

Bethia stands before it, amazed. The white marble of the double arch glows ghostly in the night. Beneath the arch, tall niches have been carved. She points. 'What is to go here?'

'Golden statutes, one of Charles and one of Philip, will be lowered into place closer to the day, for they will need guarding. Opposite will be the figures of two women, one carrying a golden trumpet in her hands, the other a golden pen in her right hand and a golden book in her left.'

Bethia stares up at the inscriptions already carved above the niches. Mainard borrows a torch from a sconce, ignoring the men at work who grumble at the withdrawal of their light.

'Immortalis fama,' she reads. 'I suppose that refers to the emperor and his son. Their fame will never die.'

'And Disciplina,' says Mainard, waving his hand to the other inscription. 'Learning and Immortal Fame – the perfect combination.'

She takes his arm and leans into him. 'I think it's what

we aspire to in Antwerp. A citizenry who are full of learning can write and speak with great eloquence and are then able to contribute fully to a civil, sorry, I mean civic, life.'

He laughs. 'I think we want them to be civil too: virtuous and engaged sinjorens.'

They walk on, arm in arm, towards the Emperor Gate, through which the emperor and his son will make their grand entry.

'I sense you feel a great connection with this city,' she says

Mainard sighs. 'I had not realised how strong until recently. It will be difficult should we have to leave.'

'Surely it will not come to that?'

Mainard gazes at her. 'Who knows. It seems the Prince of Spain is a very different man to his father, and he knows little of the Low Countries, having rarely visited, whereas Charles was born here. The city fathers will do their best, of course, and much of the pageant will give a message that, while acknowledging Philip as our future sovereign, it's best we are dealt with as a city apart.'

'But Charles is still the emperor.'

'Only for the time being. He suffers much from the gout, and it seems, most unusually, has a mind to abdicate in favour of his son, ending his days quietly in some monastery in Spain. Some say he would already have departed if he were more confident in Philip's ability to rule wisely. And, in any case, we merchants of Portugal especially need both father and son to leave us free to trade without the burden of the most recent edict.'

Bethia gasps. But it is not at Mainard's words. She drops his arm and sprints, as much as a heavily pregnant woman can. There is a tall man in front of them, taller even than Mainard. She tugs on the back of his jerkin and he turns to look down on her.

She stares up into his face to make certain it is indeed who she thinks, and scarcely believing what she's seeing, she wraps her arms around him.

Chapter Forty-Six

The Visit

Will was later to say that he received a more joyous welcome to Antwerp than the emperor. His sister hugs him tight, seemingly reluctant to let go. Her unfeigned delight warms a heart which he has done his utmost to seal off. She wants him to return with her and Mainard to their home, but when Will realises the wider family live there too, he shakes his head.

'It would not be seemly for its master to awaken tomorrow and find an uninvited guest installed.

'But you are invited. I'm inviting you, for it is my home too.'

'Best I come tomorrow and be properly introduced, rather than be discovered in my nightshirt.'

'How Grissel would shriek.'

'Grissel,' he says fondly. 'I am glad to learn she's here with you. But I will come tomorrow, in the daylight.' He can see his new brother is relieved. 'Let me begin on proper terms with the family, Bethia.'

She holds on tight to his arm. 'You promise you will not vanish, like a ghost of the night?'

'I promise,' he says, and lifting her hand from his arm, he makes a courtly leg, bows, and kisses it.

He has to give her directions as to where he is staying and, once Mainard is satisfied that Will can find his way back to the inn at the harbour, he's permitted to leave them. But he's too elated to sleep. He paces the streets marvelling at the wealth of this city. The sun rises as he stops before yet another immense structure, this time erected in the central square, where he assumes the markets are normally held. Indeed, there are some disgruntled men and women trying to set out their food stalls in the space left to them, where he stops to purchase a few apples.

'What is to be here?' he asks, in French, and fortunately the man understands him.

'Nine joys and six sorrows,' says the stallholder, and spits. 'But the joy is all for the rich folks and the sorrows for the poor working man. By tomorrow we'll not even have this cramped place to sell from, for they're to erect a large hall for the showing of the tableaux.'

He spits again, a fuller, yellower blob of mucus landing at Will's feet. But nothing can dull Will's happiness today. He leaves, thinking what a miserable fellow the man is and forgets him as he walks swiftly towards the quayside, determined not to stop or be distracted by any further wonders, for the moment.

Mainard sends a man-servant, as promised, to guide Will to the family home. He tells Will his name is Coort, his pretty face marred by a scowl when he speaks.

Will can see Coort would prefer to trail behind but he slows his pace so they are abreast, where the crowds of workers allow it. 'The city is very large.'

Grunt.

'And the preparations for the visit of the emperor most extensive.'

Grunt.

'They were erecting a giant in the market last night.'

Grunt.

'I should think Grissel must enjoy it very much. She was aye a lass who liked excitement.'

Coort turns and stares at Will, who keeps walking.

So that's how it is, thinks Will.

Bethia rushes down the stairs to greet him. He wonders how much longer she has until the birth. There's no sign of any other children, so this must be her first. Perhaps his laconic brother-in-law does not have the vigour required. Will frowns. What is happening to him? Since he left John Knox, his connection with the Lord, and proper-thinking, seems to have deserted him.

He stares at the painting hanging on the wall behind his sister's head. It's a huge rendition of Antwerp seen from across the wide River Scheldt. He's only seen paintings of such scale and size in St Andrews cathedral before, and they were, inevitably, scenes from the Bible. The de Langes must make a good living to afford such art.

He's guided into a chamber where the family are all gathered: father, mother, and a sister, Katheline. Will makes his obeisance and they respond with great courtesy. He's invited to sit and pleasantries are exchanged. His eyes keep drifting to Katheline's pretty face but, after the initial greeting, she keeps hers fixed on the hands resting in her lap. He can see the de Langes are curious about his presence in Antwerp. He's sure Bethia will have told her husband about him, and how he was enslaved on the galleys… but then he's by no means certain what Bethia knows. He curls his fingers to hide the callouses.

'My brother must stay here,' says Bethia, impetuously cutting across the small talk about the giant erected in the Grotte Market last night and how his name is Druon Antigoon.

Master de Lange recovers well and shows exemplary manners by immediately extending an invitation to Will, although Will can see the mistress of the house glancing across at her husband as he speaks. Will knows he should refuse, that it is enough that he can visit with his sister without biding in the same house, but Knox had little spare funds to give him, and those were mostly exhausted in paying for his passage here. If he had not found Bethia, he'd soon have been reduced to begging on the streets. He feels himself grow pale at the thought and accepts the invitation with every expression of gratitude.

Refreshments are brought by a plump lass with a sullen face. He wonders what's wrong with the servants in this house and hopes soon to see Grissel. They talk more about the preparations for the emperor's Joyous Entry and Will learns that the arch set up across from the giant is to have Emperor Charles and his son Philip erected atop it, personified as Hercules and Atlas shouldering the weight of the world together.

'I am most fortunate to have arrived at such a propitious time,' he says.

Master de Lange looks gratified. 'We are determined that the Joyous Entry to Antwerp of 1549 will live on in the annals of the world as the most magnificent entry ever staged. And our captain is producing an official report illustrated with woodcuts by the artist van Aelst, showing all the placements. It will be published in not one but three languages: Latin, French, and even Dutch.' His voice rises as he speaks and Will can see he's quite overcome with emotion.

There's silence in the room; no one seems to know what to say in response.

The younger de Lange shrugs. 'Not all are happy though. There is some complaint, especially from those whose livings are affected.'

'Yes, I met one of the disaffected in the market early this morning.' Will grins. 'He did not seem overly impressed by the magnificence of the structures being erected.'

Master de Lange waves his hand in dismissal and Will wishes that he'd held his tongue. 'We cannot satisfy everyone. As long as Charles and Philip are delighted, that's all that concerns us.'

His wife speaks to Bethia… in what sounds like a

strange kind of Spanish Then she smiles at Will, but it is a mere moving of the lips and does not reach the eyes. Bethia pushes herself to the edge of the settle, hand pressed at the small of her back. But before Will can move to help her, de Lange stands up, reaching down to pull his wife to her feet. He places his arm around her back protectively, leaning down to whisper in Bethia's ear. Will watches the de Lange family watching. The father gives a slight nod, the mother a half-smile, but the sister returns to gazing at her lap. Mainard releases Bethia and she looks to Will, but before they can leave the chamber the door bursts open. A woman bustles in, carrying a child, which rests on her large belly. Will tries not to stare; is she pregnant too?

'Ah, Papa, I am glad I found you here,' she exclaims. 'But why are you all lingering today, when there is much to do?' She turns around and her eyes fall on Will.

'May I introduce my elder daughter, Geertruyt,' says Master de Lange. 'You must excuse her, Master Seton, for she's always in a great hurry.'

Geertruyt ignores his words and puts the small boy down, who runs to Bethia. The younger de Lange catches the child before he knocks Bethia back onto the settle, and swings him high. The lad shrieks with delight.

Geertruyt extends her hand and Will bows low over it.

'Oh, my dear, you must be so happy to see him,' she calls out to Bethia. She looks to Will. 'Your sister has often spoken of her family to me.'

Will feels gratified, and made more welcome by this loud, plump woman in a few moments than he has after near an hour of stilted conversation with the whole family. He catches Katheline's eye and she scowls at him. It's a shame to have a pretty face marred by such a sour expression.

'I'm sorry, I cannot tarry,' says Geertruyt, 'but I would hope to have the opportunity to speak with you further. You will no doubt be here for some weeks.'

Will tries to keep his face impassive, doesn't want to reveal that he has no idea yet what his movements will be. Knox and he didn't part on ill terms, but he cannot return, especially as Knox seemed fully aware of Will's tendre for Marjorie, saying 'it was for the best' that Will go. And Will did not demur, for he'd already determined the same.

'Papa, there is such a to-do about the arch. Peter is at his wits end. Can you come and see what's happening and give us your excellent advice?'

Will catches Mainard's eye, and Mainard winks. Will realises that it's not Papa's advice that's sought, so much as his purse.

Chapter Forty-Seven

Excitement Abounds

Bethia can hardly bear to let go of Will. She wants to hold his arm, lean into him, reach up and stroke his cheek. Yet he looks so different. He's not grown any taller, thanks be to the Virgin, otherwise he'd need his own special doors cut to enter any house, but his shoulders have broadened, and when she touches him he seems to be all sinew and little flesh. She can imagine any vagrant, however desperate, would think twice before attacking Will, for he holds himself like a man who fears nothing, and one swing of that giant fist would send most men crashing.

'They should use you in a tableau vivant to play Hercules,' she says, as she leads him upstairs.

A smile flits across his face. She studies it, drawing close to him and staring up.

'Did you suffer very much?'

'I take it that Papa told you?'

She reaches up and strokes his cheek. 'Yes.'

He straightens his back. 'It was hard, but it is over. I'm a freed man and would prefer never to think of the galleys again.'

She makes the sign of the cross. He frowns, turning his head away.

'And still an adherent of the Protestant cause?'

'Of course.'

She bites down on her lip, wants to say, then why have you come here? But instead says, 'You have red-gold in your beard, like Father.'

He strokes it absent-mindedly. She opens the door to his chamber and he goes over to the bed and presses on the mattress. 'This looks to be comfortable.'

'Yes, it is a most well-appointed home.'

'You seem happy.'

She touches her swelling belly, feeling her face soften. 'Once I am safely delivered of this child, then my happiness will be complete.' She pushes away any thought of the shadow cast by the secrets of this house.

'You have no other children?'

'This is the first I have carried to full term, or near full term.' She turns her face away from him, does not want to remember the anguish of losing her babies.

Mainard appears in the doorway and the chamber suddenly feels crowded. 'I must go. Everything needs to be done and there are not enough hands to do it. Perhaps you may like to join me?'

'Yes, I would be most interested,' says Will, stepping around the bed, ready to leave.

She cannot help the look of disappointment.

'Tomorrow then,' says Mainard, glancing at her. 'I cannot deprive Bethia of your company so soon after your arrival.'

She looks at him gratefully.

'I will see you this evening, my love,' he says, kissing her on the cheek, and is gone.

'We'll sit in the salon. It'll be empty at this time, for everyone is busy, and we can have a good uninterrupted blether.'

They grin at one another over the familiar Scots word which Bethia has enjoyed wrapping her tongue around.

'I must see Grissel too.'

Ah, yes. Coort and Marisse cannot have mentioned your arrival, else she would have been among us before now.'

'Still the same old Grissel.'

She nods. 'Still the same old Grissel.'

'She'll have been a comfort to you in a strange place,' he says as they descend the stairs.

'Often more of a liability.'

'I see you have some tales to tell,' he says as she opens the kitchen door wide.

Grissel is standing at the board stirring a bowl. The spurtle goes flying, and with it great dollops of the mix spray the room. Marisse turns from the fire, angry-faced, and tugs the pap out of the back of her hair.

Grissel doesn't care. She's screaming. 'Will, it's you. Will, you great gowk, where have you come from?'

'Master Will,' says Bethia, severely.

'Aye, aye right. Master Will, where have you come from, you great gowk.'

Will roars with laughter and Bethia notices that even Marisse allows a smile to creep across her face. Marisse and Grissel, most likely both realising they had gone too far after their fight a year ago, have formed an uneasy truce. Indeed, Bethia's impressed they've managed to hold to it for so long, especially with Coort shifting favourites as he plays them off against each other – although Bethia has noticed that lately Grissel no longer returns Coort's smiles; hopefully she's finally discovered what a cunning trickster he is.

She glances over to see Coort watching from the corner of the board, a substantial repast spread before him. Bethia is certain that the roasted eggs, sliced beef, the remains of the chicken from the family's meal, and especially the dates imported from North Africa which sell for a goodly price in the market, is not fare that Mama would approve for her servants. She purses her lips and Coort dips his head, but not before she catches him glowering at her. Marisse bustles in front of him blocking Bethia's view and, when she can see again, the beef and dates are gone.

284

Grissel is hanging on Will's arm in a most familiar way. Bethia shrugs; he's enjoying the adoration. When they leave the kitchen, Grissel follows; like Bethia she seems reluctant to let Will out of her sight. Bethia understands, but she needs to speak to Will alone, and if she doesn't soon seize the opportunity the family will return, and Geertruyt will most likely insist on joining them to find out what she can. She's fearful that Will may reveal his adherence to the Protestant faith, knows this would not be well received within the house. Life here is complicated enough, she reflects, without adding a further religion to the mix.

It seems Mainard has considered the challenge she may face in speaking with her brother alone. There's a knock on the door and outside a carriage awaits, which has room for two people only, the driver sitting high in front. Grissel suggests she could join them, perching alongside the driver, but Mama appears and sends Grissel about her work.

Mama mutters that she does not know what Mainard is about; this is not a suitable conveyance for a heavily pregnant woman. Will responds, in halting Spanish, promising to take great care of Bethia.

Mama smiles at him. He has to give Bethia a pull, and Mama a push, to help her up. They squeeze in together as Mama instructs the driver he must only walk the horse and on no account trot. Bethia feels tearful to be so well-cared-for, and relief that Mama is not insisting she rest at home.

'Where did you learn Spanish?' she asks as they set off.

'In a most interesting and unusual school,' he says wryly. 'I was fettered to a Spaniard for a time on the galleys.'

She swallows. 'Mainard knows of course, but best not mention that to the de Langes.'

'I am not a fool, Bethia.'

'Sorry, I just needed to be sure.'

The carriage weaves through the workmen, around triumphal arches, past crafts guilds practising their tableaux, out the city gates and into the countryside. She remembers it's the same route she travelled with Gilbert when he visited over a year ago.

'Gilbert Logie was here.'

'I know, that's how I found you.'

She gasps. 'When did you see Gilbert?'

'Not long after he visited you, I suspect. We were transporting the wee queen to France, and I was one of her forsares.'

'You saw the queen?'

'Not only saw her, I spoke with her one day. She's a comely lass with a gentle manner.'

'That's good to know, since she will one day rule Scotland.' She strokes her top lip. 'Did Gilbert arrange your release?'

He shakes his head. 'He can manage many things with his bonny smile and suave manner, but that was beyond even him. My freedom was contrived from quite another source. Protector Somerset had a hand in it, I believe.'

'What?'

'To be honest, it was not me that England requested be released, but John Knox. Knox told them I was his assistant and must travel with him. I was of small import, so I think the French didn't overly care.' He scratches the back of his hand. 'You are no doubt wondering why I'm not with Knox at this moment.'

'I'm just happy to see you. I cannot express how happy I am to have a family member visit.'

'Ach' – he nudges her – 'so any Seton would do, even Mother.'

She smiles. 'Even Mother.'

Then they are both laughing while the driver reaches out the bag on a long stick to deftly catch the horse's dung.

'This is truly a city of marvels,' he says, which makes them laugh harder.

But what did happen with John Knox?' Bethia asks as she wipes her eyes.

Suddenly he looks weary. 'I hoped to train as his assistant, that one day I might become a priest myself.' He scratches again at his hand and she notices he's drawn blood. 'But I am no longer certain that's my path.'

She doesn't know what to say to comfort him.

They sit in silence as the carriage turns for home. She resists asking what his plans are and how long he's staying, doesn't want her questions misconstrued.

As they enter the city gates he speaks again. 'Does Father correspond with you often?'

'Of course. Although I insisted on marrying Mainard, we did not part on ill terms.'

'Did he want you to marry Logie?'

She stares at him. 'Gilbert told you he offered?'

'No, of course not, but it wasn't difficult to guess. I'm sure that everything he did to make my life more comfortable was in service of you – poor fool.'

She tosses her head. 'Why should doing things for me make him a fool? He's a kind man who wishes to help others.'

'Hah! I doubt he would go to so much effort for anyone picked off the street. ''Tis kinder of you not to string him along.'

'What are you talking about? I can hardly string anyone along… look at me!' She strokes her huge belly, feeling the child sitting high below her bosom.

'But you were not in this state when he visited last summer.'

'Nevertheless I am a married woman.'

He snorts. 'That wouldn't stop you making cow-eyes at him.'

She glares back at him. It hasn't taken long for them to have their first fight, she thinks. Will stares straight ahead, face flushed. This isn't about me, she realises, but before she can frame a question, he nudges her and grins, and she nudges him back.

Sooner than she wished, they're back at the de Langes' front door – her front door she reminds herself. She opens her mouth to speak, to ask Will what he is going to do now he's no longer following his passion, but suddenly Papa is among them, brow creased and shoulders hunched, as though he is Atlas carrying the weight of the world.

Chapter Forty-Eight

The English Merchant

Will can see that Master de Lange is deeply concerned about something but doesn't feel it's his place to ask. He follows Bethia inside trying to block from his mind that he cannot stay here indefinitely. He knows his sister is curious about what his plans are and he would be more than pleased to tell her, if he only knew the answer. And the family, they have been welcoming so far but will soon begin to wonder if they're expected to take him in as well as Bethia. And there is something strange about them. He cannot express it. The strangeness may only be that they're citizens of Antwerp, but why do the mother and pretty Katheline speak in that strange Spanish to one another?

Bethia whispers she has an urgent need of the privy and slips away. He follows Master de Lange... doesn't know what else to do. The old man seems surprised to find Will behind him, but he's nothing if not courteous and rings the bell, ordering the grinning Grissel to fetch them a drink. Will is impressed that Grissel understands Dutch. The languages spoken in this house make him dizzy as the inhabitants flow from French to Dutch to Spanish to English.

He loiters by the window and then decides he need not wait for the master of the house to speak first. Will himself is a man now, a man amongst men. 'You seem concerned, sir?'

'It's only the arrangements for the celebration, which we must endeavour to make certain is not only magnificent…' – he pauses, staring at Will from under thick eyebrows, an expression that very much reminds Will of his own father – 'you are family. I may speak freely?'

'Of course.' Will is flattered to be so addressed and draws closer to Master de Lange.

'Philip is a very different calibre of man from his father. He feels little affinity to the Low Countries; indeed, this is his first visit, made more challenging since it seems he speaks only Castilian.'

Will blinks, reminding himself there are more Castilians in the world than the group he was among who held St Andrews Castle.

Fortunately Master de Lange is too intent on his own troubles to note Will's reaction. 'He and the Emperor Charles have been travelling for near on nine months. Their Joyous Entry to Antwerp is one amongst very many and we are eager that Antwerp stand high above the rest.'

Will nods as Master de Lange's forehead creases deep as a crumpled shirt.

'In Ghent they held a battle between an elephant and a tiger, or perhaps the tiger was pitted against a cow and the pachyderm against a rhino.' He shakes his head. 'We have fireworks. But will that be enough?'

'I have heard that fireworks are a wondrous spectacle.'

Master de Lange nods, as though satisfied. 'The aldermen are anxious we retain the rights and privileges which make this city so successful – as are we merchants. But the Inquisition presses hard against our door and may soon knock it down. There's been much debate as to what saints and other religious figures we should include in the tableaux and arches.' He slides his hand under his hair stroking the back of his neck. 'Some argue that we should demonstrate our fealty to the Lord God and his Spanish prince with much display of religious allegories, and others that an absence of them will show Philip that Antwerp, while loyal, must not be interfered with.'

Will had noted the lack of biblical characters and the reliance on Greek myths among the triumphal arches as he walked the streets the previous evening and drove them today. It had been a relief and a sign, for him, that Antwerp might be tolerant of Protestants, but it seems he may have misunderstood.

A smile creeps across de Lange's face. 'Although, it has been most amusing in many ways. We traders originating from Portugal may have argued with our English counterparts over who should take precedence in the parade, but we are in complete agreement over keeping religion out of the tableaux.'

Will's mind is churning at the information given. Why would the Portuguese and English agree? Portugal is a devoutly Catholic nation. And the de Langes, with such a Dutch name, originate from Portugal – yet they speak a kind of Spanish amongst themselves. What is going on here? But foremost in the confusion of thoughts is the realisation that there must be a Protestant place of worship in Antwerp for its English residents, within a home at least, where he can connect with some of his own kind.

He realises that de Lange is staring at him, waiting for a response.

Will bows, saying, 'In this most wealthy city of the Holy Roman Empire even the future emperor will aspire to keep his citizens on side.' He thinks he's babbling but the master of the house looks relieved.

Will feels a new sense of energy. His body seems lighter, no longer weighed down by his failure with John Knox, and he will not think of sweet Marjorie… will banish her from his thoughts forever. Instead, he will seek some of his own kind. And, although this family is welcoming, they are papists. Indeed, he has never been in a home with so many crosses hung, apart from, curiously, his bed-chamber. He shrugs and asks Master de Lange where the English merchants are to be found.

'You hope to transact some business?' says de Lange.

Will nods, thinking that his host looks pleased to have determined some purpose for Will's visit. Master de Lange sends for his man-servant and gives orders that Coort is to lead Will to the exchange where the English merchants are to be found.

Bethia looks surprised when she finds Will, dressed in bonnet and short cloak, on his way out. He tells her he has an errand to run. She looks dubious, but he sidles past and follows Coort out the front door.

Will stands in the entranceway of the Bourse, where Coort has left him, feeling his shoulders constrained by his overly tight jerkin and wondering if he'll ever stop growing. He gazes around him, has never seen a building of such scale and grandiosity, even in France, and all dedicated to the pursuit of money. There are small groups of men engaged in deep discussion punctuated by the occasional burst of laughter wherever he looks in this long space of colonnades and arches. A man, hook-nosed and big-bellied, glances over at him, turns back to his companions, says a few words, and strolls over to where Will is dithering under the archway.

'Bonjour.'

'Good day,' Will responds.

'Ah, you are from… the north of England?'

'Far north. I am a Scot.'

The man's smile fades. 'And what does a Scot do here in Antwerp?'

'Flee from his papist countrymen.'

The man grasps Will's elbow and leans in to speak to him. 'It is as well it was me you spoke to. Do not assume, my lad, that all Englishmen are converts to Luther.'

'I know, having recently come from Berwick, where

many are still attached to the old ways.'

The man tuts. 'Berwick, you say... barely England, and a rough town by all accounts, laddie. But I am most remiss. I am Nicholas Chauncey, of London.' He bows.

Will bows, lower. 'And I am William Seton, of St Andrews.'

Chauncey pauses. 'Ah, I have heard of your town. There was trouble, not so long ago.'

Will nods agreement, but doesn't elaborate. The past should stay well behind him. 'I have most recently been in Berwick as an assistant to John Knox.' He stops abruptly, wants to bite his own tongue. What was he thinking to mention he was Knox's assistant, now he'll have to explain why he's no longer with him.

'A most redoubtable man, Master Knox, or so I've heard. Wait here, lad. I will conclude my business and then we can talk uninterrupted, for I see you have a story to tell.'

Will waits patiently; he has nothing else to do. He wishes Chauncey would stop calling him lad. It reminds him of Father. Yet whoever thought there would come a time when he would want so very much to see the old bugger again.

Chauncey is not long in returning and leads him along the busy street to an inn. 'You have joined us at a most exciting, and critical, time,' he says, once they're seated with a beaker of ale each before them. He sticks out his chin, stretching his neck in a way that reminds Will of that strange bird, a parrot, which his Aunt Jennet keeps in a cage in her house in Edinburgh. Beautiful to look upon, until it opens it mouth, and most odoriferous to the chamber within which it's kept.

He realises Chauncey is waiting for him to speak. This is the second time today he's had a man look expectantly at him with no idea why. He must stop wool-gathering. A yawn escapes him; he barely slept last night, nor the many before since it was decided he would leave Berwick.

Flushing, he apologises for his inattention.

'I asked what brings you to Antwerp.'

Will decides a straight answer is the simplest. 'My sister lives here, with her husband's family. You may know them, for they are merchants too: the de Langes.'

Chauncey's eyes grow large. 'Well that is most strange. You are assistant to an increasingly renowned Protestant preacher and yet say that your sister is married to a Marrano – do not be fooled by their Dutch name. They all take them to disguise their origin.'

Will blinks. He's heard the word somewhere before, but cannot remember what it means.

'A Converso, a Crypto-Jew,' elaborates Chauncey. 'What brought about such a marriage contract? Your father was perhaps in debt to the de Langes?'

Will bristles. 'My father is a most careful man and, in any case, would never exchange my sister in payment of a debt.'

A servant places a platter before them. Will stretches his clenched fingers, while Chauncey pokes at the food with his knife.

'They come from Portugal, you know. We have many Marranos from that country fleeing though Antwerp, although the emperor has not permitted any new Conversos to settle here these past ten years.' He leans forward, lowering his voice. 'Many go to the Ottomans and are welcomed for the wealth they bring... my enemy's friend cannot be my friend.'

What else are they do to, Will thinks, when they are squeezed out from one country to the next.

Chauncey leans back, arms behind his head. Will feels a strong urge to punch him in the fat belly which is so casually exposed. If Chauncey calls him lad one more time, he'll do it.

'But the de Langes have converted. They are Christian, albeit Catholics,' he says, trying to keep his voice level and calm: a man's voice.

'I know the de Langes are converts, of that there is no argument. I have seen the son in the cathedral at Mass and indeed taking confession. Most pious,' Chauncey's nose wrinkles… 'But he has the look of a Jew and all his piety cannot disguise it. It's in his very blood and cannot be expunged.' Chauncey gives a snort of laughter. 'Just as it's in your blood that you are a fiery Scotsman.'

Will stands up. He cannot listen to this arrogant Englishman one moment longer.

Chauncey also leaps to his feet, with surprising speed for a porcine man, and grabs Will's arm. 'All I am saying, lad, is take care. Charles issued an edict only last month revoking the privileges he once permitted New Christians and requiring any that have sought refuge in Antwerp within the last six years to leave. And when the Prince of Spain moves onto his father's throne he will tolerate no Jews, whether they claim to have converted or not, and no matter how long they have lived here. Your sister is in a most perilous position.'

Will shakes off Chauncey's hand and leaves without a backward glance. He doesn't know what to do with the information that Chauncey has imparted. God's blood, he wishes he'd never met him. He feels no desire to be in his company further, Lutheran or no.

He thinks of the family he's been welcomed into, and yet how Conversos are described. There are no Jews in Scotland, so far as he knows. He's never met one, never heard tell of one even among the Scottish Court, which includes peoples from many parts of the world. It is surprising there are none for it seems to him that the Jews are a most useful people to have inhabiting your country; they can be blamed for everything, saving both God and the king from responsibility.

He stops and leans against a wall, trying to calm himself. The streets are as busy as ever. He watches as a group work on yet another triumphal arch – how many does one city need to build before their fealty is assured?

He takes off his bonnet and brushes the back of his hand across his forehead, thinking the city is trying too hard. If he was Charles he'd wonder if this wasn't as much, indeed more, about the city displaying its strength and wealth as celebrating their great emperor. Interfere with us at your peril, it shouts, for we are your money-house.

He scratches at the back of his hand yet again, realising it's raw and weeping. He must get some unguent to soothe it. But it's of minor import next to the thoughts he's having, which are all wrong. It must be tiredness, for he is a faithful subject of the Lord, a follower of Luther, Calvin and Erasmus… and John Knox. No, he was once a follower of Knox but the man has lost his way, seduced by a congregation that hang on his every word, and especially by the women. He thinks of their parting. Knox actually sent him away – ordered him to Geneva. Said that Will should get some polish before he could be any use as an assistant, for he was but a laddie yet. That word again; yet there are not many men who have endured what he has and survived.

Suddenly his new brother is before him. Will looks into Mainard's open friendly face and, conscious of what he knows, cannot help flushing. His face grows red and redder while Mainard gazes at him curiously.

Chapter Forty-Nine

Ortelius

'Aye, Seton, I see you are in a brown study. Would you care to join me and I can show you the work I am engaged upon?'

Will flips the bonnet back on his hot head, saying, 'Thank you, de Lange, I would be most interested.'

And he is most interested, indeed enthralled, by the cartography that's being produced with cleverness and care, and which is displayed to him with such enthusiasm.

'We're working on a small book which will be gifted to the prince of Spain as more evidence of what this greatest city of his realm can produce,' Ortelius explains.

Will cannot believe how young they all are, and even Ortelius's sister Elizabeth is engaged in the work. Both Ortelius and de Lange are eager to explain the meaning, symbolism and boundaries of map-making. De Lange's face is alight as he describes how they scale what they draw. Will watches him. That's how I used to look when debating the works of Luther and Calvin, he thinks. He feels crumpled and small, has lost his passion. Even when he was chained to the oar his faith did not desert him. Indeed, many times he felt uplifted, knowing that he was suffering as Jesus had.

Watching them, he notices how often Ortelius finds

297

reason to pause and come stand by de Lange, leaning in close and once even draping his arm over de Lange's shoulder. It reminds him of his friend Nydie. And the bonny Elizabeth finds reason to touch her tongue to her top lip whenever she's speaking to de Lange, and once even to take out her handkerchief and pat the perspiration from her bosom. He settles back in his chair highly entertained. If Mainard had shown the slightest interest, or even awareness, of their advances then Will would've been all concern for his sister. But he seems genuinely oblivious – all attention on the task in hand, and Will thinks neither the Florenzer nor the flirt stand a chance. He's relieved to see this evidence of de Lange's devotion to Bethia, wonders if he even realises that Ortelius is likely a sodomist.

Mainard, although busy, pauses to accompany Will home once evening falls and they break their fast. 'Ortelius's family came to Antwerp from Augsburg only a few years ago,' he says as they walk.

Will nods, not much interested.

'They were suspected of a leaning towards Luther.'

Will stares at de Lange, stopping so abruptly that a portly man behind barrels into him. The streets are seething with men at work, guilds practising their tableaux, and vendors shouting as loud as they can above the hubbub so further conversation is impossible. He ponders what de Lange has told him of Ortelius and wonders if he might find a true fellow believer in him. He doubts it somehow; Ortelius is all about his maps.

Bethia is resting and the family are elsewhere so they eat alone. Will leans his elbows on the board chewing on a leg of rabbit, which has been roasted to perfection. 'I'm surprised that your father permitted you to engage in cosmography. I cannot imagine my father ever releasing me from accounting books.'

De Lange inclines his head. 'He didn't agree, not at first. Indeed he was most unhappy. I used to go at night, and learn by candlelight. It wasn't easy, and Papa allowed it so long as I was available to him during the day. But oh those ledgers and figures and the dreary dustiness of it all.'

Will can't stop his head from bobbing up and down in agreement. 'How did you gain his approval to release you?'

De Lange shrugs. 'I don't know that I have. One day I didn't go to the warehouse. Papa still talks to me of the business, and I'm interested to listen, as much for the exchange with him as anything.'

'He should get Bethia to assist him. Our father found her to be a most willing, and useful, helpmeet.'

Mainard shifts in the chair. 'Bethia will soon be fully occupied in caring for our child, and, God willing, more shall follow.'

Will stares at his brother-in-law.

'What is it?'

'It's nothing.'

'I think not with your mouth working away like a gasping fish.'

They both laugh, and in this moment Will realises he likes his new brother and thinks they could be friends, were it not for the deep pit of unanswered questions which lie between them.

'What did your father say when you returned from Scotland with a bride?' he blurts out. 'Did he know, was he expecting it?' He pauses. 'I'm sorry, that was most discourteous. But you must understand I have concerns for my sister's welfare.'

It's as though a mask has been drawn across Mainard's face. 'My family were most welcoming.'

That's not what I asked, thinks Will.

'And Bethia's happiness is my abiding concern, never doubt that. I cherish her most dearly.'

But is she safe? Will wants to ask. He thinks of Chauncey's harsh words and shivers. He chews on the meat considering what he should do, thinking of the de Langes. There is tension here that's beyond the normal family give and take. It's in the permanently wrinkled brow of the mother, the tight jaw of the father and the downward look of the younger daughter, which seems more than simple modesty... more as though she keeps something permanently hidden. Even Mainard's easy good nature cannot completely disguise an underlying anxiety.

He's crumbling a piece of bread in his fingers when Bethia joins them. He has to slide the settle out so she can ease in, her huge belly pressing against the board. She smiles at him, her hand stroking the bump, and he closes his mouth on the question. He will not probe; his sister must remain tranquil as her time draws near.

Nevertheless, he sits tugging on an eyebrow hair until Bethia reaches out a restraining hand. 'I think you are become our father.'

His laughter sounds overly loud, even to his ears. He bids them goodnight and retreats to his chamber. His bed has the thickest goose feather mattress it has ever been his pleasure to lie upon. Despite that, he tosses and turns all night, his head thick with Chauncey's words. He rises as soon as the sun pierces the gap in the thick shutters of this wealthy home and decides to seek out Grissel, is in the mood for some banter.

The kitchen is full when he pushes the door open. They stare at him fearfully. A child wails, and the servant, whose name he has forgot, moves among them dolloping porridge into wooden bowls. They spoon it quickly into their mouths, watching Will over the rim as they eat. His belly clenches. He remembers what it's like to be hungry, and desperate. There's a weary hopelessness rising from them that's palpable: their clothes ragged, faces tired and dirty.

The back door is flung open and Grissel appears, a skinned rabbit dangling from each hand. The people stop and stare, then return to shovelling food into their mouths. Grissel drops the rabbits on the hearth and pushes her way to where Will stands. She takes his arm, tugging him into the hallway.

'What is going on?'

'Ach, dinna get your breeks in a twist. We're just gieing food to some poor folks.'

He narrows his eyes and Grissel tosses her head.

'I don't think it's usual practice to bring beggars into your kitchen,' he says, realising he sounds pompous even as the words leave his lips.

'If my mither was here she'd skelp yer arse.'

'If your mother was here she'd skelp your arse for speaking to me thus. I'm no some laddie any more.'

She turns and minces back into the kitchen, wriggling her behind as she goes.

Bethia crosses the hall and smiles at him. It's a beatific smile such as those on the face of portraits of the Virgin. His new brother comes bounding down the stairs. He has a vigour about him this morning that very much disproves any thought of his sister and a virgin birth. He thinks to ask Mainard why the family are feeding beggars in their kitchen, but he is a guest. Instead, he asks where he might find pen and paper. Mainard cordially invites Will to join him at Ortelius's again, where there is an abundance of quills, brushes, inks and paper.

Once the letter is written, Ortelius undertakes to arrange its delivery. Will thinks he's done what he can, and the matter is out of his hands. Now he must look to himself and make a plan for his future.

Chapter Fifty

Joyous Entry

Mainard has arranged for Bethia to watch the activities from the house of a friend of the family. She has an excellent view of the the stage at the Grotte Market, from the long windows especially with them flung wide. Although it did take some effort to climb the many flights of stairs to reach this viewpoint and she's breathless as she takes her seat.

Following behind are a disapproving Mama and a bright-eyed Katheline. It's good to see Katheline display some sign of excitement, Bethia thinks, for recently she has become most sombre. Bethia rubs her lower back as she sits down. It's been unaccountably painful since she first awoke early this morning, but she hasn't mentioned it to anyone for she was most determined to come – when will she ever in her life again get to witness a Joyous Entry.

The hostess has welcomed Bethia effusively, fussing around to make sure she has a good view, giving her a chair and cushions for her back, but her smiles do not reach her eyes. A dozen women make up the party, with servants hovering behind. The women nod a greeting, surreptitiously staring and whispering behind their hands. No one comes to speak to her. Bethia doesn't like it but has grown accustomed; she is accepted by neither Conversos nor Christians. It's the price she has paid to be

302

Mainard's wife.

They wait for several hours and Bethia twists and shifts in her seat until Mama, eyes narrowing, stares into Bethia's face and inquires if all is well. Bethia insists all is well, and although Mama leans back in her chair, Bethia is conscious, by how often Mama's head turns in her direction, that she's being watched. She sits as still as she can with a back that increasingly feels as though hot pokers are being applied. At last the procession enters the square and all eyes turn to watch the emperor and the prince of Spain.

Charles is certainly not a bonny man, Bethia thinks. His jaw looks so long and heavy, it must be difficult for him to close his mouth. His son is as fair as Charles is dark, with a fluff of yellow beard and, although he too has a prominent lip, his face is round as an apple. He is almost, she decides, tilting her head to one side to study him from her eyrie, attractive.

Katheline has jumped up and is half leaning out of the window to gain a better view. Bethia, twisting to see past her, feels the oddest sensation deep in her belly, as though the baby is writhing like a serpent. She pushes down with her hand and, after a moment, it settles.

The first tableau vivant has begun. A woman wearing a headdress with a tower rising so high upon it that she has to reach one arm up to hold it in place leads the way.

'Why wear one so high?' Katheline asks.

The woman of the house answers in her surprisingly deep voice. 'That is a depiction of Antwerp.' She pauses as Antwerp kneels before Philip. Even though he sits on horseback, Bethia can see that the tower comes near to his shoulder in height, but then he is a small man. 'And, although all bow before the prince, the high tower shows we do not bow too far.'

Bethia stares at her in surprise.

The woman glances around the chattering group of ladies… but everyone's attention, apart from Bethia's, is on what's happening next. 'But of course we all do bow low to him,' she mumbles, and moves away.

Charles and Philip climb down from their horses and mount the steps to the stage, where they're invited to sit on gilded thrones while the oaths of allegiance are given. Bethia wonders that the oaths are not taken in the cathedral; surely it would be more usual – and more holy. Then her back is riven by another pain and she leans forward gasping.

After what feels like a long time, but cannot be for no one has noticed, it passes and she straightens up. The sky darkens and the sun disappears behind a huge black cloud. Large drops of rain are blown through the open window and blot the floor. It's as though the Lord himself is disapproving of the excess of this great entry, or at least showing his disdain for an oath-taking that's not held beneath the roof of his house.

There are cries from outside as people scurry undercover. The rain crashes down, drumming on the street below and the roof above. The rainwater pours from the roofs like myriad waterfalls and gushes along the street.

Bethia shifts in her seat. She's feeling better, the pain has vanished. Mama has told her that often there are early, but deceptive, signs that the travail has begun. This must have been one. Indeed she feels a renewed sense of well-being and stands up to peer over the sill. The rain is lessening and stops as abruptly as it began. A servant brings her a plate of food and she picks at it as the players set themselves up on the stage once more, ready for the emperor and prince to re-emerge.

But there's a sense of disquiet arising from below. She can hear, and increasingly feel, the angry muttering of the crowd. She stands up again and stares down.

'What's wrong?' Katheline asks. Mama shushes her, but the lady of the house, who seems to be an expert on all things, says that it's only a continuation of the protests which have already taken place. Bethia is puzzled, she's heard of no protest – but then she could be living in a nunnery, so cloistered is she.

'The common folk are unhappy about the huge expenditure of this visit, even though much of it has been borne by the merchants and our guilds. And the thunderstorm will no doubt confirm to the pious that the Lord agrees with them,' she says.

Eventually the programme starts up again. They watch a tableau wherein Charles defeats his enemies; the loving father protecting his children of Antwerp, who humbly thank him with bowed heads… yet never bowed too low. But Bethia no longer cares what's happening below, or indeed above. She grips her belly and a low moan escapes her.

'I knew we should not have come,' Mama hisses. 'I should never have listened to Mainard.'

'We can prepare a chamber,' the woman of the house says, but even Bethia, in the grip of another spasm, can see the woman's pursed lips.

'That is very kind,' says Mama.

Bethia grasps Mama's arm. 'Take me home… please.'

But there is the issue of how she is to reach home, through streets overfull with people, arches, tableaux, and princes. A servant is sent to find a litter. He is gone a long time, but then it takes Bethia a long time to descend the stairs. Hands pressed against the wall, she comes slowly down, step by step, with Mama and Katheline in front, although she doubts if, even together, they could prevent a fall. Indeed they'd most likely all three go tumbling to the bottom. The thought makes her smile in the space between spasms. But soon she wishes Mama and Katheline would go away, feels a rising irritation at their backs right in front of her, and how they are constantly glancing over their shoulders. And every time she has to stop, as her body is wracked by another pain, she wants to bat away the reaching hands from the gaggle of women following behind, cackling together. Bethia bites hard on her lip; she wants to scream at them all to leave her alone.

Between one gripping pain and the next, Bethia manages to plead, exhort, order her hostess, and her friends, to go back to their viewpoints. 'A child comes any day,' she says, 'but when will you again witness a Joyous Entry, and on a scale such as this?'

They protest. They cannot leave her. Nothing is more important than to help her, but already they have halted their descent and are drifting back up the stairs, calling out their best wishes for a safe delivery. The relief when they are gone, and she is no longer hemmed in by women, is indescribable – until the next great tightening comes.

The servant has found a litter, and Bethia is loaded into the seat and carried homeward, while Mama and Katheline scurry alongside as best they can, given the reluctance of the population to let the litter pass. Then suddenly Mama is in front, a staff in her hand seized from a tableau. She's beating a path through the crowd. The owner chases after her, fists raised, but when he sees Bethia writhing in the sedan he joins Mama. Now Mama and the man, who is as broad as he is tall, are leading the charge. He pushes and she whacks, and Bethia and the litter pass through the crush and soon reach home.

Bethia is helped from the seat by the combined strength of Mama and Katheline. They rush Bethia through the door, and Mama calls over her shoulder for the helper to wait and she will recompense him. More stairs to climb but soon she is in her chamber.

'Where is Grissel? I want her,' Bethia pleads. But Grissel is out amongst the throng, as is the midwife who was to assist at the birth.

'We must manage ourselves,' says Mama, while Bethia weeps for Grissel, who means home and safety.

They want her to rest upon the bed but she cannot. She must move, as the child moves within her. And surely the baby will come soon, for this has been going on for hours.

But no, Mama shakes her head, saying it is no more than one hour since they arrived home.

Bethia puts her head back and howls. 'The Virgin protect me. Please, Blessed Mary, make this end.'

There's another flurry around her, and Mama is saying she must be calm, that this frenzied writhing is not good for the baby.

Then Katheline is holding Bethia's damp face between her too hot hands. 'Be calm, be calm,' she chants over and over. 'Say it to me, Bethia,' she insists.

Bethia shakes her head but Katheline grips tighter. 'Be calm, be calm.'

Then Bethia is panting it out herself. 'Be calm, be calm, be calm.' And it does help, for a time.

She is crouching now and pushing, a long groan of effort, when suddenly Grissel is among them. She takes the arm that Mama was supporting, and Mama drops down on the kist, wiping her sweat-drenched face with the edge of her skirt.

Bethia pushes and pushes as great waves of pain engulf her.

Then Mama is kneeling at Bethia's feet. 'A boy,' she says, smiling up at Bethia.

Grissel and Katheline guide Bethia to the bed, propping her up against the bolster. Mama places the bairn in Bethia's arms and stands gazing down upon him.

His face grows red and twisted as he squalls his fury at being thrust from a warm dark shelter into an over-bright world. Bethia, cradling her son, leans to rub her cheek against the tiny face. He stops crying and lies quiet in her arms. Gazing down upon him, she is overwhelmed by love.

Chapter Fifty-One

Denouement

Will is most surprised to arrive home and find his sister safely delivered of a son, with whom she is already besotted. He, of course, is not permitted to enter her chamber, but the new father emerges with a smile that would dazzle a dreich St Andrew's day.

'He's a big fellow, eh?' says Master de Lange, nudging his own son.

Mainard nods. Will sees he's too overcome to speak, and doesn't think any the less of him for it.

De Lange calls for wine to toast his new grandson, and the three men stand in a group together, smiling and lifting their glasses.

Will turns the finely etched glass in his hand, admiring its beauty, until he realises his companions are watching him. 'I never saw what I was drinking so well before,' he says.

Mainard's father pats him on the back; it's good to feel part of a family again. Master de Lange and his son seem to be friends as well as relations. A sigh escapes him; he wishes that such a relationship was possible with his own father.

'Come,' says de Lange, 'I'll have no gloom. We're celebrating the birth of the newest Mendoza.'

Will has seemingly not masked his confusion, for

Mainard says, 'Mendoza is our Spanish name. When we came to Antwerp, by way of Portugal, it was easier take a name more familiar locally.'

Will bites his lip. This doesn't much trouble him, but what is of concern is whether they will follow the Jewish practices he has heard of on newborn boys. 'You will baptise him?'

'Of course,' says Mainard. 'My son is a Christian.'

The pride in his voice when he says my son cannot be disguised, but Will realises he's introduced a sombre note into what is a joyous celebration, and the brief moment of belonging, of feeling a welcome member of their family, has vanished because of his foolish words. 'And what is to be my nephew's Christian name?' he says, the jollity in his voice sounding forced even in his own ears.

'It is common for us…' Mainard begins, and Will hears the hesitation and knows the us slipped out, 'to name children after a living relative. I am thinking Thomas.'

Will blinks. 'My father will be most delighted, and proud, I am sure.'

Mainard's father gazes at his son. Will is fairly certain he was unaware of the choice of name until now.

'Of course, your name too, Papa. He will be Thomas and he will also be Samuel.' Mainard waggles his head from side to side in a curiously foreign-looking gesture. 'Samuel Mendoza and Thomas de Lange, I think it all sounds very well. I shall tell my wife as soon as she awakens from her well-deserved slumber.'

It is late evening now, although the streets are noisy still. Will is surprised that the curfew isn't being enforced for the comfort of their Hapsburg guests. He retreats to his chamber and sits on the bed, rubbing his eyes.

There's a knock on his door and Mainard's face appears. 'Do you want to see your nephew?'

The baby is in his cradle, quietly snuffling, while Mainard's mother stands to one side smiling. Mainard kneels at the side of the crib and strokes the child's cheek.

Will thinks of the stories about Jews murdering Christian children for their blood and wonders what Knox would advise in this situation. Then, as he watches the wonder on Mainard's face, he doesn't care what Master Knox thinks. This is an innocent, the child of his sister, a bloodline of Scots Catholics and Jewish New Christians. He thrusts his chest out. What a rich mix, and surely only good can come from it. 'He looks to be a healthy child,' he says to Mainard's mother in halting Spanish.

Her face flushes and she shakes her head, firing words at him. He turns to Mainard.

'My mother says you must not praise the child as healthy.'

Will blinks.

'She fears it will entice the souls of the dead to take him as their own.'

They leave the nursery together and Will asks, 'What part of Spain did your mother come from? Some words she uses are unfamiliar to me.'

'She speaks Ladino,' says Mainard. 'Please excuse me, I must go to Bethia.'

Will gazes after him for a moment, then retreats to his chamber.

The next morning he rises early and again finds the kitchen full of hungry souls being fed. Mainard's mother is sitting among them, holding the hand of a young woman while she bends listening to her story.

When she sees him hesitating in the doorway she rises and wends her way over. She speaks softly, but it doesn't matter if the words are soft or loud – he cannot understand them.

Katheline appears at her side and, seeing Will's baffled face, begins to translate. 'It is a greater blessing to help others than to save ourselves alone.'

Will half smiles, but he still doesn't understand.

Mistress de Lange places her hand lightly on his arm and looks up, her eyes staring with great intensity as she searches Will's face.

'Mama says she thinks you are a good man.'

'I try to be.'

'And you are of our family now.'

Will dips his head, although he's by no means certain whether it's in acknowledgement or embarrassment.

'These people flee the Inquisition in Portugal. They cannot stay here, for the Hapsburgs forbad any further settlement some years ago.'

'Where will they go?'

'Venice and Ferrara will welcome them, but only if they are rich. Unfortunately, the old, the sick, the frail, and the very young are flowing into Antwerp like a river in spate. We must help them, even though we may lose all, for the Crown will impound our estate if it is discovered.'

Will's feels a jolt run through him. His own father said the family would lose all because of Will's heretical, and treasonous, activities when he supported the siege of St Andrews Castle. But he knew he had to do what was right in the eyes of God, and his own conscience.

'The survival of our...' she stops suddenly, swallowing her words. 'We cannot sit by and allow any children of the Lord to be exterminated; we must save them.'

Will, in a strange way that is most surprising to him, feels honoured that she is speaking to him thus. 'And you will gain redemption for your good works.' He realises his words were clumsy. 'I'm sorry, I didn't mean to insult you. You are indeed as Esther – a woman of boundless virtue.'

'I'm not insulted. I do hope it will bring merit to my own soul.'

He nods. 'And I believe you are deserving of that merit.'

He leaves the kitchen, standing taller – although he has to duck to avoid hitting his head on the doorway. He's honoured to be so trusted, to be a member of the family.

Chapter Fifty-Two

Wet Nurse

Bethia is as tired as she's ever been but sleep eludes her. The baby lies next to her and she cannot take her eyes from him. He's a big baby, everyone who has seen him has said so. She only cares that he seems healthy, although Mama has tied various threads around the baby's chubby wrists against the mal ojo. Bethia doesn't want to think of an evil eye upon her son. She strokes his forehead with her pinkie, light as a feather, whispering that she will protect him from everything bad in this world, and the next.

Mama comes to take him to the wet nurse and finally she drifts off to sleep. She becomes aware of whispered voices which grow louder and more emphatic. The curtains are closed around the bed, but she knows it is Mainard arguing with Mama.

'The child must have a wet nurse,' hisses Mama.

'The character of the child is formed by the character of the mother. I have read it.'

'Hah! No doubt the meanderings of some old philosopher.'

'Who else would we look to for guidance on how to live our lives?'

'It is most wrong for Bethia to feed her own child.'

'Where have you found this woman who will have the suckling of my son? I've heard of a wet nurse who fed a baby swine milk – and in adulthood the child had the behaviour of a pig.'

'Do you think, for one moment, any wet nurse will be permitted to feed the baby outwith our sight. She'll not be left alone with my precious grandson, ever. And this nurse is of the true faith.'

'My son's character is forming, and I will have it form with the strength, beauty, and goodness that flows from his mother.'

There is a long pause and Bethia feels her heart, already overfull with tenderness, ready to burst with love for her husband that he should so describe her. She props herself up on one elbow, straining to hear what is said next.

'So be it. But these philosophers will, of course, have also mentioned that while your wife is lactating there must be no intimacy between you.'

There is a pause, then Mainard says, 'My child's welfare is the most important thing to me.'

Mama continues as though he hasn't spoken. 'And this will mean a delay before your next son is born.'

'Bethia is not my brood mare.'

Mama speaks low and soft. 'You are a loyal husband, but do not forget you have a higher duty. We must glorify God by bringing forth as many children as He wills.'

Bethia has never heard gentle Mama so emphatic before.

'And I will do my duty, to both God and my people.'

They move away, and the next time Bethia is aware of anything is when Grissel brings wee Thomas to be fed.

She stays in this burrow of contentment for many days as people come to worship at the cradle of her child. Geertruyt visits: loud, smiling, and heavily pregnant herself. Katheline will hold baby Thomas whenever Bethia releases him. Grissel is her constant companion. Papa sends messages through Mama, who seems to have accepted Mainard's decision without rancour, for the wet nurse is never mentioned again. Finally, Bethia feels she belongs. This is her family.

And, too, it gives her great pleasure that her brother visits during this time of her lying-in. She thought he might be embarrassed to be among the aftermath of birth but he's most curious. He holds the baby and talks to him, saying he can already see some red hair and Thomas will grow up to look like his namesake.

'There are worse things,' says Bethia.

Will nods. 'I think Father has always done what he considered his best by us.'

Bethia blinks, cannot remember ever hearing Will speak in such terms about their father, is far more likely to call him an old windbag than to say anything praiseworthy. She shifts in the bed, her body beginning to ache from the long lying-in. 'It's true what you say... and also that Hell is full of good intentions.'

They grin at one another.

'So what have you been doing to occupy yourself?'

The smile vanishes from his face and she immediately regrets asking the question.

'Your husband has invited me to join him, although I'm no artist, but I am learning much about cartography – and the company is most congenial.'

She knows this already, for Mainard has told her.

He taps his mouth with his fingers. 'But it's only a pass-time. I'm awaiting a response to a letter.'

'You've written to John Knox?' She knows it won't be Father, for Will has told of how he wrote to him several times from Berwick and received no reply and has now given up.

'I've been in communication with Knox, yes.'

His answer is stiff, but she senses in this moment of her vulnerability he may reveal what happened between him and his once great friend and guide. She waits, knowing any probing is likely to have Will close up tighter than an oyster in its shell.

'He changed when we were in Berwick. I know he is truly a great man, but he had his head turned by all the

314

attention. He lost humility and became a loud and boastful creature, and I didn't know him any more.'

Bethia twirls her hair between her fingers, enjoying the smell of lavender, for Mama permitted Grissel to wash it yesterday. By the time she's up and about it should have the slick of grease necessary for keeping it smooth and tidy. 'You'll not return to Knox?'

He leans back in the chair which he has pulled close to the bed. 'I have observed many things about John Knox. There is no doubt he's an inspiring preacher, his doctrine is sound and he is a leader of men…'

'But…?'

'…he is not a forgiving man.'

'That doesn't sound very Christian.'

'Even a great man has his flaws.'

'That's a serious flaw – pride is at its root. So he's unlikely to take you back, even should you wish to return?'

His mouth turns down. 'And I do not know who I am, if not the staunch believer in the need for change within our kirks… although Knox did direct me to John Calvin in Geneva.'

'I have a sense you're waiting for something first. What is it?'

He opens his mouth to speak, but before he can there's the sound of loud voices from below.

Bethia sits bolt upright in bed.

Will stands up. 'I will find out what's happening and return.'

'Please. And send Grissel to me. She should've been here this past hour.'

'I will,' he says, already sliding out the door.

She listens to the noises of the house and they don't bode well. She reminds herself that the rest of the family are full-grown and well able to look out for themselves and, tired from all the interrupted nights, she slips into a doze.

Chapter Fifty-Three

Marisse

There are loud voices coming from the salon, but Will heads towards the kitchen and Grissel, before he gets distracted. But it's deserted, the fire gone out. He's standing gazing at the ashes when the door is flung open and Mainard charges in.

'So it's true.'

Will spins round. 'Where is Grissel? Has something happened to her?'

'That's one way of putting it,' Mainard barks. 'She would've been better left in Scotland. The wench has been the cause of much resentment among the servants within this house, and now the pot' – he dips his head towards the cold fireplace – 'metaphorically, has boiled over.'

'Come, de Lange, Grissel is more than a servant. She, and her mother, are like members of the Seton family. What has she done to be so reviled... and where is she? Bethia has need of her.'

Mainard folds his arms. 'You may well ask. We're all wondering where Grissel is... most of all our servant, Marisse.'

'You speak in riddles.'

'Coort is missing too.'

'Ach, I understand. But surely all that's needed is to make certain that he weds Grissel.

'Unfortunately, Marisse has, for a long time, believed that Coort belongs to her. Grissel's arrival set the kitchens in turmoil.'

Will cannot help but smile. 'Aye, Grissel makes an art of turmoil.'

'She does and it can be amusing… but not this time.'

'Where is Marisse – why is she at least not here?'

'Marisse too has gone. We know not where, and it is a matter of some anxiety.'

Will gazes at him. 'What does she know? No, don't tell me… it has to do with the poor you feed here, in this very kitchen.'

Mainard picks up the poker and riddles the ashes. 'Mama is a good woman.'

'Are they Jews?'

'Mostly Conversos, like us, but Antwerp no longer allows them to settle here so they must go on to Venice.'

'And the Ottoman Empire.'

'Where did you hear that?'

'From an Englishman… so it seems to be common knowledge. And surely it is unwise to help the those fleeing if they are going among our enemies?'

Mainard tosses the poker in the fireplace. 'The authorities would not look kindly on it. So no, we should not render them assistance.'

'And now Marisse will accuse you,' says Will, aware his voice is loud, but he doesn't care. 'You should never have brought my sister to Antwerp. You must've known how perilous it was when you married her.'

Mainard glares at him. 'Nowhere is safe.'

'That's an over-simplification.' Will is close to shouting in Mainard's face. 'To bring Bethia to the home of New Christians was wrong – especially without her understanding what she was coming to.'

'I did tell her.'

'But she could not fully understand when there are no Jews, nor Conversos, in Scotland.'

'Imagine this was your people. They're trapped in a country which is persecuting them – even after they're forced to baptise their children and adopt Christian ways, they're neither accepted nor safe. Would you not help them? Would that not be the act of a true Christian? All we have done is to continue to support the escape route already set up by Gracia Mendes, before she, herself, had to flee Antwerp.'

Will blinks. 'Who is Gracia Mendes? But more importantly, where is there true faith in all of this?'

'I know that is a subject which deeply concerns you, but I have not the indulgence for it. Pragmatism is my watchword.'

'And so you marry a Christian.'

'I have a great love for your sister. That's why I wed her.'

'But it was useful to your family.'

Mainard snorts. 'You think my family were happy that the seed of the great and holy were mingled with a Gentile.'

Will's eyes grow wide as he takes Mainard's meaning. 'I should punch you on the nose for such a remark.'

'That is not how I think, you fool.'

Will drops down on a stool, feeling the anger drain from him. He cannot see what to do. His own future is precarious and Antwerp is only marginally safer for a Protestant than a Jew; both are barely tolerated for whatever wealth and trade they bring. The tide may turn at any moment. He knows it's not wise to align himself with Mainard and his family, yet Christ himself was a Jew, and a much persecuted one… He becomes aware that Mainard is staring at him and realises the noise he's hearing are his own fingers drumming on the board.

'My father does that,' he says ruefully. 'It used to feel as though I had the Devil stuck inside my head when I was made to stand by while he rattled the board.' He stands up. 'I understand you are indeed beset. We must make certain that Bethia and your son are protected.'

'I thank you for that we. I know you are a staunch Christian.'

'But one who has bitter experience of challenging papists' thinking, and who knows what it is to lose everything. And Luther himself said that even a Jew may truly convert.'

'Unfortunately, many do not agree with Luther. They call us Marranos here – it means swine, and it seems we have a kind of curse upon our bodies, a foeter judaicus, a Jewish stench. And if that were not enough to add to our woes, Jews are also misshapen and have an odd cast of the eye.'

Will looks up at his tall handsome brother and the flicker of a smile crosses his face.

Suddenly the door is again flung wide, banging off the wall. They both jump to find an agitated Master de Lange, waving a letter in his hand, Katheline and the mother crowding in the doorway behind him.

'What's wrong, Papa?'

He shakes his head and passes the letter to Mainard, then staggers. Mainard catches him under the elbow. 'Come, let's go to the salon. Katheline, can you bring us some wine?'

Will stays with Katheline, offering to carry the tray of glasses. She allows it but doesn't look at him as she leads the way out of the kitchen.

Mainard is still reading when they enter. He looks to his father, who sits back in his chair eyes closed, face drawn. 'Surely no one will believe the words of one disgruntled servant, especially when they learn the reason why she's aggrieved.'

'Her claims are very grave,' says the father, slowly.

Mainard turns to Will. 'A message has come from the Portuguese Merchants Guild warning Papa that Marisse has brought an accusation against us.'

'An accusation of what?' Will asks, although he

guesses the answer.

'She says we are secret Judaisers, and worse. She's accused us of stealing babies for their blood, to use for making bread.'

'What! That's ludicrous.' Will pauses, chewing on his lip. 'But no one has come. You've not been arrested, and as you say, surely they'll ignore one aggrieved servant.'

Master de Lange rises to his feet and walks up and down, bent like an old man. 'Oh they will come. Perhaps not now, but soon. The temptation is too great, for all that we have can be easily impounded with such an accusation, to enrich a debt-ridden Crown. And there is something else I must tell you… privately,' he says, looking to his son.

Katheline bursts out, 'No, let us all know.'

Master de Lange looks in surprise to be so commanded by his daughter.

'I mean' – she stumbles over her words – 'we should all understand what is before us.'

'Very well. I have heard that recently I was burnt in effigy in Portugal.'

There's a gasp from the mother, who covers her face with her handkerchief.

Will is confused; surely burning an effigy is as nothing to burning a person. 'Portugal is far away?' he mutters.

'News travels fast, especially wicked tales. They say I'm not only a Judaiser, but also a Turkish spy. And all this not helped by a false accusation last year from some painter, whom I've never met, that I commission forgeries – a minor irritant at the time, but contributing to a case against me.'

'You are indeed beset, and on all sides,' says Will, then wishes he'd held his tongue as all heads swivel to stare at him.

Chapter Fifty-Four

Tefillot

Bethia, safe in her bower, lays wee Samuel-Thomas across her lap as she changes him. She tosses the soiled clothing into the bucket and wonders again where Grissel is. Standing up, she walks around the chamber, rocking and humming to him. This wee lad is going to grow up speaking so many languages, but she'll make sure Scots is his first.

She senses a great disquiet in the house, but chooses to stay here – will not risk having her milk soured. She lays the bairn in his cradle and leans back in her chair, rocking it with her foot. She smiles, thinking of the baby's name. Papa always calls him Samuel, she and Mainard call him Thomas. One day Katheline ran the two names together and it has stuck. This is her baby of the north and the south, who will grow up an Antwerpen, although she hopes one day to take him to visit Scotland.

She thinks on the name again and a shiver runs down her spine. It is a most strange sensation. The name Samuel-Thomas is a family jest and Mainard has counselled that it must be used only within the home. To all outsiders their son is Thomas, for Samuel, he says, although in honour of his father, is not a good name for the grandson of a Converso.

All is quieter below now. She thinks she might dress

and go down. Her lying-in should be drawing to a close but she feels a strange reluctance to leave this sanctuary. Nevertheless, she slows the rocking and then stops, foot poised ready to begin again should her baby object. He does not. He's so still and silent she tucks her head beneath the hood to listen, touching his cheek with her finger. He's warm but she cannot detect his breath. She strains to listen; no, she cannot hear him breathing. She nudges his chin. He doesn't move. She pokes his cheek and he lets out a cry. Bethia chides herself for a fool as her heart starts beating again, and she rocks the cradle once more. Samuel-Thomas, it seems, has grown used to such interference and slips back to sleep.

She lifts the lid of the kist. It's strange to remove her nightgown and pull on a bodice and a skirt. Her belly is soft, where once it was taut. She pats it, would endure much worse change to her body to fulfil God's purpose. Her lips move as she sends up thanks, yet again, to the Virgin for watching over her.

Now she's ready to descend the stairs, but where is Grissel? She should be here to stay with the baby. She'll give her a tongue-lashing that Grissel will not forget when she finally reappears. Indeed, she's deserving of a beating for this desertion. Bethia smiles at the thought of trying to beat Grissel, with her mighty spirit.

There's a rumble of voices from the hall. She opens the door to find Mama blocking the doorway to the chamber of secrets, Katheline by her side. Mainard is trying to edge past them, while at his side stands Papa, arms hanging.

'No, no. You must not. No one will find it,' pleads Mama.

'Mama,' says Mainard, holding her by the shoulders and gazing down into her face, 'Marisse will know everything that happens in this house. There are no secrets hid from servants.'

'But she doesn't clean here. I do not allow it. The door is kept locked.'

'So well locked that Bethia managed to easily enter,' says Mainard, pushing Mama gently to one side. Beyond them, Bethia sees Will lingering at the top of the stairs.

Papa takes Mama by the arm. 'He is correct, my love.'

Bethia is looking from one to the other. 'What has Marisse done?'

'Grissel has run off with Coort, and Marisse has accused us of being Judaisers.'

'No, that cannot be,' cries Bethia. 'Are you certain? I do not think she likes him anymore.

'Nevertheless she has gone,' says Mainard. He holds out his hand for the key, and Mama, after a moment, passes it to him. They crowd in, gathering in front of the armoire.

'We can seal it shut,' says Katheline.

'And they will break it down,' says Mainard, studying the armoire. 'I think we should move this so the hidden door is there for all to see.'

Mama's shoulders slump.

'Stand back,' says Mainard as he and Papa heave and slide the huge cupboard along the floor until the door in the wall behind it is exposed.

Katheline rushes into the small chamber and Mama follows.

'We must set this up as a garde-robe,' says Papa. 'Easily enough done.'

'And burn everything it contains,' says Mainard.

Bethia sees Mama's face blanch while Katheline gathers up the prayer shawl and the Tefillot, clutching them to her chest. She wonders what they've done with the beautiful candleholder.

Katheline holds them tight. 'We can easily hide these.'

'Do you really want to risk it? Think what they will do to us if they are found.'

Bethia squeezes past Mainard to stand before Katheline. 'Perhaps a prayer can be said to honour them first.'

After a moment Katheline nods and, ignoring Mainard, gives the book and shawl to Papa. Mainard lays his arm across Bethia's shoulders to guide her from the room.

The sound of knocking rises up the stairwell and they all stop, looking to one another, eyes wide. Bethia can feel her heart thumping and knows she must act quickly. She snatches the book and prayer shawl from Papa and rushes into her chamber. Opening the kist, she tries to stuff them into the hidden compartment where her dowry purse was once tucked away, but they're too bulky.

'Under the mattress,' hisses Mainard.

'Too obvious.' Bethia stands over her son's cradle then kneels to slip the book beneath the small mattress, folding the shawl among his covers.

Thomas whimpers but soon falls silent.

Mainard glares at his sister.

The knocking is resumed, louder this time.

'I will answer it,' calls Will.

Mainard runs down the stairs after him and the rest follow. Bethia gazes at her son, hand over her heart, closes the door softly, and hurries down the stairs.

Chapter Fifty-Five

Another Entry

Bethia, watching from the stairs, poised to run back to her baby, sees Mainard stride forward with Will at his shoulder. He tugs the front door wide.

There's an exclamation from Will, and his shoulders tense up. Mainard stands back and bows. It's bright around the doorway as the sun streams into the dark hall. Bethia squints, but all she can see is a tall, thin figure framed against the light. Master de Lange steps forward, welcoming the visitor, who bows in return. Bethia leans over, peering as a gap opens between Mainard and Will. She still can't see.

A gruff voice asks, 'How are ye, son?'

She freezes. Then she's running forward, pushing through the family crowded around the doorway to stand before her father. He's more gaunt than she remembers, his face lined, the yellow-red beard now a peppery grey, but his eyes still grow kindly when he looks upon her.

'And how are ye, ma lass?'

The lump in her throat will not allow her to speak. She clenches her fists, must not embarrass them both by crying. Instead, she takes his hand in both of hers and cannot stop herself from kissing it. The familiar smell of Father – leather, wool, and sweat – is overwhelming. It takes all her strength not to collapse into his arms and howl. He pats her clumsily on the shoulder and somehow Master de Lange and Mainard between them move everyone out of the hallway and into the salon.

She holds onto Father's sleeve, stuck fast as a limpet on the rocks. He bows as he's introduced to Mama and Katheline. She hears a yelp and goes still to listen, then runs for the stairs. Thomas is distraught when she reaches him. His face red with rage, his body hot and sticky. She picks him up and rocks him, walking up and down as he thrashes and cries. She rocks harder and he screams louder. Eventually she sits down and feeds him, foot tapping impatiently as he suckles. She can hear voices below, rising and falling – much discussion. And then she thinks on how Will didn't seem surprised by Father's appearance. She bites her lip. He is a loving father but not a sentimental one; he will have come for a reason.

The door opens and Mainard walks in. Bethia sighs with relief. He kneels before her, wrapping his arms around them both.

'I need you to be brave, my love.'

'You're scaring me.'

He rolls back onto his haunches and rests his elbows on his knees while he tells her that Papa has been burnt in effigy and of Marisse's treachery.

She gazes into her husband's earnest brown eyes. 'But this news has only come today and does not explain why my father is here?'

'I believe Will wrote to him, saying that the net is closing in for New Christians in Antwerp.'

'Will had no right to do that. It's wrong to worry Father, for he can do nothing about edicts, effigies, or vindictive servants, be it here or in Scotland.' But even as she's speaking she knows why Father has come. She shakes her head, her eyes filling with tears.

Mainard stands up, reaching to take his sleeping son in his arms. He walks around the room whispering to him. Bethia brushes her eyes with the back of her hand and tidies herself. She opens the door to go down and greet Father properly, to tell him he has had a wasted journey.

'Wait,' says Mainard softly.

She hesitates, then releases the door, which swings shut. He lays the bairn in his cradle, tucking him in, and comes to her. She stares up into his eyes, saying, 'I will not go. Whatever you have to say you may as well haud yer wheesht.'

He smiles to hear the Scottish words, but it doesn't reach his eyes. 'Bethia…' He takes her hands, gazing down at her. 'My strong Bethia with the bluest eyes.'

'No, Mainard, I won't do it.'

'And what of our son?'

She tugs her hands out of his. 'He is a de Lange and must take his chances with the rest of us.' But she knows, even as she speaks, that she will not risk her child. She takes a deep breath. 'I will send Thomas to Scotland with his namesake. He will be beloved; my father will love him.'

Mainard takes her by the elbows and holds her close. 'A child needs his mother,' he whispers.

'And his father,' she counters. She pulls away from him. 'You must come with us. Why not? It's the safest thing to do.'

He walks to the window and gazes out, his back to her. 'I will follow, but I cannot leave my family.' He turns, raising his hand to stop her. 'And they will not let us all leave without permissions to travel and…' he mutters '…we must have good reason for going.' His voice grows stronger. 'In the meantime, I need to know that you and Thomas are safe. Please, Bethia, do not fight me on this.'

She presses her face against the door, but when she looks at him, after several minutes, she has composed herself.

There's a tap and Mama's head appears. 'Bethia's

327

father wishes to speak with you both. I'll stay with the baby.'

Father, Papa, and Will break off their discussion when she and Mainard enter the salon. Father comes to her and, placing his hand under her chin, tilts her face up to his. 'I wish we were meeting under better circumstances, my daughter.' He looks to Mainard. 'Your husband has told you?'

'I have, and we are in agreement that Bethia and your grandson will depart with you, at your earliest convenience,' Mainard says, his voice clear and strong.

Bethia glances at Will. 'You're coming too?'

Father speaks before Will can. 'I fear it's not yet safe for William to return. He would likely be imprisoned – young Nydie has recently been arrested.'

'Then how can it be safe for me?'

'Your part in the siege was minor, the risk is not great, and I have told that you were held against your will.'

'But there is some danger.'

Her father sighs. 'There's peril everywhere. It is a matter of balancing risks and, on balance, we all agree you, and the bairn, are safer in Scotland than here.'

She turns to Will, who looks so much like a younger version of the father standing next to him that she gulps. 'Where will you go?'

'Geneva, I think.'

Bethia's surprised to see him look to Father as he speaks, as though seeking permission, and even more surprised by Father's response.

'For an adherent to the Protestant faith, which I am assuming ye are still…'

Will nods

'…it's no a bad idea. And,' he touches his son lightly on the shoulder as he speaks, 'I understand Calvin to be a man of sound conscience, and some sense.'

Bethia sees Will is swallowing hard at Father's words. It's as near to a blessing that Father is ever likely to give.

At least something good has come out of all this, she thinks, and hopes Father will provide funds, for she suspects Will has none.

She goes still, feeling a tightness in her head as she tries to remember which countries surround Geneva, and how it looked in the Theatrum mapping that Ortelius showed her. She feels a flush of excitement and goes to stand before Mainard. 'Geneva, that is where I and baby Samuel-Thomas will go.'

Mainard stares at her, then walks around the chamber tugging hard on his ear as he considers. All eyes follow him, even Father's. Bethia knows it's only Mainard she has to persuade, for he is her husband. If his family take the route of Gracia Mendes and other Conversos seeking refuge then they will pass near Geneva, and she knows her husband. He will not leave his sister nor his parents until they are in a place of safety. If she goes to Scotland she and Mainard will end up far, far away from each other. If she is in Geneva, he will easily come for her, and his son. And then they can go to Italy, together.

Mainard glances at her and inclines his head; she knows his mind is following the same logic as hers. She watches her father watching Mainard. His expression is… respectful.

She goes to Father and slips her arm in his. He pats her hand, eyes still on Mainard. All will be well, she thinks. In the end all will be well.

* * *

Find out what happens next for Bethia & Will....

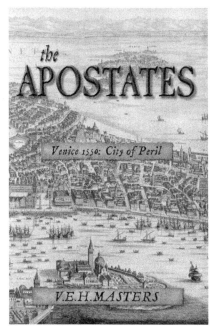

.....as The Apostates continues their story, the third book of the Seton Chronicles series.

Please leave a review

If you enjoyed this book please take a moment to share your thoughts in a review. Just a rating and/or a few words are perfect.

Reader reviews help sell more books and keep your favourite authors in business!.

Glossary

The definitions below give the meaning as used in the book

ane	own, as in my own child.
aye	always, yes.
bairn	a baby, a child.
baith	both.
bawbees	coins, money.
besom	a term of contempt for girls and women; often used affectionately.
blethering	gossiping, chattering on and on, talking nonsense.
caitchpule	'real tennis' court; oldest surviving one is at Falkland Palace
cheeky	insolent, naughty.
clout	to hit; also a cloth.
daft	crazy, stupid.
dinna	don't, as in dinna ken – don't know.
dither	to be indecisive.
dour	pessimistic, humourless.
frae	from, as in away from home.
fuffle	a disorder, a fuss.
gawking	staring, sometimes stupidly.
girning	whining.
glaikit	stupid, foolishly vacant.
glowers	glares, scowls.

gowk	a fool, stupid person usually male.
guddle	a muddle, a mess.
haar	a sea mist.
hae	have.
hirpling	limping, hobbling.
ken	know, as in 'you know'.
kent	known.
midden	dung heap, rubbish heap.
ower	too, over; as in over-much.
oxters	armpits.
scunnersome	exasperating, annoying.
skelping	smacking, slapping.
siller	silver coins, money.
smirr	fine rain
the morn's morn	tomorrow morning.
thrashing	a beating, a whipping.
tocher	dowry.
trauchled	downtrodden.
vennel	an alley, a close.
weans	children.
wheen	a lot.
wheesht	be quiet.
yett	a gate, a postern.
yon	that, over there.

Acknowledgements

Lots of people have helped me through the sometimes painful gestation of this, my second novel (don't know why I thought it would get easier…). I'd like to say a big thank you to all my friends and family for their ongoing support and encouragement and especially my daughter in law, Sarah Masters, for her help with social media. And readers and bloggers too, thank you for your kind reviews, and suggestions for what you'd like to happen next (and especially sister Jane and friend Alison for their support).

People have given generously of their time and expertise, and especially Margaret Skea. To my beta readers thanks – my daughter Zoe Masters, Esther Mendelsohn, Keddie Hughes and Hannah Faoilean – who all made wise suggestions. My editor Richard Sheehan thanks for your rock solid guidance. I'd also like to thank staff at the KBR Museum in Brussels who were incredibly helpful in responding to a myriad of questions about maps.

Hugest thanks of all go to Mike for all his love, support and help… including doing the cover, typesetting, audio book, website, and for, as ever, being a tower of strength

I researched widely and amongst many useful resources were, Andree Brooks' biography of the remarkable Gracia Mendes (*The Woman who Defied Kings*), Jane Dawson's biography of *John Knox*, Mark A Meadow's paper on *The Rhetoric of Place in Philip II's 1549 Antwerp* and Paul Binding's *Imagined Corners.*

In the acknowledgements for The Castilians I said that there wasn't much Scottish historical fiction covering this period – all blethers! I don't know how I went so long without coming across Dorothy Dunnett's brilliant Lymond series or why I forgot all the Nigel Tranter and Jean Plaidy I read in my youth.

Historical Note

I have tried to follow historical events as faithfully as I can, and in particular the fascinating *Joyous Entry* into Antwerp of Charles and Philip in 1549. Inevitably some of what happens is down to my own interpretation and, since this is a work of fiction, to the needs of the story.

For instance John Knox did toss the image of the Virgin Mary into the sea however it was rescued before it sunk beneath the waves. And *The Cardinal*, said to be the finest galley of the French fleet, ran aground on a sand bank off Cramond however Knox was not on board but watching from another galley on which he was enslaved – the phrase '*Scotland can bear no cardinals*' is attributed to him.

I have chosen to use Gracia Mendes nephew's Converso name – Don Juan Micas, but he is also more commonly known as Joseph Nasi.

* * *

Let me know if you do spot any glaring inaccuracies, or want to chat about my books. I love a good blether with readers.

You'll also find a couple of stories delving more into the Seton Family, that are free to download from my website.

You'll find me at www.vehmasters.com.

Printed in Great Britain
by Amazon